# Chapter 1

"Can this family get any more dysfunctional?" Dana Reed complained, not caring who heard her insane ranting. It infuriated her that they all expected her to put on a show for all these so-called friends. *'Playing couch potato would be more interesting than this three-ring circus act, about to unfold.'* She hated that others were forcing her to become a part of the performance.

The hours wasted pleading with her mother to hold a private setting for family only, at least for the first night, were to no avail. How unfair of her not to even listen to reasons, brushing her off as though her feelings didn't merit any consideration.

*'This is our final good-bye.'* Dana thought as tears threatened but she refused to give in to them.

Passing through large oak doors, anger touched her soul, while she struggled to control her emotions.

Briefly, she remained under an arched entrance that opened into a great room filled with on-lookers, mulling around.

Repulsed as, she absorbed the stench of death, she wanted to scream at everyone to get out and to quit the endless line that gawked down at her father's lifeless body.

*'This isn't how, he would want his work peers to remember him,'* her inner voice hollered in her mind.

Off to the side, snuggled in a corner sat her mother surrounded by friends. At least, she wouldn't have to sit by her side struggling with small talk just to avoid the real issue at hand; her father's death and the pain it left them all in.

Dana would have been happier, if the three of them could have spent the evening sitting around sharing their private memories. Even if, she somehow had managed to convince her mother into arranging a showing for the immediately family, it would have never worked. Robert would have insisted on bringing Lindsay, and of course, he would have the final say.

She glared across at him now, playing his role well as the main attraction. Standing there in his custom tailored suit with his left hand casually tucked in his pocket. From where she stood, Dana could hear the coins clicking together as he sifted them through his fingers. A habit he picked up as a young boy and one that always got under her skin. He once told her, he did it to calm down, whenever he found himself in an uncomfortable situation.

"*Huh*," everyone else may have been oblivious to his nervousness but not Dana, no matter how long he stayed away, no one would ever know him the way she did. He appeared controlled and composed, all the while shaking his free hand with the curious on lookers. He didn't fool her though, in fact seeing his discomfort, at being mobbed by a group, of people who he didn't know anymore amused her. It almost made the venture out worth it.

"I'm sorry dad," Dana immediately regretted her thoughts. It made her mad that her own family was driving her to madness causing her thinking to askew. She hated the person she became since her brother's return.

The whole scene upset her, especially since she suspected that most of the people here tonight showed up, more so, to catch a glimpse of the infamous Robert Reed than to pay their respects to the dead. Everyone, desperate to know what enticed him back to this good for nothing town, of Chiapas Falls.

*'Dammit, I can't understand his reason for returning. And, no way am I going to give him the satisfaction of asking what impelled him to come back after his big escaped.'* Dana couldn't imagine what made him come back.

It made her sick how the small crowd congregated around him like starving vultures waiting for him to toss any little piece of his story, about life away from Chiapas Falls, their way.

*'These people need a life, if the only excitement they can get is racing to a wake to see my brother who returned with an education and an estrange wife.'*

He looked more like a politician soliciting for votes instead of saying his final good byes to his father.

Dana shook her head at the way people flaunted themselves at him.

"I'd bet everything I own, which doesn't amount to much, that they'd all be dumb enough to cast a vote for him, if he ever did decide to run for Mayor." Dana whispered under her breath.

Born successful, Robert had all the typical traits of what Glamour Magazine classified as catch of the year, tall and sturdy, with chiseled features that enhanced a slight dimple in his chin.

He ran his fingers through his dark hair as another so-call mourner approached him to soak up their moment in his greatness.

Things came easy to Robert. All through his school years he excelled, being number one in the wrestling team and the fastest quarterback on the football field. Now, he could add Doctor to his list of accomplishments. He also had a personality that drew people to him, and a unique way of making them feel important whenever they were in his presence.

'Of course, the cheerleader team wouldn't miss this opportunity, still running in packs,' Dana noticed as few of them openly drool as they approached him. "Oh yes, and here comes the faithful little puppy moving in for the kill, to stake her claim." Dana grumbled quietly.

Lindsay, one of Dana's reasons why their remaining circle of three would never be the same, ran to link arms with Robert.

'You may be able to play my brother like a puppet, but I'll never fall for your fake innocents.' Dana thought as she watched the act.

Glancing at her watch, she had been there for a little under an hour and already she had enough of this night. Looking around seeing the rest of the family preoccupied, in their own little worlds, she made a run for the door.

# Chapter 2

She almost reached her destination when Robert caught her by the arm and dragged her into a room adjacent to the parlour, where they could argue in private.

"What is wrong with you? This is Dad's wake and you don't even have the decency to show up on time or to stick around for awhile," Robert glared down at her and she could see the disappointment in his chocolate brown eyes. She always wondered where his colour came from when everyone else in the family had hazel blue. "These people came here tonight to pay dad their last respect." He growled at her.

"Don't be so sure of that." Dana hissed at him. '*Does he think moving back home gave him the right to step into his father's footsteps after not showing his face in years? He didn't care about anyone when he left, so why should I care now? Dana thought.*'

Robert took a deep breath then straightened his shoulders. Running both hands through dark black hair, he looked down at her.

"Dana, it hurts to see you so sad. You used to tell me everything, now I don't recognize the girl standing in front of me. What happened to make you so angry?" Robert let out a sigh but Dana stood her ground maintaining a stiff stance with her arms folded across her chest. "If I've done anything to get you this worked up I'm sorry. I know Dad's dying is hard on you. Hell, it is for all of us, but instead of fighting, we need to pull closer together. Mom is going to need both of us to help her get through this." Dana felt her shoulders sag as she allowed his words to soften the fight within her. *'At least he's making the effort to talk to me.'*

"Robert," she started to say but stopped short when Lindsay appeared in the doorway, with a big, phoney smile spread across her face.

"What are you two doing huddled in a corner?" Dana detected a fake southern accent when her sister-in-law interrupted.

Lindsay chuckled, oblivious to the hate stare Dana shot her way. For the first time since his return, Dana wanted to open up to her brother. It drove her crazy that his wife didn't have the common courtesy to realize that they needed this time to talk.

"I guess you wandered a little too far from your puppet master's comfort zone." Dana snapped hoping her words cut through him. She ran out leaving the two of them standing together bewildered.

"Dammit," was the last thing she heard Robert say as he watched her storm out of the building.

# Chapter 3

Outside the massive oak doors of the funeral home Dana stood hoping Robert would have the gumption to stand up to Lindsay and come after her to finish their conversation.

"He won't, she surmised.

Resentment built up in her as the winds pelted chilly rain against her body.

"Is Lindsay that possessive and jealous that she can't bear seeing us together? If she hadn't barged in, we'd still be working things out. All the woman has to do is step back and allow us time to talk maybe then I could accept her into the family."

Instead, here she was huddled against a solid brick wall trying to protect her freezing flesh against the cold, allowing false hope to hold her there against her will.

'*Why am I so weak? Just leave.*' She complained, foolishly clinging to the misconception that her brother still cared enough to chase after her.

"He has too much on the go to worry about me standing out here freezing. If anything, Lindsay probably slipped the leash back on and dragged him back out to be the center of attraction, where they could both gloat over his success." Dana hissed under her breath, upset that she had resorted to talking out-loud to herself.

A small awning that hung over the entrance of the old castle-like edifice offered little protection against the elements that pounded against the large wooden doors with vengeance.

Still stalling, Dana busied her mind with a grey plaque set into the brownstone wall beside the entrance. An urge overcame her to run a finger over the print carved in the center of the stone, eighteen hundred and fifty two, the year they erected the building. Chiseled deep in the cement beneath the numbers spelt out 'Mullin's Funeral Home' the same name as the two brothers who were now the caretakers. *'This establishment reflects their personalities,'* she remembered how robotic and cold they looked mulling around the lobby on her arrival tonight.

She wondered why there would have been a need for the Mullins to construct such an elaborate place to house the dead a hundred and twenty three years ago. *'Who cares,'* she thought, getting perturbed at the minimal distraction.

"Standing out here freezing is ridiculous," Dana grumbled and turned to look back at the door she came out of.

"I'd rather die than face those two again." She shook her head. "What a stupid thing to say standing out side a funeral home." Dana knew she was being petty waiting for Robert to come out, but also new the only one hurting was herself, looking out into the darkness, she decided it was time to leave.

The light drizzle when she arrived had now turned into a raging storm. As least, flood lights attached to two post in the middle of the parking lot shed some light giving her guidance to the car.

Trying to build courage to dart out into the dark, she almost reconsidered going back inside to warm up and regretted not bringing a heavier jacket.

She had to make a decision soon, standing alone shivering in front of this old decrepit structure, in the middle of nowhere with nothing but darkness frightened her. She didn't believe in ghost but suddenly the urge to get the hell out of there sent a prickly sensation throughout her body.

Giving up the crazy idea Robert would come to her rescue, she retrieved an umbrella from her bag and popped it open. Sprinting out into the wetness, the winds quickly ripped her only protection from her hands leaving her to scurry across the parking lot uncovered.

"Stupid thing wasn't helping anyways." She thought.

Relentlessly, the rain beat down on her without letup, leaving her soaked even before she managed to reach her car. To make matters worse, when she took her keys out to unlock the door they slipped from her hand into a puddle pooling around the tires.

"Dammit can anything else go wrong?" She cursed and reached for the keys. While she knelt down to pick them up a bright flash of lightening lit up the sky, immediately followed by a thunderous clash that shook the ground, leaving her trembling.

She feared lightening may have struck the old building and braved a quick glance towards the heavens. Just as she did, another flash of light flickered across the sky, causing the towers to materialize for a fleeting moment. In that brief moment, she caught a glimpse of a figure standing in the shadows of the window in the highest peak, staring down at her.

Startled, she gaped at the spot to confirm what she witnessed, but by the time things lit up for a second time the apparition had vanished into the darkness, leaving her dizzy with fear. For a time being, she let go of the pain of her brother's success or the fact that he married a selfish woman. With her mind in a whirl, she temporarily forgot the constant beating of the rain.

Apprehension of whoever had been standing high above her in this haunted looking mansion, peering down at her, sent chills rippling through her, colder than the inclement weather could ever throw her way. She stood frozen on the spot numb to everything going on around her, as she recalled the many childhood horror stories surrounding the funeral home. As a young girl, these tales, had caused her many sleepless nights and likely would continue to do so, for weeks to come.

She shivered, as she suspected that one day, she would also end up within these darkened hallways that remained hidden behind huge, intimidating walls. A strong wind tugged at her hair and skirt bringing her back to reality. With fumbling fingers, she managed to unlock the door and without any more hesitation, she slid behind the wheel and slammed the locks down.

Shaking from both cold and fear, Dana fought to contain the tears that welled up in her eyes.

'All this anger and exhaustion must be playing tricks on my mind causing me to *hallucinate. A hot shower and good nights rest should put things in there proper prospective.'* She wondered.

"After all," she rambled out-loud, finding comfort in the sound of her own voice. "Why would anyone be watching me?" She sped away allowing thoughts of Robert and Lindsay to take control of her mind again.

It was easier to be angry then scared.

# Chapter 4

Pain shot through Dana's shoulders as she tensed up gripping the wheel tightly between both hands. Shifting positions, she tried to stretch, while she fought to maintain control of the vehicle. Heavy winds pushed and tugged hard at the Volkswagen Bug, at times they were so strong she thought the car would go airborne hurling her into a farmer's field.

With eyes fixated on the wipers, as they swept across the windshield, barley able to give a clear vision, she counted every familiar landmark that singled another step closer to her destination.

"I hate this night and everything about it." She stated. *'Maybe I should pull over until the winds die down.'* She questioned but feared the idea of sitting alone in the dark on the roadside, more than fighting the elements for the next ten minutes.

Even the blast of heat blowing from the vents couldn't prevent her body from shaking.

'What was I thinking three years ago by packing up and moving out to no-man's land," as her Dad like to refer to it? The small red brick building housing nine apartments that fringed on the outskirts of town had been her home.

Not another building around for miles, "no wonder Dad fought me all the way on my decision."

She half-heatedly chuckled at the foolishness of her situation. "Too bad your time ended before hearing those words, Dad."

Her father's constant reminders of how unsafe it would be if she broke down on the back roads, hit home tonight. At the time, she made the decision out of rebellion. Tonight, her need to cling to her stubborn notions appeared petty.

'*I have to stop making stupid decisions. Face the facts. I only move out here to get back at Dad for sending Robert off to school and making me stay.*'

Robert moved to Toronto for better education, while she followed the destiny of most people who lived in town.

If you wanted to survive and keep food on the table for your family, you headed to the Mill. Which was exactly what she found herself doing right after graduation, where she work on the lines under her father's supervision. Dana did this until Mrs. Blackwell retired and she took over the position of receptionist in the front lobby, where she enjoyed the solitude away from the plant gossip.

For the first time since she moved out of the family home she teetered with the notion of moving back in with her mother until she could find a place more local.

With Robert living only a few blocks from where they grew up, she really had to consider whether she could handle living within walking distance of Lindsay and her snooty, attitude. Seeing how her brother lived with his big house and fancy cars only served as a constant reminder of how poorly her life turned out in comparison.

In her father's eyes, spending the family savings on educating the males held the most importance. The only job the female in a family had was to nab herself an educated man with a career. The thing missing from his plan's calculations was that most of the eligible men, were spoken for before they graduated by females, like Lindsay, whose fathers sent to College or University to catch the incomes before they got out into the real world.

Her brother carried on like a freight train racing ahead with a great career and a new wife. The biggest change Dana experienced in her life was the day she packed her bags and set up house twenty minutes away from the family home.

"Maybe, Lindsay's the wrong person to be mad at, she only did what most men expect of her," Dana concluded. It's how much Robert's life aligned right along with their father's old fashion ideals the angered her most. "Lindsay is still a bimbo with her fake Southern Bell accent." Dana wasn't willing to let her off the hook that easily.

With Robert's departure to greater things, Dana drew close to her father, depending heavily on him for everything. More than anything, she regretted not telling him how much she appreciated his support and love. Instead, she foolishly wasted so much time proving her independence to him and everyone else around. With his death, she lost the opportunity to let him know what a stronghold he had been for her.

She had never been close to her mother, now with Robert back she didn't think it would improve any. Growing up, she always lived in his shadows, where her mother was concerned. He was her bragging rights. Her son, a doctor, none of her friends would be able to top that. Bringing home a beautiful wife who could produce grandchildren gave her even more boasting rights.

A deep sigh escaped Dana,

"Let it go." She encouraged herself. Lost in her thoughts she never noticed a set of headlights fast approaching, until the lights reflected in the rear view mirror blinding her.

'*Someone is in a hurry to get nowhere,*' Dana thought and slowed to a crawl and hugged the side of the road to give them all the space possible without ditching the car. "Take all the room you need." Dana offered.

To her anguish, they preferred to follow recklessly behind her flashing their high beams.

"What the hell are you doing?" For a moment, she wondered it Robert decided to come after her and caught up. '*He wouldn't be so inconsiderate and would wait until I pull into my place instead of trying to run me off the road.*

Squinting, she glanced in the rear view mirror to see if she recognize the car or person driving, but the lights were too bright.

"You're a moron if you think I'm stopping." Too many stories floated around about people foolishly pulling over in these cases only to pay with their lives.

'*What an idiot,*' she thought and braced her hands tightly on the wheel. No one in the building would drive that careless on a dirt road in this weather.

"Why now?" She complained as a growing fear built in her. She refused to, be forced, into jeopardizing her life by going faster. She tapped her breaks hoping it would slow the moron down or get him to pass.  No such luck, he seemed intent on keeping on her tail.

Finally, the laneway came into view about fifty yards away so she clicked on her signal hoping the action would cause them to slow down long enough for her to pull off the road.

She expected them to back off long enough for her to turn of the road, but they sped up in an attempt to pass her. Afraid, she stayed focused on the laneway not daring a look over to see the assailant.  'It might be view as a challenge'. Instead of speeding past, they slowed to her pace as though taunting her.

Eventually, she had to pump the brakes almost to a stop so not to miss her turn. The sound of a horn blast resounded as they sped away spiting gravel at her car.

# Chapter 5

Angry tears burned her eyes as she pulled into the driveway to find Sally her down stairs neighbour had taken her spot.

"Why expect anything different with the way this night has unfolded so far?" Dana cried as she eased her car to stop, further away from the main door. *'Mr. Walters really should put a parking light out here."* She thought barely able to see the flicker of the light over the entrance.

She couldn't blame Sally; after all, they did have an arrangement that if she stayed in town Sally, could use the spot closes to the door. *'I did tell her this morning I'd be spending the night at mom's house.'* Thanks to Robert and his lovely wife that changed. *'If Lindsay hadn't taken it upon herself to barge in to interrupt our conversation, I'd be sipping hot chocolate by a cozy fireplace, instead of having the worst night of my life,'* Dana thought.

"On the other hand, if I controlled my stubborn side, I wouldn't be pulling into the lot complaining either." Dana took partial blame as a flash of lightening shot across the sky, once again.

Knowing the security of her apartment was steps away didn't make getting out of the car any easier, while her already overactive mind began to conjure up all sorts of evils lurking in the open fields.

The engine died as she shut down the car and tossed her keys into her bag. Cold and wet she dreaded stepping out into the rain again, but time was a factor. If the moron tailing her decided to backtrack

where she turned in it could mean trouble.
The idea of some crazy person or a bunch of
kids out for a thrill catching her alone in
her car, created an image she wasn't ready
to deal with. With a deep breath before
yanking on the handle, she darted out.

Sprinting, across the wet grass
towards the dimly lit light that hung above
the main entrance, she kept imagining that
an ominous figure now chased after her.
Adrenalin spurred her on as she expected to
feel a hand fall on her shoulder any
moment.

Relief flooded her as she reached the
entrance and yanked the door opened to
stand breathless in the lobby protected
from the wind and rain. Not wanting to
waste anymore time she rushed the steps two
at a time until she stood in front of her
door.

Still dripping, she ran around turning
on lights and the radio. Right now, she
needed to hear another voice, even though
it was riding on airwaves.

After a hot shower, she curled up on
the couch with a warm blanket and a large
cup of chocolate and let the coziness of
her familiar surroundings relax her.

The newscaster interrupted the music
to issue a tornado warning. Dana pulled the
soft fleece cover across her shoulders,
glad to be in doors.

Not even the howling wind racing
through the stairwells could reach her.

# Chapter 6

Dana tied to focus on the DJ but her mind kept drifting back to the funeral home. The way her life had been going, she wondered if she imagined the apparition that appeared in the towers. In the safety of her home, things didn't have the same daunting effect they did back at Mullin's place.

Sipping her chocolate, she realized that the sensation of being watch hadn't begun tonight. She tried to pinpoint the first time she felt like she was under someone's scrutiny and really couldn't come up with an exact date. She did know that two specific things had taken take place in her life around that time.

The first, Robert moved back to Chiapas Falls, with a woman no one knew anything about until they pranced into the family home and announced that they had eloped two weeks ago.

Dana shook her head, *'I can't believe they only knew each other for only six months, before she convinced him to slip a ring on her finger. Then she dragged him off to Vegas to have a simple wedding without including family.'* She thought than said. "Who would have thought, Robert was that stupid?"

The other incident involved the delivery of an old chest that belonged to her estranged Uncle after his un-timely death.

Dana suddenly recalled the first time she believed someone had been watching her. *'Leaving the hospital after dad took ill, that was it.'* She had walked out the front doors and turned around to look up at the fourth floor where he had his room. Instead of locating it, she had seen a woman in a white doctor's coat standing in the stairwell looking down at her from the window.

At the time, she pushed it aside as being paranoid. Plenty of people came and went from the hospital that day so why would she assume anyone would be staring at her.

"Hell, things were so mess up lately I can't be sure of anything right now."

Doubt filtered through her mind again. It didn't make sense why any one would be stalking her, but trying to put the pieces together only caused her head to ache. Right now, she wanted to enjoy the comforts and warmth of the apartment. She melted into the couch, and attempted to refocus on the voice coming over the radio.

"Mother Nature is giving us a beating tonight. Over the last hour, at least three tornadoes touched down in the area, folks. The police are asking everyone to remain in the safety of their homes unless there was a dire need to go out." He had barely finished his sentence when a bright flash of lightening swept across the sky, followed by a deafening bang that silenced the warning being issued, leaving everything in darkness. Dana jumped out of her seat realizing how tense she still was. Making her way to the kitchen, she pulled a flashlight and matches from the drawer. She tried to regain composure but her hands continued shaking while she ran around lighting enough candles to brighten up a reception hall. Afterwards she drew the curtains shut and went back to the couch. She swallowed back the last bit of her chocolate.

"Why bother?" She questioned, with a quick glance around. *'I should just go to bed and get a fresh start in the morning.'* She thought and began blowing out candles when a loud rap sounded at her door causing her to knock her empty mug over to the floor.

"What the hell is going on tonight?" Holding her chest, she ran to the door expecting to find Mr. Walters, the Landlord, making rounds to see if anyone needed any help.

Glancing at a photo of her father she had sitting on the coffee table she said, "You pick a hell of a day for a wake," then hurried to open the door. Already, she missed her father and wished he could be there now.

# Chapter 7

Opening the door Dana didn't expect to find Robert on the other side, caught in a hopeless battle with an umbrella the winds ravaged.

"I give up." He ended his struggle to flip the useless piece of protection right side.

"Are you alone?" She asked peering around the corner, relieved Lindsay hadn't accompanied him on his visit. Not seeing her didn't mean she couldn't be hiding in the shadows or waiting in the car.

'Who am I fooling, I may not know much about my new sister-in-law, but would wagered every penny I own that remaining in a car isn't something Lindsay does on the best of days, let alone on a dark horrible night like this.'

"I dropped Lindsay off at home, if that who you're looking for." He set the umbrella against the outside wall by the door.

"She allowed you to come out all by yourself." She couldn't resist a jab at him.

"I didn't come all this way to fight." Holding both hands up, he took a few steps backwards. Seeing him on the defensive with a slight smile crocked up on the right side of his face, she couldn't stay mad at her brother.

Instead, she had to chuckle at how sad he looked standing there decked out in his fancy suit and tie with water dripping off him. 'Definitely, not the same confident man I observed earlier in the evening.' She thought.

"It looks like you lost the battle," she pointed to the broken umbrella, her attitude, softened by the weather beaten look he displayed.   She wondered, what would have been more difficult, the drive across town in this horrific weather barely able to keep the car on the road, or explaining to his wife that she had to stay at home. Knowing the physical and emotional fight he had to endure to get there left her with the impression he still cared a little.

"No kidding. Half way across the parking lot a massive crash occurred pitching the entire world into solid blackness.   Believe me, if I knew these legs could move as quickly as they did, I would have become an Olympic sprinter." She laughed, as his comment brought back memories of the two of them growing up together. It amused her that storms still had an effect on him. Remembering the times, the two of them would be out on one of their adventures, how the first crack of thunder would send him racing ahead of her to get home. As her memory recalled, he wasn't kidding, those legs carried him through the trees and along the trails swiftly.

'*Those days were gone.*' She reminded herself, right now they had other issues to deal with.

"After the three ringed circus you had to put up with tonight, I would have guess that you'd be at home in bed instead of running the roads at this hour." Holding the door open, she moved aside for him to come in.

"Its funny how two people can see things so differently," he smiled, "but I'm not here to discuss Dad's wake," Stepping into the apartment he kicked his shoes off at the entrance while dripping on the carpet. "You ran out of there before we could finish our talk and I'm worried about you." He looked around at all the candles flickering. "Apart from trying to burn the place down I'd say you're holding up."

"I can take care of myself." She said determined not to let him know how frightened and alone she had felt moments before he arrived. Retrieving a towel from the linen closet, she tossed it at him then sat down and watched as he dried off. *'How different he looks, not the same as the day he ventured away from Chiapas Falls.'* She thought looking at her brother.

"Nice, cozy place you have here."

"You didn't trek all the way across town on a crazy night like this just to check out what my home looks like." Putting his head down, he rubbed the towel over the back of his neck for a few seconds before looking straight at her.

"I want us to be okay. I know things are different, but I'm still your big brother and I care about you. I chased after you earlier but caught your tail lights speeding away."

"I was out there for awhile crunched under this puny canopy at first and then by the car fishing around in a pool of water for my keys that slipped out of my hand." It was her way of letting him know she gave him ample time to catch her. She was tempted to say something snide about his wife, but held back.

"It took awhile before I could get outside. I know you were upset that our conversation got interrupted." He wiped his head again with the towel. "Just to let you know, the next time Lindsay sees us talking she won't barge in again."

The image of Lindsay sulking at home after a tiff with him over what happened at the funeral parlour amused her. She didn't think he had the gumption to choose family over his spoilt wife. *'Good to see you still have your manhood in tact.'* She wanted to say but kept it inside.

"You don't need to worry about me. I'm a big girl now, besides I really don't think Lindsay liked to see us talking."

"That's not it at all." he defended, "She doesn't have any family so she tries a little too hard to fit in with ours. To be honest, once I slipped the ring on her finger and uttered I do, she became part of our circle."

"Well it would have been nice if you would have taken some time to get to know her a little more before you did." She shook her head and looked away for a moment. "Think about it, Robert." She put empathizes on his name to make a point. "What would you do if I'd walked in with a man you never met and declared we just got married after six months?" She already knew his answer. "You'd flip out on me and probably the guy."

"Of course, I'd be upset. You're my baby sister." He admitted. *'Did he think that being a male made it right?'*

Curious as to how he would justify his actions, Dana wanted to hear all his excuses.

"If you want her to be part of our family why didn't you take the time to introduce her to us or invite us to the wedding?" Dana asked, but didn't wait for his answer before she started firing another question. "What kind of woman doesn't want her soon-to-be in-laws around to witness their vows?" Dana sat back on the couch. "For someone who really wants to be part of us she sure didn't make any effort to make us feel welcome at the ceremony." Just being able to vent and express her dislike for how his relationship began relieved a lot of pressure. "What were you thinking, Robert?"

"I'm not saying we made the right choice but I can't change things now, and really, I'm not here to discuss my reasons for how or why I got married." He cut that line of discussion off.

"I realize that Lindsay can be a little pushy, but she really is a sweet person with a big heart, it wouldn't hurt for you to give her a chance," he paused for a moment, as if he were deciding whether-or-not to complete the sentence. "I'm wondering if you are taking your anger at me out on her."

"Don't flatter yourself. I was young and stupid the day you left. In case you didn't notice I've grown up some since then." Dana remembered how she had clung to him bawling her eyes out, begging him to take her with him to University.

"Whoa, I'm sorry, it's just we are being open with each other so I'm throwing out ideas. I came here with my peace pipe."

Shaking her head, a small smile caressed her lips. *'He did it again, brought her back from a potential blow up with a single sentence.'* As a young girl anytime she got upset, he would always find her with his imaginary peace pipe. She couldn't remember a time it didn't work to flip her mood around.

One time he brought a lighter and plucked two straws from a field, then, they both sat Indian fashion smoking them in the middle of the field. He always knew what to say, but things were different now. He had a wife, whom Dana didn't get a good feeling about, for the sake of salvaging their relationship, she would let the issue go for now.

"I'm sure that piece pipe got you through a lot of rough spots in University," she teased, the tension eased from her shoulders.

"It may have a few times." Laughing he tossed the towel at her. "So what's been going on in your life? Is there a mister right you're hiding from us?" He teased.

"Yeah, he's holding out in the shower until you leave." She mused. Dating was never big on her list of things to do, especially with her choices limited to the guys around town. One thing for sure, she wasn't ready to discuss her single status with her brother.

For a moment, she debated if she should confide in him about the person watching her from the towers tonight and may have if a commotion hadn't erupted in the hallway.

"It's a few minutes after midnight and the hydro is out, is this the magical hour all the neighbours wake up restless and start partying?" He questioned.

"No, it's usually pretty quiet here. Something must be wrong," Grabbing the flashlight she ran to the door while Robert slipped his shoes back on.

# Chapter 8

The neighbours right across from her were already in the lobby gathering with most of the other tenants.

"You're the Doctor maybe you should go and see if anyone is hurt," she pointed a beam of light in his face and gently shoved her brother towards the steps.

"Are you kidding me? It looks like a cult group gathering for their weekly sacrifice." He whispered, and motioned in the direction of light beams bobbing in the lobby. All were, focused on a young man screaming. "The poor kid looks like he doesn't want to go willingly." Robert winked at his sister.

"That's Phil he lives in the apartment below me with his girl friend Sally. We wouldn't sacrifice him. We only go for people who are stupid enough to return to this dead beat town." She pointed the beam of light in his face again and laughed. "I guess that leaves you." Looping her arm through his she pulled him towards the activities in the lobby.

"Can I help? I'm a doctor," Robert didn't know why he felt the need to throw his title out with his introduction and even felt a little foolish doing so, but it got everyone's attention. The murmuring stopped immediately and suddenly all beams of lights turned towards him. "You gotta help her," Phil lunged at Robert startling him.

"Before I can do anything, you need to calm down, so you can tell me what's going on." Robert placed a hand on Phil's shoulder. He looked like a frustrated child trying to get attention and no one would listen. "Who is in trouble?"

He watched while Phil stepped away and lifted his arms up only to let them drop by his sides. He looked at Robert as though he couldn't understand why he wouldn't help.

"It's Sally, my girlfriend I think she's dead." He slapped his hands over his face and a loud gasp washed over the group.

"You don't know that for sure." Robert stated hoping to keep control. Even though it was a small group, he didn't want to have this bunch running amuck in the dark having a panic attack.

Any other time this entire scene would appear humorous. A group of people standing in the dark aiming beams of lights back and forth while a young man ranted on about someone being dead wasn't quite the norm.

If the reality of the situation hadn't been so frightening he would have laughed thinking someone was playing a joke on him, but his gut told him something seriously wrong was happening, Robert wondered if drugs were involved.

"Okay Phil. Can you tell me where Sally is?" Robert asked trying to keep things calm. Phil sucked in a large breath and nodded as he pushed the air from his lungs.

"She's in her car." Phil said, looking anxious that someone was finally going to check into his issue.

"Can you call the police?" Robert called up to Dana, who was still on the steps. He hoped they would find Sally alive once they got to the car, but preferred knowing the police were on the way just in case. 'Better to explain a misunderstanding *then finding out Phil was right and wishing he called sooner.'* Robert thought as he watched Dana race up the stairs.

For some reason, Phil felt the need to explain the events that lead to his finding the girl.

"Sally called earlier to say she wasn't sure what time she would be home, I fell asleep on the couch." He rubbed at watery eyes, "I woke up late and didn't see her so I went to stand at the road to see if there were any headlights," he sniffed the air and Robert thought he would go off again. "I didn't have far to go, she was in the parking lot all this time." His voice went to a high-pitch. "Just sitting in her car with her eyes frozen opened. I got scared and ran." He hung his head and wept.

"I need to check out the situation." Robert said, *'the whole thing feels wrong but telling this group could throw them all into an uncontrolled frenzy.'*

He wondered if the two had a fight that got out of hand. He hoped not and decided to leave that questioning to the police. *'Right now, there was a girl outside, who possible needed medical help.'* He turned his attention to the group that stood around staring at Phil with tired shocked looks on their faces, behind faded lights. It surprised him at how many people actually lived in the building. Taking control, he trusted Dana would be already making the call.

"Please, please can we go now?" Phil pleaded pulling on his arm. Robert looked into his eyes, it didn't look good, and in fact he thought the boy could be going into shock. *'I'd rather pack you away in a bed*

*with two tables of Lunesta for the night.'*
Robert thought.

The mixture of determination and fear on his face told Robert there would be no cooperation until someone accompanied him to check on the situation.

He hoped that it was a simple case of too much alcohol consumption, which rendered her incapable of making the short trip from the car to the apartment.

Since he somehow, got himself elected to escort the boy out to the scene to revive his girl friend, Robert decided he would prefer some back up.

"Hi, can I ask who you are?" He held his hand out to the older man who tried to maintain crowd control moments earlier.

"John Walters, the landlord."

"Good. My name is Robert, and Dana is my sister. Would you mind coming out with Phil and me." John nodded and Robert detected a look in his eyes that told him this whole circumstance had him shaken up some.

"Sure," he said.

Robert suspected nothing much happened out this way, so something this bizarre erupting at such a crazy hour caught everyone off guard.

"Ok Phil. John and I are going to go outside with you so we can get Sally to come in. Do you know if she had anything to drink tonight?" He could only pray he would say she was out with her friends.

"No, she spent the afternoon shopping with her mother then they went for supper afterwards, you know girls day out." Phil ran a finger under his nose.

Unless her mother was a raging alcoholic, Robert didn't think she would have let her daughter drive with a blood level so high it would render the girl unconscious in a cold car. Robert stared at him not quite sure what to make of him.

"Are we ready," Robert motioned to the door. "You have to promise me that you will stay calm. Can you do that?" Robert asked and looked out into the darkness. *'The last thing I need is for this kid to start freaking out once we get outside.'*

"Yes," he shook his head. With a deep breath, Robert nodded to John and after someone shoved a flashlight in his hand he lead the way out into the darkness.

## Chapter 9

"Which way Phil?" Robert motioned aiming a beam of light in the direction of the walkway. *'Let's get this girl inside quickly so I can put this place behind me and start home.'* Robert thought, he could only imagine how pissed off Lindsay would be at him by now.

Phil pointed out into nothingness, and to encourage him Mr. Walters placed a hand on his shoulder.

"We're right behind you, son." He said and gave him a gentle push forward.

"This is insane." Robert whispered more for his own ears as he watched two shadows step slowly into the darkness. *'How the hell, did I manage to get into this mess?'* He questioned.

Once he dropped Lindsay off at the house, his intentions were to have a quick visit with Dana to put their differences aside, then after a few hugs head home to his bed. He believed they were getting somewhere until this chaos exploded.

The rain let up somewhat, but the winds continued to pound at the trees with a fury. *'I doubt even a dry cleaning will be able to rescue the Horst Dusseldorf,'* he questioned. *He could feel the 100% Merino Wool tightening across his shoulders.*

He couldn't help but remember the day Lindsay dragged him into Moore's to purchase the suit. *'Six hundred dollars and it'll probably shrink like a prune the minute it dries out.'* Robert thought as he clutched at his jacket. *'By the time this night is through it might fit a small boy.'*

Being there didn't feel right, in fact, the whole scene felt wrong, Phil appeared edgy, the closer they got. It bothered him that he felt obligated to drag himself out here to talk some girl out of a car, who probably had too much to drink and just needs to sleep it off. *'Maybe helping Dana's friend will bring us a little closer.'* Robert thought and hurried to catch up to the others.

At the end of the walkway, as if he read Robert's mind, Mr. Walters put a hand on Phil's arm to stop him.

"Why don't we give the doctor some room and wait here while he checks on Sally?" Robert had expected Phil to dart out and race to the girl, instead with the insistence of the older man he stopped a few feet short of the vehicle and stood looking back at him like a frightened animal.

Again, he wondered if the two had an argument and lashed out at the girl. Looking at the kid, he wouldn't peg him as the type to hurt anyone, but some of the most notorious killers had innocent baby faces.

"He's right it would be better if you stay here." Robert agreed, pointing his light into the darkness. His whole body trembled while his gut instincts kept telling him he would find the lifeless body of a young girl.

If nothing else this night would definitely give him and Dana a common ground to reflect back on. *'I can only hope the memory ends happy, one we can laugh at later.'* He thought.

He had to admit that so far nothing in his past compared to this.

Hopefully, Dana's call would have the police rushing to the scene. Right now, he wished that by some miracle, red, flashing lights would race into the driveway before he reached his destination.

# Chapter 10

"This shouldn't take too long." Robert filled his lungs with a breath of courage before he slipped past them.

Taking slow steps, he focused on the vehicle, all the while thinking no amount of schooling could prepare anyone for this.

Accepting the offer at the local hospital, he believed he would be coming home to a cozy position where his patients would walk in to his office. Of course, he knew death would be inevitable; *'it came with the job,'* not this soon though and definitely not under these conditions.

He pointed the flashlight through the window where he could see the young girl slumped over motionless in the front seat. At first glance, he thought his assumptions might be right. If not, he had seen enough cop shows to know, he had to take precautions. He didn't want to give anyone a reason to point a finger at him for destroying evidence. *'I bet preserving a crime scene probably wasn't top priority on Phil's agenda when he first discovered the girl.'* Robert thought.

Reaching the passenger door, he tried to find comfort in maintaining, the idea of too much alcohol, which rendered the poor girl unconscious. Carefully lifting the handle he pulled it open, a dim light flickered on giving him a clearer view.

Robert hoped that the action would evoke some kind of movement, but cringed, as she remained motionless.

"Sally you okay," He asked, "Oh no," any hopes of her being inebriated disappeared as he aimed the beam from his flashlight on her face. Looking at cold, crystal, blue eyes void of any life, he knew there would be no pulse. Regardless of his sentiment, he reached in with one last attempt. With hands shaking he placed two fingers on her juggler, her skin felt cold to his touch. He flinched at the sensation of a thin nylon rope pulled tightly around her neck.

Backing out of the car, his stomach wrenched, he moved quickly to the side and heaved. *'This girl was murdered.'* The words screamed in his mind. After a few minutes, he gently shut the door leaving the girl in peace.

He looked in the direction of his two companions, shadows behind the dim glow of light. His first instinct was to put as much distance between himself and this place.

"Where are the police," he moaned to himself, he preferred them to break the news to Phil about Sally being dead. "Why the hell didn't I stay at home like Lindsay insisted?" He mumbled under his breath. Now, he had the duty of telling Phil his analysis of the situation was right. *'It's not like I'd be telling him anything he didn't figure out already. For all I know Phil could have killed her.'* Robert reasoned.

He knew the situation, did he expect the Doctor could perform a miracle and bring her back. *'I'll go as far as confirming the death but the cops will have to deliver the part about murderer.'* From the coldness of her body, he guessed her death happened a few hours ago. *'The*

*coroner would determine the exact time.'*
Robert felt ill.

He gave himself a few moments to gain his composure back before approaching the two.

Phil couldn't wait. He wanted his suspicions validated. Even in the darkness, Robert could feel the eyes fix in his direction.

"Sally is dead, isn't she?" Phil demanded his voice shaky. John shone the light on Robert who gave a nod. He felt helpless not knowing what else he could do or say that would offer any kind of comfort for the lost of a loved one under the circumstance.

"I'm sorry." He put a hand on Phil's shoulder, expecting him to break out screaming, instead a low groan escaped from deep within.

"Let's get him inside." He motioned with the flashlight towards the building. His concern now shifted to the welfare of Phil. John immediately wrapped an arm around his shoulders in a fatherly gesture and guided him towards the door.

Robert expected he would have nightmares about this night forever. The thing that nagged at him the most was the realization that there was an eerie familiarity about the girl. For some reason he felt like he had met her before, but couldn't place where. He began to get nervous, staring out into the darkness and wondered if the killer could still be lurking out there hiding while watching on the sidelines.

For all Robert knew it could be one of the occupants that gathered in the lobby earlier. '*What kind of hellhole did Dana set up house in?*' It chilled him to think, his little sister might be sharing a building with someone capable of murder. Even before he drove into the lot, tonight, he didn't get a good feeling.

Robert formed an instant dislike for the place the moment his mother told him where Dana lived and the fight their father had trying to get her to move closer to home. No one had to tell him why she made the decision to live in the remotest area she could find. Stubbornness and pride motivated his sister to do foolish things. It was her way of expressing her independence.

Well, tonight settled it, their father may have had no luck in talking sense into her, but he would. '*If I have to drag you out of here kicking and screaming, your little act of rebellion is coming to an end, very soon.*'

# Chapter 11

What only took a few minutes to accomplish seemed like an eternity, Robert thought, as the three stepped inside the warmth off the apartment away from the elements.

"It sounds like they moved to my place." John said, pointing the flashlight towards a low murmur emitting from an open door on the main level. Robert thought the old man's face aged ten years since they went out. The wrinkles were more defined making him look older then minutes earlier, when he first met him.

His grey hair stood straight up from the wind. The trip to the car had taken a toll on him and Robert regretted not taking someone younger. Despite, everything, John still held a protective arm around the boy as he led the way to his home.

'*It looks like a gathering for a seance,*' Robert surmised in his mind as he followed them inside. He couldn't shake his earlier notion about something wrong with the occupants of this building as he watched them all assembled in the living room huddled around candles.

A tight knot gripping his stomach became a constant reminder that he walked into something evil when he came to visit Dana. Earlier they joked, but looking around at the group Robert questioned the possibility that his sister somehow got involved in a weird cult group. '*It would definitely explain her mood swings.*'

At the sight of the three men coming in, the chatter dropped-off immediately, and all eyes focused on them.

"Sally is dead!" Phil blurted out his eyes wild with fear. A gasp came from the group.

"What happened?" Someone questioned while others started to cry.

"Until an autopsy is performed we won't know." Robert decided informing the occupants a murder had been committed was the duty of the Police, not his.

Saying more than needed might tip the killer off if they were in the room. Without looking too suspicious, he tried to search out their faces through the darkened shadows of the candles. With limited lighting, fear was the only thing visible their eyes.

The idea that one of these people was possibly Sally's killer nagged his thoughts. It frightened him that someone in the room could be responsible for taken a life tonight, and were cold blooded enough to mingle with the rest of the neighbours without any remorse.

Judging people was something Robert liked to avoid, but suddenly they all looked guilty to him. Their movements looked robotic as they cleared a path so John could sit Phil down on the couch.

Right now, Robert's gut instinct told him to grab his sister and run fast and hard away from the place. A quick scan of the room revealed she was nowhere to be found, 'did I really expect to find different? Crowds were never her thing.' Robert thought.

He knew she would rather stay hidden in the solitude of her apartment waiting for him to return with his findings.

"I'm going to wait for the police with Dana. They shouldn't be too long." Robert said hoping the others would take the hint and head to their homes also.

His words had an awaking effect on Phil breaking his semi trance like state.

"Sally's dead because of me." He cried out, instantly getting everyone's attention on him.

"Did you kill her?" One of the men boldly questioned and the rest of the people stood back and stared down at him.

'Choose your words carefully,' Robert thought, 'it looks like these nice folks could easily turn into an angry mob.'

"We had a big fight before she left to meet her mother."

"What did you fight about?" A short rotund woman stepped up from behind the group and asked. She stared at him with a stern glare fixing her next move on how he answered her question.

Robert contemplated inching he way to the door but fear they might find it suspicious and turn on the only stranger on the scene.

Phil stood and scanned the room as if he were looking for someone. "Something stupid." He fell back down on the couch and slapped his hands over his face again. "Oh no, what am I going to tell her parents. They trusted me to take care of their daughter, and now she dead." A terrified boy stared up at Robert. "I have to call them." Phil turned to Robert, who had no idea if the boy just confessed or felt his actions caused her to be in the wrong place. 'He didn't really answer any of their questions.' Robert thought.

Who could know what went on tonight between them? Robert decided the police would have quite the job sorting this mess out. His duty was to make sure Phil was okay and wouldn't go into shock. He pulled two packets of Donormyl from his pocket that he brought thinking his mother might need for tonight, but she insisted on going home without any drugs.

He never imagined he would be handing them over to a young man who discovered his girlfriend was murdered.

"Let's wait until the police get here and they can decide what needs to be done." A picture of Phil blurting out to the parents that he killed their daughter would only add to the panic when they rushed to the scene.

The police would be more sympathetic. "Can I get a glass of water?" He asked Mrs. Walters who ran to the sink and came back quickly while everyone else stood back as though watching a scene of a movie unfold.

"For now, take these." He ripped the packet opened and placed two tablets into Phil's hand. Mrs. Walter handed him the glass and without any questions as to what a complete stranger handed him, he washed them back like candy."

"I don't want to tell anyone what to do but, Phil needs to settle down so it might be better if everyone waited in their own homes." Robert suggested.

Surprisingly, they slowly dispersed without challenging him. Some of them passed by Phil, and patted his shoulder before leaving, while others glared at him not knowing what to make of his confession.

"If you need anything, don't hesitate to knock on our door." A couple in their fifties offered before going. Phil stared at the floor oblivious to them all.

"Is there a place he can stay for the night?" Robert asked thinking he should be around people instead of being alone.

"We'll keep him in the spare bedroom." Mr. Walters offered.

"That will be best." Robert said. "These pills work fast so maybe we should move him now."

"Come in here my dear." Mrs. Walter's voice took on a motherly tone as she pulled on his arm to encourage him to stand.

"Do you think we should keep him awake until the police talk to him?" Mr. Walters questioned.

"He'll probably be out by the time they get here so they might have to wait until morning." Robert said wondering why there hadn't arrived yet.

"Dana's fortunate to have a brother who is a doctor. We really appreciate that you were here tonight." Mr. Walters placed an appreciative hand on Robert's shoulder.

"Thank you I'm just sorry about the circumstances I had to meet everyone under." Robert said knowing that if things unfolded differently tonight he would never have taken the time to know these people.

"Help me to get him into the bedroom." Mrs. Walters spoke to her husband. "Thank you, Robert, we can take care of him now."

"I better check on Dana. Thank you for taking care of him, just make sure he contacts his doctor in the morning." Robert suggested.

"The moment he wakes up, I'll get him to call." Mrs. Walters said and Robert watched as they disappeared down the hallway then he left.

Before he put his foot on the first step to go up to Dana's place, flashing lights lit up the parking lot. He considered calling up to Dana but thought doing so would trigger another gathering in the lobby if others heard. He doubted any of the tenants went home and crawled into their beds, the excitement would be too much for anyone to sleep.

If anything, they were probably staring out their windows at the arrival of the police. With a quick look at the door, he stepped back and went to greet the officers, grateful for their arrival.

## Chapter 12

A shrilling ring of the telephone broke through the silence of the night. Jake Turner looked up at the clock on his wall and wondered what could possibly be happening to warrant someone calling in past midnight. He pulled a double shift and was ready to pack it in and call it a night until, he noticed Helen, the receptionist, asking the caller some interesting questions.

With his office just outside the main entrance, he often heard incoming calls but this one was different. Her, voice held the same excited pitch she always maintained with the callers. The questions were what interested him and the way she repeated the information back as though what she heard was inconceivable.

"Do you know if the girl is alive?" Helen kept badgering the caller. Obviously, the person on the other end of the line refused to feed her hunger for gossip.

Curiosity got the better of him. His chair scraped across the floor as he pushed back from his desk. He sauntered out into the reception area and gave Helen a look that said do you want me to take the call but the caller hung up. She handed a pink, slip of paper out to him with details scribbled on it.

"Jake, it sounds like we might have a dead body of a young girl." Helen's voice level raised causing Bill Fletcher the only other officer on duty at the station, to leave the comforts of his office.

"What's going on?" Bill questioned and Helen turned to him please to have an audience to relate her story.

"I'm not sure but the caller requested that we rush someone over to Walter's apartment building just outside of town, on highway ten. She said something about a girl in a car that might be hurt. I think it's more serious then that." Helen's face was red with excitement and Jake knew an enhanced version of the call would be all over town before morning.

He learned a long time ago not to get too concerned about the information Helen passed along to them until he investigated it first. She liked to embellish on the stories related to her by adding her own flavour when telling things back to others. 'Calm down Helen,' Jake thought. He believed she would come in and work free for the shear fact that she heard the gossip first hand.

"Helen, let's not jump the gun or come to any conclusions before getting our facts straight." Jake cautioned. "Did the caller sound like they might have had a few to many?" Jake questioned knowing that, starting on a Friday afternoon the moment the Mill closed its doors for the weekend, Johnny's Bar and Grill, opened theirs. "This could simply be a case of someone passing out in their car, after a few drinks."

"You could be right but I don't think so. The girl sounded a little frightened but intelligent."

A loud crash of thunder clapped over the building and rain beat at the windows.

"It's a great night for this to be happening." Bill glanced out the front door at the flashes of light.

"I just need a few minutes to clear my desk then I'll head over there and check it out before I go home for the night." Jake turned to Helen who eyes lit with excitement. "In the mean time, send a squad car and put a call into the hospital, as well and have them send an ambulance." 'It could all be for nothing but its better to lean on the side of caution.' Jake thought.

At thirty-two Jake had made a name for himself as a good detective. He started out working along side his father in Toronto. A few years back he retired, so Jake decided to break away from the big city and the crimes that came with it. He put in for a transfer and when an offer came in a year ago to relocate to Chiapas Falls, he jumped on it without any hesitation.

The small town hidden three hours north of Toronto had been exactly what he wanted. The crime rate was low in the town but the higher ups decided no matter how small the precinct a detective would be available. So, under Chief Timmons, Jake was more than willing to fill those shoes and work along side seven cops and three clerks to handle the incoming calls.

It only took a few minutes to clear his desk then Jake headed for the door.

"You be careful out there, Sugar." Helen flashed him a smile that hinted she was his for the taken.

"Good night, Helen." Jake kept it cool to discourage her unwanted advances. From the day he arrived, she made little innuendos about them hooking up. He managed to brush it off but lately she pushed it more by leaving treats on his desk with notes.

So far, he avoided marriage and the women working at the station openly referred to him as the most eligible bachelor around. The other two women who shared the job with Helen were happily married. Helen on the other hand felt determined to change both their marital status.

He liked the idea of marriage, but meeting someone he wanted to spend his life with was difficult. The woman he committed himself to would have to be interested in the simple things in life, like roughing it in a tent by a campfire for the weekend. Settling for the sake of being married held no appeal to Jake.

When he did does decide to make a life long commitment to someone, Helen definitely was off the radar with Helen and her over active mouth. Jake determined as she headed to his car.

## Chapter 13

By the time, Jake pulled into the lot the squad car and ambulance were already at the scene. Surveying the area, he expected to find a cluster of teenagers stumbling around drunk. He was surprised to find an officer taping a police line around a vehicle. *'Looks like Helen's spider senses work for once.'* Jake thought.

Curiosity replaced the exhaustion he felt at the station. He slid out from behind the wheel of his car. Shoving his hands into his coat pockets, he braced himself against the wind and made his way to the cop struggling to keep the tape in place.

"What's the story here tonight, Wayne?" Jake shouted into the wind.

"Murder, there's a young girl in the car with a nylon rope wrapped tightly around her neck. The forensic team got here a few minutes ago and are working on her now." The cop shouted and Jake was sure he detected the same kind of excitement in his voice that Helen displayed earlier. Wayne was a young man who joined the force a few months before Jake packed his bags and relocated to this town.

His love for food was starting to show as his belly hung over his belt. He spoke with a country drawl and although he didn't have the typical look of a cop, Jake felt he was one of the most dedicated in the force. He took his roll seriously and whenever a case came his way he detailed even the smallest evidence.

"Do we know who found the body?"

"I think Doc Reed did, Frank's over there talking to him now." Wayne pointed towards the two men, standing in the headlights.

"Thanks Wayne," Jake nodded then headed in the direction to where a distinguished-looking man stood.

*'Very convenient,'* Jake thought, *'a Doctor just happen to be at the scene of a murder and discovered the body.* No way did the doctor set up house in this building. *Hell, even in the headlights I can tell his suit probably cost more than a few month of rent in this place.'*

The whole idea piqued Jake's interest as to why a doctor would be hanging around this neighbourhood after midnight, with a dead girl in a car.

"How's it going, Frank?" Jake turned his attention to the older cop first.

"Not too good, Jake. Dr. Reed was just about to tell me how he found the dead girl tonight."

Jake turned to face the Doctor. "Dr. Reed, I'm Detective Turner with the Chiapas Falls police station. Is there some where we can talk inside, away from this weather?" There were questions Jake needed to ask but preferred to conduct his investigation where the Doctor could concentrate on more than the winds chewing at him.

"My sister lives on the top floor. We can go there?"

"Good." *'That's one I can scratch off my list,'* Jake thought and followed Frank and the Doctor to the building. His mind raced with questions. *'Was the Doctor there to cover up something for his sister?'*

Stepping into the lobby the lights flickered on and off a few times, before they clicked on permanently.

"Good timing," Frank remarked looking more content to be in where things were relatively quiet and warm.

As though, he sat waiting for them to come in, an older man rushed out from one of the apartments to greet them.

"Hello, I'm John Walters and I own and take care of this place." He introduced himself.

"Just the man we need to see." Jake commented and turned to Frank, "no sense in disturbing anyone else tonight did you want to go and have a talk with Mr. Walters and I'll finish up with Dr. Reed?"

"Sure, I'll get a list of names for the tenants, that way we can come back in the morning to talk to them."

"Good idea." Jake said curious to chat with the Doctor.

He was interested to see what reason he had for being at a mediocre little building outside of town on the worst night of the year, looking like, someone plucked from a high fashion event and tossed out in the middle of nowhere. Add a dead girl into the equation then, you have a real mystery. Which, Jake intended to close the book on quickly.

He couldn't imagine what dire need could there be for his sister to have summoned him out there?

Frank turned to the caretaker, "why don't we step into your place?" He gestured and John nodded his approval.

"How's the boy?" Robert asked before they could disappear into John's apartment.

"He finally settled down and went to sleep."

"Good, he needs the rest." Robert said.

"Which boy is that?" Jake cut into their conversation.

"Phil, Sally was his girlfriend and he found her out there tonight." John volunteered the information.

"I thought you discovered the body." Jake wondered how they could have missed a detail like this. He searched back and forth to the two men to see if he could read anything in their eye contact.

"Phil, did…" the landlord started to give the details and Jake raised a hand.

"Frank will take your statement in a minute. Can we wake him?" Jake asked.

"I doubt he'd be helpful. He was in shock so I gave him something to settle him down so he could sleep." Robert said.

Even though Jake felt a huge disconnect between the man standing before him and this quaint little place boarding on the town's edge, he detected a genuine concern for the boy. He wondered if the connection to the place went beyond his sister.

From what he could see, the building was clean and well kept and probably would be something he might consider if he didn't prefer owing his own home. Jake found himself intrigued about the sister.

"It must have been horrible for him to find his girlfriend murdered." Jake said, wondering if the doctor deliberately ensure, the boy wouldn't be awake when the police arrived.

"Murdered," John ran his fingers across his brow. "How could this happen?" Jake watched the older man as he absorbed the knowledge that the girl's death now became a murder. It impressed him that the doctor kept that detail quiet until the proper authorities arrived. Right now, to avoid them from collaborating about the events that happened here tonight, he needed to separate the two men.

"Let him sleep tonight. An officer will come by in the morning to have a chat with him." *'I doubt the boy would be coherent enough if the doctor pumped him full of sleeping pills.'* Jake thought.

"Just make sure he doesn't take off anywhere before he talks to an officer."

"My wife and I will keep him with us." John said and led Frank to his apartment.

"I'll follow you." Jake stated, and Robert nodded as he started up the stairs. "She won't mind us barging in on her this late?"

"I don't think so."

"I have a few questions that shouldn't take too long, after that I'll head out and you can get on with your night." Jake studied the doctor's body language for any signs of nervousness but could only see a man in total control, keeping his emotions in check. *'A little too calm,'* Jake thought.

# Chapter 14

Exhaustion overwhelmed Dana but her mind refused to slow down. The whole night explode into a horror scene. *'How does a bad evening get worse? What was wrong with Sally to keep her in the car for so long?'* The questions kept flashing through her head.

Dana suspected this night would be a long sleepless one and would give anything to start the day again, so she could change the outcome.

She considered going back down to join the group but decided to pop some aspirin instead. Getting involved in all the speculation and gossip would only enhance the ache developing across her forehead.

She could picture the frenzy going on over Phil's assumption that he thought Sally was dead, *'it all sounded so crazy. He has to be wrong.'*

It bothered Dana that she ran right past Sally in her haste to get inside tonight. The idea was almost too much for her to handle, *'if I would have taken the time I could have helped Sally out if she needed it.'*

A deep sigh of frustration filtered through her lungs.

"What could be taking Robert so long?" Dana asked tying to get her mind off the what-ifs.

*'Can this night get any worse?'* She wondered as she sat down and pulled her knees tightly to her chest.

Rocking back and forth on the couch her mind raced trying to put things in their proper prospective. She searched for any logical reason for the events that went on today; there was nothing but emptiness. Her life was a mess, first her family and now where she lives. Tears took over. *'Nothing made any sense, Sally, is young and healthy. Could she really be dead? No Phil must be overreacting.'*

A familiar voice from the radio came on with a sudden blast at the same time the lights flickered.

"Thank goodness." Dana said, holding her chest as her heart race she jumped of the couch to turn down the radio and put out the melting candles. Just as she extinguished the last one Robert walked in, tailed by a man she guessed had to be with the police. Even in plain clothes and no official uniform, he held an air about him that screamed cop.

"Is Sally okay?" She demanded of her brother. His silence and sad eyes gave her the answer she feared most.

"I'm sorry Dana," Robert took her hand and sat down with her on the couch.

"What happened?" She asked, allowing her tears to flow not caring what the stranger thought.

"I'm not sure. But Detective Turner has some questions he'd like to ask." Robert motioned at Jake who took a seat across from them without waiting for an invitation.

# Chapter 15

"What kind of questions?" Dana demanded and stared into piercing blue eyes.

"I'm sorry to barge in on you at this late hour." Jake apologized sensing her irritation.

He expected to find a tall lanky woman with dark hair strutting around with an air of sophistication about her. He was pleasantly surprised to find a young pretty woman occupying the couch curled up in an insecure ball.

'The differences between the two siblings were big. *I never would have guessed the two came from the same parents.' Jake thought.*

Robert stood tall with a dark Mediterranean complexion, the typical school jock with the prom queen sister. She appeared frail with a small framed body about five feet three inches. She had long light brown hair stretching down the full length of her back and a slight tan. The only thing they held in common was they were both extremely good looking. In fact, her face verged on beautiful.

"I'm sorry this day has been a real difficult one." Jake said and Dana held up a hand.

"I just don't know how you think I can help. As far as I know, Sally was very healthy. Apart from a few colds I've never seen her sick since I moved in." Dana reached for a tissue and dried her eyes. "We never socialized much outside the laundry and summer barbecue's so if she had a chronic illness she hid it from me."

"Sally didn't die from any ailments." Jake realized that no one had time to update her on what actually happened here tonight.

"What did she die from?" She looked back and forth between the two men confused.

Jake gave a quick look in Robert's direction, if she started to act out, her brother might have a better chance of calming her down.

"I'm sorry but someone murdered your friend."

"Murdered, why would someone want to kill Sally?" She looked at Jake as though he were insane before covering her face in her hands.

"There's no answer for that now, but I intend to find out very soon." Jake said. "When was the last time you spoke with Sally?"

"This morning in the laundry room, I told her I had my father's wake tonight and she was going to spend the afternoon shopping with her mother." Dana said. Jake thought she reached her breaking point.

"Our father passed away earlier this week." Robert placed a hand on her shoulder.

"I'm sorry about your father." Jake said to both of them, now understanding the suit. "This must be stressful for you. Are you going to be okay to answer some questions?"

"Yes, what do you need to know?" Dana said wanting to help in anyway she could.

"Do you know if Phil and Sally had a fight or argument?" Jake asked.

"If they fought they kept it behind close doors. They were so happy every time I saw them together." She stated with a confidence then turned to Robert.

"Dana, Phil told everyone downstairs they had an argument before Sally left to see her mother."

"That doesn't mean he killed her." Dana stated. "You and I fight all the time and we're both still alive." Dana snapped at Robert who gave a weak smile and shook his head.

"True."

"Do both of you live here?" Jake controlled a smile at how she kept her brother in check. For a small woman she definitely had a strong personality that Jake gathered clashed with her brother's way of thinking, at times.

"No, Robert lives across town," Dana volunteered the information.

"710 Reindeer Lane." Robert related his address and Jake jotted it down.

"The weather's really bad out there. Did you drive your sister home tonight?" Jake glanced at the wedding band on his finger and wondered where his wife went.

"No, Dana left upset so I came to see if she was okay." Robert said.

"On a night like this a phone call might have been better." Jake eyed them suspiciously. '*Is little miss prom queen a tad spoilt and big brother has to cater to her,*' Jake wondered but somehow he didn't think so.

"You're probably right, but I wanted to talk to my sister face-to-face." Robert sat up defensively and clasped his hands together in front of him. "Trying to express feelings over a phone just doesn't have the same meaning." He said.

"I'd be really upset if my father died." Jake nodded his understanding. "For me though, I would want to be around family, not run from them."

"If you have to know Dana and I had a bit of an argument, and I came to make it right." Robert said.

"Were you really angry when you got here?" Jake questioned Robert.

"What are you getting at, Detective?" Dana broke in.

"I'm sorry if my questions are bothering you but a young girl was murdered here tonight and I need to cover all angles." Jake stated not holding any punches.

"I don't need any reminders about what happened to Sally." Dana stood up and a strong woman replaced the frail little thing curled up on the couch moments earlier. "My father is dead and I couldn't handle mulling around a group of people gawking down at him as his lifeless body lay on display for them all to view. I decided to leave and Robert wanted me to hang around so we argued over our difference of opinion and I left in a hurry. Robert came to check on me because that's what siblings do for each other."

"It's okay Dana. The detective is just doing his job." Robert tried to settle her down.

"No Robert. Nothing is okay. Dad is dead and so is Sally and this guy is insinuating that we have something to do with her death."

"It's late, and you're tired. Why don't I come back tomorrow?" Jake suggested. He could see that the only thing going on here was these two had family issues they needed to resolve.

"I think that would be better," Robert agreed and looked in Dana's direction.

"That's fine with me," Dana said.

"If you like Dr. Reed I can call on you at your home or you can meet me here tomorrow morning around eleven."

"My house will be better, unless, you want me here with you?" Robert turned to Dana.

"I can take care of myself besides I think Lindsay needs you more than I do." Jake detected a hint of sarcasm.

There was more to these two then they were willing to admit and he intended to uncover the story behind the scene.

"I'll drop by here around noon after I finish with Robert. Does that give you enough time?" Jake said and placed his business card on the coffee table.

"I'm not going anywhere, so I'll be here." Dana walked to the door with the two men.

"Dana if you're alright I'm going to head out also," Robert said.

"Sure, I need to get some sleep." As the two men stepped out into the hallway, Dana turned to Robert.

"Thanks for coming to see me tonight. Hopefully we can finish our conversation."

"Definitely we will do a lot more talking now that I'm back in town." With a quick peck on the cheek, he followed Jake and bumped into him when he stopped abruptly on the stairs and looked up at Dana.

"Just one question before I go. What time were you at the funeral parlour tonight?"

"My wife and I picked up my mother and were there by five and left around nine thirty then I dropped my mother and wife off. Dana showed up at six-fifty I know because I watched the clock and was upset at her tardiness. I saw her driving away at eight." Robert answered for her.

"Thanks, lock your door and don't open it for anyone. I left my card. You can call anytime if you need to."
The two men waited until they could hear the lock turning before they left.

# Chapter 16

Robert jolted from a deep sleep, the image of his nightmare clear in his mind. He forced his eyes open hoping that the daylight would erase the image of Sally's cold dead eyes staring at him. *'How long will those eyes haunt my dreams?'* He wondered, as he slowly crawled out of bed.

If this would have been one of his patience, he would have ordered them to keep their minds busy with other things, and that was just what he intended to do.

The sound of Lindsay fussing around in the kitchen, reminded him that the first chore this morning was to make peace with his wife. They were only married a short time but he knew her well enough to know that she was sitting down stairs in full battle gear waiting for him.

He opted for a shower before going to face her. This way he could combat some of his tiredness.

An hour later, he found Lindsay sitting at the table sipping coffee, catching up on the morning news. He could see by how she sat with her back straight and stiff that he hadn't been forgiven yet.

Reaching for the almost empty pot of coffee, he figured she was fully rested and running on caffeine. The only way he could possible win this battle would be to keep his mouth shut and put up with the nagging until she tired out.

Even before, he could sit at the table, she held up the front page of the newspaper at him. A surge of pain jabbed at him with the sight of Sally's smiling face looking at him. Again, he wondered if her frozen eyes of death would dim from his memory or would haunt him for the rest of his life.

"This town isn't as peaceful as you lead me to believe," Lindsay shot him a cold look. Ignoring her stares and snide remarks, Robert wondered how the press had obtained a picture of the girl so quickly. He couldn't recall seeing any news people around, last night. "Isn't murder what happens in the big city? How far away is this place?" She sneered and a half laugh gurgled in her throat as she continued ranting. "I did feel safe in my bed last night but this could have been me feathered on the front page this morning," Lindsay rambled on without waiting for any answers. "If you intend to rush off and leave me alone to defend myself we better up the security on this place."

His first intention had been to let her rant, but, she was looking for blood and he just didn't have anymore to give.

"Give me a break, Lindsay. Are you going to pull this little stunt every time I visit with Dana?"

"Your little sister poses no threat to me. I'm just stating a fact, that it could have been me. You barely slowed the car down enough for me to jump out. For all we know the murderer could have been hiding behind a hedge watching as you left me."

"You know I waited until you were inside before I drove away." Robert claimed losing his patience.

"Hardly." Lindsay said indifferently.

"It more likely could have been my sister because it happened at her building." Tired of the continuous bickering Lindsay was doing Robert decided to end it by setting the facts straight.

"Are you serious?" Lindsay stared at him with her jaw hanging down.

"I wouldn't joke about something like this. In fact, the tenants elected me to be the one to check on the girl."

"Oh my poor baby, tell me everything," Lindsay's attitude flipped from a sulking nagging mate to a tender, caring wife. Sliding off her chair, she picked up the plate of croissants and shoved them in front of him like a peace offering.

"I don't really want to discuss it right now." He sipped at his coffee glad that not only did he survive round one but also managed to end the fight. "A detective is going to show up around eleven o'clock this morning to ask some questions. So you will get the scoop the moment he arrives."

"That's only an hour. I need to shower and get dressed," Lindsay rushed to put her mug in the dishwasher before she raced for the stairs. Stopping in mid stride, she turned to Robert.

"Darling I've been thinking, we have been in Chiapas Falls for almost a month now and none of our friends have been down to visit. So I think we need to have a house warming party."

"Lindsay, how can you be thinking about parties at a time like this?" Robert felt drained and exhausted. "I'm still reeling from my father's death and trying to get settled in at the hospital and believe me, after walking into the scene I did, last night. Entertaining isn't high on my priority list right now."

Lindsay ran and put her arms around his neck.

"I know darling it must have been horrible. But, that's exactly why we need to surround ourselves with our friends and family." She gave him a quick kiss. "It wouldn't hurt Dana to let her hair down and party for awhile either."

"You'd invite Dana after the little tantrum she pulled at the funeral home last night." He smiled down at her remembering her sensitive side, and how quickly, she could forget things people did against her.

"You don't worry about your baby sister she just needs some time to get to know me. Once she does we'll be best friends." She gave him a peck on the lips. "I got your mom to love me didn't I?" He had to laugh at her confidence.

"That's true." From the moment he introduced Lindsay to his mother they clicked together. "I just think it would be better if we didn't have so much going on around us."

"Nothing, we do is going to erase the problems but we need to push them aside for awhile." Robert stared into her eyes dancing with excitement and softened. He shouldn't be blaming her for the problems that keep popping up in his life between Dana and him.

It wasn't her fault that she married into his crazy family circle. Robert told himself to ease up and to stop being so hard on her.

"You don't have to go through the trouble," he brushed her lips with his.

"Darling, your job is to make people better. My job is to be a good wife and plan your social life. It will be fun and you won't have to do a thing but show up."

"Alright, just let me know what day and time," Robert smiled down at her then gently pushed her hair behind her ear.

"You better go and get dressed before the detective gets here." He watched her run up the stairs, thinking she did have a point. He would never drive away unless he made sure his wife was safe inside with doors locked tightly.

A madman walked the streets and until the police capture this person you never know what his next move would be, or, who he would target as his next victim. Robert had no idea what he would ever do if it were Lindsay or Dana they found murdered in such a horrible way. He couldn't even imagine the pain that Phil would wake up to this morning.

# Chapter 17

Dana woke to a ray of sun spilling into her room, even the warmth couldn't remove the foreboding feeling that clung to her chest. *'Will this world ever be right again?'* She wondered.

Sitting on the edge of the bed, she eased her feet into a pair of slippers and allowed her mind to linger on the particles of dust floating on a beam of sunlight. She entertained useless thoughts of how many specs she must be breathing in. Just to avoid thinking about the things invading her life that she had absolutely no control over.

Standing, she went to the window to see the beginnings of a beautiful day unfolding. It was hard to believe only a few hours ago, a raging storm raced through chewing up the town. It saddened her to see the flowers and vegetable garden Sally had planted.

Three years passed by since Dana set up house in this building. In all that time, she couldn't remember a weekend going by without seeing Sally out back with her little pink spade and shovel digging up the earth.

Maintaining the beds around the place was a past-time Sally enjoyed doing along with Mrs. Walters.

Dana wiped the tears from off her cheeks. *'Why is all this happening now?'*

First her father dying and now Sally, what else could she expect to go wrong.

"*Oh my goodness,*" she sank down to the bed thinking how devastated Phil must be. How would he ever deal with the loss of

having Sally taken away from him? Dana
mourned her father but his death was
different. His illness went on long enough
for her to prepare for his passing on.
Sally, on the other hand, had been healthy
at twenty-six years, with plenty of life
left.

How, someone felt they had any right
to take another life angered her.
Especially, Sally who always had a smile on
her face, she was the type of girl that
looked for the good in people, no matter
what.

Dana shook her head as the sheer shock
of the reality that someone killed Sally
hit her again. She couldn't comprehend the
reasoning. *'Why would someone want to rob
Sally and Phil of a future together? What
reason would there be for a stranger to
come all the way out here to kill?'*
Questions kept pounding at her mind.

*'Was it a random act and Sally just
happened to arrive home at the wrong time?'*
Dana paced around her room, *'what if she
had been the first one to drive in.'* She
shivered at the thought. Who would be
stupid enough to hang around waiting for
someone just to kill them? Especially, with
the weather conditions last night, they'd
have to be mad, with a black heart.

Maybe Sally knew her killer but what
would push someone to the brink of murder.
Sally was a beautiful girl maybe she
rejected some guy who tried to pick her up
and crushed his male ego. *'Would that be
enough to kill?'*

Dana lived like a recluse, keeping a
safe distance from everyone. Knowing,
Sally had been the closes thing to a friend

Dana knew, mainly because they shared a few things. Both, attended Chiapas school with one other sibling, a brother the only difference, Sally's was younger by two years and she was one year older than Dana. Although their friendship had been limited to the laundry room and monthly BBQ the Walters threw, they knew each other well enough.

Apart from matching a name with faces and apartment numbers, she really couldn't claim to know anyone else who shared the building with her. For all she knew, one of the tenants could have had an altercation with Sally that ended up in murder. Dana's body tensed up at the idea. She stood staring out the window again refusing to believe that any of the individuals sharing the building could be capable of hurting Sally.

Dana shook her head, "this is unbelievable, Sally, was such a humanitarian, she wouldn't have done or said anything to cause this."

Gasping Dana raised a hand over her mouth, as she remembered the reckless driver who tried to bully her off the road last night. '*Could he have been the killer looking for another victim? Why didn't I pay more attention? It was too dark to even see the colour or make of the car.*' Dana berated herself for not being more observant.

The reality of the nightmare hit her again and her heart ached for Phil and Sally. They were always so happy, she wondered what the argument, Robert said Phil confessed to, was about. 'Maybe, Robert misunderstood what he heard.'

"Oh my gosh, this is horrible." Dana sighed.

Every thing surrounding her life seemed minuscule to what Phil had to wake up to today.

She scanned the bedroom through glazed eyes. Nothing changed, yet things had a different look to them and just didn't feel the same.

Reaching over, she pulled a tissue from the box at the same time the minute hand turned over on the clock. How strange time is, nothing but an endless entity that pushed forward no matter what, not even the death of two people could prevent it from drudging onward.

Rubbing her temples, she felt hung over as though she was suffering the effects of an all night drinking binge. *'How unfair,'* she thought, *'to be suffering without the pleasure of actually indulging, with alcohol, to get it.'*

The numbers flipped over to read nine thirty bringing her back to the reality that a detective was coming to bombard her with questions. A visit she had mixed feelings over, she wished Robert would have been able to be with her for the meeting but knew Lindsay would never put up with him leaving her again.

*'Well, I can get through this without him.'* The important thing now is to get the killer behind bars. She just preferred not to have to face the detective with his accusing stares.

His name eluded her, but not the strong feeling of dislike she felt for the way he subtly implied that her and Robert were somehow involved. She hardly even noticed him as he trailed Robert into her home without an invitation. He barged in at her weakest moment and took advantage of her at a vulnerable time. The night had gone on forever, she remembered how the feeling of exhaustion and worry consumed her, causing her to she let her guard down at the wrong time.

'*Not this time*,' even though she tossed around in bed most of the night she did eventually managed to get enough rest to be able to handle him.

Going to the living room, she remembered him leaving his business card. She stared down at the table, where he tossed it. She hesitated to pick it up, doing so made it seem like she would be giving him some kind of satisfaction. It was a crazy thought, she knew, and quickly swiped the card up and turned it between her fingers.

"Jake Turner." She let the name roll off her tongue before putting it back down. "Well, I'm ready for you, this time."

After a hot shower and some coffee, she would be ready to face him and all his questions. She went to the kitchen and set up the coffee before heading to the shower.

# Chapter 18

A headache nagged at the nape of Jake's neck as he left the doctor's house. The interview took longer than anticipated, only because his wife kept interrupting giving him the impression he was the one under interrogation. *'The woman sure can talk.'* He wasn't able to recall another time he met anyone as excited in learning what went on in the wee hours of the morning. She appeared infatuated with the details, lacking any remorse for the victim or her husband having discovered the body.

The Doctor on the other hand remained calm and oblivious to his wife's annoying interruptions.

Never had Jake ever wanted out of a place so bad. Leaving their home, it took everything he had, not to apologize to the Doctor for his til death partner.

He wondered if Doc Reed ever regretted not running in the opposite direction when he first met the woman.

Just being in the same room with her for an hour was enough to solidify Jake's decision not to settle for the sake of being married. In the past, he dated women like Lindsay and decided that being, locked, in a lifetime relationship with a woman that self-centred would become really long and mundane. *'More like a prison sentence.'*

Once in the car, he snapped open the glove compartment and pull out a bottle of capsules. Twisting the lid off, he shook four Tylenol into the palm of his hand. Tossing them into his mouth, he forced them down with the stale, cold coffee he had left earlier.

He believed the interview with the Doc's sister should pose less of a challenge, at lease not as gruelling. In fact, he found himself a little anxious to meet with her again. Something about her personality stood out as honest, not someone who would put on a phoney act to try to impress others. Jake's guess would be that the bickering between the two siblings somehow involved the sister-in-law.

He slowed the car down as he rounded a bend in the road faster than needed. Clutching the wheel with one hand, he quickly hit the brakes then shifted down to third to prevent the car from running amuck in the ditch. Mentally he cautioned himself to focus more on the moment rather then on the Doctor and his family.

The pavement ended abruptly and he swerved to avoid hitting a deep pothole that would have put his car out of commission.

'*Where the hell did that come from?'* He questioned while the car skidded on the muddy, gravel surface. *The rain must have worn away at the stones over night.* He definitely would have remembered something that big in the middle of the road leaving last night. '*It's like a bloody minefield,'* Jake warned himself.

With control of the wheel again, his mind wandered back to the Reed's, his gut told him that the Doctor and his sister were innocent and decided they just happened to be in the wrong place at the wrong time.

The forensic report showed the time of death between seven and seven-thirty. He was sure the investigation would reveal that they were all at the funeral home during the time frame.

Grabbing his phone from his shirt pocket, Jake managed to catch it on the third ring, while maintaining a good eye on the road ahead he slowed down to a stop.

"Jake here."

"Good morning Jake, Its Jim and I'm just leaving the funeral home. Edgar Mullins remembered seeing Dr. Reed and his sister talking in one of the parlours around seven-thirty."

"Well that gives them an alibi." Jake said.

"He thought they were arguing, if that helps."

"It fits with what they told me last night. Thanks for calling, Jim."

"No problem. One more thing Jake, phone records show the boyfriend Phil was talking to a buddy in town for about two hours at the time of the murder. Kinda sad, while he sat on the phone his girlfriend was having the life squeezed out of her."

"Sure is, thanks for the info, Jim, I'll talk to you later." 'The suspect list is getting shorter.' Jake thought but felt better about his interview with Miss Reed, knowing someone could confirm what time she was at the funeral home.

He slipped the phone back into his pocket and manoeuvred the car back onto the road. He pulled out his note pad and held it up to the steering wheel so he could manipulate the small sheets and watch the road at the same time. He flipped the pages until he came to where he wrote the sister's name.

"That's right Dana, and she has lived there for three years." Jake noted. For being siblings there were complete opposites, one surrounds themselves with people while the other hides away in a remote area.

He could understand why someone, would be drawn to an out-of-the-way country apartment, the area was beautiful. He would take green trees and open fields over town any day, if he could. Right now, he liked being close to the station.

Jake though the location for the building was perfect, small enough to maintain your privacy yet people around if you felt like company. He got the impression from the girl he met last night that she enjoyed her solitude.

He smiled at the memory of how she jumped to action when she though she had to defend her family. Amusing, he thought, how this timid little thing curled into a corner of the couch, as though, hiding turned into a lioness ready to pounce to protect an older brother a lot bigger then she is.

Something about her intrigued him, he hadn't figured it out yet, but he would. In fact, he was more interested in how the interview would go with her, than it did with the brother and his wife.

He tied to picture Dana and Lindsay in the same room together, the Prom Queen with an attitude and a spoilt Southern Bell. A shiver crawled up his spine at the thought and he didn't envy the Doctor.

# Chapter 19

Pulling into the lot, Jake could see the forensic team had full control over every inch of the area. He recognized one of the girls going around snapping pictures. He saw a few of them crawling around on the ground with tweezers looking for any clue. Jake doubted they would find much there, most of the evidence would have wash away during the night. These guys were a determined group, if the killer left anything behind they would find it.

Kevin waved a large palm at Jake, as he parked the car, the nickname Goliath fit his six foot seven frame, Jake thought watching large arms sway in motion with every step.

"Someone told me that you spent most of the night here. I half expected to catch you sleeping in your car when I got here." Kevin chuckled as he came around to the driver's side.

"Not this time," Jake pushed the door open. "Find anything yet." He asked.

"No," Kevin stood up straight and looked around while Jake stepped out.

"We dusted for prints but found nothing. Who ever did this knew what he was doing."

"The weather was on his side." Jake said and cursed when he landed in a puddle.

"It's too clean. My guess is whoever did it knew the girl and planned it carefully."

"I'd tend to agree" Jake said kicking mud from his shoes. "You'd think the Landlord would at least pave the lot," Jake complained as he looked down at his foot.

He'd have to clean them before he went into her apartment. The last thing he wanted to do would be track mud all over her carpets.

"How long ago did they tow the car away?" Jake asked as he looked over at a red Volkswagen soft top sitting in a spot at the far end of the lot.

"About an hour ago."

"What took them so long to get it out of here?" Jake asked confused.

"They couldn't find the keys anywhere and we checked everywhere. We even asked the boyfriend if he had them.

"How's he doing?"

"Randy's in with him and the landlord right now, trying to make sense of everything. He's still a little out of it and groggy from the sleeping pills." Kevin looked over at the building. "I guess he's still in shock.

"I image it would be devastating, was he able to get you the keys?" Jake asked, wondering how innocent the boyfriend was.

"He is positive they're in the car but ended up giving us his spare set."

"Maybe the girl had time to shove them in her purse before the killer got to her. Did anyone check?" Jake asked while jotting down a reminder to call the morgue to ask.

"Lisa from forensic did but no luck." Kevin stood shaking his head. "I think whoever did this, took them as a trophy."

"That's a possibility," Jake tended to believe with a crime this heinous the killer would more than likely take a souvenir.

Jake glanced at his watch, he was already late which never bother him in the past, but for some reason he didn't like to keep this girl waiting.

"Thanks Kevin, I'll catch up with you later." Stepping on the grass, he managed to scrap most of the mud off his shoes before reaching the lobby. Once inside, he used a tissue to wipe them down, kicking his shoes off at the door would appear unprofessional.

Confident, all the mud was left behind and he wouldn't leave a trail tracked all over her place he climbed the stairs two at a time.

# Chapter 20

After, freshened up with a shower, anger over Sally's murder gnawed at Dana. Now, she looked forward to seeing the detective. She questioned how much help she could offer, but for her own sanity needed to do whatever possible to help get the person capable of this type of crime off the streets and behind bars, forever.

In order for her to open up with the detective, a few things needed to be clarified so she could feel comfortable talking to him. She would deal with that later when he arrived, right now her mind raced with details of what happened last night.

Questioning her own insanity Dana wondered it she dreamt some of the event that happened last night like the mystical figure, she conjured up, staring down at her from the towers or Robert making a surprise visit.

*'The idiot that nearly ran me of the road was real. Robert showing up here was real, Sally dying is real.'* The realizations sent shock waves through her mind.

Her mental state had been so askew by the time she arrived home nothing made sense to her anymore. Rehearsing each step from the car to her apartment for any clue or small detail, she might have noticed but dismissed in her quest to reach the safety of the building. *'Would Sally be alive if I paid more attention?'* She felt ill wondering if the killing may have been in the car while she ran past. Could she have been the last person Sally saw? Tears fell as she wondered it Sally watched her coming home, giving her some false hope. Was she Sally's last hope for survival?

She had to let it go and focus on helping the police in anyway possible, by giving them any information she could remember, without sounding like an over exaggerating fool filled with paranoia. That means don't waste the detective's time with trivial things such as a bunch of kids having some fun hassling me on the road.

*'This is about Sally not me, so stick to the facts.'* Dana advised herself.

# Chapter 21

Dana barely had time to pour a coffee when the knock came to the door. Feeling a little nervous, she took a deep breath before opening it to greet the detective.

"I'm a little late. It took longer at your brother's home than expected." Jake gave his shoes a final scrap, across the straw doormat, before stepping in.

"Don't worry about it." She would have hazard a guess that Lindsay had something to do with his tardiness. "Please come in, can I get you a coffee?" She offered, hoping to prove she wasn't the mindless imbecile he met last night.

"Coffee sounds great, just cream. I had a bit of a headache when I left your brother's place so out of desperation I washed down a couple of aspirins with some gross, cold brew I had sitting in the car since morning." He chuckled, "A fresh one should help get the raw taste out of my throat."

She didn't understand why he felt the need to tell her his little story, but found it amusing that spending time with Lindsay had an adverse effect on him. Without knowing it, he gave her a common ground making talking to him easier.

"Lindsay has a way with people. But that's a whole other tale." Dana smiled, and poured a second cup then stirred cream into it before she handed it to him. "Please, have a seat," she offered then settled on the couch.

"Thank you" Jake took the mug from her and sat down across from her. "You look like you didn't sleep much. I can only imagine the rough week you're having." He stated the obvious.

"I think saying this has been the worst week of my life would be accurate." He looked different, then last night, younger and better looking, less threatening. His blonde scruffy hair held an appearance like a blast of wind raked through it.

"I can come back if you need more time." Jake went to stand but Dana motioned for him to stay sitting.

"No," Dana paused. "I need to do this while things are still fresh in my mind."

"Don't feel like you have to remember everything today. You can always give me a call later if anything else comes to mind." Jake sat back down and pulled out a business card from his wallet.

"You left one last night." She nodded in the direction of the stand.

"I'll write some numbers where you can reach me. I check my machine often so leave a message if I don't answer."

Her hand shook slightly as she reached to take it.

"You must get a lot of calls if you're giving your home number out to everyone you question." Dana smirked, *'for all he knows, I could be a nut case and stalk him after the case.'* She thought.

"Absolutely, I'm here to serve and protect." He attempted to joke with her but his smile faded as he reached into his pocket and pulled out a note pad. "I'm sure you have things to get done today, so why don't we get started?"

She studied his expression for any signs of what could possibly be running through his head. He was hard to read, she imagined it came with the job. Keep all personal feelings locked away. '*I do the same*'. She secretly admitted.

With a quick glance at his naked wedding finger, she wondered if his impersonal manner would filter into the marriage if he had a wife.

"I don't even know where to begin," She sighed.

His eyes held warmth in them when he looked at her, unlike last night's fiasco. Now, was not the time to be distracted by his good looks or charming smile, she cautioned.

"Why don't you start with leaving for the funeral home?" Jake encouraged. "What time did you head out and did you notice if Sally was home yet?

"I left here shortly before six and Sally wasn't home yet and we didn't met on the road into town either." Dana pushed a slip of paper across to him. "I stopped in town to pick up a few items before I went to the wake."

"Mr. Goods at six-twenty-one for potato chips and pop, quite the dinner," Jake smile at her.

"Detective! Can I ask a question before we continue?" She decided now would be a good time to clear up some of her concerns.

"Sure," he lowered his pen.

"Do you think my brother or I had anything to do with what happened to Sally?" Dana locked eyes with him.

She could see that beneath his rock like cover her question caught him of guard. He looked over at her and his eyes matched her stare as he spoke.

"The Coroner's report showed that your friend's murder took place between 7:00 and 8:00pm." He held up the receipt. Along with this, the funeral home confirmed that you and your family were at the wake during that time. Robert saw you pulling out of the lot around 8:00pm and I'd say it's about forty minutes from the funeral home to here. Factor in the weather condition would have slowed you down, adding another fifteen to twenty minutes to your drive. So I'd say you got home around nine."

"I didn't check the time but, that sounds about right." Dana said, surprised at his calculations. It felt strange knowing that a detective investigated her movements against the clock for a murder. "You checked out Robert's and my story, already." Dana asked wondering when he found the time to sleep.

"Dana, you have to understand that in the case where a murder takes place we have to look at everyone." Jake started to explain.

"It's okay, I really do understand." She said feeling stupid for asking the question when she knew he was just doing his job.

She appreciated his being straight with her and decided to let up and relax a little. *'I have to kick down my walls and quit expecting the worst from people. Trust,'* She reminded herself.

"If you're uncomfortable with me, I can get another detective to talk to you." Jake stood up again.

"I'm sorry it's just that things are so crazy lately." Dana fought back her tears. "I haven't even been able to sit back and absorb the reality of my father's death, yet."

"It must be difficult for you. It won't be a problem for me to come back later if that would be better for you?" Jake repeated his offer to hold off on the interview. She looked at him and could read concern in his eyes making him more human.

"No, please, I'm fine. I have to get through this day." She waited for him to sit back down.

A pair of arms holding her would help more than putting off this interview, but she couldn't foresee that happening soon with Robert tied up in his own affairs and her mother lost in her own grief.

Sipping from her mug more for strength to hold back tears she began again.

"The incident with Robert at the funeral home and then the struggle to keep the car on the road, the only thing on my mind pulling into the lot, last night was getting to my apartment."

"Did you notice Sally's car?"

"Yes, I keep thinking that if I weren't so frightened and desperate I may have been able to help her."

"Sally was beyond help by the time you reached home."

A chill raced through her at the idea of being so close to a murder scene and not noticing anything out of the ordinary.

"I feel so guilty, like I should have at least realized something was wrong."

"Did anything look out of place?"

"No," She looked at him through tears. After a deep breath, she decided to trust him.

An hour later, she had spilled her guts out about every incident surrounding the times she saw or spend with Sally and Phil and their relationship. Dana gave the details she could about the car that nearly ran her off the road but decided to leave out the irrelevant things about the image in the towers. She was still trying to sort out whether it was real or not.

"This will help. Jake snapped his note pad shut and stood up. "If there is anything else you remember, give me a call and time isn't an issue. I should be at the station most of the day so you can stop by there if you prefer." Dana stood and walked him to the door.

"I'll be at the funeral home again, tonight." She said and opened the door to reveal the face of Sally smiling up at them.

Jake bent down and picked up the newspaper that featured the crime on the front page with a full head shot of Sally. He handed it to her.

"We are going to catch whoever did this?" He stated with confidence.

"I hope so."

"Were you close to her?"

"Not really, we got together once in a while. Nothing outside the building though."

"I'm sorry this is happening to you."

"Thank you. It's just hard to believe that someone thinks they have a right to snuff out someone else's life." Dana said glad to be able to talk to someone about how she felt.

"I know, it's not right," Jake agreed, "please keep your door lock at all times and try to avoid being out on your own until we catch this creep."

"That's not easy to do until we bury my father."

"Would you like me to pick you up and bring you to and from the funeral parlour tonight?"

"That won't be necessary. The funeral is tomorrow so I'm spending the night with my mother."

"If you ever find yourself coming home late and need an escort, there's always a cruiser driving around. Just give the station or me a call." He reassured her.

"Do you think the killer is still around here?" Dana shivered.

"It's hard to know, so until he is caught be careful."

"Thank you detective, I will."

"Please, call me Jake." He said and pulled the door closed after him.

Dana found Jake to be nothing like her first impression of him. She found herself actually liking him.

# Chapter 22

Again, Dana found herself standing in Mullin's Funeral Home.

Looking around, she could see the small group from her apartment rallying around Phil while Sally's parents clung consolingly to each other as they stared hopelessly down at the lifeless body of their only daughter. Dana scanned the room for Sally's brother and caught a glimpse of him staring out at everyone with his arms folded tightly across his chest.

Anger filled his face and for the instant their eyes met, Dana was sure he look through her. She guessed the only thing on his mind would be avenging his sister's murder.

'*This is too much,*' her stomach tightened in knots as she scanned the all too familiar area, recalling where the exit doors were. If she were a stronger person, she would have made her way through the pockets of people and offered her sympathies to the grieving family.

She had met them a few times at some of the BBQ's the Walters held and remembered how silly Sally's father had been with the games. Seeing him, reach into the coffin to take hold his daughter's cold hand, Dana knew, a large part of him would be buried with his daughter.

She had to finish what she came to do then get out of there before madness overtook her. She feared having to view Sally in her sleep of death and would preferred not to.

It would be better to wait until her parents left the coffin before approaching them. '*I'll pay my respect to her parents and make a quiet escape. Robert can deal with his own tardiness.*'

Being there gave her a new outlook on the people she shunned at her father's funeral. If nothing else, she learned two things while observing everything going on around her, tonight. Never be so judgemental of others again. She glimpsed over at the main entrance. The other is, not to rely on Robert to be on time.

Willing her feet to move, she gained the needed courage to leave the snug little corner, she nestled into, '*I can do this,*' she encouraged. Just as she went to take a step, someone tapped her shoulder.

# Chapter 23

Twisting, she turned expecting to give Robert the same lecture, he administered to her the night she arrived late.

"Robert…" She quickly clammed up at the handsome face of Eric his partner smiling down at her.

"You wouldn't be contemplating bolting out the side door, would you?" He joked reading her well.

"The thought has crossed my mind, but I didn't think I was advertising my disdain for being here, so openly, on my face." Dana said relieved to see a somewhat familiar face.

Even though, she only met him for the first time at her father's funeral, seeing him gave her some comfort.

"Is Robert with you?" She asked, hoping to hide her frustrations.

"He's not here yet?" Eric answered her question with a question.

"No," Dana's shoulders dropped.

"I phone him before I left and he said they were heading out the door. That's why I told him I'd meet them here instead of their house." He tightened his lips and shook his head. "I should have known better, he's on Lindsay time." Eric gave a low chuckled. "Don't worry, little sis, your brother married himself a high maintenance woman who needs to calculate every move they make." Eric smirked. "From the first time I met her, I've realized that life is all about Lindsay." Eric looked over his shoulder at the entrance. "I guarantee you. She's going to time things with exact precision, so that all eyes will notice her sporting a doctor on her arm."

Dana covered her mouth to conceal a laugh, forming an instant bond with him. Knowing someone shared her thoughts on how high on herself Lindsay was, justified Dana's feelings.

"Does Robert know how you feel about his precious wife?" She questioned him.

"I've been completely honest with my partner from the moment I realized his interest in Lindsay became more than a fling. In fact, the night he flashed the rock in front of me and announced his intentions to marry the little princess, I pleaded with him to wait another six month at least." Eric stood shaking his head. "You probably know better than anyone else, that Robert's a proud stubborn man and there's no changing his mind once he has it made up. But, good grief he hardly knew the woman."

"That's exactly how I feel." Dana felt elated finally someone actually understood why she was so upset about the wedding. She looked up at Eric glad that he showed up. "You know my brother well."

"We are business partners. I make it a point to get to know someone I intend to put my name behind." Eric smiled down at her with piercing blue eyes that lit up making his face even more handsome. "And although I don't always agree with his personal choices in life he is a darn good doctor. To be honest I have to admit, his decision to marry bothered me more because he ruined my dreams of two young, good looking, single doctors on the prowl." He winked at her.

"The Don Juan's of Chiapas Falls. Just what the town needs," Dana teased and turned so he couldn't see her face flush.

"See now there's a woman who understands." He smiled at her.

"You didn't even know Sally, so why are you here?" Dana changed the subject, curious as to why anyone would intentionally come to a place like this without a necessity.

"Family, Robert is my family," his smile widen, "so I guess that makes you part of my family." He put an arm around her shoulders. "I have to admit, to discover Robert had been hiding such a cute sister away from me was a surprise. And after seeing you last week I couldn't help it, I was compelled to see you again." He flashed another smiled at her breaking the awkwardness.

"Am I actually seeing a Don Juan in action?" She chuckled at his flirting.

He looked away towards the entrance before he looked deep into her eyes and for a moment, she detected a serious tone in his voice.

"To be honest, from what I can tell, you aren't having a good couple of weeks and I think it's about time you stopped facing things on your own. Robert is occupied with a new wife and your mother is dealing with her own grief." Listening to him tears pearled in her eyes. His compassion caught her off guard. *'This guy is good but no way will I give in to self-pity tears.'* Dana cautioned.

She always took pride in the fact that she could hide her feelings and believed she had built a strong wall around her emotions. It surprised her that Eric, a complete stranger could just come along and chip a hole through the veneer, with few words. She suddenly felt extremely vulnerable and needy.

"What do you say?" Eric let his arm drop from her shoulders and took her hand. "Are you ready to start your condolences?" He asked taking control of the situation, "I promise not to leave your side," he reassured her.

Dana never met someone who could change her mood so much in such a short span of time. It was a little overwhelming, yet comforting to have him by her side.

Unsure how to react, she nodded her head and allowed him to hold her hand as she slowly moved past a group of people.

Walking forward, Dana had to admit that his presence definitely gave her strength. She appreciated his kindness in showing up, especially since he didn't have to be there at all.

Without any notice, he stopped and pulled her back into his arm so he could lean down and whispered in her ear.

"Just to let you know, I probably hate being in funeral homes as much as you do."

"I'm glad you're here for me." She said, finding it a little awkward standing with her back nestled into him while he wrapped his arm around her resting his lips slightly above her ear.

With ease, he had been able to bring out a side of her personality that she kept well protected. She hated if people viewed her as weak and helpless, and that is exactly how she was feeling right now. Yet, with Eric, she enjoyed having him take the lead. "I guess I shouldn't rely on my brother, so much, to be my strong arm, I need to realize he has other commitments." Dana hung her head a little embarrassed to be complaining about Robert to his partner.

"Robert isn't pushing you out." Eric turned her to face him so he could look her straight in the eyes. "It's what married couples do. I'm sure your parents didn't let their siblings make the rules in the house after the wedding." His words were blunt and made sense to her. She like that he did it in a non judging way.

"You're right." She got his point loud and clear.

"It's like that with every family, we may not always agree with our sibling's choice in who they decide to marry, but it's not up to us. We need to love and accept who ever they pick for a mate." Eric said shrugging his shoulders. "From what I can see Robert looks happy with Lindsay and if he's happy, I'm happy."

He had a trusting manner about him and she liked his way of thinking. He put his personal feelings aside. She could learn something from Eric and imagined he must be a good doctor to his patients.

"You're right. I should take a step back and give Lindsay a chance. Maybe it'll help me know what Robert sees in her." Dana gave in to common sense.

"Once you do you may discover she isn't the ogre you portrayed." Dana stifled a laugh, she like Eric. He had a way of turning serious talk around taking the awkwardness out of it.

"I'm glad you came here." She smiled at him.

"There is a price for my chivalry."

"And what could that possibly be?"

"Well being a lonely bachelor who is new in town, I need someone to show me around. So, after I complete my duties here you have to be my personal tour guide."

"That's a high cost, but I think I can manage it." Dana smiled enjoying her time with him. With the knot in her stomach gone and Eric by her side, she was ready to face Sally's family.

# Chapter 24

"We have company." Eric warned Dana and turned her to face Jake.

"Detective what are you doing here?" Dana asked surprised to see him.

"In murder cases I like to come and check out the crowd. Sometimes the killer likes to mingle with the decease's friends and family." Jake swiftly brought things back to reality. Dana was enjoying Eric's company so much she almost forgot why she was there. Before she could comment, Eric slipped his arm around her shoulders again.

"That's callous. What kind of sick mind would do that?"

"Someone who doesn't possess any scruples and gets a thrill out of meeting the victim's family," Jake said and held his hand out to Eric. "I'm Jake Turner, the detective on this case."

Eric took his hand. "Dr Eric Rycker, I'm a close friend of the family." Dana felt his grip tighten on her.

"Yes, Dr Reed mentioned he had a partner." Jake stated then turned his attention back to Dana. "It's nice seeing you again, and don't forget, that offer is still open if you ever need anyone to escort you home."

"No need to worry about that detective. I'll make sure she is safely behind close doors before I let her out of my sight." It bothered her somewhat that Eric felt he had to speak for her instead of letting her handle things. Thinking he may feel the need to be protective of her until Robert arrived, she didn't allow it to annoy her for long.

Just as, Jake was about to say something else Robert and Lindsay appeared beside them. After some polite small talk, he left the four of them.

Facing Sally's parents was more difficult than Dana imagined, but like, Eric, promised he didn't leave her side for one moment, given her the strength to get through it.

As they left, Dana took a quick look around for Jake and saw him off talking to Timothy, Sally's brother.

# Chapter 25

"Am I too late to temp you with dinner and a beer or two." Eric asked.

"I haven't cooked anything yet, so I guess I can be swayed." Dana said thinking the chop sitting on the counter could last in the fridge for tomorrow's meal. She was antsy sitting around, getting out might help her pick her mood up.

"Lindsay is here helping Robert decorate his office and she's badgering me to let you know they're joining us." Dana heard a chuckle from Lindsay. "She's getting violent here, so let me know where you want to eat and I'll tell them to meet us there."

"Murphy's Sports Bar has good food." Dana blurted out thinking the place would be a big f aux pas for Lindsay's rich blood. She listened as he told them and was surprised at Lindsay's squeal of approval.

"You just made Lindsay's night, it's her favourite place."

"Great, should I meet you there?" Dana said feeling bamboozled by the three of them into a cozy evening.

Well tonight, she didn't care, spending time with Robert and Eric was a lot more appealing then flopping in front of tube watching reruns all night, even if Lindsay had to be part of the package.

"No I'm leaving now to pick you up."

"Okay," Dana hung up.

A month ago, if someone told her Robert's partner would be picking her up and bringing her to join her brother and his wife for dinner and drinks, she would have vowed not to let it happen. *'I feel a crack in my shell, and I'm starting to like my new outlook on things.'* She chuckled as she headed to the bedroom to change.

## Chapter 26

Eric parked the car and jumped out to open her door.

"You ready?" He smiled and cupped her hand in his to help her up from the seat.

"I guess so," Dana smiled, amazed at how comfortable she had become with him in such a short time.

"Make you a deal." Eric said releasing her arm.

"Oh don't tell me you're a deal maker too." She laughed.

"Now that really hurts." He clutched his chest in mock pain. "Just as I was going to reveal my deepest secret on how to avoid being with someone when it becomes unbearable to be in the same room with them." Flipping his thumb at the restaurant, she knew exactly who he meant without having to mention any names.

Having dinner with Robert and Lindsay never made her top ten list of things to do but for her brother's sake she was willing to try to get to know his wife. Dana would never openly admit it but she might be able to learn a few things from hanging out with Lindsay.

Having Eric by her side, knowing he had her back, made things easier.

"Okay, I made a terrible mistake, please accept my apology and disclose your most intimate plans." Dana laughed and pleaded at the same time.

"Since you asked so nicely, I'll divulge my secret." Eric smiled down at her and winked, "You ready?" He asked.

"Absolutely!"

"Blackout, you lost me," Dana gave him a confused stare.

"We keep drinking until we are pissed face drunk and nothing she says to us will matter or even be remembered the next morning." He stated it with such seriousness causing her to laugh, something she did a lot around him.

"That's quite the method."

"As soon as we get seated I'll order a jug of beer, maybe two depending on the situation." He stated and held the door opened for her. 'This is exactly what I need for tonight.' Dana thought walking in the door, excited to spend time with their small group.

# Chapter 27

Spotting Robert waving his arm in the air to indicate where they sat was easy. Dana couldn't help but notice a huge, silly grin pasted across his face. Of course, he'd love the idea of the four of them meeting up for dinner. Having Eric bring her would only be icing on his cake. '*I hope he isn't reading too much into Eric and my friendship.*' She thought as he watched the two of them approach the table.

Robert had to understand that sharing a meal together didn't mean an instant bond would form between her and Lindsay either, these things take time. There was still something phoney about her that grated on Dana's nerves.

Seeing Lindsay's arm wrapped around Robert as if staking a claim made Dana wonder if she ever let him come up for air.

"Don't you two make a sweet looking couple?" Lindsay called out, and Dana saw a few heads turn in her and Eric's direction.

Eric grinned at Dana and caught a Waitress passing by.

"Would you please, bring us two jugs of beer?" He asked while Dana, who was finding it hard to contain a laugh, slipped into the booth.

Within minutes, two pitchers appeared in front of them. Eric filled two glasses handing one over to Dana he clicked her glass with his.

"To blackouts," he winked at her and she chuckled knowing exactly what he meant. "There's nothing like a cold beer to relax you." Eric chugged half it down.

"I have to agree with you," Dana said. Enjoying their secret, she took a good drink of her ale, ignoring Robert's questioning stare.

By the time their meals arrived, Dana had started on her second glass.

"Robert, you never said how you met Lindsay." Dana feeling braver with each sip ventured a question, she at one time vowed never to ask.

Robert laughed and pointed over at Eric.

"Don't blame me." Eric shook a hand in front of him and Dana raised eyebrow at him.

"He pointed Lindsay and her friend out." Robert stated.

"I'm innocent." Eric laughed refusing to take the blame.

"Okay, it was spaghetti night and we decided to buy fresh veggies down at the market. Eric noticed these two beauties roaming around picking through tomatoes." Robert related and took hold of Lindsay's hand. "First look at Lindsay, I headed over to get my own tomatoes. We all know what happened after that." Robert said before, he planted a quick kiss on her hand while Lindsay giggled away like a star struck little schoolgirl.

"What he doesn't know is my girlfriend and I had them in our sights first, they just played into our plans." Lindsay added her own touch to the story.

"And where's the girlfriend." Dana turned to Eric and asked.

"I don't know. What was her name again, Jessie or Jenny?" Eric cocked his head trying to recall the name of the friend.

"That's right lover boy, it started with a J, and her name was Jenny. By the way, she's engaged to a very nice man now and is doing fine. In case you were wondering." Lindsay tossed her napkin at Eric and everyone laughed. Despite herself, Dana was enjoying the company.

A band came out and started to set up, while people began to pack the place. A couple of women, who shared a table with two other men across from them jump up, one held a napkin and frantically waved towards the entrance.

"Jake, Jake over here." She called out.

Dana looked back towards the door to see Jake making his way towards them.

# Chapter 28

"Dr. Reed," Jake nodded at Robert once he reached his table and turned to Dana. "We keep running into each other."

"It's a small town, for sure." Dana said trying not to sound too stupid.

"Enjoy your evening." Jake said before he sat down with his group.

They had finished their meals, and the Waitress started to clear the table just as Robert and Eric's beepers went off at the same time. Taking his out of his pocket Robert turned to Lindsay.

"It's the hospital, we have to run can you drive Dana home?"

"It's dark out and you know I don't like driving at night especially down the back roads alone. Besides, you need the car to get home." Lindsay snapped as though the emergency was an inconvenience to her. "I don't think Eric is going to feel like coming all the way back here to drop you off." She rolled her eyes.

"I can call a cab and Dana can wait at the house with you until I get home?" Robert's words sent shivers through Dana. She would have to chug a lot more beer before spending an evening alone with Lindsay. Robert had no right to make plans for her. Holding her hand up she began to protest.

"Robert, I have to do laundry…." Dana started to say before Lindsay cut in.

"Why don't we just ask our detective friend? I'm sure he won't mind dropping me off then running Dana home." Lindsay came up with the plan so fast that Dana wondered if she disliked the idea of the two of them being trapped in the house together for who knows how many hours, as much as she did. Dana realized this was the first time she actually agreed with her sister-in-law.

Hearing the beepers go off Jake joined the commotion.

"Is everything okay?" He asked Robert.

"We're fine but Eric and I have to run to the hospital I hate to bother you but could you possible drive my wife to our house and Dana back to her apartment?" Robert asked.

"Sure, I can do that." Jake stated without any hesitation.

"Give me a few minutes to use the washroom and then I'll be ready. Is that alright with you Dana?" Lindsay requested.

"That will be fine." Dana said thankful for Jake's willingness to give up his evening to help them.

"Don't wait up for me Babe." Robert kissed Lindsay.

Eric surprised Dana by leaning into her and whispering in her ear.

"Be careful. I think the detective has a crush on you." "Don't worry. I can take care of myself." She smiled hoping
Jake didn't hear Eric's comment.

"Can I call you tomorrow?" She could feel her face go flush and was glad it was dark enough so no one would notice.

She didn't know what to make of Eric or her own reactions to his openness and flirty attitude towards her. She had to admit that he was a charmer and being around him made her feel like she can come out of tough situation unscathed. Without him, she would have never made it through Sally's funeral.

"Sure," was the only word she could squeeze out with everyone watching, the little display being acted out between them.

Eric threw a handful of bills on the table, then the two raced out, and Lindsay grabbed her bag. "I'll be right back." She said and headed to the restrooms.

"Sure, I'll meet you outside." Dana reached for her purse.

Jake turned to group at his table. "I'll catch up to you guys later." One of the women looked past Jake and shot Dana a look of dislike. Dana had to suppress the urge to tell his female to relax and give her some reassurance that her only interest in Jake was a ride back to her house. The next time, she wouldn't be so willing to leave home without her car.

Instead, she turned to Jake. "You know, I can call a cab and drop Lindsay off then borrow her car. I don't want to put you or your friends out." Dana avoided eye contact with the girl. This way she only had to endure a short time with Lindsay.

"That's an offer you can't refuse Jake, especially since the band is starting up and my feet can't stand still." The woman, who moments earlier shot daggers at her, now smiled an approval of Dana's decision, to find her own way home.

"Maybe another time, Helen." Jake smile at her and she looked like she would melt, but, once he turned his back, she managed to give a quick warning glared at Dana before she shrugged her shoulders and turned her attention back to her group.

# Chapter 29

Never in his life had Jake ever met a woman who could continue to talk without taking a breath. It gave a whole, new meaning to someone talking your ear off. To make matters worse, she kept prying for confidential information surrounding the case.

"Like I said before Mrs. Reed, I'm not at liberty to discuss anything." He repeated for around the fifth time. She didn't know how close he came to slamming on his breaks and dumping her out on the curve.

Up until now, he always considered himself a patient man, but he was losing it quickly. He looked to Dana for any kind of assistance to help turn the conversation to a different subject. She continued to stare out the window with her lip curled up in a slight smile, if anything she appeared to be enjoying his predicament.

"It's actually Mrs. Dr. Robert Reed." Lindsay corrected, while she appeared to get the point turning her attention to something in the bottom of her oversize purse.

Jake enjoyed a brief interlude of silence that lasted for less then a minute before he felt a dark sense of cold eyes piercing the back of his head. He regretted glancing up at the rear view mirror to find her staring him down.

"Are you married detective."

*'Dammit,'* Jake cringed, *'don't tell me she's going into an area I have no interest in sharing with her.'* He should have known she would be the type of person to take

things to the next level by delving into his personal life, since he refused to entertain her with details of a crime.

"No, I'm not and never was." He had no idea where her probing would lead to, so he offered a little more hoping to shut her down.

"Are you seeing anyone?" She persisted.

"My personal affairs really aren't anything you need to concern yourself with."

"Have you always lived in Chiapas Falls?" Lindsay asked without missing a beat.

"No, I haven't. Are you always so inquisitive?" He turned the table around on her before she dragged his life history out into the open. She's the type of woman who could get men to open up and reveal the darkest secrets if they weren't careful.

He glanced over at Dana again, hoping she would be a little sensitive to his situation.

"Some help here, please," their eyes met for a moment in the reflection of the glass.

"Are things getting a little too personal, detective?" Dana turned to him and smiled.

"You're enjoying this, aren't you?" He stated the obvious and knew he was right when she shot him an innocent smile.

"A little," she held her thumb and finger up to indicate how much before turning her attention back to the window.

'Cute,' he thought, she's probably glad that Lindsay targeted him and not her. He was about to tell her that but Lindsay cut in. She probably didn't like sitting back there being ignored.

"I would hope you aren't offended by me asking you these things. I just like to know the person whose car I'm driving in." Lindsay sounded a little insulted. She probably heard the small exchange of words between him and Dana. "Even though you are with the police force, I don't know you at all.   You could be the killer." Lindsay made her defence.

Dana laughed out-loud this time, and Jake stepped harder on the gas. He almost let out a shout of joy at the sight of the street sign for Reindeer Lane, a few more minutes and it would all be over. A drive that only took ten minutes seemed like an eternity.

"Let me set your mind at ease right now, I can definitely say I haven't killed anyone." He eased the car into the laneway, "not even in the line of duty." He offered trying to keep one-step ahead of her questions.

Once he pulled in front of her home, her interest in his life ended along with the bombardment of questions.

"There you go, safely home." He turned to her in the back seat, '*I need to get the guys down at the garage to install an ejection button for the back seat.*' Jake humoured himself.

"I'm not inside yet and it's dark out. Someone could be hiding behind the hedges or may have broken into my home. So how safe can I be?" Lindsay complained. Jake forced a smile at her before he let out a small sigh, he didn't need to be told what she wanted from him.

Instead of trying to argue with her in a battle he knew no male in the world would have a hope of winning, he snapped the release button on his seat belt the same time he shut down the engine.

"Please, let me walk you to the door to make sure you get inside without anyone jumping out from behind the bushes." He offered. '*I wonder how quick she would be to have me follow her into the house if she knew I lied about killing someone, in the line of duty.*' Jake contemplated telling her but decided against it.

"It was nice getting together with you and Eric." She fired, what Jake felt was an obligatory good bye, to Dana who just waved a hand in response and Lindsay stepped out of the car.

There was definitely some tension between the two women. He looked back at Dana who didn't even attempt to hide the grin on her face. For reasons he couldn't explain, knowing she had been obviously enjoying his plight, an urge to make her laugh struck him.

"If, I'm not out in five minutes call for backup."

"I'll start my clock now." Dana glanced down at her watch and laughed.

"On second thought I think you better come in with us. Sitting out here in the dark can't be too safe." He teased.

"I'll be fine right where I am, thanks for the concern though." Dana waved a hand at him, then looked past him and nodded. "She's almost at the door. You better hurry before some pour soul attacks her from behind." Dana pointed towards her sister-in-law.

"Lock the doors. I'll be right back." Jake chuckled before he slammed it shut.

He rushed over to a bush and pretended to pull the branches apart, then looked back at Dana and shrugged his shoulders before he followed Lindsay into the house.

At Lindsay's insistence, he did a quick sweep of the place then left her content that no one snuck in to get her. Leaving, he heard the bolt slide into place, behind him.

He didn't waste any time getting to the car in case she got a last minute notion to haul him back in, to search something else.

More than likely, she'd be rushing for the phone to call her friends to boast about the nights events and how she needed a police escort home, while, her Doctor rushed away to save lives.

# Chapter 30

Sitting behind the wheel, Jake pulled his belt around, locked it into place, turned the key in the ignition, then took a deep breath and back out of the laneway without a word.

"So did you find any bad guys lurking inside?" Dana chucked.

"You're sister-in-law can sleep soundly. I even checked under the beds. If anything I think it's you're brother we need to be worrying about." Jake looked over at Dana and shook his head. He liked the sound of her laugh.

"Don't worry about Robert, from what I see he is smitten with his wife." Dana said in a way that made Jake think she finally accepted the fact that Lindsay belonged to her family.

"One good thing is. He never has to worry about not having enough to talk about." Jake tried to keep the humour in their conversation.

"Lindsay is a rare gem and my brother just happened to be the lucky man to find her." Dana sounded snide, and Jake decided to see how far she would allow him to go with questioning her personal life, so he braved asking something he felt he already knew the answer to.

"I take it you don't get along with her." He stated and Dana let out a sigh.

"I shouldn't be so hard on her. I find it difficult to get over the idea they only knew each other for six months before she had him slipping a ring on her finger. It hurts a little that the family she's so anxious to be part didn't get an invite to the wedding. I can guarantee, showing up and saying I do was the only thing Robert had any control of." Dana sounded irritated, and he understood why she would be.

"The crazy thing is, we didn't even hear about it until he brought her home to meet us a week before our Dad died." Dana looked over at him and shook her head. "Don't get me wrong, I'm happy Robert found someone, I can see he loves her." She admitted.

"The few times I've seen them together they both look happy. From what I see Lindsay is a woman who needs lots of attention and Robert fills that need." Jake wanted to say spoiled and demanding but didn't think it would be appropriate. He could only imagine what living in the same house with Lindsay would be like.

"I need to trust Robert's choices. One thing that bothers me is I wonder how long he would have waited to tell us he had a wife if he didn't have a reason to come home." Dana sounded hurt. "I guess it would have been soon enough because he had bought their house, which was another thing they kept to themselves. Everything around their relationship is so secretive, that can only be revealed in small increments."

"It's not uncommon for people to marry after knowing each other a short time." Jake offered the little tit-bit hoping to make her feel better about her brother's choice. Even though he probably would have reacted the way Dana did if he had a brother who did that to his family. "If it brings you any comfort, from my experience in the force, most of them end up in divorce within a couple of years." He tried to make light of the subject.

Dana chuckled. "I don't really want Robert's marriage to end. I just wish he would have taken more time to get to know her." Dana shrugged a shoulder, "or at least let the family know, but he skipped the girlfriend part and went straight to the wife bit.

"Robert is a smart man. He knows what he's doing." Jake said.

"You're right. I need to keep reminding myself that he is." She agreed.

Since, they had the conversation flowing so well he decided to push it to a more personal limit.

"Eric seems like a really nice guy, I can tell that he and Robert are good friends."

"He is nice." Dana smiled.

"Are you dating him?"

"I'm not my brother." She sounded definite. "I need to get to know the person before I agree to date them." She sounded determined. "I met Eric for the first time at my father's funeral, two weeks ago."

At least she answered him without telling him to mind his own business.

"Is that right, I would have guessed you knew him a lot longer than that." The way they were hanging off each other at the funeral, Jake thought.

"It feels like we do, he showed up at a really difficult time for me and gave me the support I needed." She turned to look out at the darkness again. "That makes him a good friend."

"We all need friends like that." Jake agreed realizing their conversation put her back at Sally's funeral.

"Truthfully if he didn't show up when he did I don't think I would be coping with everything going on." Dana sounded, a little irritated, almost as though she felt she had to defend Eric to him, so he took the clue and backed off. Especially, since Dana and Eric's relationship, whether casual friends or lovers had nothing to do with the case, or him.

Watching how Eric flirted around her whispering in her ear, Jake figured they would be a couple within a month.

He found the man over confident, and wasn't sure if he liked him or not. He hoped Dana would be more than a trophy for him to hang off his arm at public appearances.

# Chapter 31

Dana withdrew into herself and turned to staring out into the darkness again, leaving Jake to regret bringing up Eric to end the conversation he was enjoying. It would be better to let her be to sort out her thoughts.

To break the silence he reached out and clicked the button to the radio, where Jailhouse Rock blared out over the airwaves.

"Sorry, I didn't mean to blow your eardrums out." Jake apologized and quickly turned the sound down. "You can change the channel if you like." He offered.

"No, I love this station. It's the only one I tune into at home. Believe me I blast it as loud as possible without having the neighbours bang on the ceiling." Dana smiled looking more relaxed discussing a less personal subject.

Blue Berry Hill started to play as they turned into her lot. Even though it took longer to drive across town to take her back to her place, the company was definitely more pleasant then the first ten minutes. Pulling along side the building, he noticed something disturbing.

"Is that Sally's car?" he turned to Dana and nodded at the red Volkswagen parked in front of the apartment. Dana turned quickly and followed where he indicated.

"No, that's my car." She let her breath slowly escape from her lungs. "Sally and I always laughed at out taste in cars."

"They're identical." '*How did I miss that detail?*' Jake wondered.

"So are you taking over the spot?" He asked thinking it strange that she would move right in.

"No, this is where I've always parked." She said and as if reading his mind. "It's closer to the door, Sally and I had an understanding, that if I wasn't going to be home for the night, she could use my spot. Earlier that day I met her in the laundry room and told her I'd be spending the night at my mother's." Dana became quiet for a second then turned to Jake. "It could have been me who died that night." Big eyes filled with tears looked at him. He had no explanation as to why he felt a strong need to protect her. Reaching over he covered her hand with his.

"Don't think like that. It's possible that the killer saw her somewhere and followed her back here." Jake offered comfort hoping she wouldn't think him to forward for touching her hand.

"Do you really believe that?" She asked.

"Yes, I do. That's why it's important to be aware of your surroundings at all times, especially if you're out late at night." He stated and pulled his hand back.

"I just can't believe it sometimes. It's such a horrible thing, I felt so sad for her parents and brother." Dana said and opened the door. "Thanks for the ride home but I don't need you to search my place." She attempted to joke, but her smile held sadness to it.

"I don't mind walking you inside."

"I'll be okay." She shut the door.

He watched her start up the walkway then turned his attention to her car in the headlights.

*'What is that all over her car?'* Jake noticed something looked wrong, and jumped out.

"What's that on your car?" He called out before she could reach the door.

"What do you mean?" She questioned as she hurried back. "Someone keyed you," walking around, he noticed a few scratches on the other vehicle as well.

"Who would do that?"

"Are there any kids in the area who would have done it?" Jake asked.

"No, I'm pretty sure that I'm the youngest one living here and there aren't any houses close." She ran her fingers over the scratches. "What is going on? Nothing like this happens here. It's always been so peaceful and quiet." Dana sounded like she was searching for answers that were beyond her grasp.

"I'm going to walk you up to your apartment then I'll check with the landlord to see if he saw anything." Something about this didn't strike him as a prank. If he had to hazard a guess right now, he would think someone was targeting the building. The idea was disturbing and one he didn't want to share with Dana.

He scanned the grounds as they walked towards the building but the single light above the door barely made the walkway visible for the tenants to make their way to the main entrance. If kids did this, more than likely they would hide out close by watching but Jake's gut told him differently.

"What's down there?" he pointed to the basement once they stepped inside the building.

"One apartment and the laundry room with a bit of storage." Dana said and followed him down the stairs. "You're beginning to worry me a little." Jake detected a nervous tone to her voice.

"Don't be I just like to be thorough. If kids marked up the cars, it's possible that we interrupted them and the closes hiding place is inside the building. The landlord should have locks on the doors." Jake said while he took a quick scan of the laundry room and peered inside the storage rooms.

"This is clear." He said and led the way up to her apartment, he didn't like how they had dual set of stairs for the back and front of the building. It was great in case of a fire, but offered hiding places for someone who wanted to remain hidden.

Jake waited for her to unlock the door.

"I know I'm being pushy but do you mind if I take a look around before I leave?" He didn't know why but seeing that her car resembled a dead girl's and had been scratched up, left an uneasy feeling in him.

"Sure, I doubt you'll find anything." She stood back for him to pass by. After doing a quick sweep of each room, he checked the locks on the windows.

"It's always a good thing to keep these bolted." He said while snapping the leaver into place.

"I'm on the second floor. I don't think anyone is going to crawl through them." Dana looked at him as if he were a little on the crazy side.

"If someone wants something bad enough they find a way." He pointed out the window at the ground under the light shining over the back entrance. "See that little covering over the back door."

"Yes," Dana said looking to where he pointed.

"It's really not that high. Anyone can scale it, if they wanted to."

"Good another thing to keep me up all night."

"You'll be okay." Jake decided to let up before he got her so paranoid to feel safe in her own home, especially since she wasn't the target. "Sorry, I don't mean to frighten you. I just like to take extra precautions. You should see my place. I have bars on the windows." He laughed trying to ease her tension.

"I don't think I'm ready to replace my curtains with bars, unless they make designer ones that will match my decor."

"If I see any I'll let you know." Jake laughed and made his way to the door. "Just keep the bolt in place and don't open to anyone you don't know." He picked up his card from the stand and held it up to her. "Call if anything happens that is out of the normal. I'd also recommend you stay in and don't go out anywhere."

"You're scaring me again." Dana stood before him with big deer like eyes staring at him.

"It not my intention to frighten you, but there's a killer on the loose and I always get a little overly cautious until we catch them." He smiled at her and decided to ask a question that had been bothering him. "Why did you choose to live out here in such a remote place?"

"You're beginning to sound like my brother." She smiled her lips pressed firmly together in determination. "I love the area and until now, it has always made me feel safe."

"I agree it a nice place, but is there anyway you'd consider staying at your brother or mother's place until we find the killer. I can take you there now if you like."

"My mother has been staying at my Aunt's house since the funeral and I can't picture me and Lindsay sipping coffee by the fire place while we wait for Robert to return." Her honesty about Lindsay made him laugh.

"Just what I thought, but I'm serious don't go out unless you have to and even then be aware of who is around you."

"I promise." Dana said and bolted the door after him.

# Chapter 32

Being inside the apartment should have made Dana feel secure, but Jake's search of the place, made her uneasy. She hated feeling spooked in her small one bedroom. Even though he just left, she picked up his card and considered calling just to hear another voice. Shooting, a quick glance at his number, she decided he was probably heading back to be with his friends and her call might be construed a nuisance.

She opted to curl up on the couch and flicked on the television, for company instead.

A news flash came on featuring Sally's death, the host advised people to travel in pairs until the street were safe. It pained her to see Sally's face posted in the background, a shiver coursed through her body. It was still very difficult to accept.

"That's enough for me," she grabbed the remote and shut it down, "no more reminders."

Murder in Chiapas Falls was rare, so Dana figured the news would sensationalize the story for as long as they could. She didn't see the reason behind putting senseless fear into everyone. *'The killer probably moved on to another province by now and is watching all the hype.'* She guessed.

Anger replaced all other emotions she had built up, she got of the couch determined not to allow the media or insane people she didn't know invade her life. *'Why should I be the one trapped within the walls of my apartment I didn't do the crime, yet it's like I'm the one under house arrest?'* She surmised.

She had things that needed to be done and to get back any kind of normalcy to her life she had to get routine going again. Running around, she collected things to do a laundry, tossing the items into the hamper.

Grabbing her keys, she stepped outside the apartment and dropped her basket to the floor to lock up. She hesitated, looking down the stairs things took on a different feeling once on the other side of the door. The cockiness she had mustered up while running around like a mad man faltered somewhat.

"What the hell am I trying to prove?" She questioned her actions as her heart pounded hard pushing on her chest.

She considered sucking up her pride and running back in with her tail between her legs, until the murmured voices from her neighbours across the hall gave her the courage needed to continue her mission to do laundry. Picking up her basket, she made a slow descent to the machines.

On the main level, she fought an urge to stop by the Walter's place to let them know she would be in the basement.

"Don't be an idiot." She chastised herself. She gave a quick look out the front door into darkness. Jake was right, a locked would make her feel safer.

She would mention it to Mr. Walters the next time she saw him.

Dana regretted isolating herself from her family. She used to enjoy coming down listening to the hum of the machines as she read in a corner. *'There would be no reading tonight,'* she thought; her concentration limited to zero.

She hit the light switch then made her way slowly into the room, it felt cold and damp but pride prevented her from backing out now.

She picked a machine then placed her basket on the floor and began loading her clothes in without bothering to sort them. After sprinkling detergent over the pile she closed the lid down and eyed the storage doors, gaining comfort, knowing Jake had check them earlier.

A muffled thud hit the floor sending her heart into a panic. Every inch of her skin crawled with fear, she jumped letting out a small scream that almost send her racing out of the room.

"Get a grip." She told herself feeling foolish. "I'm being stupid." She picked up the box of soap on the floor then grabbed a magazine to use as a dustpan to scoop up the spill. Her hands were shaking while she tried to balance the paper with the soap weighing it down. She almost made it to the trash can when the storage door opened with a creek that filled the room.

She froze on the spot, her eyes fixed on the door while trying to justify any reason, besides someone hiding behind it, as to what would cause it to open on its own. *'Would kids stay that long in a room? Impossible, I watched Jake check it.'* She thought.

"This is ridiculous. I'm not going to go through life afraid of everything." Tossing the magazine into the garbage, she strutted over, with a new found bout of courage, and slammed the door closed, then twisted the handle to make sure it was tightly shut.

She stood listening to the chugging sounds coming from the washer as an unbalanced load whooshed around taking on a whispering sound. Her moment of confidence ended the moment she flipped the lid open. Coming from behind her, Dana swore she heard what sounded like a voice whispering in tune to the washer winding down. "Sal-ly, Sal-ly." It repeated in a low tone, turning she imagined the door opening again. Barely able to breath, she held onto the washing machine and considered loading the wet clothing into her basket and running.

'These can wait until morning,' Dana decided and raced out the door leaving her laundry.

## Chapter 33

A short, sharp scream escaped from deep within Dana, as she rounded the corner.

"Henry, what are you doing here?" She had run straight into the occupant of the basement apartment.

"I actually live down here." He pointed to the door across from the laundry room.

"I'm sorry Henry. I wasn't expecting to find anyone out here." She forced a smile while running her fingers across her forehead.

"Are you okay? You look like you saw a ghost." He asked.

Henry was the one person in the building that she knew the least. The most interaction they shared had been a nod at each other while passing in the hall, nothing more until now. He was about the same age as some of the younger tenant, yet kept to himself most times. None of that mattered now, at this moment he saved her from having a premature heart attack.

"I guess things are just getting to me." Dana said gaining her breath back along with the sensation in her body.

"I think they are getting to everyone." Henry said. "Are you washing your clothes?" He asked.

"Trying to but I talked myself into a frenzy thinking someone was hiding in the storage room." She gave a half laugh not caring how foolish she sounded.

"I can check it out?" He offered and looked into the room.

"No, it's alright. But would you mind waiting until I get my things?" She asked.

"No problem, I'll walk you to back to your place if you like." He smiled at her.

"Thank you so much." Dana said thinking he probably thought she was nuts as he helped her to load soaking clothing into her basket, but she didn't care.

"I'm not doing anything right now so if you like I can stay with you until your clothes are done." He offered. She considered it for a moment before turning it down.

"That's kind of you, but I just want to get back home." No matter how uncomfortable she felt in her apartment, it was better than what she just went through.

Henry carried the basket to her door and waited until she pulled her load of wet clothes into her place.

"Thank you Henry, I'm okay now." Dana turned and gave him an appreciative smile before shutting the door.

It amazed her how quickly things turn around. She hardly knew Henry and now a connection was formed between them, one she would never forget.

Still shaky, she dragged her basket to the bathroom and dumped the basket in the tub. She'd deal with the mess in the morning when things were clearer. Going back to the living room, she picked up Jake's card and reached for the phone. It rang just at the moment, startled she grasped the receiver.

"Hello." Her voice had a crackle to it. "Eric?" Dana asked surprised. "No, I'm considering retiring for the night. Yes, the detective dropped me off and headed out." Hearing his voice had a calming effect on her. His call came just in time to save her from losing her mind.

## Chapter 34

Jake woke with a heavy feeling pressing on his chest. Groaning he rolled over. "Get off me Nelly." He pushed a grey Siamese to the floor.

The night was dark, with about an hour to go before daylight would filter in. Awake, his mind instantly drew him back to the case and Dana. "Thanks Nelly, now I can't get back to sleep." He petted the animal as she crawled back onto his bed. Something nagged in the back of his mind like a missing puzzle piece.

Seeing what he thought was the dead girl's car spooked him, but not as much as finding out that Dana had the identical vehicle. He had to start over from the beginning, clear everything from his thoughts. *'I need a hot coffee and the file.'* Pushing the covers back he got up, jumping from the bed Nelly took her clue and followed him to the kitchen.

"Meow", the cat complained rubbing against his legs while he rinsed the pot under the tap. He nearly tripped over her while reaching for the sugar bowl above the stove.

"Come on Nelly, its five in the morning you can't be hungry now." At the feline's persistence, he pulled the box of Cat Chow down from the cupboard and emptied some into her dish. Purring, she munched away content to leave him to his work.

Flicking the on button to start his coffee, he picked up his brief case left by the front door last night then headed into the dining room adjacent to the kitchen. The stove light cast a dim glow, enough for him to see a silhouette, in the Garden Doors of himself standing barefoot in black cotton pyjama bottoms. He looked past his image into the darkness.

It bothered him that someone had dared to wander into this town to upset the peacefulness of it. Being, an outsider who moved in he had a different kind of love for the place. He had been welcomed and set up house here.

As a young boy, he geared himself up to, follow in his father's footsteps. His dream never wavered all though school causing him to go straight from graduation to the police academy and then the sixteenth precincts, on his father's recommendation.

He ran his finger over an aged scar on his left bicep, almost invisible, covered up by the muscles that now filled a more mature body. The memory of, how it got there would always be clear in his mind, he and his partner had been dispatched to a domestic battle in the early morning hours. They found a big burly man beating on his wife after a drinking binge. With a knife held over her head, he threatened to slice her to pieces for not having food on the table.

Jake remembered seeing the fear in the woman's eyes as her fragile body crouched on the floor squeezed into a corner, begging her husband not to hurt her.

He fixed his eyes on the weapon while his partner tried to reason with the man. His gut told him there was no talking to this brute. Something in his cold, uncaring eyes told Jake he intended to follow through on his promise to kill his wife.

Even though he stepped away from her, Jake could tell that the battle wasn't over.

His partner let his guard down, but not Jake, he could read the fierceness in the eyes. In an instance, his arm raised and he let out a yell that still rang in Jake's mind, before plunging the knife downward.

Without thinking how his next act would affect him, Jake leaped in front of the victim. The blade sinking deep into his flesh would never leave his memory, or the gunfire that brought the crazed man down.

The man later died in the hospital giving his widow a second chance. The Review Board considered it a clean shoot but Jake's partner couldn't take the stress and quit the force, while Jake had been dubbed a hero.

For a few moments, he wondered what kind of life the woman lived today. He hoped that if she remarried her choice would have been smarter.

In his decision to transfer from the force in Toronto to Chiapas Falls, he had hoped to get away from this kind of crime.

One thing, for sure, plenty of good officers protected this town. If the animal responsible for killing Sally still walked their streets it wouldn't be for long, he would be caught and punished. Jake made that promised to himself.

Pulling out the chair to sit, he stepped on one of Nelly's squeaky toys bringing him back to reality.

"What did I tell you about leaving your toys around?" He picked it up and tossed it towards her but the cat continued to munch on her food oblivious to his movements.

Sitting down he pulled a green file folder from his case and started to read the report over again.

"What am I not seeing here, girl?" He spoke to the cat, something he always did while trying to solve a case.

He mulled over the words until the gurgling sound of the machine indicated the brew was ready. Closing the folder, he went and poured the hot liquid into a mug. He took a moment to inhale savouring the scent before he went back to work, only to find Nelly claimed his chair to curl up.

"Not this time girl." He balanced his coffee in one hand while he picked her up with the other, a move he instantly regretted. Intending to put her on the floor, she surprised him with plans of her own. With one leap, she managed to escape from his grip dragging her back claws across his bare stomach. Landing on the table, she sent the file and all its contents flying to the floor.

"Jeez Nelly," Jake murmured under his breath while placing his mug down. He ran his fingertips over the fresh scratches while he watched as she skidded around the corner.

"I should have gotten a dog." He threatened, bending to retrieve the papers scattered all over.

A chill raced through him as he stared down at an eight by ten photo of Sally staring up at him. The answer to his nagging questions lay right in front of him causing an instant assault of fear to attack his insides at the realization it brought him.

"Why didn't I notice before?" At first glance, he would have sworn he was seeing a picture of Dana. The long blonde hair and soft features had such a resemblance that they could have been sisters.

His mind raced back to the similar red Volkswagens the girls drove and how they shared a parking spot, which Sally used the night she died. Then seeing the car keyed, it all made sense, he finally knew what had been nagging him. A sick feeling gnawed at him as he realized the truth.

"The killer got the wrong girl." He needed to get to Dana to warn her. Chances are she knows who they are and interacts with them on a regular basis. He hoped his assumption was wrong but didn't think so.

If he was right, the keying could be a statement, or a thrill for the killer to see how close he could get to the real victim, keeping her in his sites waiting for the perfect moment. Jake held onto a slight hope that whoever it was, got careless with his little act of vandal last night.

The clock on the stove showed five thirty.

"Dammit it, I should have sent someone out there last night while things were still fresh." Instead, he allowed the Landlord to talk him into believing that the grandchildren of one of the tenant's may have done it on their visit.

He needed to get someone out there now, hopefully before anyone woke up.

Picking up the phone, he dialled the office to hear Helen's cheery voice answer after the second ring.

"Good morning, you've reached Chiapas Falls Police, how can I direct your call?"

"Helen, you're still there." Her shift ended at three in the morning and he expected someone else to answer.

"Lois is coming down with a bug of some sort so I'm taking a few of her hours and Judy said she'd come in early to cover the rest of the shift."

"That's nice of you to help her out, how are things going?" Helen was like a shark in a blood-filled pool when it came to information. She had an innate ability to hone in on the tone of the caller's voice, and used it as an indication on how serious the situation was. Asking her, to transfer immediately, may have caused a small frenzy, so he tried not to change up the natural routine.

"We had a quiet night, so far it has been quite boring, but the room just lit up now that you called, Sugar. What are you doing up so early?" She queried.

"Couldn't sleep and decided to work on the case for a while." He ignored her comment choosing not to feed her obvious interest. "Is Mike around?" Looking at the clock on the stove, he knew Bill would be gone by now.

"Sure is, Sugar, let me put you through." She said and then as an after thought added. "If you can't sleep I'm clocking out of here in half an hour and can come and make you breakfast if you like." She chuckled into the phone.

"I'll pass on that offer Helen, Nelly's all the company I can handle right now." Jake bent and picked up the rest of the file Nelly kicked to the floor. He hoped his preferring a cat over her invitation would be enough for Helen to realize he had no interest in her. If she didn't get the hint soon, he would have to spell it out to her, even if it meant being rude.

"Well if you ever get tired of cuddling up to your pet, you can always give me a call. Oh, and don't forget you still owe me a dance or two." She managed to say before she transferred the call.

"Morning Jake, what's up?" Mike's voice cut through the silence, diminishing any thought of Helen.

"Last night someone key Miss Reed's car along with one of her neighbours can you have Dennis run out and dust for prints."

"Sure, I can get him out there this morning." Mike sounded confident. "We don't usually do much for that sort of small crimes. Do you think it has something to do with the case?" Mike questioned.

"It's only a hunch for now but I'll fill you in once I figure it out."

"No problem, talk to you later."

"Thanks Mike." Jake hung up the phone then rushed to change.

He berated himself all the while he headed up the back roads to Dana's place. It had been two weeks since Sally's murder and he was only cluing in now on the similarities. He felt an urgency to get to Dana.

# Chapter 35

Passing the open fields getting further away from civilization, again Jake enjoyed the scenery. The place was serene in the morning light as a slight fog hovered over the fields, a pleasant contrast from the darkness of last night.

Nice but dangerous, for some reason a killer attached himself to the isolated haven and Jake believed it had something to do with Dana. He would feel better if she were in the village where her family could keep an eye on her, at least until the case is solved.

He questions his findings wondering how to tell her that the killer got the wrong girl. Sally wasn't the intended victim. Maybe, it would be a mistake telling her what he suspected until he had solid evidence. No matter how he looked at it, he had to warn her, give her a fighting change.

It might be enough to give her motivation to move back in to her mother's house until things cooled down.

If Robert is right about her being stubborn, Jake doubted that relocating wouldn't be listed in her immediate plans, Jake thought as he tried to play out how their meeting would unfold this morning.

"Dammit," things were getting complicated." He stepped on the gas feeling a sense of urgency. He needed to spread his search to the Mill where Dana worked. The personnel records would show the new hires, from there he they could narrow it down to transients passing through town picking up temporary jobs to earn enough cash to move on.

This could be as simple as Dana turning some drunk down for a date, while at a bar. Although she didn't look like the type to sit around hammering back brews all night.

Ten minutes away from the building, his phone rang.

"Hello." Jake expected to hear Mike on the other end.

"Hello, this is Dana." Her soft voice had a slight tremble to it.

"Is everything alright?" Jake asked as a lump formed in his stomach.

"I feel a little foolish and I'm probably being over paranoid but I went to get something from my car this morning and there's a man fussing around it. I didn't want to confront him so I high tailed it back to my apartment."

"He's from the police station." Jake let out a sigh pleased that she turned to him. He hoped she would for other situations that might arise. "I sent him over to see if we could get some prints of the cars. I thought he would have been done before anyone woke. I'm sorry, it was too early to call and let you know ahead of time."

"Don't apologize, I'm relief to know it's an officer."

"Is everything okay?" Jake thought she sounded too shaky for just seeing a stranger in the parking lot."

"Nothing but a bad case of nerves," she gave a short chuckle that didn't sound convincing and he wasn't about to let her push the issue aside.

"Did something happen after I left last night?" The line went silent giving him the answer before she did.

"It all seems so irrelevant in the morning light, but after you left I decided to brave a trip to the laundry room and while there I allowed my imagination to take me on a roller coaster ride through hell."

"You should have told me you needed to wash your things. I would have stayed with you." He offered concerned that she didn't listen to his warning to stay inside.

"I can't ask you to baby sit me." She sounded a little insulted but changed her tone immediately. "But, I learned my lesson, next time I'll heed your words and remain behind lock doors like a prisoner." She let out a soft chuckle that didn't sound real. "If Henry, my down stairs neighbour, didn't get home when he did you may have found me curled up on the laundry room floor in the fetal position sucking my thumb."

"What happened?" Jake asked curious as to Henry's timing.

"I worked myself into a frenzy with an over the top imagination," Dana offered then changed the subject. "I'm thinking of picking up a bottle of wine and giving it to him as a thank you. What do you think?" She asked Jake's opinion on the gift.

"If some guy did something to stop me from curling up on the floor and sucking my thumb, I'd probably pick him up some liquor." Jake liked that she still had a sense of humour despite all the trouble.

"Good. Once the officer is done with my car, I'll run into town."

"I'm just down the road and should be there in a few minutes I'll check out the locker room once I get there."

"Okay, would you like a coffee?"

"Coffee sounds great."

"I'll meet you at the car. I left a few things in the back seat, including coffee." Dana said and hung up.

Just as he turned into the lot, Dennis was pulling out. Jake stopped and rolled his window down.

"Good morning, Dennis, I really appreciate you getting out here so fast."

"Glad to be able to help. Although, it looks pretty clean. Like it had been put through the car wash or someone wiped it down with a rag."

"What about the other car?" Jake questioned.

"There were a few more there, but I'm guessing they belong to the owner."

"Let me know, I'll talk to you later." With a wave to Dennis, Jake watched him drive away.

# Chapter 36

Jake pulled into an empty spot at the end of the lot and stepped out just as Dana exited the building. With her hair pulled back in a ponytail, *'I bet this girl has no clue of her beauty,'* Jake thought as he watched her approach.

He enjoyed seeing the smile on her face and couldn't imagine what about this girl could cause someone to want her dead. Once he found the motive, finding the killer would be easy.

"Your man is fast. In the short time I went to call you to complain he disappeared." Dana called over as she walked to meet him. For a moment, Jake wished they were meeting for something other than police business. *'Keep it professional,'* he warned.

"You just missed him. We crossed paths I drove in as he pulled out." Jake smiled and followed Dana to her car and watched as she unlocked the door.

"I have to admit that there is something about day light and having a detective by my side that gives me a different prospect on things." Dana said with a slight laugh. She put on a strong front but the dark circles around her eyes told Jake a different story.

"Night always brings out the shady side of people." He stated.

"That's strange. I left the bag right here the other night". Her voice softened as she popped the latch to the back door.

"Is something missing?" He watched as she rummaged around feeling under the front seats.

"Only my mind… I left a bag here yesterday and now it's gone… It doesn't make sense." She pointed to the floor.

Her car was immaculate, not even an empty coffee cup, so when Jake saw a small white slip of paper neatly spread out on the floor behind the driver's seat it stood out of place.

"What's this?" He picked it up carefully.

"At least I have proof that I actually purchased the stuff. It must have fallen out of the bag."

"Coffee, sugar, music box." Jake read the items off.

"You're positive you didn't bring these upstairs."

"I check around my place which isn't that big. I parked the car yesterday and rushed out totally forgetting them." Jake walked around running his fingers over the locks. Looking for any tell tale signs of a break-in.

"Do you always lock your doors?" He asked wondering if maybe, she didn't and whoever took the items thought it would be a funny gesture.

"Always!" Her answer was definite and he believed her.

"My guess is the culprit who keyed your car somehow managed to get into it without leaving any marks and took your things." This only added to confirm Jake's theory making him think the killer was making a game out of stalking Dana. '*A game she doesn't even know she's playing. Well I'm about to even the playing field.*' Jake thought.

"I'm amazed at how good these kids are at crime." She went to take the receipt but Jake stopped her. "If you don't mind I'd like to take this to the lab for testing."

"Why?"

"Whoever did this they may have left prints." He had to tell her. "I woke early today and started going over Sally's file again."

Looking into deep blue eyes, he detected a hint of fear and knew there wasn't any way to break the news to her without causing more.

"I came here to talk to you about a few things regarding the case." He made the decision to be honest with her and tell everything, but not in a parking lot where Sally died.

Dana followed him to his car, and watched him take a clear, plastic bag from the glove box and slipped the paper in before sealing the top.

"I guess my invitation for coffee is out." Her smile weakened as she looked around the open fields surrounding her building. "I use to love this place so much, now I'm not too sure what I'm feeling."

"It is beautiful out here but a lot of badness is hanging over it, maybe you should considering moving back into town for awhile." Seeing she openly admitted her doubts, maybe now would be a good time to bring up her relocating.

"Things like this never happen here. Why now?" She stared at the ground and kicked at the gravel. He thought she did it more to conceal the tears she dabbed away with her fingers.

He wanted to put his arms around her for comfort instead he looked away.

"Who knows why these things start," he let his eyes wander around the property, "It is a remote area and with no one around it easier to do the crime."

"I guess. It's just hard to believe things can change so quickly."

"There's no stopping change. We just have to learn to adapt to it." Jake smiled, "Why don't I take a quick look through the lockers?" He felt like the two of them were standing in quicksand, and the more they struggled the deeper they sank.

"I hate to think that some brats are now enjoying my coffee and sugar. To make matters worse they are probably enjoying it to the sounds of my little music box." Dana motioned towards the car and managed to laugh.

"Did you have plans for the next hour or so?"

"Just a trip into town to buy some coffee and sugar, I can forget replacing the music box. I got the last one from the shelf." Dana complained. It angered Jake that the thieves took something so personal.

"Why don't you let me drive you into town and we can talk over breakfast, afterwards I'll take you over to the grocery store so we can at least replace the coffee and sugar."

She looked like she was mulling his offer over and Jake wondered if she would accept.

"Us sharing a breakfast should be good for a few rumours." She rebounded back and chuckled.

"I'm always up for a good rumour." He enjoyed seeing her smile again.

"Well you're in the right town for that."

"If you like I can stop and pick up a squad car and drive you around in the back seat with the lights flashing."

"Try to explain that one to my boss on Monday." Dana laughed hard at his offer.

With a lighter mood, they headed inside to the laundry room before heading out.

# Chapter 37

"How do you do it?" Dana decided to be bold and delve into his personal life. He knew almost everything about her and she knew very little about him. She wondered what kind of person it took to do his line of work.

Being a detective solving cases and facing un-timely death was an important job, but how many could do it and come out unscathed at the end of it.

'*He seems to have a handle on it*,' she thought while quickly examining his profile to see if any signs of premature ageing were present. None even hinted at his strong handsome features. Except for the darkened shadow of an unshaven face, his skin looked smooth. Taking in his good looks, Dana had to fight a crazy urge to run her fingers along his cheekbones.

He appeared to possess an inner strength that gave her the sense that she would never have to worry about someone trying to harm her with him around.

"Do what?" He queried looking away from the road for a brief moment.

Embarrassed at her own thought, she pretended to be interested in a group of horses grazing in a passing field to avoid him seeing the slight blush rushing through her cheeks.

"Balance your hectic job and your life."

"Knowing what I do brings a sort of comfort to the victim's family helps. But, more than anything, putting useless creeps behind bars where they can't hurt anyone else is reward enough."

"You're continually surrounded by crime. Do you ever get away from it?"

"Truthfully, it doesn't happen, all that often in Chiapas Falls." He smiled at her. "You might find this hard to believe but I do have a social life," turning to her he smiled, "and of course Nelly keeps me busy enough at home."

Her eyes shot to his naked ring finger. She recalled, Lindsay drilling him on his marital status and was positive he claim not to have a wife. A feeling of awkwardness swept through her. *'Not having a ring on his finger didn't make him single.'*

"She doesn't mind you rushing out of your bed in the early hours, to rescue strange women before you take them to out breakfast." Dana questioned.

"She might have been if I didn't feed her first."

"Really," Dana said. *'I feel like the fool flirting with a man who has a girlfriend sitting at home stuffing her face,'* Dana thought.

"Nelly and I have a special relationship, I do my thing and she does whatever she wants." He surprised her with a laugh.

"You don't need to explain your personal life to me." Dana felt uncomfortable despite his obvious enjoyment. *'Believe me mister you're not doing you're little thing with me.'* Dana thought, and was about to change their plans and ask him to let her off at her mother's place.

"I'll have to introduce you to her," he grinned over at Dana, "she the best cat every."

"Nelly's a cat?" She understood his humour now.

"She doesn't think she is." He smiled looking quite pleased to have put one over on her. "I'm sorry were you thinking something different?"

"I knew you weren't married because you told Lindsay, but you had me believing you and a girlfriend had some weird little agreement to do your own thing despite being together, as long as you fed her." Her lips curling into a smile at the sound of Jake's laughter, *'it is nice to see he has a humorist side and isn't all work.'* Dana thought.

"I assure you that if I had a wife or girlfriend at home I definitely wouldn't be spending time alone with a beautiful woman." Jake turned his stare back to the road.

"That's good to know." Dana's face flushed at his complement. She found herself enjoying the innocent flirting between them now his marital status had been confirmed.

"But it would really give the natives something to flap their jaws about." She teased.

"Ah, you're the type who likes to give people a good reason to gossip about."

"Believe me. The people in this town don't need a reason to natter about."

"I take it you don't like living here." Jake noted.

"Don't get me wrong, I love where I live," Dana sighed, "and contrary to popular belief, I don't mind the town." She rubbed her hands over her bare arms, she felt chilled even though the morning was warming up. "What I don't like is the lack of privacy, everyone knows your business. I just think living in a larger city would give you more freedom to be yourself." Dana said.

"No matter where you go you're going to find insecure people who need to talk trash about others." Jake glanced over at her. "Not everyone is like that. Usually, the ones who have low self esteem and the only way they can feel good about who they are, is to demean others."

"You're right. Working at the Mill everyone knows the whole town's business. The place is one big Soap Opera and I really don't need to know whose cheating on their spouse, or which best friends are punching it out over a guy at the local bar."

"It's not like that every where."

"I know not everyone is bad, most of my workmates have been very supportive with my dad dying and I'm changing my thinking." Dana said remembering all the cards and flowers left on her desk at work. "I guess another reason I feel stifled is the town is stale, there's nothing else to do."

"I don't know about that, I'm going on my second year here and I haven't been bored yet. In fact, there's a lot to do." Jake defended the town.

"Sure, if you don't mind watching reruns at the local theatre, where if you go early enough you can get the same seats your grandparents carved their names in when they were young. Or, you can always spend the night at your favourite pub getting so drunk you can't remember how you got home until you get to work the next day. Where, everyone is more than happy to fill you in on your night." Dana stated, 'that must have sounded bad.' She thought. "Just to let you know I'm not speaking from personal experience."

"I didn't peg you for a binge drinker." Jake smiled. "I can't say I've done the movie thing or the binge drinking but I have taken advantage of the beautiful provincial parks around here." Jake said.

Dana remained silent for a moment before turning to Jake.

"I haven't gone camping in so long I almost forgot about the great parks." She said with a more positive attitude.

"All you have to do is look in your own back yard." Jake smiled over at her.

"I could probably enjoy a peaceful weekend sleeping under the stars." She wondered why it would take a stranger to the town to remind her of the good things right close by. It's funny the things you take for granted, pitching a tent and sitting by the light of a fire for the weekend sounded like something she could use in her life right now. "My mother probably has all the equipment stashed away in the attic. Thanks Jake. I might bundle up some warm clothes and head out to spend the weekend under a moon lit sky." Dana smiled.

"That's the last idea I want to put in your head. Send you out on a camping excursion to a secluded place. I don't think so with Sally's killer still out there."

"Do you think he's still around?" Dana quivered. It angered her that someone she never met could control what she did.

"It's hard to say. So, for now let's play it safe." Jake suggested and Dana nodded. With their topic of conversation changed and the reminder of why they were together, Dana withdrew staring out the window.

"You had to be up early to have caught Denis working." Jake mentioned hoping to keep the communication open.

"I love my mornings too much to sleep in." Dana said allowing Jake to draw her back into a conversation.

"I do too. There's nothing like watching a sun rise with the smell of a campfire drifting on the morning air." Jake said.

"I agree."

"When this is all over, I'll personally drive you out to the campground. I might even pitch a tent beside yours."

"What about Nelly?" She teased.

"I'll bribe her with a box of chow mix and treats and she'll be good." He chuckled.

"Nelly sounds like quite the girl." Dana laughed at his apparent love for the animal.

"Believe me, Nelly thinks I'm the pet and she's the master. About four this morning she got this insatiable hunger and decided her belly was more important then my sleep." Jake laughed.

"You don't strike me as a cat person." Dana surmised.

"After this morning I had my doubts. I fed the feline and she thanked me by raking her back claws across my stomach, believe me, I considered trading her in for a dog." Jake rubbed his hand over his mid section then pulled into Granny's Kitchen.

# Chapter 38

"It smells great in here." Jake said as he ushered Dana to a booth.

"I love this place." Dana confessed.

A cheery waitress approached their table, with two menus and a pot of coffee. She flipped over the mugs and filled them without asking if it was what they wanted.

"Do you need a minute to look at the menu?"

"Two eggs scrambled with sausage and brown toast." Dana ordered handing back the menu.

"I'll have the same with an orange juice." Jake said. Taking a sip of his coffee, he sat back. "We've got company." He nodded towards the back of the restaurant.

"So this is where you're hiding, I've been trying to call you all morning." Eric slid in beside Dana, without an invite.

"What for?" She looked at him questioningly. "I wanted to see if you would come house hunting with me and Tina today." Eric nodded towards his table where a tall, blonde, gave a quick wave and smile. "But I can see you already have a date for today." He looked over at Jake. That was a little flippant Dana thought.

"I wouldn't actually call having breakfast a date. I had some business at the apartment and invited Dana out for something to eat so we can talk." Jake wondered if Eric was showing signs of jealousy or if it was just his manner.

"What happened?" Eric asked concerned.

"Someone decided to take a key to the neighbour's and my car and helped themselves to a few items I forgot to take in from the back seat."

"Dana you have to get away from that place." Eric stated and Jake like where this conversation was going. Finally, something he could agree with Eric on. "What do you think detective?" Eric threw the question over to Jake.

"I don't think it would hurt for you to move into town for a bit," Jake backed up Eric.

"There you go." Eric slapped the table to prove his point.

"I don't need you two ganging up on me. I'm not ready to let a bunch of prankster kids, out on a nightly spree, chase me away from my home." Dana held a hand up in front of her.

"You're probably right but why take chance. I'm sure Robert and Lindsay would love to have you stay with them for awhile." Eric suggested.

Dana almost chocked on her coffee before she turned to give a crooked grin at Eric.

"Wouldn't that be a volatile situation," Dana turned to Jake, "how long do you think Robert would last with his two favourite women living under the same roof."

"I see your point, but what about your mother's?" Jake asked.

"Jake, I thought you were on my side." Dana turned back to Eric. "I haven't live at home for so long I don't know if I could do it again, and I'm sure my mother appreciates her alone time."

"You could always bunk up at my place for awhile." Eric offered flashing a sly grin at her. Jake watch Dana's face turn red but she came back quickly.

"No thank you. That could be even more deadly than living under the same roof as Lindsay."

Jake sat back and smiled, hearing her refuse Eric's offer made him want to laugh but he kept it quiet. Hazarding a guess, he would think the doctor didn't get too many refusals in his life time.

"Ouch, that hurt, so I guess its mom's house." Eric laughed not allowing her quick rejection to bother him.

"Don't you have a house you have to look at?" Dana gave him a gentle shove in the side. Eric was about to answer her back just as the waitress came with two plates.

"Can I get you something sweetie?" She flashed a bright, white smile at Eric, obviously pleased with him being there.

With a glance over his shoulder at Tina, he stood up.

"No thanks, I think my order is ready for me at the other table." Before he left he turned back to Dana.

"If I can't get you to move in with me can I at least get you to come house hunting with me this morning after we finish eating?" Eric asked.

"I would love to but I have plans already." Dana said without giving any indication as to what they were.

"Ouch, two rejections in less then five minutes," he teased. "I should have given you more notice. What about tomorrow." He asked not giving up.

"Sure tomorrow is better for me." Dana smiled up at him.

"Good, I'll pick you up around nine and if Jake doesn't mind I'll get breakfast tomorrow." Eric smiled over at Jake.

"I'm only working a case here. What Dana does is her own business." Jake said, the brief connection he felt with the Doctor to get Dana to move disappeared, he decided the more he got to know Eric, the less he liked him. In Jake's opinion, the Doctor was too arrogant and cocky, probably due to the nature of his profession. Jake found the attitude unique to Eric, Robert, he found more humble.

"I'll see you tomorrow, then." Eric winked at Dana before he left to go back to Tina.

Jake shoved a mouthful of egg into his mouth and watch Eric make his way back to Tina who looked irritated as she flashed a phoney smile in their direction.

## Chapter 39

Jake and Dana finished their meal and the waitress was refilling their cups when Eric walked past to leave.

"You two have a good day, and I'll see you tomorrow." He pointed to Dana.

"You enjoy house hunting." Dana said and Jake just nodded.

It was obvious that the doctor wanted to make sure Jake understood his interest in Dana. It may be a good thing Jake thought, both of them keeping an eye on her would make it hard for anyone else to get her alone.

That wasn't enough though, to ensure her safety, more had to be done, Dana needed to be aware of the possible dangers so she could look out for herself. Not telling her would be unfair.

"I agree with Eric, you know." Jake tried to ease into how he would break the news to her.

"What about?" Dana asked.

"Staying with your mother for awhile," Jake knew she would refuse but he had to try.

"Like I mentioned earlier, I'm not going to let a bunch of kids run me out of my home." Dana stated with a determined look. This wasn't going to be easy, Jake thought so with a deep breath he looked straight at her.

"Dana, we need to talk, but not here." He glanced around the restaurant. Telling her that he believed a killer was stalking her somehow, didn't seem appropriate in a crowded area.

"Okay." Dana gave him a sceptical look. He had to be honest with her so she would believe he had her best interest at stake.

"Come with me." Jake got up and threw some bills on the table.

# Chapter 40

Jake drove to a roadside stop and parked. A few couples strolled pass the front of the car while out walking with children who ran ahead picking up dried leaves.

"Dana, I'm going to tell you something and I need you to trust me." She looked at him confused.

"I do trust you." She stated with confidence.

"This is hard." He rubbed a hand through his hair.

"Dana I also need you to promise to keep this between us, at least until I know for sure." He locked eyes with her, hoping she would understand the seriousness.

"Not even Robert." She questioned.

"No, not Robert, not your mother, best friend, not even Eric." He put a hand on her shoulder. "Do I make myself clear?"

"You're scaring the hell out of me, but if you don't want me to say anything, mom's the word." Jake waited for her to promised, before he reached into the back seat and pulled out the case file.

Dana sat in silence as he took out the picture of Sally and held it up for her to view.

"I'm only telling you this so you will be more aware." Looking at Sally's photo, he turned to Dana. "I hope I'm wrong about this but I need to take precautions." Jake hated having to tell her and knew he had her worried, but knowing would at least give her a fighting chance.

"What are you getting at?" She sat with her back against the window.

"I was going over the file this morning and came across Sally's picture. I looked at this a hundred times and can't believe I didn't see it sooner." Jake held it out for her to look at. "Do you notice the resemblance to you?"

"Everyone thought that." Dana gave a nervous chuckled. "In fact, Phil use to tease us about being twins separated at birth. Where are you going with this?" She searched his face.

"There's no easy way to say it," Jake inhaled, "I think the killer is after you." Dana stared at him with eyes wide open.

"No, no, are you saying Sally died in my place." She covered her face with her hands.

"Dana, listen to me." Jake took hold of both her hands. "I know Sally's death is extremely tragic, but the reality is, if I'm right, your life may still be in danger." There was no going back now he thought as he looked at the fear in her eyes.

"Why would someone want me dead?" She looked shocked.

"I don't know but I promise you I will soon." He stated with determination, he wouldn't rest until he did. "You have to tell me everything that's been happening in your life no matter how minor you think it is."

"I will." She sat back and started to talk.

Listening to her relate events that happened from sensing someone watching from higher locations at the hospital and then towers at the funeral home. The incidence in the laundry room and, the night someone almost forced her off the road had Jake convinced that he his gut instinct was right.

"Why didn't you tell me all this when I first interviewed you?"

"It seemed irrelevant at the time. I didn't want to make it about me."

"You can't think like that." Jake sighed and stared her straight in the eyes. "You have a hard time trusting people, am I right."

"A little," Dana admitted.

"You're going to have to open up to me otherwise I won't be able to help you."

"Okay." Dana gave in and Jake felt that something changed between them. They now shared a secret that only one other person knew, '*the killer.*' Jake thought. He hoped his conclusion evened the odds, because the killer wouldn't know he figured it out or that Dana knew.

# Chapter 41

Daylight outside faded as darkness slowly crept its way into the apartment. Curled up on the couch, Dana sat in semi shock, not believing Jake's words that echo in her head.

Rehashing the day's events, the fantasy side of her brain convinced her Jake had to be wrong. While her heart rationalized with information, she stored up since her father took ill, forcing her to admit that he only confirmed an idea she toyed with herself.

What she needed right now, was to forget everything and get some of the old emotions and feelings back, at least for a few hours.

Picking up her plate, she got off the couch and tossed a half-eaten ham sandwich into the trash. Her stomach felt tied in too many knots to hold any food.

She winced at a sound coming from her living room window that sat directly over the building's back door. Remembering Jake's tale about someone scaling the wall, she quickly pulled it shut and locked it, after a quick check to ensure no one was on the landing. She shivered while trying to block out the image of a person climbing the poles to reach the small roof that sheltered the entrance. From there it would only be an easy reach for her window. It would be great in case of a fire, but not under her present paranoia.

Shutting the blinds gave little comfort. Turning on lights and television for company, she questioned if she ever felt so much fear while in her own home.

The reassurance, she had knowing Jake searched the building from the storage sheds in the laundry room right up to the closets in her apartment had vanished. *'It's becoming a habit every time he comes to the apartment now.'* Dana thought.

She was content to believe some kids sabotaged the car, why did he dramatized it to make her think Sally's murder evolved around her. Especially since, he based his theory on a picture of Sally that resembled her.

The only purpose it served was to make her feel like a mouse trapped in a cage, knowing a cat prowled the grounds in wait for the perfect opportunity to attack.

Things were starting to settle and get back into routine again. Of course, she had a few issues, but she was working through them.

It made her a little uncomfortable that he was able to nailed her trust fears, causing her to feel weak and vulnerable. *'Is it because he's trained to pick up on these traits or do others read me like an open book and Jake was the only one who called her out on it,'* she wondered. Whatever the reason, his ability left her feeling naked, as though he could see all her flaws.

What did Jake think he was accomplishing by waltzing in to fill her head with foolishness.

If he was trying to keep her on her toes by putting fear in her, it worked. *'Lately, seeing my shadow scares the hell out of me.'*

Maybe she should get away from here and spend a few nights with her mother. She considered tossing a few things in her suitcase and heading there tonight. The only thing stopping her was her mother's voice, lecturing her about how she should have listened to her father.

She hated having to admit defeat. Damn her pride, why did she always feel it necessary to fight what was bests for her. Dad had been right and if she heeded his words, she wouldn't be in this predicament. She felt like a child desperately clinging to her pride. The only thing it ever did for her was segregated her from the family and made her feel like an outcast. 'Lindsay a complete stranger moved in and bonded closer to mom than I ever have. 'How *pathetic!'*

It was like she view being happy as a weakness, as though she didn't want others to think she settled with how her life turned out. Why should she feel like that, she lead a good life and enjoyed her job, so why carry on as though she was a failure? If only she had come to this realization before her father died.

Going to the hall closet, she though her mind was made up as she pulled out a suitcase.

"Who am I fooling? If Jake is right, this was going to happen regardless of where I lived." Leaving the case in the middle of the hallway, she walked to the kitchen and pulled a bottle of Baby Duck from a wine rack she had sitting on the counter. With a futile attempt at twisting the cap off, she gave up and paced back and forth between the kitchen and suitcase trying to decide what to do.

"Stop!" She told herself and went back to the kitchen. If she let her guard down, she would probably end up crawling into a corner to cry and feel sorry for her predicament.

"The only thing that would change, if Jake's theory were right Sally would still be alive." She opted to sit on the couch and stare blankly at the television screen.

"I need to stop thinking or I'm going to go mad." Dana managed to take a deep breath and pulled her feet up under her.

"More than that, I have to stop listening to Jake." He could at least have more to go on before he surmised that someone was out to kill her. She didn't appreciate his method of keeping her informed and would let him know that the next time she talked to him. In fact, it might be better for her mental state to put some distance between them and only contact each other with concrete proof.

# Chapter 42

Grabbing for the phone, a chill ripped through her spine as a shrill ring echoed through the apartment.

With a voice that sounded shaky even to her ears, she answered and fought to control her emotions.

"Hello."

"Hi, it's just me." Eric's cheery voice came over the line putting Dana at ease. She didn't know what she would have done if Jake had been on the other end.

"How did the house hunting go?" Dana smiled allowing his familiar voice to calm her down. It surprised her how he always seemed to be there when she needed someone.

"There were a few I want to check out again…..are you okay?" Eric asked changing the subject abruptly clueing in on her fears.

"Yes, I'm good." She said not sounding too believable even to herself.

"Who are you trying to kid? Your voice could probably hit an 8.5 on the Richter scale. Did our detective friend do something to upset you?"

"No, I'm just reflecting on all the crazy things going on and wish they would end. My car being keyed and the fact that they took my personally things set me back somewhat." Dana semi lied, unsure why she kept her promise to Jake to keep the secret between them.

"I hate that this is happening to you. What did they take?" Eric empathized with her situation.

"Just a few food items I replaced, this morning, and a little black music box that happened to be the last one." Dana complained.

"Why can't people just live their lives and leave others alone." Eric sounded upset.

"That would be nice, but I doubt it will every happen." Dana agreed.

"I just finished putting a cast on a kid who thought he was a superhero and broke his arm by trying to fly off the garage roof. After I hang up with you, I just need to advise a hangover patient to take two aspirins and sleep it off. Then I'm all yours and can be there in an hour, to keep you company." She laughed at the breakdown of his duties.

"I can't have you drive all the way across town just to baby sit me." Dana chuckled. Just hearing his voice settled her down making the monster she built in her head less intimidating.

"You're not asking me. I want to. And believe me being with a beautiful girl isn't my idea of babysitting," Eric complemented her. His offer sounded tempting and she almost considered letting him but her reasonable side couldn't do it. He would either have to spend the night, which she was definitely not ready for, or he had to leave shortly after he got there and drive back to town. That wouldn't be fair to him.

"Thanks, but I'm going to take a hot bath and get to bed early." She declined.

"You sure, I don't mind making a house call to tuck you in." Eric teased causing Dana to laugh. His call made things seem less ominous.

"If I need a doctor you'll be the first one I think off when I pick up the phone, but thank you for the offer." Dana smiled.

"I can't wait for that call." Eric chuckled into the phone, "You still up to looking at houses tomorrow?"

"Sure, nine o'clock right." Dana confirmed.

"I'll be there." Eric said.

"You don't have to come all the way out here. I can meet you in town." She offered.

"Unacceptable, how am I going to compete with your detective boy friend if I make you drive to the restaurant?" Eric laughed.

"If you're talking about Jake, the only reason we were out was to discuss the case." Dana stated not wanting to think about him.

"So are you saying that you're definitely unattached?" Eric asked.

"That's right, I'm not seeing anyone." Dana laughed into the phone.

"I bet the detective would like to change that." Eric teased.

"I thought we were discussing housing and breakfast. How did the subject suddenly turn to the detective?"

"You're right, I'm sure we can find a better subject to entertain ourselves with." Eric apologized, "So do you mind going to the same place to eat?" Eric asked changing the topic.

"Won't that look good?" Dana chuckled.

"What" having breakfast with me?" Eric sounded surprised.

"No, having breakfast two mornings in a row with two different men."

"Ah! You little hussy, are you afraid of rumours?" Eric teased.

"Not at all," she laughed.

"Good maybe I'll cuddle up close to you and really give them a story." Eric joked.

"The way the waitress was drooling over you, I'm sure she would prefer it if you cuddle up with her."

"I didn't notice at all, maybe I'll give her a big hug instead of a tip." Eric teased.

"You never know, she might enjoy it more." Dana laughed feeling better.

"So I'll pick you up at nine."

"If you're sure." Dana said.

"Do you have a pen handy? I'll give you my number at home." Eric offered.

"Sure, what is it?" Dana said thinking how strange it was that she and Robert had a mutual friend.

Eric rhymed of the number. "So if you change your mind about having company you can give me a call." He said.       "Thanks but, I'm just going to go to bed, you have a good night." Dana paused for a second, "And Eric, thanks for calling."

"It was my pleasure. Oh before you go Robert just stepped into my office and said to say hi. Can you hear him?"

"Yes, tell him hi back and to give me a call someday." Dana smiled into the phone.

"I will, area you sure we can talk you into joining us for a beer."

"No tonight but thank for asking."

"Okay, I'll just have to wait until tomorrow to see you. Have a good night." Eric said then the phone went dead. A smile covered Dana's face as she cradled the receiver. She liked Eric, he was becoming a good friend. Her mind drifted to Jake and before she realized it, she found herself comparing the two men.

# Chapter 43

Even thought the differences between the two men were night and day they were both pleasant to look at. Eric had a love for life and could not only find the humour in things but helped others to laugh along with him about a situation, as well.

Jake on the other hand was serious a little too much. Although, there were a few times, he let his guard down and she actually found him funny, especially when it involved Nelly.

She knew he wasn't all work because he met up with a bunch of friends at the bar and he did tell her he like to camp.

She could picture him roughing it and he definitely had the rugged outdoor look about him. She wondered what it would be like to spend a weekend with him sitting under the stars. She allowed her imagination to wander for a moment before she reminded herself that she was still angry with him, so roasting marshmallows over a fire under a star filled sky was out of the picture.

Life was strange. She dated a few times in high school and twice she accepted invitations to go for drinks after work on a Friday night. The first guy ended up getting so drunk she snuck out of the bar embarrassed to be seen with him. She thought the second one would be more responsible because he was a Supervisor, but he ended up competing in a tequila binge and got mad when she refused to chug back shots so she left. After that, she promised never to waste time with anyone she worked in the same building with. She was beginning to think there were no good men available in this town.

She knew Jake was only doing his job, under different circumstances she might have enjoyed getting to know him better. '*He'd have to ditch the serious side more often,*' she thought it would become strenuous in any relationship.

Eric on the other hand confused her. One minute she got the impression he felt sorry for her and befriended her for Robert's sake, on the other hand she found him flirty, a little too much at time. Whatever his motive, Dana appreciated his friendship and loved his ability to make her laugh.

'*I need to stop thinking and get these two out of my head.*' Dana thought. A hot bath and a good night's sleep should help things to be clearer in the morning.

With the tub filling, she slipped into her housecoat then went back into the kitchen where she picked up the wine again. This time with more determination, she succeeded to pop the cork.

After a healthy sip, she headed to the bathroom with a lot less tension then before her call with Eric. She chuckled at some of his comments thinking he picked the perfect profession. If he could bottle his personality, he would be a rich man. His patients must love him. She wondered if Robert had the same bedside manner.

She adjusted the water temperature and was about to slip out of her housecoat when the phone rang again. Thinking Eric might be calling back to try to convince her to let him come over she turned the tap off and ran to answer and contemplated letting him.

# Chapter 44

"Hello." Dead air wasted away. "Hello, who's this?" She asked trying to make out the muffled sounds in the background. At first, she thought it could be Eric but it sounded more like music playing softly. She was about to hang up when she recognized the tune to be the same as her jewellery box that someone heisted from her car. Her heart dropped deep within her chest.

"Who is this?" She pleaded, not knowing why she didn't just hang up. "What do you want from me?" Fearful tears filled her eyes.

She almost threw up when a low whisper sounding almost robotic came over the line.

"Sally died for you." Dana had to strain in order to hear, but the words were definite. The music grew louder just before the connection went dead. A tune she played repeatedly, for the melody now terrorized her.

Dana covered her face with her hands and rocked back and forth on the couch, as her insides shook.

"Why is this happening?" Her stomach felt ill.

"Who could be doing this?" She cried into her pillow. *'I'm a loner and stick to myself most times. Why would anyone want me dead?'* The biggest question in her mind was if she was the intended victim, *'why kill Sally?'*

The questions kept coming, but none of the answers.

No matter what this definitely proved Jake right, someone wanted her dead. Dana berated herself for not taking him serious.

If she wasn't such a coward she would pack up a few things to leave tonight. The idea of going out alone and driving down a dark, remote road by herself frightened her, this guy could be hiding outside hoping she would run right into his murdering arms. She found it all too much to handle.

She, barley found the strength to move around her apartment, if made her sick thinking the caller could be watching her right now.

Maybe she should call Eric and take him up on his offer she thought and reached for the phone.

# Chapter 45

"Please answer." Dana pleaded as the answering machine kicked in on the fourth ring.

"You've reached Jake, as you guessed I'm not in at the moment so leave a message along with a number I can call you back on."

"Why are you not home?" She cried and hung up. "So much for getting you in a moments notice," 'what if she had been downtown and needed him. I'd be pouched.'

At least in the apartment she could look past her fear somewhat, knowing she had some safety behind concrete walls.

She considered calling, her first choice, Eric but her vow of secrecy to Jake took president. With Eric's innate ability to read her thought, she would probably spill her guts. The last thing she needed was him running to Robert and the two of them getting involved in this mess.

Her instants told her that since Jake was unreachable she should at least call the station.

"I'm so confused, someone wants me dead and I can only talk to one person about it because I can't trust anyone else. "Where the hell is Jake?" Dana felt hopeless.

A noise in the hallway startled her and her eyes shot to the door. Noticing she had been hiding out all this time with only the twist lock on the door, she leaped from the couch and raced across the floor. "Dammit." She fell against the door and turned the latch to the dead bolt. She stood there listening as an animal trapped in a cage would, for more sounds but there was nothing.

Crazed with fear, her mind created all sorts of evils. She had to pull herself together, but the memory of the distorted voice kept echoing in her head. She even contemplated going to one of the neighbours but remembered Robert telling her how uncomfortable he felt in the Walter's apartment, with all of them, wondering if one of them could be capable of murder. At the time, she thought the idea ludicrous but not so much now. Her killer might be in the building knowing her every move, waiting for her to flee.

Somehow, she managed to land in the middle of a horror movie. The scene was just as horrifying only more real. What was happening to her couldn't be stopped by shutting down a camera. She had no idea why some mad man decided to drag her into his insane game. Knowing why, might help to understand better, at least give her a fighting chance.

He had to have been stalking her since her father took ill. It was then she started to get the feeling of being watch.

This person could be hiding out in back yard, right now, spying on her every move, for all she knew. Turning down the living room lights, she pulled the curtain back far enough to peer out. Nothing but darkness blanketed the area. She let the drape fall back into place. If he was out there, she didn't want to give him the satisfaction of knowing how frightened he had her.

"This is too crazy to take in. Where could Jake be?" Dana complained losing her confidence in her so-called protector. '*I didn't ask him to take on the roll, he designated himself.*' Dana thought, thinking he could at least make himself available.

"He's probably out with his clingy girlfriend from the bar."

Trying to fight her fears Dana grabbed a fashion magazine, and curled up on the couch and stared blankly at the pictures.

At least flipping through the pages gave her mind something to focus on instead of running wild. Her tension eased and she considered leaving her comfort zone to go to her bed with the magazine.

Before, she had a chance to unravel her legs from under her the ring of the phone shrilled through the apartment sending her back into a wild frenzy.

"I can't take this." Her hand shook as she threw the magazine down beside her. Emotionally, she couldn't handle a repeat of the call she had earlier. She jumped and ran to unplug the cord from the wall.

"What if it's Jake?" She didn't leave a message but maybe he could tell she phoned. Pushing the plug back in, she raced back to the phone, she felt stupid running around not knowing, what the hell, she was doing. She managed to grab the receiver by the fifth ring.

"Hello," she said praying to hear Jake on the other end. Instead, dead air greeted her. "Not again." she cried and slammed the receiver down before any music could play.

Immediately, it began again. She held two throw pillows over her ears in a poor attempt to drown out the ring. She counted six muted rings before it stopped.

She contemplated answering it the next time to scream at the tyrant trying to scare her. She wasn't that brave so instead, she unplugged it from the wall again. Then went to the bedroom and slipped into a pair of jogging pants and sweatshirt. It would make it easier to run if she had to.

Back in the living room, she picked up the magazine again, and curled up on the couch hoping to lose herself in its pages, once more.

# Chapter 46

Despite Dana's fears she managed to doze off, she woke to a banging on the door causing her to bolt from the couch. Grabbing the phone to dial 911 she remembered, she unplugged it and the cord now lay on the floor. Her whole body shook while she searched for the end of the cable.

"Dana it's Jake. Open up." Recognizing his voice, she ran and fumbled with the locks before pulling the door opened to see him standing there with a look of terror on his face.

"You left a message that didn't make sense and I tried to call. Why aren't you answering your phone?" He demanded.

"Because I thought it was him," was all she could say before breaking down in tears from the mixture of stress and relief.

"What is going on?" Jake walked in and flipped the locks behind him while Dana dabbed at her eyes.

"You are right." He remained quiet as she began to relate the night's events.

"You're shaking. Let's sit down so you can tell me everything." He motioned towards the couch and sat down beside her.

"Sally's killer called me tonight."

"I should have made you go to your mother's." Jake slapped the arm of the seat. "What did he say?" He asked calmly but Dana could tell the news upset him.

"At first nothing and I almost hung up. Then the music started, faint in the back ground and grew louder, as though someone purposely moved it back and force from the receiver." She sat back and took a deep breath.

"What kind of music?" Jake asked.

"I'm positive it was from my music box that the thief stole from my car." Tears welled up in her eyes and slid down her cheeks "His voice was mumbled, I could hardly make it out. He told me that Sally died for me." She sniffled into a tissue.

"Dana did you recognize the voice." Jake asked.

"No, it sounded robotic and not real. It frightened me so much I hung up and tried to call you."

"Why didn't you call the station when you couldn't reach me?" Jake picked up her card and turned it over to see a blank back.

"I couldn't find the one you wrote the other numbers on." "It's okay. I'm here now."

"Thank you so much for coming." She looked at Jake relieved not to be alone anymore. "I guess knowing someone wants me dead is turning me into a mess."

"Can you think of anyone it could be?" Jake asked taking on his detective role she expected to see him pull the little note book from his pocket.

"Nothing makes sense anymore." She looked intently into his eyes, as though the answers were hidden behind them.

"You might think this is crazy, but his calling is a good thing. He exposed himself, so we know he is still around. He's getting sloppy and desperate, which, also makes him more dangerous." He turned to her. "We need to get you out of this place and the sooner the better."

His tone was firm, even if she wanted to stay Dana knew, she wouldn't win this battle. The fight was gone from her and staying held no appeal.

She glanced over at the clock in the kitchen.

"It would shock the hell out of mom if I showed up at her door at one o'clock in the morning with you tailing behind me." Dana forced a weak chuckle. "I don't think she'd quite understand if I told her I need to hide out at her house so the person who wants me dead won't find me."

"Point taken, but you have to go tomorrow." Jake insisted. "I still think it's best not to involve anyone else outside the station." He locked eyes with her until she nodded her agreement.

"I'm sorry I doubted you Jake." She dried her eyes with a tissue. The place didn't seem as ominous with him there.

If he hadn't been sitting on her couch she wouldn't have the confidence go to the kitchen. "Thank you for coming." Dana said pulling herself together.

"Dana we are going to catch this guy. I promise." His determination reassured her trust in him. *'I just hoped Jake nabs the creep before he carries out his mission.'* Dana thought.

"It's late and you need sleep, I'm going to do a check around the building." Jake looked at his watch and stood up and Dana jumped up with him.

"You aren't thinking of leaving me here alone, are you?" Dana held back from grabbing his arm and pushing him back to the couch.

"I'll be right in my car, if you need me I'll be seconds away."

"What if you fall asleep and the killer ambushes you. I couldn't live with knowing two people died in my place." Dana nervously rubbed her hands up and down her arms. "My couch would be more comfortable than trying to curl up on the front seat of your car."

"I'm not so sure of that." Jake looked at the half size piece of furniture and smiled. Dana gave a half hearted chuckled knowing exactly what he meant.

"I wasn't thinking big when I furnished my small one bedroom apartment." For the first time, she began to questions her living quarters. "You can use my bed and I can use the couch." Dana offered.

"I'm not going to take your bed while you try to twist yourself up on this. But I will take some blankets and stretch out here." Jake moved the coffee table away. "This way, I'm close enough to come running if you need me."

"I never dreamed I'd be afraid in my own home." Dana felt awkward exposing her fears. Things were getting serious and she couldn't afford to keep her old habits of blocking others out of her life. "Can you come with me to get some blankets?"

"Sure." Jake said and followed her to the bedroom and waited as she rummaged through her closet. In minutes, she pulled a couple of comforters and sheets that balanced a pillow on top.

"These are plenty." Jake quickly took them from her and carried them to the living room.

"I really appreciate you staying." Dana said as Jake help her place the last blanket down.

"I love a sleep over." He teased.

"Next time I'll give you more notice," Dana said, feeling less stress knowing he didn't intend to leave her alone.

"Good idea, that way I could pack an overnight bag with my jammies." He joked.

"I have a pink pair I can lend you." Dana laughed at the idea of him squeezing into her flannels.

"Not that I don't appreciate the offer, but I think that's one I'll have to pass on. Thanks though." Jake laughed.

"Let me know if you change your mind." Dana chuckled and remembered the wine she opened earlier on the counter and decided she could use a glass. "Would you like a drink?" She held up the bottle.

"Sure," Jake walked to the window and pulled the curtain back far enough to peer out into the darkness.

"So this is why you didn't answer my call." He picked up the end of the jack. Turning the phone upside down he plugged it back in.

"Well let's see if you get anymore calls tonight."

"You're answering if we do." Dana said.

"I can do that."

"I hate that I can't even stay in another room without feeling spooked." It felt comfortable carrying on a conversation with Jake from the kitchen.

"You're probably going to feel like that until we catch the guy and maybe for some time afterwards." Jake sat on the couch and kicked his shoes off looking more relaxed.

She poured two large glasses then took a good sip from hers and topped it up again before she joined him on the couch.

Already, she could feel a calmness wash over her. Handing a glass over to him felt so natural, her face flushed at her thoughts, being here with him felt more like a date. She curled a leg under her and faced him. She had to remind herself that he was a detective and wouldn't be there if she hadn't place her desperate call. *'I didn't think I stayed on the line long enough for a message to go through.'* Dana thought grateful he understood the mad ranting.

"Will I ever get over the fear of being alone?" Dana put her wine down thinking she better slow down before she started rambling on in stupid chat.

"You have a lot of good people in you're life. Who I'm sure will surround you after this is all over and eventually the memory will fade." Jake said, even as she nodded her head in agreement, she wondered if she would ever be free of this nightmare.

"I know, I just feel bad not being able to tell them." She said. "Robert's already thinks I don't trust him."

"The moment this is all over you can tell Robert, Eric and anyone else you want everything. Right now, I think it would be better to keep it between us. What do you think your brother or Eric would do if they knew?"

"Go on a man hunt," Dana suppressed a yawn.

"Exactly, and the last thing we need is for two of our local doctors chasing around town trying to catch a killer."

"I know. Do you think he knows you're here now?" Dana asked.

"Possible, but not likely," Jake said.

"That's good to know." Dana sighed relieved.

"You should get some sleep. Jake suggested.

Dana looked at the pile of blankets on the floor.

"I feel bad for you, why don't you use my bed and I can sleep here." She offered again.

"I'll be fine right here." Jake stood up. "It will be like roughing it under the stars, only with a ceiling." He smiled.

"Are you sure?" Dana asked. She felt foolish having dragged him out of the comforts of his home.

"Yes, now will you go and get some rest?" Jake looked at her and she wondered if he went above, and beyond for everyone.

"Do you do this for everyone one who is in trouble?" Dana turned to stare into his eyes. She drank more wine than she should have and to fast and felt a little light headed when she stood up. He was handsome and she wondered why a woman hadn't snatched him up yet.

"No." Jake answered quickly. "And probably will never do it again."

"Why did you do it this time?"

"It couldn't be prevented because of the late hour."

"How would you be able to prevent the situation if it happened again?"

"You ask a lot of questions, but if this scene ever happens again I will refuse to listen to the stubborn person and force them to leave the apartment sooner to stay with relatives."

"Good answer," Dana smile and fought a strong urge to reach up and kiss his lips. "Thank you for everything, Jake." Dana walked away before she did anything she'd regret later.

## Chapter 47

Dana woke to the sharp shrill of the phone penetrating her dream. She jumped out of bed and ran to the living room where she almost tripped over the temporary bed. She hurried over to where Jake stood by the phone slipping his shirt over his head. If she wasn't in such a panic about having to answer the call, she may have taken some time to enjoy the sight of his bare muscles.

"Do you think it could be him?" She questioned.

"I doubt it, go ahead and answer it." Jake said, and Dana nodded then lifted the receiver to her ear.

"Hello." She drew strength from Jake presents and gave a sigh of relieve, at the sound of Eric's voice.

"Good morning, did I wake you." He asked.

"No, I was getting up anyway." Dana felt guilty. *'Damn I forget Eric is picking me up to view houses.'* She glanced at the kitchen clock. Eight thirty he was probably on his way.

A new wave of panic filled her. The makeshift bed and Jake running around half dress certainly would be hard to explain. She might be able to toss the blankets into her room but that would make it appear as though Jake slept with her. With not being able to reveal why Jake stayed with her all night, the only reasonable thing would be to stall Eric.

"I'm not quite ready. Are you on your way out now?" She asked while trying to sound calm.

"No, I have to ask for a rain check. An emergency came up at the hospital and I'm heading over there now. Can I make it up to you another time?"

"I hope it's nothing serious." Dana tried to sound concern and not as though she just dodged a bullet.

"You sound relieved."

"I'm sorry, it's just I didn't sleep well last night and have a bit of a headache." She rubbed her fingers over her temples. At least she told the truth, a small reminder not to chug two large glasses of wine in less than an hour. She quickly replayed her scene with Jake last night and although she acted a little stupid, she had enough sense not to follow through on her notion to kiss him.

"Remember I make house calls."

"I haven't forgotten," she smiled.

"So I have to change our house hunting date. Is that okay?"

"Sure, thank you." Dana said, happy she avoided a near disaster.

"Why don't I drop by tomorrow and we can make some plans."

"Actually, I have decided to go to my mom's for awhile." Dana tried to sound casual.

"Why the sudden change? Did something happen?"

"No," she answered a little too quickly." She took at breath "It's just staying here spooks me." She said.

"I agree and it wouldn't hurt you to spend some time with Mom."

"You're right."

"Glad to hear that, so let me get back to you with the time on the house hunting thing. Maybe we can pick a morning so we can bring Mom with us for breakfast." He laughed into the phone.

"We'll see." Dana chuckled at the image. Bringing her mother out on a breakfast date with her brother's partner somehow seemed a little to cozy for her right now.

"I'm at the hospital now so I better let you go." Eric said.

"I'll talk to you later." Dana said and hung up. She looked over at Jake who busied himself trying to figure out the coffee machine in the kitchen. She appreciated that he kept quiet while she talked to Eric.

She didn't understand her need to hide that Jake was there, especially, since it was no ones business who she had spend the night.

She knew Eric for only a few weeks and they were becoming close, but apart from his joking with her about dating, he never came right out and asked. Last night was the first time he offered his phone number to her.

She couldn't even say for sure dating Eric was what she wanted. Right now, she needed to focus on finding out who wanted her dead and there were only three people who knew her plight, Jake, the killer and her.

Maybe Sally knew the killer and discovered his intentions to kill her so he made sure her secret died with her. Dana agreed with Jake, it is better to keep this between them.

# Chapter 48

Dana packed up a suitcase and Jake took it to the car while she locked up.

Deciding to exit the back entrance, she scanned the area, for what felt like a last time. It was beautiful here, a haven nestled amongst the trees, especially now with the burst of colour the leaves displayed.

The flower gardens, Mrs. Walters and Sally spend so much time in, showed signs of neglected. Dana guessed that there would be too many memories for Mrs. Walters to enjoy again.

She considered running back in to let the Walters know she would be staying at her mother's for a while, but decided to call them later. With a deep breath, she slowly walked around the building to find Jake leaning on her car, patiently waiting.

Seeing him, casually resting against the vehicle reminded her how handsome he is and the image of him standing in her living room shirtless flashed back to her causing her face to flush.

"You ready?" He asked as she approached him.

"It's not like I'm leaving forever," she said not believing her own words.

"That's right, and things are going to come together. I know it doesn't seem like that now, but they will." Jake consoled her.

"True." She agreed knowing all to well how to piece together the shattered remains. It was something she learned after Robert left for school. Being older, she now understood that he made a smart career move. This town would have destroyed him if he remained. Like her, he would be stuck working at the Mill.

She wasted too many years sulking over the fact that she didn't get the same opportunities her father afforded, Robert. It all seemed so meaningless now. Dwelling on the past and what ifs, change nothing.

"Come on, I have a stop to make before I drop you off safely at your mothers." Jake sounded cheery as he held the door opened for her.

"I'll follow you, once we reach town pull to the side for me to lead," he directed.

"Do I get hint as to where you're taking me?" She like the easy-going attitude he displayed once the detective hat came off.

"Nope, you must be patience." He teased and shut her door before he hastened to his car.

Briefly, her mind drifted to how Sally sat in this very spot on her last night. How terrified she must have been at the realization of what was happening. The comprehension of what actually went on still hit Dana with a small shock wave every time she tried to wrap her mind around the act.

At the sound of Jake tapping his horn, she backed the car out. An urge to flee from this place never to return overwhelmed her. It wasn't the first time she felt it, but now a sense of urgency followed the feeling. She really believed that if she stayed any longer she would die.

Driving out of the laneway, it astounded her, how the contrast between night and day were so strong. In the early morning, the grounds wrapped, in the warmth of a deceptive beauty could lure anyone in, until the fingers of darkness slowly caressed the night with evils that left the occupants frozen in fear.

Dana couldn't recall ever being as frightened as she had been in this building over the last few weeks. Last night reached a pinnacle that she never wanted to face again and doubted she could ever return to live a normal life within these walls.

Her eyes shifted to the rear view mirror many times to assure herself that Jake still followed behind her. It was almost eerie to have someone she hardly knew tailing so closely. For all she knew, he could be the killer. Her mind played tricks on her as she mentally reviewed his profile of how most of these offenders like to make a game of hanging around the family members and friends of the victim.

Being a detective, he would know first hand what was going on with the case. He put the pieces together about how she was the real target making her promise to keep the news between them. Then the call came through, confirming everything and he showed up even though she didn't think she left a message. Maybe he was taking her somewhere to finish the job and she like a fool willingly followed him off to who knows where.

"This is crazy." Dana immediately shut down her insane thinking and checked the mirror again.

"Trust," 'I really have to work on trusting people. Jake is a good detective whose agenda is to protect her.' She reminded herself that she called him to come over last night. He had every opportunity to complete the task while they were alone in the apartment.

Once she reached the town limits she eased the car over to the side of the road and allowed him to pass, with a smile and wave, he drove ahead of her. She chuckled, *'wouldn't you think I'm a wacky case if you knew moments earlier I toyed with the idea that you could possibly be the killer.'* Dana smiled back and followed him until he pulled up in front of a cottage like house, a few streets from where her mother lived.

# Chapter 49

Jake pulled into a dirt laneway and Dana parked behind him. She took a moment to absorb all the sweetness of the home, the ivy climbing up weathered cedar siding to the chimney and a big elm tree in the middle of the yard with a swing attached by long thick cords hung down motionless. Dana smiled at the scene, there was no way a thief of life would live in something this cozy. She thought as Jake walked to the car and opened her door for her.

"Is this where you live?" She stepped out enjoying the scenery.

"This is home," he pointed to the house with a sense of pride.

"It's so cute."

"Cute!" He gave her a quizzical look that made her laugh.

"Hum," Dana said feeling a little flirty. "I don't know about this. Am I going to be safe going in there?" She teased.

"You just spent the night with me so you know I'm harmless, Nelly on the other hand is female and hungry." He laughed. "So I can't speak for her."

At the sound of a pot crashing to the floor of the porch, Jake positioned himself to stand in front of Dana.

"Well isn't this cute." Dana recognized the woman from the night Jake drove her and Lindsay home. She stood in red jeans and a white halter-top, and stepped off the porch looking like she was ready for a fight. Dana felt like she was caught cheating with a married man. The freeness this woman spoke to Jake with led

Dana to believe there was more to their relationship then he wanted to admit to.

"Okay, well thanks for everything, Jake but maybe we should do this another time." Dana back up towards the car wanting to get out of there before the fireworks started.

"Wait a minute Dana. Jake took hold of her arm to stop her from leaving. "Helen, this is my house, what are you doing here?" Jake demanded sternly.

"This came in for you and I tried calling but you didn't answer," she held up a large brown envelop. "I'm smart enough to put two and two together to see what kept you busy." She made a huff sound and threw the item down on the step before she pushed past Jake and stopped in front of Dana.

"Funny how some women are. They'll share their bed but not their car." She hissed at Dana whose feet stood frozen to the ground.

"Helen, be careful of what you're saying." Jake warned and moved between the two.

"If anyone needs to be careful Jake, I'd think it would be you. Or have you forgotten miss beauty queen is a case file." Helen managed to spit out before stomping her way back to the porch showing that she wasn't going anywhere.

"Helen, the case I'm working on isn't about Dana." Jake clarified.

"Well she's involved in it." Helen hissed at him.

"Helen, living in a building where a crime took place, how does that make her a part of it?" Jake questioned.

"For all you know she could be the killer." Helen's eyes squinted as she nodded in Dana's direction.

"Helen, stop for a moment and try to remember what your position is at the station." Jake tried to control her while Dana stood with her mouth gawked open.

"What are you going to do Jake? Arrest me."

"Helen what is this all about?" Jake demanded.

"Up until now I always thought you were being a gentleman by not inviting me over." Helen looked at him with such hurt. Her voice took on a calm sadness different from the crazed ranting she greeted them with earlier.

Now would be a good time to take advantage of this unexpected mildness Dana thought, as she took slow steps to put some space between them.

She wondered how someone could go from a screaming raging fool to a timid woman within seconds. Split personality and not someone Dana needed involved in her life right now or ever for that matter. Whatever Jake had going with this girl he was a fool not notice how deep her feeling were for him.

"Listen, I'm going to leave and let you two sort this out." Dana said to Jake." She opened the car door and slipped in behind the wheel while Helen stood with a victory smile spread across her face.

"I don't know where this is coming from." Jake held the door before she could close it.

"It's not me you have to explain things to." Dana nodded to where Helen stood with her arms folded across her chest glaring at them.

"I'm sorry about this." Jake gave a weak smile. "Maybe another time?" He said.

This whole morning could have turned out so different, yet again another person change the outcome. Dana felt sad for Jake. For some reason this woman attached herself to him and believed, she had dibs on him.

"Don't be, I should get going anyhow." Dana looked over at Helen who now looked lost while she waited for Jake. She felt pity for her. She probably had her own visions of what would happen after Jake got home, while she patiently waited for his arrival.

Whether or not Jake returned this woman's feelings, in her mind there was something between them.

"This is awkward and a little embarrassing." Jake held the top of the door and looked down at her. "There really is nothing going on here, not now or in the past." Jake tried to explain the situation but Dana didn't feel it necessary.

"It's okay, it's really none of my business."

"I should really take you over to your mother's."

"It's just around the corner. I can manage the two minutes drive from here."

"I'll call later." Jake whispered.

"Okay, and thanks again for coming to my rescue last night." Dana whispered as she looked over at Helen who stood rubbing a hand down her red jeans as though she had just won a lover's spat and was getting ready to make up. Dana thought then pulled out of the laneway.

# Chapter 50

'*Talk about walking into a bad dream,*' Dana thought as she turned up the street towards her mother's home. She didn't envy Jake and his situation. She was a little curious as to how the scene would unfold now that he was alone with her.

'*What would cause someone to become so possessive over another person?*' Dana wondered.

Especially, since Jake was adamant that they never shared anything together. '*Obviously, they do go to the same places maybe, they had a few too many and ended up in a one night fling and that was enough for Helen to stake her claim.*' Dana knew for sure.

'*That definitely was a mood breaker.*' Dana chuckled to herself as she manoeuvred her car around the corner.

She actually enjoyed being with Jake, for a brief moment she felt like life could be normal again. Meeting Helen gave her a reality check helping her to realize life has changed for her. Jake had his own issues to deal with and she intended to give him all the space he needed to work out his own problems.

Instead, of worrying about other people's drama Dana had to concentrate on getting her mind accustomed to moving back home and fixing her own affairs.

Being on the familiar street with all her childhood memories a sense of security rushed her. It felt good coming home.

She may have appreciated it more if her father had been around to enjoy her revelation.

Having two people, you know die in the same week definitely had a profound effect on her. Especially, Sally's being the most senseless, just because she happened to be in the wrong place. The last few weeks have been life altering to Dana, giving her a different prospective and an urgent need to re-evaluate her way of thinking.

Getting mad at the things you have no control over was such a waste. It made her ill knowing the killer made it clear that Sally died because of mistaken identity. *'Why me? What did I do for someone to want me dead?'* The whole thing overwhelmed her.

Not only was it time to relocate her living quarters, but she also needed to start forming solid friendships.

# Chapter 51

*'Great, first I'm accosted by some crazy person who believes I'm stealing her man and now I get to chit chat with my snobby sister-in-law. Can the day get any better?'* Dana questioned then pulled into the driveway.

She preferred to fill her mother in on her decision to move back into the house without an audience. Then unpack and settle in before implementing her new leaf on life.

Walking into the house was strange, and despite the rays flowing through the windows, it felt cold. This was her first time home since her father died, how different not to have him rushing to greet her at the door. Even with him gone, his presence felt strong and she half expected to see him coming down the stairs or pop his head out from the kitchen. Dana wondered how long it would take to lose the feeling.

A muffled conversation replaced the familiar laughing of her parents.

She put her cases down and followed the voices to where the two sat sipping tea.

"Good morning, Dana," Lindsay spoke first, "we are having some tea and scones. Would you like a cup?"

Despite her resolution to change her attitude, her guard went up. If a stranger walked in, they would have thought Lindsay lived here and everyone else was her guest.

She fought the urge to lash out, realizing how difficult implementing her new plan to fit into the family would be.

# Chapter 52

"Hi Mom, it's nice to see you have company." She stated more of a hint to Lindsay as to who the real visitor was.

"Tea would be nice, thank you." Dana acknowledged Lindsay and turned to her mother who look drained with dark circles under her eyes. "Are you feeling okay?" She asked worried that her father's death was taking a larger toll on her than expected.

"I'm just a little run down, lately."

"Mom's been feeling a little under the weather, but she going to be just fine." Lindsay said. "How do you like your tea?" She asked Dana, who felt a little peed at how casual Lindsay referred to her mother as mom.

"Black, thanks." Dana waited for her to leave before going over to sit on the couch beside her mother.

"With everything going on I must have caught a flu bug or something silly like that, but Lindsay's been wonderful coming over every day to keep me company." She smiled at her daughter.

"I'm sorry I haven't been around much." Dana said as a tinge of guilt gnawed at her. It gave her some respect for Lindsay.

"I know you're busy and have a lot going on in your life with that horrible killing at your own back door. I worry about you dear." Her mother looked at her with sad eyes and Dana was happy for her decision to move back home.

"Well you can take the problem of me living outside of town off your plate because if you don't mind I'd like to move back home for awhile."

"It's been what I've been hoping for." Her mother clasped her hand around Dana's arm and laughed.

"I must say that I haven't seen you this happy since your son, relocated me to this quaint little town, Mom." Lindsay said coming in holding a teacup out to Dana. "Are you the bearer of good news?" She flashed a row of perfect white teeth Dana's way.

"My daughter is moving back home." Her mother smiled at Dana while maintaining her grip on her.

*'Maybe my decision would be a healing time for both of us.'* Dana thought.

"That's wonderful news." Lindsay said.

"Have you seen a doctor yet? Dana asked ignoring Lindsay.

"Don't be such a fuss bug, dear it's only the flu and I'm starting to feel better."

"Do you even have a doctor?" Lindsay asked.

"I've always been healthy so I haven't needed one."

"Mom, does Robert know you're not seeing anyone?" Dana asked, wondering why he hadn't taken care of this.

"No and there's no need to tell him." Her lips pressed firmly together to display her determination. *'She wonders where I get my stubbornness from,* Dana thought.

"Maybe you should have Robert look at you." Lindsay suggested.

"I'm not going to have my son probing at me." Her mother protested.

"If you're against Robert we need to get someone else to get some medicine prescribed." Dana stated, knowing there would be no way she'd pick Robert to be her doctor either. She didn't push it.

"I could ask Robert's young handsome doctor friend." A gleam hit her mother's eyes just before she turned to Lindsay and they gave each other a look as though they held a secret between them.

Dana wondered how much Eric had been talking to Robert and what Robert was repeating to Lindsay who in turn fed it back to her mother.

"What was his name again, Dana." She toyed with her daughter trying to restrain a smile.

"What are you two up to?" Dana wasn't sure she like where this was going.

"Oh it's no secret that Eric likes you. You're all he ever talks to Robert about." Lindsay laughed.

"I'm sure there are a lot of women in Eric's life." Dana said feeling like she, time travelled back to her grade school days.

"Is that a confession that you have mutual feelings?" Lindsay dared to ask and Dana's mother sat back as though she were anxious to hear her response.

"Don't get excited Mom, we're barely friends." Dana's face felt warm as the blood raced to her cheeks.

"He is a good catch, my dear." Her mother laughed leaving Dana feeling like she was being lured into a private girls club. Confused by mixed emotions she couldn't tell if she liked the chattiness or resented her mother and Lindsay discussing her personal life.

"I think the five of us should go out to dinner tonight to celebrate you moving back home." Lindsay recommended and picked up the phone to call Robert before anyone had time to reject.

"That was easy." Lindsay said a few minutes later, looking like she saved the world from total annihilation. "Robert was in his office and Eric just happened to be with him." Lindsay flashed a deviant smile at Dana. "And guess what Mon, Eric already knew our Dana was. He also said they were going to go house hunting and had to reschedule."

"Interesting, why would you and Eric be looking at houses?" Her mother asked with a silly grin plastered on her face.

"It's nothing Mom." Dana held up a hand, thinking her timing couldn't have been worse for coming back home. "He wants a woman's input. That's all."

"I think we should go to the lovely new French restaurant that opened up last month. Is that okay with everyone?" She asked picking up the phone to make reservations before anyone could protest.

"When did a new place opened?" Dana questioned glad that Lindsay had the decency to change the subject away from Eric.

"A few months ago, I think it's called Chez Petra's." Her mother said.

Dana nodded as she listened to Lindsay asking the operator to put the call through for her. She was determined to make friends with her brother's wife but hearing her on the phone she had to grip her jaw shut.

When she got through to Chez Petra's, Lindsay developed her southern bell accent again. Dana wondered if Robert landed himself a woman with duel personality.

"Hello, this is Mrs. Doctor Reed," each word rolled off her tongue, "I would like reservations for a party of five for tonight at six." She requested. "Yes, it will be under Doctor Reed's name." Lindsay studied her nails waiting for confirmation. "That will be wonderful." She smiled at the two of them and hung up. "Well I better leave you two so you can catch up. Robert and I can come by and pick you up later if you like. She stood and ran her hands down her dress to smooth the creases.

"No, I'll drive us over." Dana said thinking she would probably have to take a loan out to pay for the meal, but had no intentions, of letting Lindsay know her financial state.

# Chapter 53

After Lindsay left, Dana talked her mother into going to bed for some rest, then lugged her things up to her old room.

Alone, unpacking the realization of everything hit her like a brick wall. Sitting on the bed, she forced back tears. If someone were to ask her what she felt, right now, she would have to say isolated.

How did she get to this point in her life? Most girls her age had friends they could turn to. Not her, she couldn't think of one person she would be able to unload her disaster of a life on.

The sad part is, she didn't know how to change her social misfit status around.

She could start with Lindsay by showing some interest instead of pushing her away every time she tried being nice to her. Eric was becoming a good friend. Dana started to feel some-what better as she itemized the people she could possible construed as a friends. I can't forget Jake, she doubted they would ever see each other once the killer was caught.

*'Hell, maybe I could make friends with his wacky lady friend.'* Dana made herself laugh. *'The red jeans would have to go.'* An image of the two of them strutting down the main street with Helen decked out in those red jeans and white halter-top, did not work for Dana. *'Unless I get a matching set, but that would probably tick Helen off, and that's the last think I want to do.'* Dana amused herself with idol thoughts.

The potential list was short but at least there was one. Dana drew in a deep breath of air and looked around her room. It felt a little odd being back in her old surroundings but something about it felt safe.

With her things put away in drawers, she ran a tub and eased her self into water as hot as she could possible stand. She must have dozed off because twenty minutes later, she woke to the chimes of the grandfather clock in the hallway.

The short power nap rejuvenated her. An urge to go out and enjoy the sunshine caused her to throw on a yellow flowered dress and flats. It might be too late in the year for the outfit but she didn't care. Slipping the strap of a tan shoulder bag over her arm, she grabbed a sweater then headed to her Mom's room.

# Chapter 54

"You okay Mom?" She sat on the edge of the bed and rested her fingers across her forehead.

"I've had better days." She rolled over to face Dana.

"I'm sorry I haven't been around much for you." Seeing her mother's condition saddened her. It made her decision to come back home seem right.

"You have your own problems to worry about, my dear." She said and patted her daughter's hand. "With your father dying and that young girl you knew. You need to heal too."

Tear threatened Dana's eyes, it was the first time anyone mentioned her father since his death. Dana didn't understand why, talking about him would be a good thing to help bring the family closer.

"Do you miss Daddy?" She dared to ask.

"Very much," her mother said and her eyes glassed over as though she were remembering a memory they shared. As quickly as she let her mind wander, she changed the subject. "You look lovely, are you going out?" She asked and pinched the material of Dana's dress between her fingers.

"Yes, I thought a walk around town would be nice, maybe go by the bank and rob it so I can pay for dinner tonight." Dana chuckled at her mother.

"The banks don't open on Saturdays."

"I'm joking Mom, I'll just have to get them to up the limit on my credit card." She teased with her mother.

"It's probably expensive but I'm sure that young doctor friend of Robert won't let you walk out of there paying for your own meal."

"Mom, I hope Lindsay isn't putting all these ideas in your head. Eric and I are only friends and I don't want him to think I'm going around telling everyone we are more than that." Dana cautioned her mother.

"Do you like him?" She asked ignoring her daughter's warning.

"As a friend, yes, but I don't know him enough to be anything else. And I don't buy my friends dinner whenever we go out so I don't expect him to pay for me."

"A relationship has to start somewhere." She persisted.

"I have to go." Not wanting to discuss Eric any more, Dana got up and planted a quick kiss on her mother's forehead. "I'll be back around five to pick you up." Dana waved at her and closed the bedroom door before she left.

# Chapter 55

Such a beautiful day made it hard not to feel good, regardless of all the craziness going on. Anyone planning on turning over a new leaf in life, today, would be the ideal time to do it. Dana felt like she stepped out from behind a big, black veil that had been blurring her vision of the world.

It surprised her at how anxious she was to walk around the town she forced herself to detest, until now. The fresh scent, of autumn, filled her nostrils as she walked past her neighbours out raking the leaves of their lawns. Had she forgotten how beautiful her childhood neighbourhood was or could it be, she finally opened her mind to it. Either way, being here now she couldn't help but smile and wave as she past the neighbours.

The streets were teeming with people sauntering through a sidewalk sale running full tilt. She easily fell into step with every one around her. Everything, she could think of lined tables along the main road. She paused at a selection of hand made ceramics and ended up purchasing a locally made tea- cup and saucer covered with bright red roses, for her Mom.

A rack of clothing caught her eye drawing her into the next store. She tried on clothes for the longest time before deciding on an amber coloured cardigan to put over a cream blouse she purchased. She cringed at the price of a pair of two-inch heel ankle boots, but they matched the chocolate brown mini skirt too well not to sacrifice her budget. *'What the hell,'* she

told herself as the left with her packages.
*'I'll pay it off with the last month rent once I move out.'*

She managed to make her way to the end of the street, where she took a moment to congratulate herself for making it through both side of the sale with out pushing her credit card over the limited.

## Chapter 56

A lone chip wagon, sitting at the entrance of the empty fair grounds, caused her stomach to growl as a reminder that she hadn't eaten anything today. Looking at her watch, she was surprised that she had been wandering the little shops for over two hours.

It would take about fifteen minutes to get home and half an hour to change and get her mother into the car. The drive to the restaurant should only be five minutes, giving her plenty of time to grab a small fry.

The reservations were for six but she doubted any food would reach the table before seven. '*My stomach won't last that long.*' She thought as she approached the window.

"What'll it be young lady." An older man called down to her. By the size of his belly, Dana guess, he ate a few of the profits before the day's end.

"A small fry and Cream Soda, please," Dana answered and reached in her purse for some change and placed it on the counter.

"It'll be about five minutes. You can wait over there and I'll call you." He pointed in the direction of an old weather beaten table sitting at the entrance of the empty fair grounds.

"Thank you." She answered, getting off her feet sounded like a good idea, grabbing her can of pop she headed to the comforts of a seat.

The streets were thinning and only a few people wandered around as the shops slowly pulled their goods back inside.

Feeling a little chilled she placed her bags on the table and slipped on her sweater. She peaked in at the outfit and decided to wear it tonight.

She would never admit it but she was a little excited to get out tonight. Robert had been so busy at the hospital she hardly talked to him. It struck her as funny that, over the last few weeks she spoke more with Eric then her brother.

"Fries are ready Miss." Dana heard a shout from the wagon and jumped up to get them. After shaking salt and vinegar over them she looked up and was taken back to see someone sitting with her packages.

'How rude,' she thought as she rushed determined to grab her bags and say something snide. She stopped in her tracks when Henry turned and smiled at her.

"Henry, you surprise me?" She stated relieved when she recognized him.

"Hi Dana, I hope you don't mind, if I sit with you. I noticed you were getting your food and left the packages. So I thought I'd watch them until you got back."

"Thank you, I guess I was so hungry I didn't think much about leaving them here. Anyone could have walked by and snatched them up." Dana sat down feeling a little foolish for her near attack on Henry.

Even though they shared the same apartment building, they were strangers. She had to admit that he was more of a recluse than she had been. He never attended any of the summer picnics the Walters held, even if he were home.

The only time she ever spoke to him was the night, she nearly ran him over fleeing the laundry room. Maybe he felt that incident warranted a friendship.

"You look a little more relaxed from the last time I saw you." He smiled at her and bite into a hotdog.

"That was a bad night. I tried to get a few chores done but my imagination got the best of me and I created a boogie man in the storage closets." Dana confessed feeling a bit foolish looking back on how she reacted.

"It happens to all of us. I get spooked being the only one living in the basement." He chuckled. "Thanks for the wine by the way. You didn't have to do that."

"I know, but you really save me from a break down so I wanted to say thanks."

"Well if you ever feel that way again you can come and see me." He washed the rest of his hotdog down with a chug of his pop.

"I'll remember that." Dana said, grateful for his offer, although she couldn't imagine ever seeking him out for anything.

"Truthfully, I don't think I'll be living there much longer." He surprised her by his confession.

"How come?" She questioned.

"Since Sally died I've been planning on moving and have been apartment hunting most of the afternoon."

"I know what you mean. The place just doesn't feel the same anymore." Dana agreed thinking there was something different about him. He was exposing a side he kept hidden from most people, she actually found him more appealing.

"I filled out an application for a place over on Daton St."

"Poor Mr. Walters, I kind of moved back in with my mother and was going to call to give my notice tomorrow." Dana admitted. "Seeing his tenants leave is going to hurt them."

"I wouldn't worry about it. I talked to him this afternoon to give my notice and he told me they're putting the place up for sale."

"Apparently, the police let Phil leave because they were able to validate his alibi. I believe he moved back in with his parents a few counties north of here.

"Wow, Sally's death has changed so many lives." Dana's heart felt heavy, she always had a hard time accepting change.

Hearing that the Walter's were selling the apartment hurt a little.

"Change is good sometimes. I moved in there five years ago." Henry said.

"I've been there about three. I love it out there." Dana looked at him and wondered what about the secluded apartment would appeal to a young active man.

"Can I ask you something?" She asked feeling comfortable enough.

"Sure."

"If you loved it there so much, how come you never joined any of the BBQ's?" She expected him to tell her it was none of her business but surprised her by a saddened look in his eyes and a shy smile touched his lips.

"You wouldn't believe me if I told you." He looked out over the empty fields.

Almost like, she was touching on a subject he kept protected in his own thoughts.

"I can understand if you're shy." Dana said.

"It has nothing to do with being shy." He made direct eye contact and held her stare. "Can you keep a secret?" He asked.

'Not another secret,' Dana thought almost afraid to hear what he had to say.

"You're the only one I have ever told this too. By you're reaction I guess she kept the secret as well." Henry said confusing her even more.

"Who are you talking about?" Dana asked and Henry took a deep breath and scanned the area as though to make sure no one else would hear his confession.

"Sally," an ache stabbed at Dana's stomach. She didn't know if it was at hearing Sally's name or how comfortable the word flowed out of his mouth.

"We use to date many years ago." His eyes were intense watching her. If he was waiting for a response, Dana had no problem giving him one because her eyes bulged at the news.

"What?" She managed to say a little louder than necessary. She looked around hoping no one heard, fortunately, the streets clear out and even the Fry Guy closed up his truck. "She never mentioned anything." Dana said.

"She and Phil moved in about a year after she ended it with me. I found out when, she was doing her laundry one morning after Phil had gone to work. She begged me not to let on to anyone, especially Phil." His story just flowed while Dana listened in shock.

"So you avoided any place they were at." Dana said putting the pieces together. "That must have been terrible for you. Why didn't you move out then?" Dana could read the pain he felt on his face.

"I didn't end our relationship, she did. I loved her and would have married her." Henry confessed. "That's why I stayed away." Large fingers wiped at watery eyes.

"That's terrible." She said.

"I lost her twice. At least the other way I could steal a glance at her once in awhile." Taking a deep breath, he rubbed both his hands down his face. "Life goes on." He said cynically, leaving Dana speechless. *'What a horrible way to exist.'* She thought.

Hearing how he lived in the shadow of his love for Sally touched Dana deeply. It helped to realize her life wasn't all that bad.

"She is the reason I stayed in the building. I'd rather see her in the arms of another man then never see her again." He looked away from Dana. "Insane, isn't it. In a strange way her death set me free." Henry looked at her through pained eyes.

Hearing how he felt Sally's death was a release made Dana uncomfortable. It was a bizarre way of viewing someone you loved demise. He must have noticed her change of attitude, as if they never had the conversation about Sally his facial expression changed, and with a deep breath he went on to another subject.

"I should get going, I have a birthday dinner to go to and I haven't even wrapped the gift yet." He grabbed his package from the table. When he did a soft tune familiar to her sang from the bag. He reached in and quickly pulled a little box and shut the lid. "You'd think I'd be more careful with this thing after all the trouble I went through to get it." Dana's froze in her seat at the sight of the music box.

It was the perfect replicate, if not the same one stolen from her car. Even if he had managed to purchase the item before she got the last one, chances of him getting the same tune would be difficult since all played different melodies.

Had Henry been playing with her all this time? First, he tells her about his love for Sally who didn't return his affections then he shoves her stolen item in her face.

'*What tenacity*,' all she could think about was getting away from him without tipping him off.

She forced a smile in his direction.

"I better get going a few of us are meeting downtown for dinner." She made a point of letting him know a group of friends were close by.

"You look a lot like Sally." His eyes looked sad. "A few times I though you were her doing your wash."

"I know," was all Dana could think to say to him. "I'm late and really have to go." Dana said realizing she spent longer then intended.

"Thanks for listening." He smiled.

"You're welcome." Dana tried to remain calm but a vivid image of him killing Sally haunted her thoughts.

Gathering her bags, she jumped up from the table and scanned the area. Suddenly it looked darker out and the people wandering around were fewer.

"You look a little nervous would you like me to walk you to where you are meeting your friends?" Henry offered.

"No, I'm good, it's just up the street. She managed to get the words out without sounding to awkward.

"Well you have a good night."

"You to." She forced a smile again and once he stared towards his car, she hurried to put as much distance between them as possible without running.

# Chapter 57

The restaurant was only three blocks over, maintaining a steady pace should get her there in ten minutes, five if she cut across the empty play park.

A car engine echoed over the empty grounds, Dana assumed it was Henry. Knowing he was leaving didn't ease the tightness in her pounding chest as she speed walked down the barren streets.

How could so many people vanish in minutes, she questioned as she chanced the shortcut through the park.

It was there that she realized that someone tailing her.

Positive the footsteps resounding behind her belong to Henry she increased her pace. He must have notice that she clued in on his connection in Sally's murder and wanted to silence her before she met up with anyone. She reached inside her bag and wrapped her fingers around a comb. If she had to, she would use it to protect herself.

She quickened her step and whoever was tailing her matched her movement. The view of the restaurant's neon sign gave her some hope of escaping Henry's grip of death. Hearing her assailant closing in on her she began to sprint. Just as she went to round the corner, a hand gripped her shoulder.

A scream escaped from her, as she pulled away she bumped into someone.

"Dana what's going on?" She recognized Eric's voice. She clung to him and braved a look back at her stalker.

Instead of Henry, she found Helen standing there with a smug look.

"How many men do you have sniffing around you?" Helen hissed at her. Eric moved between the two women.

"Who the hell are you?" He questioned Helen.

"Oh look at you playing the big hero. You're nothing but a sucker to her. She probably won't tell you that you're the third man she's been with today. She spent the night with Jake and five minutes ago she left her afternoon boyfriend, now she's decided to give you what's left over." An evil smile curled up on her lips as she glared at Eric.

"Why don't you get your jealous ass out of here?" Eric said and put an arm around Dana. "She won't hurt you while I'm here." He bent down gave Dana a kiss on the forehead. His arm felt strong and safe around her shaking body, she willingly let him take care of the problem.

"Don't let this bitch seduce you. In this town a girl who jumps from one man to the next in a matter of hours is nothing but a tramp." Helen stated.

"What's going on here Dana?" Robert and Lindsay came up behind them.

"Little miss jealous face here decided to chase your sister down and is giving her a hard time." Eric filled Robert in.

"I think we should call the police." Lindsay said and took hold of Dana's hand.

"I am the police." Helen laughed "So don't bother, I won't waste my time on a low life like her. If you guys had any brains you wouldn't either." She said and headed into the darkness.

Shaking and in shock from the fear of discovering Henry and Sally's secret and then being chased by a mad woman through the streets was more than Dana could take.

"Robert, can you please take me home? I'm not really hungry." Dana pleaded.

"I'll drive you." Eric offered but Robert spoke up.

"You and Lindsay go ahead inside and I'll be back in a few minutes." He gave Lindsay a quick kiss before he escorted Dana to his car.

# Chapter 58

From his office, Jake could hear a commotion going on in the front area. He didn't expect to find Helen draped over the reception desk looking like she had been mugged.

Out of curiosity, he stayed and listened as she rattled off some tale to Lois, about how some people ganged up on her.

After her stunt, this morning, he could see her causing a commotion to upset people enough to attack. He witnessed it first hand at his house and put up with her bawling and carrying on for an hour after Dana left. Desperate to get her off his property he offered to drive her home.

Before she got out of the car, he made sure she understood that whatever she conjured up between them was strictly in her head. With a hug, she accepted to be friends only.

From what he could see, the assault wasn't physical. Knowing, Bill could handle the situation, he turned back to his office but not before, she caught sight him.

"Oh Jake." She ran to him and wrapped her arms around his neck. "It was terrible." She cried on his shoulder. Reaching up he took hold of her hands and untangled them then pushed her towards a chair.

"Seat down and Bill can fill out the complaint." Jake ordered, wishing she had latched on to someone else who stood around watching her fiasco.

"Lois can you get some tissue? Jake asked and she grabbed a box from behind the reception area and placed it in Helen's lap.

"Please don't be mad at me, Jake. I was only trying to be nice." She pleaded gaining Jake's interest wondering why she felt it necessary to seek his approval. "I tried to do the right thing and it blew up in my face." She stared up at him with desperate eyes and his gut tensed up as he started to piece things together.

"Does this involve Miss Reed?" He eyed her with distrust.

"After you drove me home this morning I felt so good about our talk and I wanted to make things right." She wiped a tissue across her cheeks spreading the streaks of make up further down her face.

"You didn't answer my question." Jake tried to be patient but tired of her display to get people to side with her.

"I went down to the street sale this afternoon and practically ran into your friend from this morning. I wanted to apologize. I thought you would want me to do." She blew her nose in the tissue, while Jake waited for her to continue. "She was having a cozy moment sharing fries with a male friend, so I decided not to disturb them."

Pulling a handful of tissues out, she let out a sob and dabbed her eyes before beginning again.

"I decided to just go home and notice her walking alone through the play park on the corner of Tweed and Duncan. I don't know where her friend went but I thought it would be a good opportunity for me to make things right." She turned to Bill who soaked in every word. "I called out to her but she didn't hear me or decided to ignore me."

She sipped at a glass of water, handed her.

"Thank you Lois." She managed to say then turned to Jake. "I caught up to her at the new French restaurant, Chez Petra's and tried to talk to her there. But she met up with another man." She empathise her words.

She jumped into his arms and acted as if I tried to kill her.

"I started to reason with her but this man pushed his way between us and wouldn't let me say a thing." She took a deep breath. "I never met anyone so rude. He kept kissing her and called me a jealous bitch." She wiped at her eyes again, Jake was sure the man would have been Eric. "I don't understand why he would think that I'd be jealous of her and him." Jake shook his head at how ridicules she sounded.

"To make matters worse her brother showed up with his wife and threatened me." Jake could tell she enjoyed the attention as she looked around at Bill and Lois.

"So you started a fight with Miss Reed and two of our local Doctors."

"It wasn't my intentions."

Jake couldn't believe what he heard, of course Dana would be frightened. It upset him that the poor girl couldn't even walk around town without an incident. If anything, it should be a lesson to be careful at all times especially in the evening. Tonight she was fortunate to run into Eric.

"You had no right chasing the woman." Jake fought to control the anger building up in him.

"I only wanted to apologize." Helen said.

"I'm not so sure." Jake stated.

"How could you say that?" She challenged him.

"It's okay Helen." Bill stood over her like a Jungle Cat protecting its litter. "Don't you worry, I'm going to ride over to that fancy restaurant and show those Doctors that they aren't above the law." Bill sided without knowing the full story.

"Bill, Helen chased the woman through a park. Don't you think we should give Miss Reed a chance to give her details of what happened?"

"What does she have to hide running from the law when all Helen wanted to do was apologize to the woman."

"We need to get their story. Did they assault you physically?" Jake questioned Helen who shook her head.

"No. I left before it got to that point."

"You did the right thing by leaving." Bill put his hand on her shoulder, "this is one of ours." Bill spoke directly to Jake who wasn't in the mood to argue with anyone over Helen.

"You stay and take care of Helen, I'll deal with this." Jake offered and Helen took it as a sign that he was going to defend her honour.

"Thank you babe." Helen smiled up at him, her face streaked with mascara. The sight of her disgusted him.

At first, he intended to ignore her comment so as not to add to the dramatization Helen created, but he didn't like how the others gawked at him as if they all agreed that it was his place to defend his woman. He didn't know what gossip Helen spread around the office but he had to end the rumours now.

"Helen we talked about this when you invaded my privacy this morning. I don't know what crazy idea you've concocted in your head about what you think we have together." He looked around at the others who stood with blank expressions on their faces. "I've never gone anywhere alone with you and never will. I try to treat everyone with the same respect. If my being nice to you confuses you then I'll stop."

There would be no mistake, if Helen couldn't get the point, this time, at least Bill and Lois would.

"So get it through your thick head there never was or never will be anything between us. I'm not interested in you Helen."

She looked at him in shock with her mouth gawked opened in disbelief while Jake cleared up her confusion.

"So are you clear on this. I'm not your babe."

"Yes." She nodded and tears started to stream.

"Another thing if you ever come to my house and create a scene like you did this morning, I'll charge you. Do you understand?"

"I understand." She whimpered.

Jake waited for her response before he turned to Bill and Lois.

"Now everyone knows that there is nothing between Helen and me." All three of them stared at him as if he suddenly went mad.

He wasn't one who liked to draw attention to himself but this was unavoidable. He had enough of Helen and her crazy antics, right now he needed to check on Dana.

"I've been here way too long for one day. Lois, I'm going out to hear Miss Reed's side then head home." He detected a smile on her face when he walked past her.

# Chapter 59

A sharp pain stabbed at the back of Jake's neck indicating signs of a headache about to settle in for the night.

"What the hell was Helen trying to prove going after Dana?" He always considered her a little flighty but never expected her to have the gall to chase someone through a park at night. Dana must have been petrified.

Passing Chez Petra's, Jake slowed down, seeing a fire engine, red Porsche reading "Dr. Eric" confirmed they were still in the restaurant, Jake suspected Dana would be in there with them, maybe even musing over the tenacity of Helen.

Jake had to chuckle at Eric's plate, definitely not something he could ever see himself doing no matter what career choice he made. Somehow, it suited the Doctor's personality, cocky and confident and why shouldn't he be. The years these men had to dedicate to their education to help others, they earned the right to have a bit of attitude.

The people in this town are fortunate to have two Doctors move in when most people were streaming to the bigger cities.

The few times he met Robert and Eric, he definitely wouldn't categorized them as trouble-makers. Eric obviously has feelings for Dana so when he saw Helen going after her he reacted. *'I would have done the same thing in his place.'*

Pulling out of the parking lot Jake decided the four of them could do without him interrupting their evening. The last thing he intended to do, was feed Helen's insatiable ego by causing a scene on her behalf. He would wait and call Dana in the morning.

Jake drove towards home but found himself steering his car down the street where Dana lived. He looked for anything suspicious or someone hanging around that didn't belong, a clue or sign, anything to help close the case. It had been almost a month and so far, they had nothing. He needed to talk to Dana about getting a tap on her mother's phone.

"What did he want from her, and why Dana?" Jake questioned as he scanned the area. He was sure the killer began stalking her way before the phone call. Maybe he could catch a break and be fortunate enough to see him in the act.

Nothing but a few leaves flutter up and down the street pushed by a light wind. He stopped in front of her place and let the engine idle a few minutes before shutting it down. He could park here unnoticeable to anyone coming along the street.

If he were thinking, he would have picked up coffee before his impromptu moment to stake out the place. The Coffee Shop, a few blocks over, should still be open. It would take two minutes to whip around the corner. He was about to turn the key when the porch light flick on and Dana stood in the open door waving at him.

He didn't expect her to be home, stepping out of his car he headed up the walkway feeling like a kid caught spying. His stomach felt an anxious fluttering at the site of her standing there. He always considered her pretty but tonight he found her beautiful.

Maybe he should get someone else to take over the investigation, he thought as he managed to wipe sweaty palms along the inside of his pockets. For the first time ever, he was getting, emotionally attached to someone involved in a case.

If he couldn't control these feelings and be professional it could cost Dana her life.

## Chapter 60

"I heard a car pull up and notice you sitting out here." Dana knew she sounded shaky. "I thought it might be Robert and Lindsay." When Robert dropped her off, they decided not to worry their mother about the incident at the restaurant but he made her promise to call the police the moment their mother retired for the night.

Alone with Robert, she came so close to confiding in him about everything going on in her life, but fear and confusion kept her mouth shut. She desperately, needed someone she could talk with.

"Helen dropped by the station. I wanted to see if you were okay." Jake said, getting right to the point.

"No, I'm not, and not because of Helen." Dana rubbed her forehead, relieved to see him. "Okay she may have added to my stress somewhat, but truthfully, seeing that it was her chasing me was a relief."

"It must have been frightening," Jake said.

"I was going to call you once my mother retired for the night." Dana held the door opened for him. "I haven't said anything to her about Helen and don't feel it necessary for her to know. So please don't say anything."

"She won't hear it from me," he followed her into a large living room where an older woman sat on the couch looking very pale and gauntly.

"Mom this is Detective Turner. Detective this is my mother, Nancy." Dana kept the introduction professional.

"Is everything okay?" She eyed Jake suspiciously.

"He just came by to talk, that's all."

"A little late for a police visit," she glanced up at an old Grandfather clock getting ready to ring its chimes in a few minutes.

"I have a few questions for your daughter and since I live around the corner I thought I'd make a quick stop in." Jake said.

"Is he the reason you don't like Robert's friend?" She blurted out and Dana stared at her with widen eyes while she sat there with a sly smile.

"Its business, Mom," Dana could feel her cheeks heat up and figured she had better get her mother out of the room before she said anything else to embarrass her.

"You look like you can use some sleep so why don't you go to bed so the detective and I can talk." Dana turned of the television and helped her from the couch to the stairs.

"I can understand that you kids want to be alone." She stopped in front of Jake. "It's a pleasure to meet you detective."

"It is nice meeting you too and I promise not to stay too late." Jake smiled and Dana could tell he fought back a laugh.

"You take all the time you need." Nancy managed a smile at him before she climbed the stairs towards her room. "Good night dear." She stopped short of the landing and gave a sly smile in Dana's direction the only thing missing was a wink to indicate her approval.

"Good night." Dana said thinking whatever sickness she had was causing her to be delusional.

"I'm sorry. She hasn't been herself lately and I think its causing her to lose her mind." Dana tried to make light of her mothers innuendos.

"Don't worry about it," he smiled. "She doesn't look well, is she going to be okay?" Jake asked.

"Since my dad died she has been ill. I think she's worn out." Dana said.

"Maybe she should have someone look at her." Jake suggested.

"I wanted Robert to but she's stubborn and refused to have her son treat her. Lindsay and I managed to get her to agree to see Eric." Dana said.

"That's good." Jake said.

"I'm sure it's nothing that some rest and a bit of medicine won't cure." Dana looked up the stairs, satisfied that her mother wouldn't make a quick turn-about and head back down to embarrass her again.

"Can you stay for a coffee? I need to talk to you about something."

Her body shook from the inside out and started to ache from the tenseness she held in since her encounter with Henry.

Especially since she had to bottle her emotions all night, first from Robert and then sitting with her mother trying to pretend everything was good.

With the only person who could possibly understand her predicament, standing in front of her, she fought to maintain some composure so she wouldn't start blubbering like a moron.

She had to sound rational when she accused her neighbour of murder. Once she told Jake, there would be no turning back so any doubts must be push aside.

"I'm sure Nelly won't mind." He tried to lighten the mood as he followed her down a hallway to a large country kitchen that had another set of servant stairs leading up to the bedrooms.

"Nelly sounds spoiled." Dana chuckled enjoying the moment of idle chat as she pulled two mugs from the cupboard. She like how he loved his cat it showed a caring side of his being. She always thought you could tell a person by two things; how they treat their parent and animals.

"She's good company." Jake twirled his mug around before getting to the point of why she invited him in. "So do you want to tell me what went on today that led to Helen chasing you through the park?"

She had to be candid with him. "I know who the killer is." With no other way to explain it, she just blurted it out.

"And you know this because…?" Jake asked giving her a look of disbelief causing doubt to fill her. She couldn't recant her story now. She could only hope he could help her sort it out.

"Downtown today I met someone from my apartment and he told me that him and Sally use to be a couple and that he still loved her." Dana's hands shook. It felt good to finally, be able to get everything out.

"Who was it?" Jake straightened up giving her his full attention.

"Henry."

"Henry? Isn't he the guy you bought the wine for?

"Yes and he happens to live in the only basement apartment across from the laundry room."

"Did he confess that he did it?" Jake asked.

"No, he just confided about the relationship they once shared and how they mutually decided to keep it a secret."

"That doesn't mean he killed Sally."

"He told me her death set him free and that I remind him of her."

"Okay, that is a little strange."

"There's more."

"What did he do?" Jake questioned."

"He had a gift in a bag, for someone's birthday." Her hands shook as she played with her coffee mug. "I'm positive it was my music box."

"Dana, are you sure?"

"Yes, it was the same colour and tune and it was like he wanted me to see it."

"It definitely fits the profile. He wants to get close to you to gain your trust at the same time he's taunting you." Jake look agitated. "Dana, it was too easy for him to get close to you. You can't go out alone any more."

"I know." The tears she struggled to hold back all night while with her mother finally won the battle. "I thought it was Henry chasing me." She stood up, and grabbed a paper towel from the rack and covered her face with it while she leaned against the counter. The next thing she knew Jake was holding her in his arms.

"It's okay, Dana. We are going to get him."

"I was so frightened." Dana stated and Jake released his hold on her and stood back.

"I know but a least we have someone to go on."

Dana nodded and he sat her back down at the table. Being in his arms felt safe and she hated that it ended.

"Did you feel like he was threatening you?" He sat back down, and pulled out his note pad and scribbled some things down in it giving him a more professional attitude, which gave her strength to fight the tears.

"No, I actually felt sorry for him, at first." Sitting with Jake across from her only confused her more. Maybe, she was wrong about Henry. His love for Sally was so sincere and when she thought about it, nothing made sense.

"Could I be wrong, what if he bought it somewhere else. The store could have restocked them."

"That's a possibility I'll check out before we make an arrest. For now avoid going anywhere alone, especially walking." Jake cautioned.

"I can't be a prisoner in my own home." Dana complained.

"Only until we get this guy, and trust me it won't be long." Jake promised.

"What if I'm wrong? It was like he trusted me with a precious secret that only he and Sally shared." Dana sighed. The idea of sending an innocent man to jail would haunt her for life.

"Dana, don't feel sorry for this guy. Maybe Sally was going to expose something about him and he had to keep her quiet." Jake suggested.

"This is getting to be too much for me." Dana said.

"Henry could have wanted to rekindle their relationship and she refused and he had to silence her for good."

"But the caller said that Sally died for me."

"You reminded him of her." Jake said trying to set a possible scene and Dana nodded anxious to hear how he would piece her connection. "His original plan may have been to get Sally to go back with him. When she refused, he might have pulled you into the scenario because of the resemblance between you two and wanted to use you to show Sally he, meant business. He could have blackmailed her into thinking he would kill you if he didn't get his way. Sally could have threatened to tell you or the police and he had to kill her."

"So, in his mind, he feels Sally died for me and now he has to follow through." Could Henry be that cold, she wondered. "I'm so confused I don't know what to do anymore." Dana looked at Jake. "What if I'm wrong?"

"Until we have solid proof, this is all theory, but it's a start." He put a hand over hers and made direct eye contact. "Dana I can't stress this enough if you need to go anywhere and don't have anyone to go with give me a call."

"You're a hard man to reach. What if I can't get you?"

"Then you call Robert or Eric, even Lindsay if you have to." He waited for her to nod her answer.

"It's late and I better get going before your mother comes down and kicks me out." Jake pushed his chair back and stood up.

"I doubt she'd do that." Dana felt a headache creeping along the nap of her neck as she walked him to the door.

"And don't worry about Helen. I made sure she won't be bothering you again."

"Thanks." Dana said and waited to see if he would give her some explanation about his ordeal with Helen, but he stepped outside instead.

"Lock the door tight and call the station if you notice anything suspicious."

"Sure." Dana said wondering why the sudden coolness towards her.

"I'll try to call you tomorrow after I speak with Henry. If you don't hear from me another officer will get in touch." Jake said before he stepped off the porch.

"Good night Jake, and thank you for coming tonight," Dana said.

"Lock your door," was all he said as he waited on the step for her to shut him out. She watched out the window until he drove away. Something change between them tonight, at first he took his detective hat off long enough to hold and comfort her and now it was like he took a step back to put distance between them. She wondered if he got scared off, thinking she would misread his action and react like Helen.

# Chapter 61

Dana hung up the phone and watched her mother coming down the back stairs to the kitchen. She felt good despite all the trouble surrounding her. Being back home turned out better than she imagined, she had routine in her life again.

"Well it is official." Calling the Walters was the thing she dreaded most but she had to do it. Prolonging the conversation any longer would have only weigh on her mind.

Knowing their schedule, she decided to make the call before her workday began. Mrs Walters informed Dana, that her husband was out making his morning rounds. She confirmed that they were selling and that other tenants were giving notices as well. She didn't suspect anyone would be staying. Dana promised not to move her things out without saying her good-byes. She hung up refusing to allow herself to be sad by their conversation.

"I just talked to Mrs. Walters and gave my notice."
Nancy went over and kissed the top of her daughter's head.

"Having you back home makes me feel a lot better."

"I have to admit you are looking much healthier than when I first moved back in." Dana felt as if she woke from a nightmarish dread that went on for way too long, and she was ready to bust out of her cocoon life style.

Today was to beautiful to sit around, Jake not calling her since the night Helen chased her through the park didn't bother

her either. He had, another officer phone to let her know he was following up with Henry but hadn't been able to track him down. Officer Mason believed Henry fled town but gave her the usual warning to watch her back and stick to crowds.

Knowing that Sally's killer would soon be behind bars comforted her. It angered her that his selfish act forced so many people into a major life change.

"Can I make you a tea?" Dana asked and got up from her seat.

"Maybe a coffee, tea upsets my stomach lately."

"Do you mind if I store my furniture here?"

"Of course not. Most of your things will fit in your bedroom," Nancy stated, reminding Dana how small her apartment was. Knowing her mother's ability to organized things she could see her blending the few items Dana owned in with the rest of the furniture and still leave the room with an uncluttered look.

"You know my coming home is only temporary, and once I find a place in town I'll be moving out again?" Dana felt a little guilty for being so blunt. Especially since, her mother appeared so much happier with the present living arrangement.

"I know dear, but at lease you'll be closer and we can do more things together." Nancy sipped her coffee. "I hated driving down those dirt roads to visit. I don't know how your father managed it at night."

"I'm sorry I gave you guys such a difficult time." Dana patted her hand, regretting the stubborn attitude she clung onto for so long. "Seeing Dad and Sally die has really forced me to look at things differently."

"Death can have a very profound effect on us, but looking back and dwelling on the past won't change a thing." The look in her mother's eyes held such love Dana struggled not to cry. "What we do with our lives going forward is what counts."

Dana listened to her words of wisdom and wondered where the frail woman sitting in front of her, pulled her inner strength from.

"That true and I promise things are going to be different."

"With all these men coming around lately I didn't think you'd be staying forever." Nancy chuckled lightening the mood. Dana laughed at seeing the silly side of her mother come to life again.

"We had this talk the other day mom, so whatever idea you have swirling around in your noggin, forget it. I'm not seeing anyone." Dana stood up and placed her mug in he sink.

"I'm not talking about that detective who showed up unannounced the other day. I just don't understand why you are so against Robert's friend Eric." She waved her hands.

"Mom, I don't have anything against Eric. He's a nice man, which I'm sure a million other women would agree. To him I'm Robert's kid sister and he's being kind to me."

"Perhaps, but Lindsay is positive he would like it to be more."

"Mom, doctors don't marry girls like me. They go for the Lindsay type. And believe me I'm definitely not the Lindsay type." She clarified. "Besides, he never gave any indication that he's interested in anything more than friends."

"If he did would you be interested."

"I haven't given it much thought so don't get any ideas." Dana lied. Of course, she thought about what it would be like dating Eric, she just didn't want to give her mother something to run to Lindsay with so she could go back to Eric.

"Maybe you should talk to Lindsay."

"I wish you wouldn't discuss my life with Lindsay, she's the last person I want to confide in about men and I don't want her filling your head with plans about my future either." Dana felt like an old, spinster, woman, her mother desperately wanted to marry off, so she enlisted Lindsay's expertise.

"Lindsay is a lovely girl and only wants to be part of the family. You should give her a chance." It didn't surprise Dana that her mother used the same argument Robert did the night he tried to reason with her about Lindsay being family. Picturing the three of them huddled around a table discussing her made Dana feel more like the outsider.

"I'm not disagreeing with you. For Robert to marry her there as to be some good there, but I don't need the two of you interfering in my life."

With a quick look at the stove clock Dana jumped up.

"I better get going or I'll be late for work." With a quick kiss planted on her mother's cheek Dana grabbed her knapsack and ran for the door. "I'll see you tonight."

# Chapter 62

All Dana wanted to do when she arrived home from work was to shower and fill her head with mindless games shows while she stuffed her face with dinner. She cringed when she walked into the foyer to find her mother holding the phone out to her. The last thing she needed was a lengthily chatting session, especially if Lindsay was on the other end, she thought as she took the receiver from her mother. She wished her mother would allow her to form a relationship with Lindsay at her own pace.

"Hello," she said, thinking this is a set up her mother planned for the moment she walked in the door. Putting the phone to her ear, she expected the cheery voice of her sister-in-law. She shot her mother a warning stare at the sound of Eric's voice.

"Hi, how are you doing?"

"Good, thanks." Dana answered while her mother frantically waved her hands in front of her.

"I had nothing to do with him calling." She whispered then scurried off to the kitchen.

"I'm sorry I haven't called you since the crazy lady accosted you, but I thought you might need some time to regroup."

"It was a little bizarre. I should have called to thank you for being there." Dana shivered imaging what Helen might have done if Eric hadn't been around the corner.

"Well it's over, so we just have to put it behind us and use the incident as a growing opportunity and push forward with our lives, hence, the reason for my call.

Eric said and Dana could hear his smile over the phone.

"This is going to be interesting to see how you equate the Helen episode with moving on."

"You have to find the positives even with the bad things that confront us from time to time." Eric said causing her to laughed thinking how much he sounded more like a doctor now.

"I'm having a difficult time trying to pick the good out of the bad with this one. So help me out here." Dana teased, although she had passed Helen's act off as a jealous wanna be girlfriend, she was curious to hear how Eric would turn it into a positive.

"Think about it. Didn't I come to your rescue?" He said sounding proud.

"Yes you did and I thank you for doing so."

"So I'm your superman." Eric claimed. She laughed hard at the image of him flying around in a tight costume with a large "S" etched on his chest.

"That's so funny."

"It's also makes us more like family." Eric said.

"Family is good." Dana had to admit that out of all the people who ever passed through her life, Eric was the only person besides Robert, who could swing her mood around instantly and put a smile on her face.

"In some countries that act of heroism would make you mine." Eric said.

"I thought it was the other way around. That the hero had to become a slave to the one who benefited from his heroism until they paid back the act."

"That sounds just as good because I've found a way you can repay your hero."

"And how is that." Dana questioned almost afraid to ask.

"I'm still looking for a house and do recall someone saying they would join me in the tedious hunt. I'll even bribe you with food." He teased. Dana really didn't feel like house hunting but couldn't bring herself to say no to him.

"There's no way I can refuse after that." She chuckled.

"Good, so when should I pick you up?" He asked.

"I'm just getting in the door now and would like to freshen up a bit. By the smell coming from the kitchen, I'd say mom has supper cooking already. What time did you have the appointment set up for?" Dana asked.

"Seven thirty."

"Can we make dinner another night?" Dana said.

"Rain check it is, I'll pick you up at seven." Eric said.

"I'll be ready." Dana said, and hung up the phone. She tried to avoid the silly grin spread across her mother's face as she started up the steps.

"Just friends, Mom." Dana laughed and ran up the stairs before the drill session began.

## Chapter 63

The doorbell rang just as Dana finished putting the last of the dishes away.

"That will be Eric, I shouldn't be too long." She told her mother.

"I'm going to make a cake while you are gone so you can invite him in later for some dessert." Her mother offered.

"He probably won't have time, but I'd love some." Dana smiled and grabbed her purse of the counter and headed to the front door with her mother on her heels.

Dana unlocked the latch. She wished her mother would go to the parlour to do her spying; instead, she hung around the door, like a giddy schoolgirl.

"Okay mom, I'll see you when I get back." When she ignored the hint to leave Dana pulled the door open intending to rush down the porch steps with Eric.

"Hi, you ready to go?" Eric stood with a smile that lit up at the sight of Nancy standing behind Dana. "I almost didn't see you. How are you doing Mom?" He said ruining any plan she had of making a quick exit.

"I'm good, thank you for asking." She replied looking happy at the attention, he shoved her way.

"Robert said you haven't been feeling well lately and you don't want him to look at you. He also said you might be okay with me running some test on you."

"I've been thinking about it."

"I hoped you would have called by now, but can understand if you still need time to consider it." Eric said. Dana smiled as she watched Eric work his magic on her mother. "It wouldn't be much more than some blood work that I can rush to the lab.

"I intended to call but I have been feeling better lately." Nancy gave a sheepish grin.

"Good, so you won't mind me taking some samples and running a few test because I'd really love to be your doctor if you don't mind."

"That would be nice." Nancy smiled and Dana could see her face reddened even in the dim lit hallway.

"Good, if you're free tomorrow morning I'll come by with my doctor's bag, unless you'd be more comfortable at the hospital." Eric offered.

"I can't ask you to come here, I'm sure Lindsay will drive me to your office. If not I'll grab a cab." She chuckled.

"It would be no trouble but if you prefer, I'll see you tomorrow at the hospital, for now we're off to look at houses." He said and took hold of Dana's arm as they started down the steps. Then as an after thought, he turned. "We aren't going far if you wanted to come with us." Dana's heart sank when he invited her mother to join them.

"Your car won't hold three people and I really think she should get a bit more rest before she starts running around." Dana answered before the invitation could be accept. She wasn't ready to start romping around town with Eric while her mother rode in the back seat waving at her friends.

"Maybe another time," Eric said rewarding Nancy with one of his killer smiles.

"When I'm feeling a little less wobbly on my feet, but thank you for asking," she said and Dana wished she wiped the silly grin off her face.

"I'm making a cake if you'd like to stop in after you look at some houses." She invited Eric and Dana couldn't believe she asked him. Especially since only moments ago, she told her not to. She may not have come right out and said the words but she did think she made it clear she didn't want to invite Eric back for cake. She shot her mother a stare which went unnoticed because she was too busy bonding with Eric.

"Cake sounds great." He said.

"Good, I'll see you two kids when you get back."

In one swoop, her mother managed to shatter her plan to get back home and curl up on a comfy couch to hopefully fall asleep watching Clint Eastwood telling someone to make his day. She just had to convince Eric to buy this place whether she liked it or not, that way there would be no need for him to drag her out on another hunt.

"Well let's get going." Dana said, wanting to get this night done with.

# Chapter 64

Driving into the neighbourhood Dana had to admit that the area was beautiful. Being an older part of town, the trees lining the streets were mature and shaded the road in a protective arch.

"This is beautiful." Dana looked around in awe. Floodlights lit up the yard, as they pulled through a huge cast iron gate with a bronze oval plaque nestled in the middle, displaying the name of the former owners. 'Weets' with the house number inscribed with fancy script on it.

"How come they're selling?" Dana wondered why anyone would want to give up such a beautiful home.

"Because the owner grew old and passed away, and no she didn't die in the house." Eric answered her next question before she had a chance to voice it.

"How sad." Dana said as Eric pulled his car in behind Tina's Mazda. He went to open Dana's door but she jumped out before he got there.

"Well, do you like it?" He pointed to the old colonial mansion, with a proud expression.

"It's amazing, and the grounds are wonderful." Dana had to admit. "I feel under dressed in blue jeans and sweatshirt with runners." Eric laughed at the comment about her attire.

"It is a classy place." He said.

"It's like taking a step back in time." Dana slowly turned around trying to take in all the sights. She envisioned great social gatherings with old fashion cars lining the roads and eloquent women in long flowing dresses gracing the place.

"I love the history." Excitement rang in Eric's voice as he looked around with pride. "I did some research and it use to belong to an estrange mistress old man Mullins kept." Eric related the tale to Dana.

"Are you talking about the Mullins with the funeral home outside of town?" Dana asked even more intrigued by the story.

"Those are the ones."

"So are they selling it?" Dana asked curious as to why they would be getting rid of the home.

"Apparently they don't have any stake in the place. Old man Mullins left everything in his mistress' name. Their illicit affair produced a daughter who left along time ago. The rumour is she got pregnant by someone who didn't quite live up to their standard. I think he toss her out after that."

"How unfair," it angered Dana to think that old man Mullins gets away with an affair and sets the woman up in luxury. The offspring of the relationship gets pregnant by someone not of his social standing and he gives her the boot.

"Things were tougher back then, apparently she moved away to have her baby, which I believe was a son. I'm hoping to bring a new kind of life to the place."

"How did you find all this information? I've lived here all my life and never seen this place before, let alone heard the tale behind it." Dana wondered how she could have grown up in the town and been so oblivious.

"When I first saw the place I fell in love with it and went to the library. Tina did her homework, as well." Eric said.

"Where is Tina?" Dana wondered why she didn't greet them when the drove in.

"I told her I was bringing someone who could give me a second opinion so she's probably waiting inside so I can show you around the grounds." Eric took her to the back of the house where a huge pool spread out across the back patio.

"This is amazing." Dana gazed over the yard as far as the light could shine.

"It's dark now, but during the day you can follow a path down to the lake where you can sit and watch boats go by." She could tell he already made his mind up about the place.

"Could you see us living here?" Eric's question threw her off. That would be more of a thing a husband would ask his wife or finance, not the sister of a friend.

"Who wouldn't?" Not knowing what else to say she pretended not to notice his comment. Maybe she was reading more into it then he meant.

"True, let's go find Tina." Eric turned the handle of the large garden doors and pulled them opened. He paused and gave Dana a strange look.

"I have an urge to carry you through the threshold."

"I don't think so." Dana pushed her way past him to a large room. She definitely didn't sign up for that even if it was in fun.

"I'm only teasing, kid," he laughed, reminding her that she was only Robert's little sister, to him.

His laugh echoed across the empty chambers.

"Tina, we're here." He called out. When she didn't reply, he led the way into a enormous entrance hall where two staircases arched in a horseshoe to create a cozy little nook between them. Dana never saw anything so magnificent in her life.

"Where could she be?" Dana asked.

"It's a big place maybe she's on the upper level." Eric headed up one side of the massive oak steps.

"Tina," he called out again. "She might have gotten tired of waiting and went outside looking for us." He smiled at Dana. "So let me give you the tour and she can catch up to us." He placed a hand on Dana's back and guided her towards the end of the hall where another staircase ran through the back of the house. She guessed, it was there for the servants so they wouldn't have to use the main ones.

"I love these old places." Eric said as he opened a door to a master bedroom. A huge picture window displayed a view of the back yard.

"So do I," Dana opened the door off to the side where she found a bathroom larger than her bedroom at home. "Look at this Eric." She couldn't hold back on her amazement any longer. Eric's earlier question about seeing herself living here took on a different meaning as she pictured herself stretched out in a bed of bubbles sipping wine in the tub that stood on four brass legs while looking out over the garden, through the two oversized windows.

"Now that's a tub." Eric stood behind her looking over her shoulder. His breath felt warm against her cheek and the slight pressure of his body pushing against her back aroused feelings she had suppressed for years. Control, she told herself when a temptation to turn around and kiss him overwhelmed her.

The slight musk scent of his aftershave filled her nostrils as he placed his hands on each of her shoulders. She wondered what he was waiting for. He moved even closer and his hands slid down to her hips as he gently pulled her body against his, causing her insides to feel like they were on fire. Pull away, her inner voice screamed but the rest of her wouldn't comply.

It had been a long time since she had wanted to be with a man.

"I love the place." Eric's mouth was right by her ear, his voice heavy leaving her to believe he was feeling the same way. When his lips slightly wisped across her cheek, she took a deep breath and fought her urges. Slowly she managed to move away from him.

"Just when things were getting interesting," He smiled and Dana could tell he knew the effect he had on her just then.

"Yes, and Tina walking in would have made it even more so." She chuckled feeling her face go flush.

"Tina's a big girl. I'm sure she'd understand, especially since I'm going to buy the place." Eric winked at her.

"You intended to buy the place even before I saw it didn't you." Dana gave him a look that let him know she was starting to catch onto his plan.

"You caught me. The offer is already done up. I just need to sign on the dotted line." Eric said.

"Then, why do you need me to look at it?" Dana questioned, while she managed to lessen the effect of being so close to him.

"I wanted a woman's opinion," he said, "and yes I know Tina is a woman but she also has a stake in me buying the house." Eric stated as though he could read her mind and knew what her next question would be.

"Okay, then lets find Tina so she can give me a professional tour. But, I have to admit that if the rest of the place shows like the bathroom I'll hand you the pen." Dana waved her hand around the room and headed out from the bedroom with Eric following closely behind her.

# Chapter 65

"There's a light on at the other end of the hallway, maybe she's in there." Dana pointed out the direction.

"Lead the way." Eric placed a hand on her shoulder and took it off when they reach the room. "I know the house is big Tina so you don't have to play hide-and-seek to prove it to me." Eric grinned at Dana "In fact me and my lady friend here decided to buy the place." Eric winked and pushed the door open and jumped back when Dana screamed.

"Eric what's wrong with her?" Dana stood at the door and watched Eric run to where Tina's body lay sprawled out on the floor.

"I don't know." He pressed his fingers against her juggler. There's no pulse," Reaching into his pocket he pulled out a phone and slid it across the floor to Dana who stood looking on in shock. "Call 911 and tell them we need someone here immediately." Eric yelled the orders at Dana. Her hands trembled as she pressed the numbers.

"Please we need an ambulance right away." Dana's voice quivered despite her efforts to remain calm while Eric performed CPR on Tina. "The address is 18 Rose Blossom Lane, please hurry… I'm not sure Doctor Rycker is trying to revive her now."

Dana watched in horror as Eric unravelled something from around Tina's neck. "Oh no, this can't be happening again." Dana thought as the woman on the other end of the phone kept asking her questions, she had no answers to. A few

minutes     later,     she     heard     sirens
approaching. With Eric doing CPR, she ran
down the hallway to wave them to their
location.

# Chapter 66

"We are up here." She greeted the paramedic at the front entrance. In moments, they rushed the stairs and followed her to where Eric frantically worked over Tina.

One of the men went to replace Eric.

"I've got it." Eric sounded desperate as he snapped at the man. Leaving Eric to continue with the CPR one of the men took hold of Tina's hand and checked for a pulse, he slowly placed it back on the floor and shook his head at his partner.

"We're too late." He said to Eric.

"We can't be." Eric pushed on her chest a few more times.

"Dr. Rycker, what happened here?" One of the paramedic recognized him. Eric sat back and ran a hand gently across Tina's head before he stood up with a look of anger on his face.

"We're going to have to get the detective to answer that one for us." Eric glared over at Jake who entered a few minutes after the ambulance. "What's going on Jake?" He walked over and took hold of Dana who stood in shock. "How many women are going to die before you catch this bastard?" Eric demanded bringing everyone's attention to Jake.

"We haven't even examined the evidence so the cause of death hasn't been determined yet." Jake remained calm despite the verbal attack Eric threw his way.

Eric released his hold on Dana long enough to strut over to Tina's body where he picked up the nylon rope he unravelled from her neck earlier.

"I would say this matches the murder of the girl that lived in Dana's building. Wouldn't you say so?" Eric tossed the rope at Jake's feet.

"I'd appreciate it if you didn't disturb the evidence." Jake stated not letting Eric's accusations affect him.

"Tina was my friend detective, what has to happen to make you do your job?" Eric walked back to Dana side. "Does Dana have to go next for you to speed up the process?" Eric put a protective arm around Dana's shoulders. "Don't worry Dana. I won't let anyone near you." Eric's words filtered back to her sounding like, he was speaking through a hollow tube.

She hoped this was only a bad dream, *this can't be happening again.*' She looked around at everyone in the room in disbelief. A coroner arrived and started snapping pictures of Tina's lifeless body.

"Dana, you're very pale, I think you should sit down." She looked at Jake who somehow moved from the doorway to her side.

"I need to get her to the hospital." Eric said.

"No I'm fine. Why is this happening again?" She turned to Jake.

"I don't know, but we are going to get to the bottom of this." Jake gave her a look that made her feel like she was still safe despite the scene before her. Eric loosened his grip on her and faced Jake.

"I shouldn't be taking my frustration out on you Detective." His tone softened. "I just don't get it, why anyone would do this." Eric stood shaking his head.

"Don't worry about it." Jake looked at Dana. "I hate to say this but I'll need you two to follow me back to the station for questioning if you can handle it.

"I can," Dana nodded embarrassed to make eye contact with Jake for fear he could tell what went on between her and Eric in the house earlier.

It sickened her that she not only let Eric so close to her but also encouraged the action all while Tina lay dead in another room. Tina might have been alive and Eric could have saved her if they found her sooner.

What the hell, was she thinking, she wasn't even sure getting involved with Eric on a romantic level was what she wanted and yet she carried on with him like a cheap trick.

All she wanted was to go home and hide away in her room.

# Chapter 67

Jake led the way into the precinct and shot a look at Helen who eyed the group following him. Her smug expression vanished with his warning glare.

"Bill I'm going to take Miss Reed to my office, Dr. Rycker you need to go with Detective Mason. He's just going to ask a few questions about what led up to you finding Miss Wakefield's body."

Since the night at her mother's, Jake purposely kept a distance from Dana, which helped to keep him on track with the case. He would have questioned Eric and put Dana with Detective Mason but needed to clarify a few things with her.

"I prefer to stay with Dana." Eric took hold of her hand.

"It's okay Eric I can handle this." Dana slid her hand from his grip.

"As long as you're good with it," Eric bent down and brushed her temple with his lips causing her to pull away from him.

"It's best that we talk to you separate." Jake said, realizing something had changed between the two.

"Sure, I understand." Eric said then followed Officer Mason to another room while Jake escorted Dana to his office.

"Coffee," he took a pot of a burner and held it up to her.

"No thank you." Dana said her voice almost a whisper.

"Are you going to be okay?" He asked thinking she looked strained and wondered how much more of this she could take.

"At one time I thought so, but not anymore." She looked at him. "What is happening in this town?" She sounded desperate and frightened.

"I wish we had an answer to that question." He couldn't even say he got in touch with Henry. Now he struggled to deal with the fact that Miss. Wakefield may still be alive if he had.

"Did you fine Henry, yet?"

"No, it's like he did a disappearing act right after he spoke with you. It's likely he realized you figured him out and went into hiding."

"Do you think Henry is capable of doing this?" She questioned.

"It does resemble the method Sally's killer used and he is our prime suspect so far. We'll know more when the forensic team are done."

"Why Tina?" Dana looked visibly upset.

"I've been asking that same question." Jake tapped his pen on the desk before he looked up at her. "Somehow, he knew you and Eric would be at the house."

"I didn't even know I'd be there until Eric called at five after I got home from work."

"There has to be a connection between Sally and Tina that ties in with you."

"How? Apart from seeing Tina at a distance, I've never met her."

"Henry may have known her already. Did you ever see her or her car at your apartment?"

"I don't think so, but I can't be sure."

"Did you notice anything strange when you arrived at the house?"

"No, the place was beautiful. I did think it a little odd that Tina never came out to meet us, but Eric thought she was giving us time to look on our own." Jake wondered if she and Eric were looking at the house with the future in mind.

"How long were you there before you found her?"

"I'm not sure, maybe twenty minutes."

"That's a long time, what were you doing?" He questioned and noticed her cheeks flush. There was definitely something different about her.

"We were checking out the bathroom in the master bedroom." She admitted and looked away when their eyes met. "We were joking about the size of it then Eric said he was going to buy the place so we went to find Tina." Seeing how uncomfortable the subject made her, Jake guessed they did more then check out the bathroom.

"Dana do you think anyone could have been in the house watching you and Eric?"

"No, I don't think so." Dana looked away. "They were really quite if they were."

"If I'm right, he wouldn't have been able to resist you and Eric's reaction to his job."

"I would never have suspected Henry to be this insane."

"Dana I need you to remember every time you saw him, also what happened when you did. Maybe, it goes beyond Sally and you offended him somehow."

"He's a loner, remember, so I never got the opportunity to see him in action. so there is nothing I know about the man that I can tell you." Dana snapped at him.

"Think, Dana." Jake slapped the desk causing her to jump in her seat. "This guy wants you dead and is making a game out of it." Dana's eyes watered over and he felt bad for having to play the tough guy but he didn't think the true seriousness of how in danger she actually was had sunk into her brain yet. "I guarantee you he was in the house soaking in the moment of shock you and Eric felt at finding his latest victim. The fact that Miss Wakefield and Eric were friends would only have heightened his pleasure." Jake waited for her reaction and had no idea what he would have done if she broke down.

Instead, she sat straight up and looked at him with the fight he knew she had.

"What if, Sally knew something about him and threatened to expose him and he thinks she told me and now he needs to get rid of me."

"That's possible but why Miss Wakefield?" Jake stood up and paced behind his desk. It made sense if Henry had a history he wanted to keep secret he might kill to keep it hidden.

"Until we find the tie between Henry and Tina this is only speculation." Jake sipped his coffee, knowing she wouldn't like to hear what he had to say next. "In the meantime you need to take every precaution. I assigned an officer to watch you."

"I refuse, there's no way this guy is going to control my life. I'm tired of looking over my shoulder every time I leave my home and I don't want someone to waste their time following me around." She stood and stepped away from the desk and for a moment, Jake thought she intended to end their conversation and leave. He had to convince her that having someone keeping an eye on her was a protection.

"Dana, I'm not the enemy here, somehow this guy is stalking you and he's very good at keeping one step ahead. In fact, he's able to know where you are going to be even before you do." Dana sat back down with a sigh. "Once we can find the strings that tie Henry to Miss Wakefield we can make an arrest."

"Is my family safe or is he going to start killing them off?"

"He's trying to show you he is in control and what he intends to do you. Right now he's attacking people you know but who aren't particularly close to you."

"Could Eric be in danger?" She asked and Jake could see how real her concern for him was, confirming his decision to keep distance from Dana was the right thing to do.

"It appears that women are his target for now, so you don't need to worry about Eric. But if he does decide to make it personal going after your boyfriend might be where he starts." It was a bold statement to make concerning her and Eric's relationship but Jake refused to make this pretty for her. Even if they weren't dating, someone watching from the sidelines might conclude that they were.

"Can I go home, now?" Dana stood up and shot an indignant glared his way, not confirming or denying if they were a couple.

"Sure, we're done here. Let me see if the officer is finished questioning Eric, if he needs more time you can wait in my office." Jake recommended.

"I'm tired and really don't want to hang around here." Her tone softened.

"If they need more time, I'll get a ride for you." Jake held the door for her. Except for Helen, the place was empty.

"Helen is there anyone around who could drive Miss Reed home."

"Just Bill, and you and me." Jake detected a bit of attitude in her voice but she kept it professional without looking up.

"The guys are over at Johnny's breaking up a brawl." She smiled and looked up at him. "I'm available if you like." She flipped the page and went back to her magazine when he ignored her comment.

"Wait over there. I'll let Eric know I'm taking you home." He motioned to a seat away from the front desk.

Jake knocked on Bill's door and stepped inside it leaving Dana alone with Helen.

## Chapter 68

"It must be nice to have a doctor and a detective chasing after you."

"Listen, Helen I don't know what you're talking about and really, I'm not in the mood for your stupidity."

"That's right you never had time for anyone, except to tail behind your super stud brother all through school."

"What?"

"Oh look, Miss innocent. Flirting with all the men pretending you don't know what you're doing. Just like Robert."

"How do you know my brother?"

"It's a small town with one school." Helen smirked "You haven't changed a bit you're still playing the shy little girl who needs all these strong men to protect her."

"You don't know me."

"I know all off you, even that Sally girl. You two were the same, snobby, always elevating yourselves above everyone else."

"You know nothing about anyone of us." It angered Dana that this woman would disrespect Sally.

"More than you know." Helen stared her up and down with such hatred Dana thought if she came around the desk at her, she would barge into the room where Jake and the other officer were talking with Eric. This woman was crazy and the fact that she knows everyone associated with Dana scared the hell out of her.

"And trust me when I say stick with your Doc friend because Jake isn't interested in your type." He might make you think he is, like he had me believe, but when it comes right down to it, he runs."

"I'm not interested in anything you have to say." Dana moved towards the door and tried to remember her school days or any recollection of Helen. There was none, she would have to dig out her old year books, when she got home.

"You may want to listen, because chasing after Jake could be unhealthy." She flashed an insane glare towards Dana.

"What?" Dana turned wondering if Helen just threatened her, but decided the woman's thoughtless ranting stemmed from a deep jealousy.

She intended to say more, to Dana, but quickly flipped around in her seat when the door opened and Eric rushed out with Jake trailing him.

"I brought you here and should be bringing you home. Why don't you wait for me?"

"I'm sorry Eric, I feel terrible and need to get out of here." Dana stood in the middle of the floor on the verge of tears.

"How much longer will this take." Eric questioned looking agitated.

"You can leave anytime, but if we want to get Miss Wakefield's killer of the streets before someone else ends up dead, I need to ask a few more questions." Bill stated and Eric hung his head then looked up at Dana.

"I'm sorry Dana but I need to do this for Tina."

"It's okay." She gave a weak smile in his direction.

"You go home and I'll call you tomorrow."

"Alright,"

"Tina was my friend." Eric broke down and Dana ran to hug him.

"I know and we'll get through this." Her inner strength not wavering Dana consoled him then backed away.

"That's why we need everything you can possible remember." Eric nodded at Jake's words.

"I know, get her home safe." He said to Jake before following Bill back into the room.

# Chapter 69

"Will this night ever end?" Dana complained when Jake pulled in front of the house to see Robert's car parked in the laneway.

"You're fortunate to have a brother who cares about you." "I know."

Jake felt sorry for her thinking she must feel like she had the weight of the world resting on her shoulders.

"I checked into Henry's past and it ends five years ago when he moved into the apartment. I don't think he's from around here."

"Can't you just arrest him?"

"Not without more evidence. We can't even prove he broke into your car."

"I'm so sick of this. I have no control over my life anymore. And now you want to put a tail on me."

"Dana, he's watching you and I think he has something bigger in mind for you." Jake sighed. "You really need to watch your surroundings and make sure someone is with you every time you go out."

"I'm sure everyone has nothing better to do than baby sit me." Dana sat shaking her head in disbelief.

"If you promise not to go out alone I'll hold off on having an officer watch your every move."

"Can I call you if I need an escort?"

Under different circumstances, Jake would have loved to take her into his arms and promise to protect her. Instead, he had to give her news he didn't think she'd appreciate hearing.

"I have to leave town for a few days."

"Why. You're the only one who knows what's happening." She started to panic.

"The envelope Helen brought to me the day she harassed us at my home, contained some information that may have a bearing on this case."

"Where are you going?" She questioned.

"Toronto." I pulled my father out of retirement to see if he could dig up some things on Henry. He decided not to tell her what the contents of the envelope were that his father sent him. "He's very good and still gets called in to consult on cases all across the country.

"How long are you going to be gone?"

"I'm hoping Thursday, Friday the latest, no more than a week. Here is the number where I'm staying. Don't lose it and don't hesitate to use if at any time."

Taking it, she tucked it into her wallet and looked so vulnerable with tears pearling at the tips of her eyes.

His control began to waver, Jake leaned towards her intending to wrap a protective arm around her and moved back when the door whipped opened.

"Dana what are you doing sitting out here?" He ignored Jake at first.

"I'm making out with the detective." Dana threw a snide answered at Robert.

"Everyone is waiting inside for you."

"Robert what are you doing here?"

"Eric called to tell us what happened, Lindsay and I rushed over to be with you." Robert popped his head in the car.

"Detective, what's going on in this town?"

"I'm hoping to be able to figure that out soon."        "I hope so." Robert stated and held the door opened for Dana.

"Until then don't let your wife or sister go anywhere on their own." Jake knew Robert would let the seriousness of the situation sink in.

"Believe me, I intend to put them both under lock and key until this is over. I just need you to help me make it clear to my stubborn sister who has a problem with people talking care of her." Jake like Robert, and knew he could trust him to make sure the women surrounding him never went out alone.

"We just had a conversation concerning this and she was about to make a promise…."

"I get it, so give me a break," Dana stepped out of the car cutting Jake off. "Let me know when you get back." She said and walked to the house.

"Thank you for bringing her home safe."

"Anytime," Jake said and headed towards home to pack a few things before heading out. '*I better put some distance between Dana and myself, and get out of town before I do something I regret.*' Jake thought.

He found Dana unlike any woman he ever met, her strong qualities drew him to her. She wasn't clingy and seemed to thrive on being independent. Also, she was chatty speaking only to hear the sound of her voice. Dana was definitely someone he would like to get to know more if the circumstances were different.

# Chapter 70

Jake woke to the aroma of coffee brewing and tantalizing scent of bacon lingering throughout the house. Growing up he couldn't remember a day going by when his mother hadn't cook a breakfast. After a quick shower, he joined his parents in the kitchen.

"Some routines never change." He wrapped his arm around his mother's small, frame and took in the slight scent of her musk perfume as he bent and planted a quick peck on her cheek before taking a seat at the table with his father.

"What can I say….I'm a creature of habit." She chuckled and placed a coffee down in front of him then went to get his plate.

"What time did you get in, son?" Thom asked folding the newspaper together and placing it down by his plate.

"A little after midnight."

"That's not too bad."

"It's an easy drive." Any other time Jake would have loved to carry on with idle chat but right now, he was racing time.

The last time he spoke to his father was shortly after Henry revealed his secrets to Dana. A lot changed and he was anxious to update him and to hear if he had any leads for him.

"Were you able to get any information on Henry Nairn?" Jake looked over his shoulder waiting for his mother to voice her distaste about where the conversation headed." He laid the file he brought from the bedroom, on the table.

"Hum, seven fifty six," she glanced at the clock on the stove. "Not in the house two minutes and you're already talking shop." She produced a slight frown on her forehead. "You know this kind of talk around the table is unhealthy for the digestion system."

Even though, he grew up with his mother's theories imbedded in his brain he learned at an early age not to take the words serious. After all, dying from taking shop at the dinner table was less likely than having a speeder shoot a cop at a routine stop.

Out of respect for his mother, he and his father always abided by her wishes and only broke the rules on rare occasions. Right now was one of those times.

"I'm sorry, but someone is killing young women back home and I believe it started here." Jake talked openly with his mother, knowing she always respected the confidentiality of the things they discussed in the privacy of their home.

"He's right Lila we can't waste time on this." Thom sat back in his chair and Jake covered a smile at the familiar tone his father used whenever he needed to break the family rules.

"When have I ever been able to stop you, Thom?" Lila playfully tossed a rolled up napkin at her husband as she sat down.

"Thank you for being so understanding, my dear," he flashed a smile across at her and tipped his coffee at her before turning to Jake.

Taking their playful bickering as a sign to continue, Jake opened the folder and pushed it in front of his father.

"This is the girl who was murdered." He pointed to the eight by ten of Sally. And this is Dana the other girl I mentioned to you." He pulled the picture from the file.

"The resemblance is uncanny. Did you check out the possibility that one of their father's had an affair with one of the mother's and produced a twin."

"The blood types are different." At the onset of the case, he questioned the relationship between the two girls and had some test done.

"Well, that eliminates the parents as suspects."

"Especially, since one of the fathers just passed away."

The fax machine beeped and Jake jumped up. "To make matters more complicated another woman was killed last night." He came back with a picture.

"I asked Bill to send a copy of her photo once he got it." He handed it to his father.

"Tina Wakefield, our second victim and hopefully the last."

"Can you tie her to the other girl or this Henry fellow?" Thom scratched his head.

"She was a real estate agent showing a house. Guess who discovered the body?" Thom looked over the edge of his glasses that balanced on top of his nose giving Jake his full attention. At 63, his father was more fit than Jake could remember, his height beat Jake's by two inches and except for the hint of grey touching the sides of his head, he could easily be mistaken for Jake's brother.

"Should I know this?" He looked intently at his son for the answer.

"Her boyfriend intended to buy the house." Jake held up Dana's picture. "He brought her to look at the place and they stumbled on the body with nylon wrapped around her neck, similar to Sally and the other women whose pictures you mailed to me."

"So far the only connection is Dana. Have you checked her out?"

"Both her and her brother we at their father's wake across town the night Sally was killed." Jake picked up a slice of bacon, breaking it in half with his fingers he tossed one piece on his plate and shoved the other into his mouth.

"The case is getting weird and complicated."

"Why is that?"

"Dana received a call from the killer."

"Oh the poor girl, do you think she could be next?" His mother covered her mouth and gasped.

"He told her the first girl died instead of her, so I'd say it's a good possibility."

"That must be horrible for her." Lila stated.

"Did you hear the call?" Thom questioned.

"No. She called me after it ended and I went over." Jake shook his head. "We checked the phone records and it shows a call was made to her house, at the time she gave us, from a payphone downtown."

"Did he only call that one time?"

"I thought he might call back that night and waited around to see if he would but he didn't."

"You stayed the night?" His father gave him a questioning glance.

"She was too frightened to stay alone, and I couldn't drop her at her mother's at two in the morning, so I stayed the night." Jake stared across at his father regretting that, he allowed him to corner him into admitting that he spent the night with Dana. Seeing his mother sitting across from him with a raised eyebrow didn't make things any easier.

"Cops stake out places all the time."

"Where was her boyfriend?" She suddenly took more of an interest in Dana's picture twisting it around with her fingers to get a better view.

"They weren't dating at the time and I was there as a detective." He moved the picture away from his mother. "So don't get any wrong ideas going through your head." He could hear his father chuckling.

"Is there something wrong with her?" She baited him for more information.

"Thanks Dad." He turned to his father who had a grin on his face. "I'm not going there with you, Mom." Jake said avoiding one of the many lectures, he was sure she rehearsed in her head, about him and marriage and grandchildren.

"She is very pretty." She gave a sheepish smile in her son's direction.

"I think now would be a good time to get going." Jake suggested to his father who sat laughing at his predicament.

"What time will you be back for dinner?" Lila followed them to the door.

"I'm not sure, I'll call you later."
Thom gave her a peck and followed Jake to
the car.

# Chapter 71

Thom waited until they were driving before he went into more detail.

"The profile definitely fits a string of murders in the area that go back a few years. The trail went cold on us and the killings just ended."

"I vaguely remember the case?" Jake admitted.

"You were just a rookie at the time. I gave the case to Jones and Dunlay. They interviewed and chased around town and kept coming up empty handed. I guess we were all hoping the creep either died or got killed himself." He shook his head and Jake could see the stress in his father's eyes. "Looks like the bastard just went into hiding for a few years."

"I tend to agree with you."

"You remember Pete down at the station?"

"Sure do."

"I asked him to look into things while I tie up a few loose ends on a case over in Whitby. He's real excited to heat things up again."

"I appreciate all the help I can get." It felt good to be back with the team, Jake thought.

"All us old guys down at the station are hungry for this one and don't intend to let this creep slip through our fingers again if it's the same culprit." Thom's face held a familiar determination that Jake knew well, he reacted like a hound dog that just picked up the scent for the first time. If he had any chance of finding this killer, he needed the experience of his father behind him.

# Chapter 72

"Hey look whose back in town." Jake's ex partner Dave called out as he ran and wrapped vice grip arms tightly around his shoulders. "Tell me small town living got too boring for you and you finally come to your senses."

"Not quite Dave." Jake laughed as he shook himself free from his grip.

"My shift ends at six. Want to grab something to eat and a few beers after." Dave suggested.

"Sounds good," Jake gave him a friendly slap on the back before he followed his father into the Sergeant's office.

A tall man in his mid fifties towered behind the desk as the two men entered. Except a for a few crows line scratching at his eyes he hadn't changed much.

"Great to see you again, Jake, how's it going?" Reaching over the desk, he clasped Jake's hand in a bear grip.

"Good, thanks,"

A few months before Thom's retirement, he recommended Pete as his replacement for the Sergeant position.

Pete was a good man who held a deep respect for his former boss, and still consulted him on a few cases that had gone cold. Jake remembered dinners at their home in his rookie days. After the meal, the women would chase the men into the den where they spent the rest of the evening mulling over unsolved murders.

"I never believed in ghost but many times I go down to the tombs and stand among the boxes and vow to find an end to their stories." The Sergeant stated.

"I know some of them have been there way too long." Thom agreed.

"It kills me that the victims and their families have to live with no resolution." Pete's eyes revealed a pained look and Jake was sure the man lost sleep over these cases. "Right now, there are six women who hold positions in that room and my gut is telling me that finding Jake's guy will put these girls and their families to rest."

"Let's hope so. Did anything come in yet?" Thom asked.

"A few things, I was able to pick up a trail from McCory School where Henry Nairn attended and spoke with the principle who vaguely remembered the name. Apparently, he was some kind of jock.

The school secretary is back today and he's going to get her to dig the file out from the archive which is in the basement." Pete offer. "He had a teacher drop this off yesterday." He showed them the school yearbook where Henry graduated nine years ago."

Flipping the pages, he pointed out a younger version of Henry in a basketball jersey. "There's your boy, right there." He slid the book across the desk. Jake stared down at Henry smiling for the camera.

"He looks like your typical kid sporting his team name with pride." He ran his finger over the picture with Henry Nairn written below it. Out of curiosity, he flipped some of the pages to see if he could find one of Sally. He didn't think he would because her parents were locals of

Chiapas Falls and as far as he knew they never step foot out of it. "Can I take this book with me?" Jake asked.

"Sure,"

"I was able to get some info on his mother but we won't be able to question her." Pete stated.

"Why not?" Jake asked.

"She died of cancer when Henry was seven."

"How did you find that out, if the school had nothing?"

"Okay, let me see this for a sec. I started leafing through this and found something that should pique your interest." Pete motioned to Jake to give him the yearbook back.

Flipping the pages, he turned the page to face them and pointed at another boy around the same age of Henry.

"Read the name."

"What the hell." Jake couldn't take his eyes of the picture. It was the splitting image of Henry.

"Can you believe it, this kids name is Hank Nairn. Does Henry have a brother we don't know about?" Jake asked and slid the book around so his father could see the resemblance.

"Could it be a mistake?" Thom asked looking across to Pete.

"I'm thinking it's his brother." Pete stated looking like he found the national treasure.

"You might be right, so why would a mother give her two sons the same name?"

"Sounds like daddy had an affair and got both women pregnant and maybe the mistress wanted to make a statement and gave her boy his father's name also. I'm betting the old man's name is Henry." Thom gave a short laugh while giving his opinion.

"I'd be careful with what your placing your cash on, my friend." Pete pointed at Thom.

"Who knows, is there anyway we can track this Hank down?" Jake asked.

When a sly smile covered Pete's face, Jake had to chuckle.

"What kind of cop couldn't uncover a small detail like that?" Pete laughed.

"It would save a lot of time and we all know how precious time is on these types of crime." Thom said.

"Do you know how many Nairns are listed in the phone book?"

"Not really, but I'm sure you know." Jake shook his head knowing Pete already had the answer while he held up his index finger.

"One and not in the white pages, I just had to pick up the phone and dial and can you believe it, on the first call I hit the jackpot." He turned the phone book to face them and flipped it open to the yellow pages. "Right here, Nairn Law Firm." He tapped a huge index finger over a full page add.

"Great, daddy is a lawyer." Thom admitted.

"Hank Nairn and I spoke very briefly, he refused to answer any questions, but let me know his father was out of town on business." Pete looked between the two men sitting across from him. "I thought he was going to lawyer up, so when I received a call this morning, it surprised me to hear

Sr. Nairn on the line." He turned to Thom. "You might want to consider your earlier bet, because he introduced himself as Dennis Nairn." Pete looked like he was gunning for mayor with this one and Jake was ready to cast a ballot for him.

"Did he give you anything?" Jake questioned.

"I told him we were investigating Sally's murder, he admitted that Henry is his son and he dated Sally a long time ago. He also said Henry's mother passed away when he was seven. He's out of town right now, but will be back Thursday and agreed to meet with you at his son's home at eight, Thursday morning. He wants it early because he has to leave town again. Wanna bet after he hung up with me his next call was to Henry."

"Let's hope it's to tell him to drop by the nearest station for questioning." Thom said and stood up.

"That leaves the rest of today and tomorrow." Jake hoped to be heading back before then. "Do you mind if I spend some time going over the files of those women?"

"Whatever you need, just name it." Pete's face lit up, Jake expected he was please that he might get closure on the women.

"Thanks Pete, I owe you for this."

"If we can prove this guy is responsible for those six girls in the tombs and I can help their families get closure that will be payment enough." Pete slid a piece of paper over to Jake with the address.

"Thanks Pete, eight on Thursday." Jake repeated.

"That leaves the school." Thom said getting up.

"The principle is expecting you this morning." Pete said.

"Looks like we're going for a ride across town to visit McCory," Thom shook Pete's hand. "We appreciate everything you've done.

"I won't forget this Pete." Jake smiled please with the leads given him.

"You're doing a good thing, Jake. You know I could use a good man to help empty the tombs."

"I'll think about it," Jake said knowing he could never leave his home in Chiapas Falls.

"You got a good boy here, Thom." Pete slapped Jake's back.

"You don't have to tell me," Thom's face beamed with pride as he looked at his son. "Drop by with the wife sometimes soon."

"Will do, in the meantime, let me know how tomorrow goes. We really need to get this creep." Pete followed them to the door.

"Sure will, thanks again Pete." Thom said.

""I'll meet you over at Settler's bar and grill around six thirty," Jake call out to Dave as he left.

# Chapter 73

Young teens crowed the schoolyard as they pulled up in front of main entrance. Jake ignored smiles from some of the young girls as he walked past them, the last thing he wanted to do was encourage unwanted attention.

Jake felt strange thinking, he could have wandered the same hallways as Henry, if his mother hadn't insisted on him attending Pearson's across town.

They might have even crossed path at one of the many rival sports events between the two schools. For all, Jake knew, he could have warmed a seat during a basketball game Henry played in.

Pockets of students smoking in groups stared with distrust at the two unfamiliar men coming up the large cement steps. Jake was sure their appearance screamed out cops as he caught a boy tossing a joint to the ground before he stomped on it.

Another time, he might have issued a warning to the kid, if he didn't have more pressing matters to deal with. Drugs were the one thing he had no tolerance for, even in school he had no desire to experiment with them.

They easily found the Main Office where a rotund Ms. Tolley stood her full four foot eleven, to greet them with a smile.

"Good morning, please have a seat and I'll let Mr. Denson know you are here." She buzzed the principle's office to announce their arrival.

"Good morning officers," he came out immediately and towered over his secretary.

"Ms. Tolly please, do you have the files we need."

"Right here," she scooped up a pile from the corner of her desk and handed them to him.

"Thank you, He took them from her then ushered Jake and his father into his office closing the door behind him.

"I have to apologize I haven't had time to review these before your arrival." He flipped open the folder and shifted through the pages. "It looks like we had three Nairns around the same time." He opened the first file and licked his finger to separate the pages. "Wendy Nairn, has a letter written to the school, from her parents, after two young women were killed, informing us that they were moving her to another school for her own safety. They strongly felt the killer was a student." He set it aside to open another one. "Here we go, Henry, I guess he preferred to go by Hank because the name has been crossed out and replaced with the shorter version." He handed it across to Jake before picking up the last one.

"We believe their brothers." Jake offered, somewhat surprised that the mother of Hank would allow her son to attend the same school as the boy from her husband's affair. He knew an affair was only an assumption, but it all pointed to one father and two mothers, what else could it be.

"I think you're right. This one is Henry but the address is different." The Principle pushed the page over to Jake "From the dates here your Henry looks to be about six month younger."

Mr. Denson looked a little confused for a moment. "Well isn't that strange?" he gave a weak laugh, "It looks like Hank's family must have taken Henry in because the address changed shortly after he started.

"Does it say anything about his mother passing away?" Thom asked.

Mr. Denson gave a look of sorrow towards Thom and shifted through some more papers in the file. "Oh yes, here it is. How sad for the boy, he was fortunate Mr. Nairn was so kind."

"Yes he was." Jake felt it better not to divulge any more information than necessary.

"Oh here is the original application for the boy. Interesting the mother had two last names. We don't see that too often. She signed it Mavis Weets-Mullins on the form." Jake quickly looked up from the folders he had.

"Did you say Weets-Mullins?" Jake's heart started to race.

"Yes" The principle nodded.

"Can I see that, please?" 'we got him' Jake thought controlling his excitement and shot his father a look.

He picked up the green folder and flipped it open. In dark bold lettering the name 'Weets-Mullins' jumped out at him, the mother's name Mavis Weets-Mullins. It just kept getting better as he read the pages. Not only was the Toronto address there but a secondary one. Eighteen Rose Blossom Lane, emergency contact was Martha Weets, Grandmother. Henry has ties to the house Miss Walkfield's murder took place.

Jake wanted to jump up and slap his father on the shoulder. '*Henry is related to the Weets and Mullins,'* he found the missing link needed to connect Henry to Tina's murder. He shot a look over at his father, who had remained silent until now, letting his son control the meeting.

"Will we be able to get these files copied?" Jake asked.

"I figured you'd be asking for copies so I had Ms. Tolly do it earlier." He leafed through the files and pulled out three white folders. "Will you need Wendy's file as well?"

"If you don't mind," Jake said anxious to read over her parent's letter.

"Thank you, I think we took enough of your time." Jake stood up and his father followed suit. "You've been very helpful. I'll need to keep the yearbook you had dropped off at the station for a little longer." Jake said clutching the file. Thank goodness for school records. This tied Henry to both the murders, and gave enough evidence to make an arrest.

Excitement flowed through Jake's veins. He was close. He could taste it.

"I'm glad to help. Don't hesitate to call if you have anymore questions." The principle walked them to the hallway and shook their hands before they headed back out the large oak doors, a lot wiser, than when they came through them earlier.

"What did you find in there to get you so excited?" Thom asked once they got in the car and away from the earshot of the kids mulling around the yard.

"Weets is the name of the person where the second murder took place and the Mullins just happens to run the biggest funeral parlour establishment in Chiapas

Falls." Jake said pleased that the pieces were coming together.

"I assume Weets is Henry's Grandmother." Thom said.

"That what it say in the file."

"You know what that means, son?"

"Henry is connected to the house Miss Wakefield's murder took place in." Jake said elated to be a step closer to closing the case.

"Good work."

"That would explain how Henry had the info on where Dana would be even before she did."

"There's one piece missing from the puzzle." Thom looked over at Jake. "Motive, find that and we can close this case."

"I'm hoping our talk with the father tomorrow will help us out there." Jake glanced over at his father. It felt good to be working along side him again.

"It'll be interesting to see what the other Henry, alias Hank Nairn is up to lately. Thom said.

"Maybe they are in it together. It would explain the other murders."

"I'd also like to know where Sr. Nairn heads to when he goes out of town." Jake took a deep breath, he was close he could feel it. Once he got all the pieces together, he would make sure Henry is behind bars and the key melted down.

# Chapter 74

"Hello,"

"Hello, this is Detective Turner."

"Oh Detective, how are you doing?"

"Good, thank you and are you feeling any better?"

"A little, I guess." Nancy's timid voice spoke.

"Have you seen a doctor yet?"

"Oh yes, Eric has been taking care of me, in fact he dropped of a prescription the other day for me and is coming for dinner tonight. They must be magic pills, without them I would never have gotten out off bed." She chuckled.

"Do you know what is making you ill?"

"Since my husband took sick, I haven't had much rest so my immune system is weak and I caught a virus."

"That does happen, just get lots of rest."

"Robert and Eric say the same thing."

"You listen to them."

"Did you need to talk to Dana?"

"If she's there and can come to the phone."

"She's in the kitchen. I'll get her."

"Thank you." He waited a few minutes for Dana to pick up the phone.

"Hi, where are you?" She asked hoping he would say back home.

"I'm still in Toronto. It looks like I'll get back Thursday. How are you holding up?"

"I'm still alive."

"Let's keep it that way. We're getting close to making an arrest."

"Did you find something?"

"I'm hoping to get more details when I meet with Henry's father and his brother Thursday afternoon."

"You found his family. How did you find them so fast?"

"A lot of people down here are interested in this case." The phone went quiet for a moment and she could hear the soft breathing of his breath. "There's more."

"What else is there?" Something in his voice caused a knot to form in the pit of her stomach.

"The house you and Eric found Tina's body in belonged to Henry's Grandmother."

"Are you kidding me?"

"Tina must have told Henry that you and Eric were viewing the house and that's how he knew."

"It makes sense, except for why he decided to kill her." Dana asked.

"Who knows what is driving him. Until we get him I want you to watch like you have eyes in the back of your head."

"I intend to. Do you know where he is?"

"No, I called the station earlier and still haven't been able to locate Henry for questioning."

"Do you think he left town." It frightened Dana that Henry could be hiding out there watching her.

"It's possible he's here in Toronto with his family."

"So I don't have to keep watching over my shoulder." She gave a weak chuckle.

"Let's not make any assumptions. Even if we knew his where-about, we still need more evidence to bury the key after we lock him away, so until we know for sure be careful."

"I feel more like the prisoner." She was so tired of looking over her shoulder.

"Just one more thing, until we do make an arrest I am going to have a detective watch the house."

"I'm too tired to fight you on this anymore.

"It's only until I get back, and remember you can go out anywhere you want as long as someone is with you or you stay in with the crowds."

"You sound like Robert. Just to let you know how desperate things are here, I spent an entire afternoon sipping wine and checking out the stores, with Lindsay just to avoid going mad from sitting at home alone.

"I'm sure that went over well." Jake laughed hard into the phone. She like the sound of his laughter, and for a moment felt tempted to clear up his misconception about her and Eric's friendship.

"The good thing was. I didn't have to do much talking."

"I believe that."

"Do you have any plans for tonight?" He asked.

"My mother invited Eric for dinner." She wanted Jake to know the invite came from her mother and not her. "I would prefer to watch reruns but Mom felt like company."

"Well you sound busy and I'm about to head out to meet an old friend for dinner so I better let you go."

"Thanks for the update." Dana said wondering if the old friend was female.

"No problem, I'll try to call you again Friday."

# Chapter 75

Dana mulled around the kitchen stirring the sauce for the spaghetti while her mother tossed a salad. If her mother insisted on pushing Eric her way, something would have to done about it. Being sick for so long, maybe she is trying to make sure someone is there to take care of Dana in case she dies.

Her chances would improve greatly if she worked on Jake. In Dana's mind, *'he was a better fit and more her type'*. She allowed her mind to fantasize about what it would be like if he was coming to dinner instead of Eric. Hearing his voice tonight was nice. An image of him sharing a romantic dinner sipping wine with a tall beautiful woman slapped a reality check into her.

Once Henry goes to jail and she gets her life back, more than likely, Jake will fade away. He'll go back to dodging Helen and she'll go back to her same hum drum life… how sad she thought.

What's the point of stewing over something that will never be? Dana lectured herself. She wanted to talk about Jake and was tempted to discuss him with her mother who kept shooting, side, glances at her. Dana knew her mother was dying to interrogate her about the call, and she would have loved to discuss Jake with her. She just didn't trust her mother not to blab everything she said to Lindsay.

A shiver went through her as she remembered Eric leaning up against her. She allowed herself to get, caught up in a moment and promised herself never to let things go that far again. He was family and kissing him would be like making out with a brother.

Eric was the typical lady's man and she wasn't sure he would be able to commit to one woman for the rest of his life. She saw how women stared at him while with her and his smiles back to them didn't go unnoticed either. Being with a man like him would take a lot of energy and stamina neither of which she had.

At first, she thought he was playing the big brother to fill in where Robert was lacking but after they almost locked lips, she wasn't sure.

'*Men are so confusing*,' she thought, '*right now, I have too much going on in my head to allow myself to be preoccupied with such foolishness.*'

"Mom," she called out when she noticed her mother left the kitchen. "What are you doing out here?" She found her sitting in the parlour looking tired and drained.

"Nothing much," she said looking pallor with dark circles around her eyes. Seeing her mother's frail tiny frame perched on the couch, Dana realized how much weight she loss over the last few months.

Had her parent's marriage bond been so strong that Dad's death left a deep void?

"Are you okay?" Dana knelt by her, feeling a tinge of guilt for not being more sensitive to her mother.

"I thought the detective might have told you something bad again and it frightened me." Tears filled her eyes and Dana noticed her hands shake.

"I'm sorry mom. There's no reason for me to keep you in the dark. I just don't want to worry you with anything else." She took hold of her hand. "I promise to share more with you." Dana smiled up at her. "In fact, the Detective actually told me some good news."

"He did." She smiled through her tears.

"He thinks they're going to make an arrest soon."

"That's wonderful. It's horrible what's happening in this town. I get so worried every time I think of you and Lindsay being out on your own."

"I know, but you don't have to worry about us. If anything all this is bringing us closer, remember Lindsay and I spent the afternoon together, so that should make you happy."

"Yes it did." She pulled a tissue she had tucked away in the cuff of her sleeve and dabbed at her eyes.

"That proves things are getting better." Dana patted her hand and stood up. "You sit here and answer the door for Eric when he gets here, I'll set the table."

"Thank you, dear."

"You going to be okay?" Dana asked feeling like a heel. "Yes."

"Good, I'll bring you a tea."

# Chapter 76

Jake woke to the familiar scents and murmurings of his parents, going through there morning routine. He sat on the edge of his bed and reflected on the cold cases he and his father rummaged through most of the day before.

Everything fit the murders, in Chiapas Falls. The murderer quit and went underground after his last victim, a young girl in her mid twenties.

He pulled open the file and even though all the victims looked to be in there early twenties there ages ranged from twenty to twenty-six. Interestingly, the two girls from the school both went back after taking a few years off. One because she had a baby and the other just decided being a high school dropout got her nowhere in the work field. *'How sad,'* Jake thought looking at the young face smiling up at him. *'A young pretty girl gets her act together to improve her lot in life only to die.'*

Everything fit the crimes back home. What happened, Jake wondered, did the cops get close and the coward got frightened and fled?

Why did he wait so long to start again, what triggered him to go on the rampage? More importantly, how did he end up in Chiapas Falls stalking Dana, and why hadn't he killed her like the others? He needed to find out what made Dana different.

Those answers would come in time, right now, he was anxious to get the interview over with the Nairns so he could head home to keep an eye on Dana.

He jumped out of bed and after a quick shower packed up his few things before joining his parent's at the breakfast table.

Henry running around free didn't set well with him, neither did knowing his family gave him the heads up that the police were looking for him. It gave Henry an advantage.

"Good morning, son." Thom greeted Jake.

Once he sat down his mother planted a kiss on the top of his head then placed a coffee in front of him.

"You haven't stopped since you got here. Do you think we'll be able to find some time to sit and chat so I can catch up on life in Chiapas Falls?" She patted his back then went to get his plate.

"Not this visit mom, I'm sorry but I really need to head back after the meeting." Being the only offspring, Jake knew his mother missed not having him around. Seeing her look of rejection bothered him. "I promise, after all this is over, I'll take some time from work and come and talk your ear off."

"That would be nice."

"I'll warn you, it's going to be boring since, nothing has changed from how I lived here." Jake said, putting a smile on her face. At least she didn't pull the guilt trip on him about how all of their friends have grandchildren now.

"A mother never gets bored with what's going in her son's life. I'm interested in who your friends are." Lila said and Jake knew she was probing to see if there was a girl in his life.

"Quit pushing the boy, Lila. He'll tell you soon enough when he meets a girl he's willing to let tie a ball and chain around his leg." Thom chuckled and winked at his son.

"Oh you keep quiet. A mother should be able to talk with her son." She made a face at Thom.

"You can ask anything you want. My life is an open book." Jake smiled at his mother.

"You let loose a whole can of worms there son." Thom laughed.

"I'm interested in my son. What's wrong with that?"

"If you're so anxious to find out if your son has a group of woman stashed away that he isn't telling us about, maybe we'll need to take a bit of a holiday and go and check the place out." Thom came up with the idea and Jake knew it was because he wanted to follow the case.

"You're welcome to come but I can't guarantee that I'll be around anymore than I've been here. There is a lot that needs to be done once I get back."

Jake always enjoyed when his parents visited but he didn't want his mother to think he would be touring her around. From the determination, in his father's eyes, he didn't think he would be spending much time carrying her shopping bags either.

"I understand, it'll be fun, you two can run around while I wander down town checking out the quaint little shops you have." Lila's mood changed from one of rejection to excitement at her husband's plans. "When can we leave?"

"If that's alright with you son, you go home when we're done today and your mother and I follow later tonight."

"That would be great." He could use a fresh pair of eyes back home and appreciated his father's offer.

"Alright, it's settled then, so start packing mother, cause' we're going on a trip." Thom stated.

"You don't have to tell me twice. I'll have everything packed up and the cases by the door before you get home." She chuckled and started to hum as she cleared the table.

"Now that's settled we should go I have a few things to check out at the station before we make that appointment." Thom looked at his watch.

"I'll see you later tonight." Picking up his suitcase, Jake gave her a quick peck on her cheek.

# Chapter 77

With her mother spending a few nights with Lindsay and Robert, the house felt too big and empty, by four thirty, boredom settled in so she decided a short walk to town wouldn't be too unsafe.

If Jake had been back, she might have asked him to accompany her to the fair, but with him tied up in Toronto she didn't expect to hear from him before Friday. *'He's been so stand offish lately, I doubt he would come, he probably would get one of his police friends to fill in for him, again.'* She thought.

Robert would be furious if he knew she ignored his warnings to go out alone. The streets had people strolling along them so all she had to do was stay with the crowds, this way she could justify that she wasn't really alone. She was willing to chance that whoever was stalking her, would not want to bring attention their way by trying anything with a mob of people strolling up and down the streets.

She intended to keep to herself to avoid drawing undue attention her way, but if needed her lungs could conjure up a scream loud enough to turn some heads her way.

The sound of a band playing brought back memories of younger days when she tagged along after Robert. Thoughts of riding the, Ferris Wheels at night with the lights all lit up caused butterflies to tickled her stomach as she neared the fairgrounds.

Things were changing with Robert back in town, she even found herself opening up to Lindsay. Shopping with her was actually more fun than Dana anticipated. She had to admit they did a lot of laughing over lunch. *'Although, the carafe of wine may have helped the situation,'* Dana thought.

Her visions of the big exciting cities dimmed, by the fact, that they weren't thrilling enough to keep Robert from coming home. Even Eric and Jake left it all behind for the serenity of a small town.

The grounds were teeming with people eating cotton candy and screaming kids, as they were being toss around in a tilt-a-whirl. It all sounded so alive. She followed the tunes, riding the airwaves, of a local band to a beer tent. Her stomach growled as she walked past a group of vendors cooking up batches of wings and ribs along with a chip wagon. She opted to get a small fry to hold her over while she listened to the group sing their rendition of Legs by ZZ Top. *They're actually doing a pretty good,'* she thought as she stepped up to the line.

She counted out her changed and jumped when she felt a hand land on her shoulder.

"Hi Dana." She turned sharply to face two girls who worked in the factory.

"Oh hi, Jenny and Sue, how are you guys doing?" Dana felt a little awkward but relieved at the same time.

"We're good, thanks, are you here with anyone?" Jenny asked.

"No, I walked over from my mom's house.

"There's a few of us from work here, why don't you sit with us." Dana's first inclination was to turn down the invite.

And if she hadn't vowed to change her social habit she may have this time, as well. '*At least she could tell Robert she was here with group from work, when he hounded her about going out alone,*' she decided.

"You don't mind?" Dana asked.

"Of course not, it'll be fun."

"Okay, I will." After getting their orders, she followed them to their table.

"Look who we found." Jenny called out. Ten people sat around a large table, most of whom Dana recognized from work. She felt obligated to put her small bag of fries in with the rest of them when the girls put them on a plate beside a stack of ribs and wings.

"Have a seat over here." Matt one of the guys from shipping pulled a chair from another table and squeezed it beside him.

"Don't worry Linda your new boyfriend's seat is safe, even though he's very late." He teased one of the girls Dana didn't recognize.

"If anyone should be worried, it should be Dana if she's sitting beside you." Linda teased and the rest of the group chuckled, their agreement. Matt laughed along while he poured her a glass of beer from a pitcher.

Before long, Dana found herself enjoying the company. After starting her third glass of beer, she allowed Matt to talk her into a dance when the band slowed things down.

"I hope you wore steel toed boots, because I've been known to step on a few toes in my day." Matt laughed and slipped an arm around her waist.

"I have enough beer in me, that I shouldn't feel the pain until tomorrow morning, at least." Dana teased back.

"Aren't you a cheap date. Give the girl a beer and I can walk all over you." Matt tightened his hold on her.

"Funny guy, it will just leave me having to explain a bunch of bruises at work tomorrow."

"I better get a tight grip to make sure you don't fall taking me with you." Matt laughed and swirled her around causing her to laugh louder than she was use to. They were enjoying themselves until someone tapped Dana's shoulder.

"Excuse me, but I'd like to dance with my girl." Dana turned to face Eric.

"Your girl," Dana questioned as she looked from Matt to Eric. "When did that happen?" Dana asked surprised that Eric would have the gumption to walk up and interrupt giving the impression they were a couple.

"Okay, she's not my girl, yet." Eric lips spread into a slow smile, while Matt stood looking confused. "Help a fellow out," he turned to Matt.

"You okay, Dana if I go back to my seat?" Matt asked.

"I'm sorry Matt, I'll be fine." Dana shook her head as he walked away.

"Are you mad at me?" Eric slipped an arm around her taking over the dance.

"More shocked, about what you said." This is exactly why Dana avoided calling him earlier; he was too carefree and took too many liberties. "How could you just come out and say I was your girl? What makes you so sure Matt isn't my boyfriend?"

Dana wanted to make sure he wouldn't pull a stunt like this on her again.

She was enjoying her time out getting to know some of her peers. *'How did he find me anyhow?'* She wondered.

"Remember, you told me you are single. Did that change in the last few days?" He smiled.

"No but could have."

"I'm sorry Dana, you're right I shouldn't have been so stupid." Eric apologized letting go of her hand. "These are your friends and here I'm barging in and making a fool out of myself." Eric said.

"Don't worry about it." Dana softened accepting his apology. "Besides this is the first time I ever did anything outside of work with them. So I can't really call them friends yet." Dana sighed, "I'm hoping they will be though." She added as an after thought.

"For someone who you hardly know, Matt over there certainly had you in a tight hold." Eric said as he wrapped his arms around her and swayed to the music until it ended.

"I hadn't noticed." Dana said.

"Would your new found friends mind if I joined the group?" Eric asked.

"If you behave yourself, they probably won't mind." Dana smiled and nudged him in the side.

"Ahh, that was a cheap shot." He bent over holding his side pretending she hurt him.

"Faker," Dana laughed and led the way back to the group. She stopped a few feet away from the tent and turned to face Eric.

"Eric I can't go back there." She clung to his arm.

"What do you mean?" Eric stared down at her as though she suddenly lost her mind.

"There's someone there I really don't want to be around." She was almost ready to cry.

"Who?" Eric demanded.

"The guy sitting beside Matt."

"Who is he?"

"His name is Henry but I can't tell you anything right now." Dana's voice shook.

"Do you want to leave?"

"Yes please but I have to get my purse. Come with me, please." Dana pleaded and took a tight grip on Eric's arm.

"You sound terrified, of course I won't leave you." The foolish side of Eric completely disappeared and the same protective man who stood beside her at Sally's funeral came through.

"I don't want to make a scene. I just want to get my purse and go home." She said grateful that Eric showed up when he did. She didn't know what she would have done if she went back with Matt and saw Henry there.

"No problem." Eric assured her taking hold of her hand he led the way to the table. "Hi everyone one, I'm Eric a friend of Dana's. We were going to come and have a few beers with you guys but won't be able to after all." Eric reached over and pickup her bag. "This is yours, right hon." He snatched the bag from the table.

"Yes it is thanks." Dana struggled to keep her voice from cracking. It concerned her that the boyfriend Linda was waiting for happened to be Henry. How could she warn her without sending everyone into a panic? *'I have to call Jake and tell him.'* She thought, still holding on to Eric's arm they started to leave when Henry called over to her.

"Hi Dana, I hear a friend of yours is interested in knowing how I knew Sally." Henry's eyes glared at her. Dana's heart sank when all eyes turned to her. Her mind stumbled for the right words when she heard Eric's voice.

"Isn't that nice, you and Dana have mutual friends. Well you guys enjoy the rest of your night." Eric clasped his hand over Dana's and walked away.

# Chapter 78

Dana felt like all eyes were on her, even after she got in the car with Eric.

"You're shaking." Eric notice and reached into the back seat and pulled out a black bag.

"How many beers have you had?"

"Not many, two at the most," 'maybe three,' Dana thought not wanting him to think she was on the verge of being drunk.

"Take these." He grabbed a small bottle and popped the lid, before he shook two little green pills into his palm.

"What are you giving me?" She put them in her mouth and washed them back with a bottle of water he had sitting in the cup holder.

"Something to help you relax. Then I need to make a quick stop at the pharmacy, before I get you home where I intend on making you a nice hot tea and bed for the night."

Pulling up in front of her house she noticed a strange car off to the side with a man sitting in the front seat with a book opened. If Jake hadn't told her someone would be sitting outside her home she wouldn't have given the car a second thought. Seeing it gave her a sense of safety.

Obviously, Eric didn't notice because he was busy tending to her and raced to her side to open the door before she had time to get out.

She decided not to bring it to his attention and rather liked the idea of sharing a secret with Jake. 'Once I get in *the house and Eric goes I have to call Jake.'* She hoped Eric wouldn't stay long.

Stepping out of the car, she felt a little dizzy and grabbed Eric's arm to help her up the steps.

"I didn't drink that much." Her words sounded like an echo in her ears.

Eric helped her to the door where she rummaged through her purse for the longest time before she found her keys. Then she fumbled with them until she separated the one that unlock the front door from the rest. Trying to slip it into the lock became a challenge.

"Those pills work fast." She laughed and covered her mouth when she snorted.

"It's probably the beer." Eric said taking the keys, he easily fitted them in the lock and pushed the door opened.

"I only had three small glasses." Dana said but had to admit that the shock of seeing Henry with her new friends didn't bother her as much now.

"You told me two."

"I lied, I'm sorry." She laughed.

"Stay here while I get you some water." He helped her to the couch in the parlour."

"Eric you're so nice but you don't have to stay." Her body started to feel rubbery and her words slurred making her sound goofy even to herself, but somehow it didn't matter. "I'm sure you have a lot of other places you'd rather be than baby sitting me." Eric took her face in between his palms and looked directly into her eyes.

"Dana, when are you going to start believing in yourself? This is exactly where I want to be right now." He bent her head towards him and placed a gentle kiss on her forehead. "If I wanted to be somewhere else, that's where I'd be." He got up and patted her hand. "I'll be right back."

Dana rested her head on the back of the couch. *"What did you give me?"* Dana questioned, feeling very relaxed like her body was slowly melting.

It made her ill thinking about what Henry could be telling her co-workers about her. They would probably hate her by the time she showed up at work tomorrow. *'So much for making new friends,'* she chuckled thinking it all seemed pointless.

The kettle whistled, bringing her back to the realization that Eric was in her kitchen. He was so kind, better than a big brother, maybe, they could have a romantic relationship. She laughed at the ideas going on in her head. *'It must be the beer and those stupid pills are messing up my thinking, I wish Jake were here.'*

## Chapter 79

An urge to talk to Jake overcame her and she attempted to reach the phone, but it was too far away. She tried to remember why she needed Jake. Nothing made sense anymore. Just the act of thinking hurt, it didn't matter when Eric came around the corner holding a tray.

"You look more relaxed."

"I think your little green pills are doing their job." She said. "Just like Jake is only doing his job." She rambled on comparing the pills to Jake.

"Is there something going on between you two?" Eric asked.

"No, he doesn't like me." Dana held her head. "I need to sleep." She lay back on the couch.

"Let's get you upstairs and into something more comfortable." Eric helped her off the couch.

"Alright," she tripped over her feet and Eric scooped her up in his arms.

"Maybe two were too much." Eric said while heading up the stairs with her. "By the way, where is your mother?"

"At Lindsay's house for the night," Dana chuckled. "Eric put me down I can walk."

"Once we reach the top of the stairs I promise to let you walk the rest of the way." Eric said. "I never would have guessed that such a tiny little thing like you would weigh so much." Eric laughed as she attempted to slap at him.

"Have you ever considered, you might be out of shape?" Dana felt giddy.

"Ouch that hurt, after I carried you up all those steps.

"I know you're being so kind to me." She held onto him as he walked to her room where he placed her gently on the bed.

"Nice girly room." He looked around.

"I think so."

Lifting her legs over the side of the bed, she started to undress and stopped when she saw Eric still looking at her. "Do you mind?" She asked and waited for him to turn around.

"I am a doctor." Eric reminded her as he folded his arms across his chest and turned faced the door.

"Not mine." Dana chuckled then stripped down and slipped her pyjamas on. "Okay, I'm changed now."

"Good, now let's get you under the covers." Eric pulled the covers back. "Feel better now?" He asked.

"Eric, thank you for being such a good friend," Dana said and the words sounded slurred, but it felt good having someone to take care of you.

"You don't get it do you?" Eric walked over to the other side of the bed and lay down. She turned to face him.

"Get what?" She stared into his deep blue eyes, when she did he lean over and kissed her cheek.

"How much you affect me." He said softly before kissing her on the lips.

"What are you doing?" Dana slapped his chest and tried to push but let her arm drop, it felt too heavy to lift.

"Dana I know you feel the same way. At the house I knew you wanted me to kiss you then."

"That was back then, I don't anymore," Dana protested.

"You're right," Eric said and gently rubbed the hair from her eyes. "Why don't you tell me about this Henry guy who scared the hell out of you today?" Her mind shifted and she had to think for a second before Henry's face flashed before her eyes.

"I don't want Henry to kill me." She whispered, and Eric leaned over her.

"Why would he want to do that?"

"Henry killed Sally?"

"What?" Eric sounded shocked.

"I can't tell because Jake told me not to tell anyone." Dana gave a weak smile in Eric direction. "I need to sleep now."

"You sleep. And believe me this Henry guy isn't going to hurt you as long as I'm around." The last thing she remembered was Eric rubbing her head until her eyes remained closed.

# Chapter 80

No one noticed the black Chevy Impala parked two doors up. How could they with the big folding sunglasses propped up on the dash of the car window.

'It's like being in army fatigues hidden behind a blind spot. Even the cop sitting across from the house thinking no one notices him while he hides behind a book, can't see me. How, Mickey Mouse.'

"Peek-a-Boo,"

'I see you coming home Miss Dana, clinging off the cocky Doc. Well Doc, don't think I won't take you or anyone else out, who gets in the way of me getting the cash. This is going to be a long boring night'

The sound of an engine jumping to life resounded through the air disturbing the silence.

"Dammit I fell asleep." 'What the hell, is happening?' The mystery person watch, unnoticed.

"Ahh, did the big bad cop get tired of serving and protecting the innocent." The car occupants held up some opera binoculars Maybe, wondering what's going on in the bedroom at 3 a.m. is too much for you to handle." A low laugh sounded within the car.

'This town is a joke,' a gut wrenching laugh, escaped as the cop passed the car unaware of the occupant hiding behind the cardboard mask.

"Hey cop I see you. Can you see me?" 'You stupid ass, I'm sitting under the damn street light. How much easier do you want me to make it for you?'

The perfect camouflaged with peek-holes big enough to see everything but small enough to conceal a body hiding behind it.

"Just call me, Genius." The self-proclaimed Genius said as the officer drove away.

"Whoa, what are you up to Doc?" Genius questioned.

'Sneaking out of the house the minute the cop leaves his post. Well now might be a good time to tell you how this game is being played, Doc.' Genius though and was about to open the door.

"What the hell is that?" Movement behind a bush caught the eye of Genius just in time to stop from blowing their cover.

'Who are you? And why are you hiding in the bushes almost making me do a big f aux pas.' Questions kept running through the silent observers head. 'Why are you watching the Doc.'

"Interesting," Genius said. 'The moment Doc drives away this guy just shows-up out of no where.'

"I believe Miss Dana isn't the sweet innocent little girl she likes people to think she is."

'Well, well, if I had known it would get this exciting I would have brought popcorn.' Genius thought.

'I was beginning to think I made the long drive for nothing, now I get a show I can sit back and enjoy.'

# Chapter 81

Dana jolted awake to a room completely engulf in blackness. Easing her legs to the edge of the bed, she sat up and turned on the side light.

She cupped her pounding head between her hands.

"Aah," The vague recollection of Eric carrying her up the stairs to bed made her groan. She ran a finger across her lips. *'Did Eric really kiss me?' She questioned. 'Maybe I dreamt he did.'* She remembered pushing him away. *'Thank goodness. Maybe it upset him and he went home.'* Dana thought.

Slowly she stood and had to do a balancing act before making the trip to the washroom.

"No more beer and little green ones." She looked in the mirror at how rough her face looked. *'There has to be aspirin in here somewhere,'* she thought rummaging through the medicine cabinet. Giving up her search, she was about to head back to bed when a noise came from downstairs. Eric must still be here. *'He should have something hidden in his magic little case to handle a headache.'* She surmised.

"Eric, is that you?" She slid her hand along the wall as she descended the stairs. "Half way down she leaned her body forward to see. The place was in darkness, if he spent the night why would he sleep on the couch when the spare bedroom would be more comfortable.

"Eric," she called out again. Instead of answering, something hit the door. "What are you doing out there?" Dana felt her heart pounding in her chest. Switching the lamp on by the phone emitted a dim glow, then, she flicked the wall switch for the outside light.

"Typical, it's burnt out." She hesitated then remembered Jake's man sitting out in front of the house earlier.

Eric must have locked himself out, *'the door is opened,* she thought as she turned the handle and stared into darkness.

"Eric, answer me." Maybe he went to his car. She stepped out to check the driveway but the street light shone on an empty spot in the lane way.

"Eric," she whispered, the last thing she wanted was to wake her neighbours at three in the morning by calling out to a man who brought her home. That would be a great story to have to explain to her mother. Although, her mother would be more thrilled that Eric spend the night.

She couldn't wait until Henry was in jail, then all the people who looked at her like she had the plague tonight would understand her crazy behaviour.

His car was gone. He left her alone with the doors unlocked, *'if Eric went home, what or who banged on my door?'* Panic filled her. Looking across the street, she realized the officer had called it a night and left. She had to get back into the house. She jumped when the dim light from the hallway revealed a tall shadow blocking her entrance.

## Chapter 82

"Dana we need to talk." A moan escaped her at the familiar voice of Henry. Suddenly, she wished she would have gone and spent the night at Robert's house with her mother and Lindsay.

*'I can't let him know I'm frightened.'* She thought. He had to believe she was stronger than she looked.

"Henry you need to leave before Eric gets back." Maybe she could convenience him that Eric would be pulling into the laneway any minute now.

"Not until you tell me why you sent the cops after me?" He demanded. "I trusted you with something very personal," he slammed his fist against the side of the house.

"The police are questioning everyone from the apartment, about Sally's murder. Including me," Dana didn't know what else to say and moved back when Henry stepped towards her. She though about running but in her groggy state he would easily catch her.

"My father called and told me your buddy cop called and he's going to his house, tomorrow, to inquire about me and Sally's relationship." He came at her again. "You're the only one I told."

"I don't know what the police are doing." She backed away from him.

"Do you really think I killed Sally?" He questioned her.

"I don't know who did," Dana avoided making eye contact with him.

"Don't lie!" He raised his voice and Dana hoped it was loud enough to wake the neighbour. 'Where the hell, did the cop go whose suppose to be watching the house?' She thought unable to hold back tears. "You think I'm a killer. I see it in your eyes." Dana was afraid but took a deep breath.

She wouldn't go without a fight.

"Henry, go home."

"Why so you can call your buddy cop or your doctor boyfriend." He caught her off guard when he lunged at her and grabbed her arms between his fingers.

"Dana, you have to believe me, I loved Sally and would never do anything to hurt her. I want to find her killer more than anyone." His voice softened leaving her confused.

'No, I won't let him fool me, all the evidence points to him. His closeness to Sally and being the owner of the house where Tina was murdered, he is the killer.' Dana thought.

"The thing that hurts the most is that I finally told someone how much I loved Sally and now I might go to jail for it." He released his hold. "I don't even mind going to jail. What cuts me the most is everyone is going to think I'm the one who robbed her of her precious life." Dana stood in front of him with tears streaming down her cheeks as she listened to him. "I won't let that happen." Henry shoved her against the door.

A beam of light pulled into the laneway startling Henry.

"You're wrong," he shouted before he leaped from the porch clearing the steps, he fled into the darkness leaving her standing petrified.

Eric had her in his arms. "What the hell is going on here?" I go to get a coffee and come back to find some guy accosting you on your front step." Her legs felt like elastic so when Eric picked her up and brought her to the couch in the den, she could only cry. She had never been happier to see anyone in her life, as she was when Eric showed up.

"Henry was here." She managed to say.

"Did he hurt you?" Dana sat shaking her head. "I'm calling the cops right now." Eric grabbed the phone.

Caught up in the antic of Henry's attack on Dana, neither of them noticed a figure, someone they both knew, lurking in the shadows watching the scene unfold.

The lone figure didn't escape the eagle eyes of the "Genius".

"A round of applaud for the new guy," Genius gave a slow clapping of hands. *I couldn't have planned this out any better if I tried.* A slow laugh escaped as the star of the show fled in different direction with an unknown assailant in hot pursuit.

# Chapter 83

At exactly eight, they pulled up in front of the Nairn's house. Jake took his phone out and turned it off. He wanted nothing to interrupt this meeting.

"Business must be doing well." Thom commented as they pulled into the laneway off a large colonial style home, set back on a well, manicured yard stretched out to cover at least four acre that ended on a green belt.

"I wondered what happened with Henry. They live like kings and he rents a small one bedroom apartment." Jake rang the doorbell. "Quite the contrast compared to what he goes home to every night. It could be reason enough to be tick at the world." Jake stated.

"Maybe step mommy prefers not to have him around." Thom ran his fingers along the carvings in the oak doors.

"Fits the profile," Jake said as a watched through the bevelled glass as a distorted shadow approached.

"Detectives please come in. I'm Hank Nairn, my father is waiting in the den." No one needed to tell them the man answering the door was Henry's half brother, the resemblance was remarkable.

They walked into a large entrance, where a row of paintings from the group of seven stood out against antique white walls.

They followed him into a den where Sr. Narin sat in a high back leather chair in front of a wall of books. A fire tickled at logs piled tepee fashion in a brick fireplace. The only thing missing was a silk robe and Sherlock Holmes pipe.

"Thank you for coming detectives. I'm Dennis Nairn." He stood and held his hand out. "I have to admit that we were taken back to have the police contact us about Henry, especially without giving any details." He pointed to two chairs. "Please have a seat."

"Can I offer you a coffee?" Hank asked, they declined, and took their seats.

"After the call we've been trying to reach Henry but to no avail, has something happened to him?" Dennis asked. For a man who wasn't sure why the police were after his son, he appear strangely calm. *'It must be the Lawyer in him.' Jake decided.*

"No, but he is being investigated?" Jake said. Telling these two men that a member of their family was the prime suspect in at lease two murder cases would be difficult.

Jake's first image of Henry's family was to find a divided household living in a lower income district. Even when he heard, they were lawyers he thought they'd be the ambulance chasing type. He didn't expect to find a cohesive father and son team financially set.

After Henry's mother died, he may have felt abandoned and had to adjust to being dumped on by his father's other family. Jake wondered how Mrs. Nairn took to having the offspring of her husband's affair pushed on her. It may have been a constant reminder of her husband's infidelity, causing her to treat him poorly. The results-Henry's kills imagining the women to be his stepmother.

"Henry is a good boy, what are the accusations." Hank demanded.

Jake glanced over at his father grateful for his support before relating the details.

"Two women have been murder in Chiapas Falls over the last few months. Both of the girls have a connection to Henry." Jake said.

"And you think Henry did it." Hank stood up abruptly and defended his half brother.

"We have evidence that point to him as a suspect."

"If you're talking about Sally, Henry loved her and would never have hurt her. Any thoughts of him killing her are absurd."

"Hank, sit back down and let's listen to what they have to say." His father spoke in a stern but kind tone.

Jake found Hank a little too quick to jump to Henry's defence.

"Are you familiar with the house on Rose Blossom Lane in Chiapas Falls?" Jake questioned and waited as Dennis stared off as though travelling the road back to a more painful past.

# Chapter 84

"Is Henry in trouble?" An older woman, Jake suspected was Mrs. Nairn, entered the room, and stood behind Dennis placing her hands on his shoulders.

"They suspect he is involved in two murder cases and I'm sure it's a misunderstanding that we can clear up." Dennis responded to her question.

Jake's eyes locked with Dennis, "The questions could get personal." He watched Mrs. Nairn circle around the chair to sit beside her husband. Her face held a strong determination that told Jake she intended to remain by her husband's side.

"If you're referring to my husband's affair, I know all about it, detective." She smiled over at Dennis. "So please, ask anything you need to. We have no secrets in this family."

"You want to delve in my past to see if Henry has become a killer because you think he was traumatized in his youth?" Dennis asked.

"Talking to you might help us to eliminate your son as a suspect." Jake said, even though he didn't believe anything could change the facts.

"Nancy and I married very young." Dennis began letting out a sigh before continuing. "Work was scarce and shortly after the wedding I got scared, not knowing how to provide for a young bride." He looked at his wife with sorrow and love showing in his eyes.

"I've made some horrible mistakes." He spoke more for his wife's benefit.

"The blame lay as much on my shoulders as yours." Nancy assured him. He shook his head, before beginning.

"I abandoned my wife to look for work and ended up in Chiapas Falls as a hired hand for the Mullins." Jake's ears perked up at the mention of the Mullin name.

"Twice a week Edward Mullin would get me to drive him to his mistress' home, on Rose Blossom lane, so in answer to your question, I know the address quite well." He stopped long enough to pick up a glass of water.

After pressing it to his lips, he turned to his wife who still held his hand in hers. "I hate for you to have to hear this, my love." He said while stroking her hand.

"I didn't stay loyal to you, either. I ran back to my father's house like a spoilt brat. I can't remember how many times he turned you away from the door while I stood hidden at the top of the stairs allowing him to." She comforted him ignoring the fact that others were listening. Jake sat in amazement at the love and complete honesty these people openly displayed for each other and wondered how Henry fit in with the family.

"On one of the trips I met Alice, their illegitimate daughter. Not a lot of people knew of her existence, very seldom did she leave the home. It was as though she was their big secret.

Edward Mullin had a great love for Sylvia Weets, but apparently, their class of people look down on her social status.

They arranged for Edward to marry someone else, which he did but he never abandon his first love. When Sylvia got pregnant, he set her up in the home on Rose Blossom Lane for her to raise their daughter.

"Does Henry know he is related to the Mullins?" Jake asked.

"Like we said earlier, our family have no secrets." Dennis smiled up at his wife.

"I think the better question here would be do the Mullins know Henry is related?" Thom asked.

"I've never approached them about it. But, I suspect Mrs. Mullins knew where her husband hung his hat on the nights his side of the bed remained empty." Dennis said.

"Do you know if she is still alive?" Thom asked.

"Yes she is." Hank who remained silent while his father struggled with relating his past, answered.

"Thank you," Jake scribbled some notes on the page.

"I know this is hard on you, Mr. Nairn but please continue." Jake gently prodded.

"After a few trips to the Weets' home Alice and I started to spend time together. She was like a prisoner in the house, trapped away from the rest of the world, their hidden treasure. She was lonely and I was stupid. We ended up spending one night together." He looked at his wife who smiled and nodded at him.

"It's okay." She said.

"The next morning I felt so guilty I ran from the house and didn't stop until my feet landed in front of Nancy's door. This time, I stood up to her father and threaten to camp outside on their doorstep, until I heard from Nancy's own mouth, not to come back.

It took a few hours but he finally agreed and called her down to the den. I've never seen anything so beautiful, she face me with a swollen belly.

Three month later Hank made his entrance into the world. I will never forgive myself for running away like a coward instead of standing up to her father. How sad and frightening it must have been for you." He rubbed her hand between his.

"I was three months pregnant when you left. I never should have hidden it from you." She looked at him with tenderness and Jake peg this family as survivors.

"When did you find out about Henry?" Jake was curious to hear more, about their history. So far, there had been no, mentioned, as to how Henry fit in with this family.

# Chapter 85

"After Hank was born, Nancy and I went back to Chiapas Falls. I needed the money Mr. Mullins owed me. I told Edward about my wife and baby Henry. He was generous paying me three times my wage and told me to stay away from Chiapas Falls and his daughter. He threatened to tell Nancy about Alice and my affair. Afraid, I would lose her again I agreed. He never told me that Alice conceived a child." Dennis took a sip of his water before beginning his nightmare. Jake could tell the past still haunted him.

"He told Alice after we left about my wife and baby and when she gave birth she named the boy Henry after Hank.

"She never told us why she did and we never asked." Nancy filled in the small detail before Dennis continued.

"We didn't find out about Henry until six years later. With the money, I received from Edward I went back to school and studied law. Thanks to Edward Mullins I now run my own law firm."

'*At least Henry would have good counsel behind him. So you need to advise your son to give himself up,*' Jake though.

"I was on a business trip when Alice showed up at the door." Dennis went on to relate the tale.

Dennis stopped to take another sip of water and Nancy took over for him.

"I have to admit that, when I first opened the door to this frail beautiful woman standing there with a shy, timid little boy who resembled my husband more than my own son, I was shocked and furious. No one had to tell me that Dennis was the father. I also knew how to count and figured out that it had to have been around the time we were separate.

Something about the girl touched me. Her eyes were dark and lifeless. I invited them in and called my Henry down to play with the scared little boy who clung to his mother's skirt. I couldn't believe it when my Henry asked the child his name and he spurted out that his mother called him Henry. I don't know why but when I looked down at the little thing my heart ached for them so I turned to my Henry and said I guess we'll just have to call you Hank. Without even a second thought, he turned to face little Henry and said, you can call me Hank. Then they ran off to play." She smiled at her son before continuing.

"Once they were gone I took Alice into the den and she started talking and by the time she finished tears were streaming down my cheeks." She pulled a tissue from a box on the end table and dabbed her eyes at the memory.

"She was so strong and I envied her courage. It wasn't easy for her to come and face me. To this day, we probably wouldn't know Henry existed if it weren't for her health. Alice was ill and dying from cancer with only had a few months to live. She did what any mother would have done for her son." She sighed before beginning. "We moved them in with us and Alice and I became good friends. Dennis and I held her hand until the end." Nancy dried her eyes again as Dennis rubbed a gentle hand across her back.

"So the boy stayed with you after his mother died?" Jake confirmed.

"At first we feared that Ms. Weets would demand to have little Henry, Alice had papers drawn up giving custody to Dennis and me. She also had a will stating she wanted Henry raised by his father.

The funeral was held here but Mrs. Weets took Alice's body back home and buried her there." Dennis said and Jake could tell the memory pained both of them.

Jake's admiration for Nancy Nairn grew the more she related how she met her husband illicit son.

"Did she fight you for the boy?" Thom asked.

"No, she did the complete opposite. At the funeral, Ms. Weets approached me. She complained about being too old to handle a child especially a rambunctious boy of seven. Before I could say anything, she placed an envelope in my hands. She gave a very generous amount in the form of a cheque." Dennis said.

"Dennis told her to keep the money and that he would take care of his son. She insisted saying it was her daughter's inheritance and it now belonged to the boy." Nancy backed up her husband.

Jake scanned the room, remembering how Henry lived compared to the mansion his stepbrother resided in.

'That would explain the life style,' Jake thought, losing some of his admiration wondering if they had him leave with nothing once he got old enough to fend for himself.

"It's not what you think." Hank finally spoke up as though he read Jake's mind. "I see you looking around my home. I worked hard to finish school and earned everything I own." He looked at Jake and Thom with pride.

"I don't understand." Jake said. "Why is Henry living in a small apartment?" Hank let out a laugh and Jake sat back waiting to hear what he found so funny about his question.

"Henry is a free spirit. He has as much education as I do if not more. Job offers poured in even before he received his diploma, but none of them interested him, the idea of being lock up behind a desk never appeal to my brother. His education only took a small portion of the money Ms. Weets left him. The rest sat in the bank building interest."

"You didn't use it to help the family?" Jake asked. The more he listened, the more respect he felt for these people.

"No." Dennis sounded determined. "That money belonged to Henry. "Many things were sacrificed to give Hank the same education, but not Henry's money." Dennis drew in a breath before he began again almost as though he wasn't sure if he should divulge the next bit of information. "After Edward died he left Henry a small fortune which we also put aside for him in a trust account." Dennis said and Hank cut in.

"His fortune increased just a few months ago when Ms. Weets left him the house and fortune she had. Henry is a very wealthy young man, who knows how to invest." Hank stood and paced the floor looking offended.

"Just because he prefers not to flash his wealth doesn't mean he isn't a part of this family. He's my blood brother and best friend, and I assure you that you're absolutely on the wrong track if you think he had anything to do with Sally's murder or anyone else's. He loved Sally." Hank defended his half brother.

"He shared the same apartment building with Sally and her new boyfriend. If he loved her so much seeing them together may have been very stressful." Thom stated.

"He also hid the fact that he knew Sally from the police and the second victim was discovered in the home he inherited." Jake knew his words, impacted Henry's family. Hank sat back down slowly dropping his head in his hands while Nancy gasped. Dennis stood up and looked Jake straight in his eyes.

"I know it looks bad detective but I know my son is innocent and would never hurt anyone, let alone murder them. Has he been arrested, yet?"

"We haven't been able to locate him do you know where he is?"

"No we don't."

"You know it will look better on him if he comes to us." Jake said. He had a hard time believing they didn't know Henry's location, and wondered if Henry might be hiding in the house listening to them right now.

He doubted these people would be that careless to stow away a murder suspect.

"You should be looking at Old Lady Mullins she had more motive than Henry." Hank said. "Her husband had a child with his lover, the woman he would have preferred to marry. Maybe she wanted the house and did it to deter people from buying it. I wouldn't put it past her to have Sally killed. It would benefit her in two ways." Hank gave Jake a defiant look.

"How is that?" Jake questioned curious with the answer.

"She could get back at Old Lady Weets by having her grandson's girlfriend killed and it brought business to the funeral home." Hank sat down and folded his arms across his chest.

"Are you suggesting that the Mullins go around killing people to keep the business going?" Jake though the idea ludicrous, but couldn't afford not to listen, no matter how far fetched they were.

"Hold on, no one is accusing anyone of such a crime." Dennis stood up and pointed a finger at his son to be quiet.

"Henry is a caring boy and would never do anything to harm anyone, and I'm sure once you get all the evidence together it will prove him innocent."

"That's why we're investigating every angle, including the Mullins." Jake jotted a note to follow up with the Mullins when he got back.

"We've taken enough of your time." Thom said.

"If you do talk to Henry, tell him to report to the nearest police station." All three stood and followed Jake and Thom to the door. "One more thing, another woman received a call saying she is next." Jake stared at them wondering if they were pulling something over on them. "If it is Henry, I will stop him."

Jake and Thom left the house with more information than they counted on getting, leaving Jake anxious to talk to the Mullins.

# Chapter 86

If nothing else, the Nairn's put on a good front. They were a good solid, tight knit, family with no secrets, '*almost too perfect.*' Jake thought as he pulled into a Truck Stop. '*I need to read my notes again and maybe grab a sandwich.*'

The restaurant was pack with truckers, at first Jake wasn't sure he would get a seat until a cheery young girl approached.

"Just you, honey?" She picked up a menu from a podium standing at the entrance to welcome guest.

"Yes, thanks," He never understood why some women felt it necessary to call complete strangers, honey.

Maybe, he equated it to Helen who finally got the message and stopped once he set her straight at the station.

He followed the girl to a table in the back.

"Will this do Hun?" He considered asking her to stop referring to him as Hun or honey but decided the time and energy wasted to explain wouldn't be worth it. Instead, he just nodded and took a seat. Looking around he thought the term probably landed her lots of tips.

"I'll have a chicken salad sandwich and ice tea." He placed his order before she could run to another table.

"So, you won't need this?" She chuckled and tucked the menu under her arm.

He immediately took out his notes and appreciated it when she quietly, placed his order in front of him ten minutes later.

'*What am I not seeing here? Sally, Dana and Henry shared separate apartments* in the same building. I can see Henry killing Sally because he got tired of seeing her with Phil. Could I be running with the wrong ball. What if Phil put things together about Sally's secret past, and confronted her about it then killed her out of anger. The only problem is how does Dana fit in with the triangle?' Jake thought.

'The killer said Sally died for her. Somehow, Sally got in the way. The girls looked like twins, especially in the dark and she parked in Dana's spot in an identical car. Mistaken identity, the killer believed Sally was Dana. It's the only thing that makes sense. So what is the connection between Dana and Henry? I need to talk to Phil again.' Jake thought.

He was about to close the book when Ralph Reed's name jumped out at him, he jotted it down as a side note. The estranged uncle who died in an accident only weeks before his brother dies, 'could it be coincidental.'

It was only a shot-in-the-dark, but maybe the hospital wasn't where things started for Dana, only she didn't realize it.

'The uncle lived in Toronto, where the first killings began.' Jake thought as, he flipped his note pad shut and reached for his phone.

"Dammit," he said when he realized it went dead. He got too reliant on using the phone at his parents and neglected to charge the thing.

Throwing a ten dollar, bill, on the table he headed out to the pay phone.

"Hi mom is Dad there?" He asked as soon as she picked up.

"Yes dear, he's just gathering a few more things for his suitcase. Is everything okay?" She asked.

"Yes, I just need to talk to him for a minute." He could hear her calling out to his father.

"He'll be right here. Oh, by the way a fellow named Bill has been trying to reach you all morning. He said to tell you to turn your phone on."

"Thanks Mom, I'll call him when I'm done with Dad." Jake found himself getting irritated and knew it came across in his tone to his mother.

"Alright dear, he's on his way."

"What's up son?" His father's voice came through.

"Did you talk to Bill?" Jake asked.

"No, he called when we were out."

"I'll call after I hang up. I need you to do something for me before you leave."

"Sure, what is it?"

"I stopped to look at my notes and Dana had an uncle, Ralph Reed, who lived in Whitby. He died in a car accident about two weeks before her father died. Can you dig into it a little before you come down?" Jake expected it would be a wild goose chase but would feel better knowing he checked it out.

"I'll get on it right away. Your mother's going to be a little disappointed because I don't think we'll be able to leave tonight, like we planned, but we can be on the road tomorrow."

"Thanks dad, and tell mom I'll make it up to her with a trip down town."

"She'll like that son. See you tomorrow."

# Chapter 87

"Chiapas police station, how can I direct your call?" Lois' cherry voice rang through the line.

"Good afternoon Lois, can you put me through to the Sergeant?" Jake asked knowing Bill's would be home sleeping by now.

"Sure, I can do that." She said and hold music started playing.

"Jake, I've been trying to reach you since this morning."

"My phone went dead. What's going on?"

"The prints came back from the house the Real Estate girl got murdered at and they belong to Henry."

"It's his house, so it's not enough to make an arrest."

"Well, the fact that he attacked Miss Reed at her home early this morning should count for something."

"What the hell happened? Wayne should have been out front watching the house." Jake demanded.

"He was and left around three in the morning." Sergeant stated.

"Why didn't he stay and do his job?" Jake was furious.

"Calm down Jake, Wayne did his job. He stayed even after her doctor boyfriend drove her home. At 3 a.m. he figured she was safely, tuck in bed with the boyfriend.

The idea of Eric next to Dana holding her left a dull ache in his stomach. He quickly shrugged if off. He knew all along that Dana and Eric would end up together. He just hated that the inevitable didn't wait until after the case was closed and they went their separate ways.  The fact, that, he had allowed his feelings for Dana to grow disgusted him even more.

"Is Ms. Reed alright?" Jake asked in a calmer manner.

"A little shook up but the doc gave her a pill then drove her back home. He said he is going to stay with her. I told him to call if he has to leave and I'll send one of the guys back over to watch the house."

"Thanks, I should be there in about an hour." Jake hung up the phone, with the image of Eric's arms wrapped around Dana supporting her at a very vulnerable time for her. It only made him more determined to put this case behind him.

# Chapter 88

It didn't take much for Thom to pull up the information on the accident that killed Dana's uncle. With a little digging, he found himself standing in front of a cozy brick bungalow ringing the doorbell.

"Hello, are you Margaret Lewis?" He questioned a woman in her mid fifties who opened the door.

She looked as though she had been expecting him. Her hair was perfectly styled and the dress had a snug fit over a well, maintained figure. She was beautiful. *'If anyone dropped by his house without notice, they would find Lila dressed down with garden dirt somewhere on her clothing.'* Thom chuckled to himself at the image of his wife.

"Yes who is asking?" She stared at him with sunken eyes.

"I'm Thom Turner, a detective." He flashed an I.D. badge.

"I was hoping I could ask you a few questions about Mr. Reed."

"Are you with the police department?" She looked at him suspiciously.

"I'm retired a little over a year ago. Now, I have a private practice, occasionally I get called in by the police to help out with a few cases." Thom felt he was intruding on this woman and wanted to get this over quickly. "Do you mind if I come in for a minute. You can call the station to confirm my identity first, if you like." He suggested. She stared him up and down as though considering his offer to do a reference check. He prepared himself to stand on the stoop until she returned but she suddenly pulled the door back for him to enter.

"It's cold out and you look honest." She said and moved to the side for him to pass by. He sniffed in the sweet sent of perfume as he stepped past her.

"Thank you."

"Please have a seat." She offered and he waited for her to sit.

"Thank you I appreciate you taking the time to see me." He sat and looked around a well, maintained cozy den.

"I don't know what else I can tell you that I haven't already told the police." Her eyes saddened at the mentioned of Ralph Reed.

"It must be difficult for you. The file said you were dating when Mr. Reed had the accident."

"Ralph and I were engaged, dating sounds so childish." She chuckled.

"I'm sorry for your loss."

"It's not your fault." Thom picked up a hint of anger in her tone but he couldn't blame her. He would be upset if Lila had been stolen from him by an accident. He looked over at a picture of her posing with two younger people. Standing beside one of her and an older man he assumed was Ralph.

"Are these your children?" Thom asked picking the frame up to get a closer look.

"Yes, I was married before and he died of a heart attack twenty years ago. The children, they have grown up and gone their own separate ways, my son moved to the States somewhere and my daughter is in Ottawa with her husband. Its funny how things go, you spend most of your life raising them and they grow up and forget you exist." She stood and took the picture from Phil and rubbed her fingers over the glass.

'*No wonder her eyes hold a hint of sorrow, everyone in her life abandon her, either through death or running away.*' Thom thought.

"Can you explain the accident to me?" Thom reeled the conversation back to the reason he was there.

"Not really, apparently he had a few drinks and he ran into a tree while trying to make his way home." She gave a slight sigh and put the picture of her and the kids back on the side table. "Did something come up about his death?" She stared across at him.

"No, I'm just here to tie up a few loose ends." He assured her.

"That's good. I don't think I'm strong enough to rehash that nightmare of his death again." She adjusted a doily on the table before she looked up at Thom with tears in her eyes. "Our wedding date was set for next month. It hasn't been easy for me." She picked up a glass of water she had sitting on the end table and took sip. "We were going to get married in St. Joseph's church. Instead, I had to hold his funeral there." She dabbed her eyes with a tissue.

"I'm sorry it must be very hard on you." Thom sympathized with her situation. "Maybe you should try calling your kids.

Thinking of her kids made him appreciate Jake he would never block his mother out of his life.

"Yes, maybe they will return the call this time." She said and stared off.

"Thank you for you time." He stood up not sure what Jake expected him to find here but from his point of view it was a dead end.

"Thank you for coming detective." She held the door for him.

"If you have any questions please don't hesitate to call the station. There is always a detective there who can answer any questions you have."

"I will." She smiled at him and closed the door once he reached his car.

# Chapter 89

Phil had been stalking Henry every since Sally spilled her guts about their great love affair. It killed him to know they shared that secret. Sally betrayed him, Phil wondered how many times she lied to him saying she was doing a laundry when all the while the snuck into Henry's place across from the machines. *'How convenient,'* Phil thought as he watched Henry lurking around Dana's place so late. The two of them deserved each other. Phil strained to hear what they were fighting about on her porch.

*'She probably found out you were playing both her and Sally and moved on to the fancy car guy. I hope it hurt because you need to pay like Sally did.'*

From what Phil could see Henry was playing the Casanova to all sorts of women.

Watching them now, he could see Dana seems to be the one who gets under his skin the most, the one that would hurt Henry more if she died.

Henry would have to pay first. Phil jumped back behind the tree as the coward Henry ran past him when the car light flashed on him. *'The new boyfriend to the rescue,'* Phil thought as he chased after Henry.

He followed Henry back to the apartment. There was no turning back now, Phil thought as he banged on Henry's door and waited for him to open it.

"What do you want?" Henry questioned.

Phil pulled back his arm and landed a fist at the side of Henry's head.

"Sally's dead because of you." He screamed and lunged at Henry.

"You're crazy." Henry moved and shoved Phil to the ground and ran up the stairs. Mr. Walters and a few of the neighbours must have heard the commotion. He almost ran into them at the top of the stairs.

"He confessed to killing Sally and the other woman and Dana's next." Phil was yelling as he came after Henry.

Henry didn't waste any time, he fled out the door towards the woods.

# Chapter 90

The police station was in turmoil when Jake arrived. The last few months have played havoc on the small precinct. The place teemed with every officer available for miles around plus most of the towns occupants, everyone desperate to capture the killer, regardless of guilt.

"What's going on Wayne?" Jake questioned the first officer he met in the lot.

"Sergeant called every man available and enlisted a group of civilians. He wants to get this Henry guy before it gets dark.

"Do we know where he is?"

"I heard he was at the apartments of highway ten."

"So he went back home after accosting Miss Reed." Jake was tempted to remark on Wayne's inability to stick it out at the house. He opted not to go there with him.

"He's inside briefing everyone." Jake thought pulling the locals in was a bit much but not his call.

Jake entered the building to find Sergeant Timmons standing in front of a group of about thirty men that Jake would describe more as a mob of angry citizens. Jake recognized some from the force in another county.

"Remember to stay in groups of three's and report any findings to one of the officers." He slapped a rolled up paper in his hands. "Officer Williams, here, is in charge when you are out searching through the woods, he will be accompanied by officer's Tyler and Conroy. You'll follow their lead." He nodded at Jake when he saw him come in. "Keep in mind, that the boy will have a trial so don't take matters into your own hands, otherwise you may be charged." Sergeant threatened, than turned to the tall young man beside him. "It's all yours Williams."

"Thank you sir," he said before rallying the men outside to the parking lot. Jake waited until the room cleared before approaching the Sergeant.

"What makes you think he's hiding in the woods?" Jake asked.

"A call came in from the Landlord saying the first girl's boyfriend, Phil and Henry went cuffs to fist and Henry confessed to killing the two girls and even said Miss Reed is next."

"His father is a lawyer in Toronto. I'm going to place a quick call to him and then I want to check out another lead.

"Hopefully the father can make it here before they bring him in. What's the lead you have?"

"Mrs. Mullins, while in Toronto I discovered some interesting things.

"Like what?"

"That Henry is the grandson of Edwards Mullins from an affair he had with the Weets woman."

"The same Weets woman, they found the dead real estate girl?" He questioned.

"And that's not all."

"What else is there?" Sergeant gave Jake a look.

"The Weets woman had an affair with Mr. Mullins and produced a child and she gave birth to a son. Can you guess who the grandson is."

"Are you kidding?" He looked at Jake as though he wasn't sure he heard him right.

"I wouldn't kid about that, Henry is the grandson." Jake confirmed. "So I'm going to take a ride over to there." Jake suggested.

"That's crazy. Did you want to take someone with you?"

"No, I won't be long." Jake said.

"I'll call if anything changes here."

"Thanks." Jake said nodding to Helen who gave him a sheepish smile, on his way out.

Before driving away, he placed call to Dennis Nairn.

# Chapter 91

Jake pulled into a large circular driveway in front of an old colonial home about ten blocks from the Weets home. '*Old man Mullins liked to keep his women close*.' Jake thought.

The house made the one the Weets woman lived in look like a miniature, '*the price of being a mistress instead of the wife*,' Jake guessed.

He had to wait several minutes before anyone answered the door.

"Can I help you?"

Jake immediately recognized Edgar Mullins and flashed his badge. His facial expression remained empty as though he were greeting a mourner at the funeral home.

"I'm detective Turner." Jake introduced himself. "I'm hoping I could speak with your mother." Jake stated.

"May I inquire what this is about?" Even though he maintained his professional tone, Jake noticed tiny beads of sweat formed on his forehead.

For a moment, Edgar hesitated staring at Jake as though contemplating his next move. Until he pulled the door back, Jake wonder if Edgar Mullins was going to turned him away.

"She's in the den, please follow me." He stated and Jake followed him down a long hallway past a parlour to a den.

A frail looking, Mrs. Mullins sat prim and proper in a high wing back chair watching the news with a picture of Henry on display. When they walked in Simon Mullins immediately turned the sound down.

The resemblance of the two brothers was uncanny, without the moustache Simon had, no one would be able to tell which one they were speaking too.

"Mother, this is detective Turner. He would like to have a word with you." Edgar announced him.

"Please, have a seat." She pointed a boney finger to a chair, and the brothers waited for him to sit, before they followed suit. There was an eerie calmness in the room, almost as though, they expected him.

With a brother sitting on either side of their mother, like hawks waiting to swoop in at the first sign of harassment, Jake wasn't sure where to begin his questioning.

"Are you here about the boy, Henry?" Mrs. Mullins easily took the lead speaking with an air of authority.

"Yes." Jake answered with a nod of his head.

"You're good detective." She smiled over at him. "I thought it would take some time before anyone connected Henry to our family."

Jake watched her closely to see if he could spot any signs of resentment when she mentioned Henry, but her expressions were blank, something, he assumed was a trait learned in their line of business.

"I spoke with Dennis Nairn yesterday." Jake said. He detected a slight reaction from her when he mentioned the name.

"I'm sure he filled you in on everything and there is nothing more I have to add." She gave a cold stare in his direction. "So what is the purpose of your visit Detective?"

"Has Henry tried to contact you?" Jake asked.

"Do you think we would harbour a criminal?" She demanded then sat back while her lips curved up into a slight smile. "Or do you think that I feel some kind of kinship with the boy because he is the product of my husband's affair?"

"Truthfully I wasn't sure what to expect." Jake watched this small frame woman before him thinking she was anything but frail.

"Did you come here to rub my father's indiscretions in our faces?" Before Jake could answer, the old woman raised a hand to him.

"Edgar, mind your manners." She cautioned and he took a tissue out of his pocket and dabbed at his forehead. *'Why is Edgar sweating so much?'* Jake wondered if Henry made his way here and his unannounced visit was unnerving Edgar causing him to sweat. If that were the case the band of men chasing through the woods were on a wild goose chase.

"I have no ties to Henry, and I am also not a woman who lives a petty life where I would resent a child who has no control over how he entered into this world."

The similarities between the two families were uncanny. Tight knit with no secrets, *'I bet a little bit of digging would product some deep, rooted secrets.'* Jake thought.

"I see you are keeping up with the events surrounding Henry." Jake pointed to the television and decided to ask a loaded question. "Do you think he killed Sally?"

"He has Mullins blood running in his veins and one thing for sure is we would never do harm to another being." She looked at her two sons who sat silently by her side. "It's the complete opposite. We do everything possible to ensure people are treated with the every bit of respect due to them after they have passed on."

"I appreciate the work you and your sons do. But a lot of things point to Henry's guilt." Jake was surprise at how she mimicked the Nairns in her willingness to defend Henry. When he left the Nairn's home, he was sure he would meet a cold callous old woman who would be anxious to put Henry behind bars.

"Have you ever met Henry?" Jake ventured a guess.

"He helps out at the home every once in a while. Although he doesn't have to because Edward left him a substantial amount of money." She stated.

"Does that bother you?" Jake asked thinking that solved Dana's mystery person in the tower.

"Even if it did, Detective, I am an old woman, and don't have the strength or stamina to kill anyone." She pointed around the room. "Besides, the family has more than enough."

"Does it bother you two?"

"We are not lacking anything." Simon spoke for both of them while Edgar continued to sweat. "We have nothing against him."

"The boy didn't ask to be born through a linage of unfaithful, men. Mrs. Mullins cut in. 'She *obviously knows about Dennis Nairn's affairs as well.*'

"Who made the first contact?" Jake asked.

"When, he first discovered who his Grandfather was he contacted us." Her lips pressed into a slight smile. "He is a persistent lad, determined to bond with his blood roots." She reached over to a small round table and gently took hold of a small black box. "He comes by a few times a year and never misses my birthday." She opened the lid to a soothing melody. "I turned the page of another year in my life recently and this is the gift he brought me."

No one had to tell Jake that the box was the one Dana saw Henry with when he confessed his love for Sally.

"Would you mind if I take it with me." Jake asked.

"Heaven, what for?"

"As you can see Henry is suspect in the murder of two women." He pointed to the television. "I believe this music box was stolen from another woman's car and could implement Henry."

"Hog-wash, Henry wouldn't hurt a fly. Take it if you must but I insist you return it once it served your purpose."

"Absolutely," Jake said unsure he would be able to keep the promise.

"I'll get you a case to put it in." Edgar offered to take the item into another room.

"If you don't mind, I'll keep it here while you get the case. Edgar nodded and left.

"If Henry contacts you, I would appreciate it if you call me immediately." Jake handed his business card to her.

"We don't harbour fugitives." She sat with lips pressed together with determination. "You're wrong detective, Henry is innocent." She said with conviction.

Edgar returned with a small container and Jake carefully placed the music box into it.

"Thank you." Jake said and Edgar went to show him out.

"Mullins is a good strong name in this community, detective. A situation like this could cause a lot of useless gossip if it were to leak out." Mrs Mullins stopped him before he could leave the room. "We would appreciation if you will handle it with discretion."

"The best way to ensure discretion is to have Henry turn himself in if he does show up here." Jake said not so sure he wasn't already stowed away in one of the rooms already." Jake hoped they would heed his words as both Simon and Edgar walked him to the door.

## Chapter 92

Robert had been away for a week, next year Eric could make the trip to the convention. His house felt strange to him when he unlocked the door and stood in the entrance. Lindsay's car was in the driveway when the cab dropped him off, but the place looked deserted. He should have called and told her he'd be home early but wanted to surprise her.

Setting his bags down, he headed to the kitchen. Except for the tell tale signs of a massive tea party, Lindsay and his mother had last night, the place was quiet.

He smiled at the image of Lindsay and his mother having a girl's night and wondered if Dana showed up. *'I doubt it.'* He thought.

They must have gone to bed late because Lindsay left everything out on the counter. Robert reached for a croissant and pulled his hand away quickly as it rubbed against the kettle. *'It's still hot someone must be up.'* Robert massaged his knuckles.

He took the stairs two at a time, anxious to see his wife.

Passing the room his mother spent the night in, he was surprised to see Lindsay sitting on the side of her bed.

"Please, mom, drink this, you'll feel better." Lindsay held a cup to his mother's lips.

"Lindsay's, what's the matter?" Robert rushed in. He definitely surprised his wife, who nearly dropped the mug.

"I found her in the bathroom this morning being ill. She doesn't look too good. I phoned the hospital and left a message for Eric."

"Lindsay, get my bag by the door." Robert ordered trying to keep the situation calm.

"Mom, where does it hurt?" He asked, placing a hand on her forehead. She was burning up and could hardly speak as she slowly ran her hand over her stomach.

"My stomach," she whispered."

"I'm going to get you to the hospital." Robert grabbed the phone and dialled 911.

In less then twenty minutes he helped the nurses to settle his mother into a private room.

Lindsay quietly took a seat beside the bed and sat with tears rolling down her cheeks.

"We had such a fun night." She watched Robert draw three vials of blood while a nurse hooked up an IV.

"I know sweet heart she's going to be okay." Robert reached and patted her hand. "Honey, I'm going to see if I can reach Eric, will you be okay with Mom?" Robert was furious. Eric told him she had eaten some bad food mixed with a viral infection that he was treating. *'From the looks of Mom, he is obviously wrong.'* Jake thought.

"I'll take care of her until you get back," Lindsay grabbed hold of Nancy's hand. Robert gave Lindsay a reassuring smile before turning to the nurse.

"Get these samples to the lab immediately." Robert scribbled some things down on a paper and handed it to the nurse. "I want results within an hour." He said then ran out of the room.

"Where the hell, is Eric?" He questioned as he rushed the stairs up to their adjoining offices. 'He told me he had things under control.' Sometimes, it takes a second pair of eyes to check over the results.

'I should have taken her illness more seriously and followed up more with Eric. It's my own fault, I allowed her to push me away as her doctor.' Robert beat himself up. He foolishly attributed all her symptoms to mourning the loss of her husband. 'Mom wonders where Dana gets her stubborn streak.' Robert pushed opened the stairwell doors. 'Well it stops right now, I'm taking control.' Jake determined.

# Chapter 93

"Damn it" Eric rummaged through the cupboards for the second time since he tucked Dana into bed with another pill.

*'What is with this family? They have millions dropped in their laps and they act as though it's nothing.'* Either they don't know about the money yet or fear of what to do with it is holding them back from using it.

*'I will find it even if it means killing the whole family off.'*

*'It all depends on you baby sister.'* Eric thought when the floor, boards creaked above him.

His plan is working out better then he expected. Who would have thought the girl he strangled off by mistake would have a secret.

The memory of hearing cries for mercy slip from her lips with her last breath excited him. Sally wasn't his first. No, although it had been ten years ago, he would never forget, his first, beautiful Alisha. In the beginning, she reminded him so much of his mother, it could only end in her death.

The other five girls were to fill a desire, that can't be filled. There would have been more but the cops got too close, so he went to school to keep himself occupied. It worked until now. *'How did I last so long without killing?'*

Tina was a self, indulgent killing. He couldn't resist the milky smooth neck and the instant flash of fear in her eyes when he confessed the murder of Sally. *'She knew her time was up.'*

He looked up at the television again to see a shot of Henry's face pasted beside Sally. Ex lover tired of seeing girl with new boyfriend.

"Dam, she looks identical to Dana." Eric surmised again. "I can't tell how much you scared the hell out of me when I spotted you at the funeral home struggling with your key." *'You had me believing in ghost, but I bet you were scared more when you caught me spying on you from the towers.'* Eric chuckled as he remembered the first time he saw Dana after he thought he killed her.

*'Well plans have changed, thanks to Henry.'* Eric quickly looked around him and pulled a bottle of Riesling from a small wine rack that sat on the counter.

"All you have to do is say yes. Maybe, I'll let you live long enough to tell me where the money is hidden." He laughed and headed up to Dana's room. "Then we'll have a very sad case of genocide when our poor local Doctor and his spoilt wife end their time on this earth with a terrible accident like Uncle."

From the frantic message Lindsay left him, he was sure Mother Reed would be dead by nightfall.

"Being the grieving best friend I will have to flee this hell hold of a town. There is no one who won't understand."

# Chapter 94

Robert intended to give Eric a blast the moment he laid eyes on him. He wasted time trying to reach him at his home and even called his mother's place to see if he was with Dana, but there was no answer there either. "Why does he have his phone turned off?"

He pushed his chair back determined to make sense of everything and get things back into perspectives.

He fumbled around with his key and unlocked the locker holding the spares for both their offices. He had to get to his mother's file. The key to his office was hanging there but the one to open Eric's door was missing.

"Where the hell did it go?" Robert cursed.

With a quick glance at his watch, he realized it would be too early for the lab to have the results yet. He planned his next steps, heading down the hall to the elevator he stopped at the nurse's station.

"Judy has Dr. Rycker called in today?"

"Sorry Dr. Reed he hasn't."

"Please page me if he calls in."

"Certainly, Dr. Reed, is every thing alright?"

"No my mother is ill and he has been treating her so I really need to speak to him."

"The moment he calls I'll let you know."

"Thank you Judy," Robert said and hurried to the elevators to check on his mother. After a quick stop, he would root himself in the lab until they gave him the results. Without them, he was helpless to know what treatment to start.

He found Lindsay in the room still holding his mother's hand. He loved her loyalty to his mother, *'I need to take her away for a while when things get settle here.'* He promised.

He considered himself, fortunate to have found Lindsay, and wondered if her relationship with his mother filled a void for her. Losing her mother to cancer at a young age and then to have an uncaring father abandon her to a sick aunt was hard on her. Yet his wife turned out with the kindest heart he ever knew.

"She's sleeping now." Lindsay whispered through tears.

"You okay?" Robert stood behind Lindsay and messaged her shoulders.

"It's not me who has to be better." Lindsay wiped at some tears. Robert pulled a chair up beside her.

"I'm going to find out what's wrong and make her better." Robert promised and kissed her hand." He reached up and adjusted the saline solution.

"I know you will because you're the best doctor around." She attempted a smile but he could see fear in her eyes. It really showed him how real, her feeling were for this family.

"Have I told you lately how much I love you?"

"You're always telling me." She smiled between tears.

"Good, and I'm sure my sister will change too." Robert said.

"Dana's coming around." She managed to smile, "we had a girl's day out shopping and then had a late dinner and shared a bottle of wine. We actually laughed a lot."

"You didn't tell me that." Robert smiled at her.

"I wanted see how it went first so I could surprised you with the details when you got home. If it didn't go well I wouldn't have said anything. She actually opened up and we had fun together." She gave a half laugh.

"You're so sweet it would be hard for anyone not to fall in love with you." Robert kissed her. "Will you be okay here while I run to the lab?"

"Of course, I will."

"I won't be long." Robert checked the IV and his mother's pulse before leaving.

The pale greyish tint had left her and a slight rosy colour showed on her cheeks. He smiled at Lindsay. "She's going to be fine." He said and left.

# Chapter 95

A young girl looked up when Robert entered the lab.

"Hello Doctor. I'm just logging the results here."

"Thank you for rushing them."

"No problem, but something doesn't look right to me."

"What do you mean?" Robert stood over her. She pointed to the last entry on the page.

"Traces of poison," Robert read the results. "It is only small amounts but enough to eventually kill her, if not treated soon."

"Poison," Robert said a little louder than necessary and took the log from her.

"Yes, it looks like a common rat poison." She paused and looked up at him. "But Doctor, I'm not talking about the poison when I say something doesn't add up."

Robert turned to her unsure what could be worst.

"Explain to me what doesn't add up."

She pulled the book back to her and flipped the pages to a few weeks earlier.

"Doctor Rycker brought these samples and told me to make sure we did a through checked because it was your mother." She pointed to the results.

At first, Robert wasn't sure what she was getting at until she pointed to the page.

"Look here." She sounded almost annoyed with him for not seeing what she obviously found clear. "This is the sample you gave me this morning." She showed him the last entry she just added again.

"Okay." He said, wishing she would make her point, so he could start treatment.

"Now here are samples Eric submitted for your mother a few weeks ago."

She turned the pages to the first entry. "This is the first one he submitted." She took a deep breath and sighed before she began again. "I have this quirky little thing I like to do whenever a Doctor's family member needs blood tested." She looked a little embarrassed as she confessed. "I track the samples," She pointed to the one she logged. "I tag it with your initials, DRRM#603 it stand for Doctor Robert Reed Mother office #603, in case there is more than one Doctor with the same initials." She showed him the other entries and they were tagged the same."

"Interesting," Robert said realized how young she was.

"It doesn't always work because I don't always know if the sample belongs to a Doctor's family member, unless they tell me, or if another nurse is on duty when the sample is brought in." She smiled at him. "Doctor Rycker made it very clear that we had to be through with your mother's sample."

"I'm very busy so why don't we quit the guessing game and you tell me what you're seeing." Robert asked a bit perturbed with the girls rambling.

"I'm sorry, but the samples are from different women." She gave him a smug look.

"What," he frantically flipped the pages. "Could it be a mix up?" Robert questioned finally seeing what she was getting at.

"I asked that too, so I checked back a bit further and there were five samples taken. I can see maybe, someone logging it wrong once but all five are from different women, none of them match, the only similarities are that the women are about the same age."

"That has to be a mistake." Robert picked up the ledgers and examined them. She was right, the blood type didn't match.

Numbness started to crawl over Robert's skin. *'What the hell is Eric up to?'* He questioned.

"I need to look into this some more." He realized how much he didn't know Eric, and if he was up to no good Robert didn't want anything to tip him off.

"I understand." She gave Robert a smile that showed him she was pleased to be able to show off her findings.

"What is your name?" Robert asked promising never to get annoyed with the Lab Technician ever again.

"Jennie Harwood."

"Thank you Jennie, you have a very smart system, can I ask you not to mention this to any of the other nurses or Doctors."

Her eyes were big and brown as she stared at him realizing the seriousness of what she just discovered. "You can trust me. I won't say a word to anyone, not even my family."

"Thank you so much Jennie." Robert said and left the room. *'I have to get into Eric's office and get my mother's file.'*

Robert thought as he headed to his office to call security.

# Chapter 96

Nothing made sense to him. Why would Eric mess up so badly? *'There had to be an explanation.'*

When he got to his office, he picked up the phone and tried to call Eric again. When the answering machine came on, Robert slammed the receiver down so hard it cracked the ear piece.

The question why, kept pounding in his head. He had to get into Eric's office. He picked up the phone, this time he called security.

Ten minutes later the guard had the door open and left Robert with instructions to lock it up after he was done.

Robert felt like an intruder rummaging through Eric's desk, but he had a gut feeling that his partner was up to something bad.

He didn't have to wait long before he pulled out three files from under a pile of books. It disgusted him, how sloppy and unprofessional Eric was with the patience's files. *'Looking at this mess is there any wonder, why the samples, are so screwed up.'* He questioned. He didn't recognize the other two people's files but the third belonged to his mother.

Opening the contents, he realized that the three women were the same age. On further examination, he guessed two of the blood samples came from these women. What he was seeing frightened him but not as much as what he saw in his mother's file.

Eric has notated the margins with strange two to three word statements that made less sense to Robert than why Eric swapped blood samples.

Why would he put things down like 'another one gone.' 'easy money' 'predicted death' Robert slammed the file shut. This was too eerie.

*"Who the hell are you Eric?"* Taking the file, he went back to his office. *"I need to get the police involved."*

# Chapter 97

"You finally decided to join the rest of the world." Eric walked into the room to find her sitting on the side of the bed.

"I'm beginning to think I should just curl up and stay asleep forever, with everything going on."

"Things will get better." *'If you do what I say,'* Eric thought. *'If she refuses, then she'll join her friends in girly heaven.'*

"I can't believe Henry had the nerve to show up here last night." Tears filled her eyes. "I'd probably be dead now if you didn't show up."

Eric sat beside her on the bed and held her in his arms.

"Don't worry I won't let Henry kill you." Eric slid his fingers along Dana's neck. *'So, smooth, what kind of fight would you give me.'*

"The news showed the police chasing him through the woods." Eric felt her shoulders sag. "It won't be long and trust me, there is no way, I'm leaving your side until he is behind bars."

"I owe you so much." She took his hand.

"Since you feel that way, there is something I've been meaning to ask you."

"Of course."

"I want you to ride off into the sunset with me, so I can protect you from all the dangers in this crazy world." Eric took her hand before he slid down on one knee in front of her. "I want to be your protector for as long as we live."

"Eric, what are you doing?" Dana groaned.

"I'm asking you to be my wife." He kissed her hand then pulled a tiny black velvet box from his pocket. When he snapped the lid open, a huge diamond flashed. He held her hand up and slipped the ring on her finger.

"Eric, it's beautiful." Tears quickly filled her eyes. "But I can't accept it."

"What do you mean?" He snapped. "I'm asking you to marry me and you're turning me down." *Who the hell, does she think she is?*

He didn't know what pissed him off more, this no body girl who had nothing going for her rejecting him, a doctor, or her ruining his plan after he revised it.

"We haven't even dated." Dana looked at him, as though, he was some kind of idiot.

"We've been on lots of dates." He could take her now but he must be patient.

"We don't really know each other. That was the reason I was so upset with Robert for getting married so soon. Remember."

"Well a short engagement didn't hurt them. They both look very happy."

"They were fortunate." Dana looked down at him. "I can't do things that way." Dana slipped the ring off her finger and handed it back to him.

"Fine." He stood up and sat on the bed. *Remain calm, I need to get her out of the house and then make her pay.* "I guess we won't need these." He gestured to the wine and glasses on the dresser.

"I'm sorry," he took her hand in his. It was hard but he had to make her believe he was okay with this.

"Can I officially ask you to be my girlfriend?" Eric had been so sure Dana would have jumped at his offer. He messaged her neck. *'I could take you right now, if I wanted to.'* He thought.

"Can we just keep going the way we were. Things are so messed up in my life right now I'm not ready to commit to anything." Dana sighed.

"Wow, not even willing to date. Did I mess things up that bad." Eric rubbed his hands together. "Am I drowning here?" Eric wondered if the cop had anything to do with her decision.

"You're more like a brother to me."

Eric could feel his blood rising and the desire to finish her off was almost too much for him. *'Control, he reminded himself.'*

"I understand." He looked at her and actually felt hatred. Rejected by a small town nobody he thought. *'You don't know it missy but you just sealed your fate. Killing you will be the best out off all the girls.'*

Who would have guessed Dana wanted another brother instead of a husband.

None of this had to happen if her crazy Uncle wouldn't have backed out of his promise to marry his mother. Or, if she hadn't been stupid enough to have him killed before telling her where he hid all the T-bills and Bonds worth millions.

Ralph Reed had to have sent them here. *'I will find them.'* Eric thought. *'For now, I need to take care of Dana.'*

"Can I at least get my new baby sister to help me glue the broken pieces of my pride back together?" Eric forced a laughed then wrapped her in a bear hug and kissed the top of her head.

"Thank you for being so understanding."

"No problem, sis." He grinned at her. "I need to call the hospital. Why don't you go and shower then I'll take you out and we can celebrate the birth of my new sister."

"That will be nice."

# Chapter 98

Leaving the Mullins place, Jake made a quick stop to the lab to drop the music box off and then to picked up some groceries. Nelly probably munched through the box of Meow Mix he left her. He grabbed a squeaky mouse toy, 'a *treat for being a good cat.'* He tossed the object into his cart, wondering what kind of mischief she got into while on her own. The last time she decorated the house with the toilet paper. *'Not this time though, I hid it all away.'* He thought as he pulled into the laneway to find his parent's unpacking suitcases from the trunk.

"I thought you weren't going to be here until tomorrow." Jake grabbed the case from his mother.

"You know your mother doesn't wait for anything. She had the bags on the porch for me the minute I got back from the interview."

"Well, I'm glad you're here."

"Thank you my dear." His mother said making a face at her husband, while Jake unlocked the door.

Once the suitcases were out of sight, Jake and Thom sat in the living room while Lila put the groceries away and made sandwiches.

"How'd it go with Ralph Reed's girlfriend?"

"Nothing there, but a woman grieving her loss," Thom sighed, "I can understand why, the wedding they planned turned into his funeral."

"That would be difficult, instead of meeting at the church to say I do, she had to say her good byes." Jake agreed.

"Especially since, Margaret Lewis is a good looking woman," Thom winked at his wife as she came into the room. "I'm sure someone else will come along." He teased.

"Are you getting a wandering eye, my dear?" Lila placed a plate of sandwiches on the coffee table.

"I may look once in a while but you're the one and only apple of my eye." He planted a kiss on her cheek before popping a sandwich square into his mouth.

"I expected something like that, but my trip to the Mullins turned out a music box that Henry gave Mrs Mullins for her birthday."

"Does it belong to your girl?"

"I dropped it off at the lab. All I need is one print of Dana's to be on there." Jake said, then got up to answer the phone.

"Hello." He looked over at Thom, "I'm leaving now."

"What's up?" Thom questioned.

"They caught up to Henry and are bringing him in now."

"Good, let's go." Thom said and grabbed a handful of sandwiches for the road.

"I'll see you men later." Lila said and followed them to the door.

# Chapter 99

Jake and Thom arrived the same time a cruiser pulled in front of the station with Henry.

Two officers from the other County help Frank and Kevin maintain the mob control while a camera crew from the local television station ran around filming and interviewing anyone who wanted to give an opinion.

"These guys look hungry for blood." Thom said.

"So much for being innocent until proven guilty," Jake said, while four officers forced the crowds back to form a make shift gauntlet as Conroy and Tyler took the lead.

Williams followed closely behind with a frightened Henry in hand cuffs.

Jake scanned the crowd for Dennis Nairn, if planned right we can question him before he has time to lawyer's up. '*I really want to know if he went to Dana's house to kill her.*' Jake wondered.

A spectator reached towards Henry and shook a stick at him.

"Put that thing down." Jake stared into the eyes of a man in his fifties.

"After what he's done he doesn't deserve to breathe another day." The man said as he slowly lowered his weapon.

"We aren't running a kangaroo court here so until he has a fair trail and is found guilty we won't be playing judges." Jake stated.

"So much for getting to Henry before he lawyers up," Jake said as Dennis Nairn greeted them at the main door. "Can we get the cuffs off?" He gestured to Henry's hands. Williams looked at Sergeant Timmons. "Not until we have him inside." He said and pushed Henry forward.

"Dad, I didn't kill anyone." Henry ran towards his father, but Williams pulled him back.

"Don't say anything." Dennis said.

"No, Dad, I want to tell my side."

Jake stood back, nothing about this guy would lead anyone to believe he was a cold killer, but neither did Mary Bell when she kill two young boys at the age of ten.

"Jake you have a call on line two. It's a Doctor Reed and he says it's important.

"Thanks Helen." He said without looking at her. "I have a call coming through, let's go to my office." Jake said to his father.

"Jake here,"

"Hello detective, this is Doctor Reed." His voice sounded a little unsure.

"How can I help you?" Jake waited curious to see if Robert intended to ream him out for not watching Dana better.

"I'm not sure, but I found something that is disturbing in Eric's office, that I think you should take a look at."

"Can you give me some details?" Jake's ears perked up.

"Well, I had to rush my mother to the hospital this morning. I tried to reach Eric to get his file on her, since he has been treating her and couldn't reach him." Robert sounded perplexed.

"Is she okay?" Jake asked worried about Nancy.

"She will be, but her lab results didn't add up, so I had security open his office. I found my mothers file along with two other women." The line went silent for about a minute and Jake wondered if Robert was trying to decide how to say what was bothering him.

"What did you find?"

"I'm sure Eric has been falsifying documents but the worst are the notes he left in my mother's file."

"What kind of notes?" Robert definitely had his interest.

"Things like another one gone, and easy money. There's more but I think you should come to the hospital to see it for yourself."

"I can be there in twenty minutes." Adrenalin raced through Jake's veins as he ushered his father out of the office.

# Chapter 100

Hospitals weren't Jake's favourite place to visit, they held too much of an eerie feel. Even the hallway they stepped into after exiting the elevator had the lights dimmed.

He could never decide which bothered him more, a funeral home where the body was prepared for final resting or the hospital where the person retired their last breath of life.

Rounding the corner, he could see a pocket of light at the end of the corridor. A nurse greeted them with a smile as the stepped up to the counter.

"Are you looking for someone?"

"Yes, Dr. Reed asked us to meet him here. Can you show us where his office is?" Jake smiled at her.

"It's on the next floor up, but he just went in to see his mother a few minutes ago." She pointed down the hall. "Room 418, it's only a few doors that way."

"Thanks," Jake said. "I don't want to upset any of his family, so if you could let him know he is needed out here." Jake was sure Dana would be in the room and didn't want to barge in and cause a scene, upsetting everyone, when her mother lay sick in bed.

"Sure, give me a sec." She jumped up and flashed a smiled at Jake before she rambled towards the room. Within a few minutes, she came back with Robert behind her.

"Thanks for coming so quickly, detective." Robert held out his hand and shook both their hands. "I just hope I'm over reacting."

"You never know, do you have somewhere we can go and talk." Jake asked not bothering to introduce his father.

"Yes, we can take the elevator up to my office." Robert offered, and started walking. He stopped when he heard Lindsay calling.

"Robert, honey." She hurried up to him.

"Oh, good evening detective. What are you doing here?" She questioned looking surprised.

"I was just about to inform your husband that we have Henry Nairn behind bars." Robert's face clearly showed relief when Jake covered his reason for being there.

"That's good to hear, but do you always personally go around telling people?" Jake detected a hint of snobbery in her voice.2

"No, I just thought you would like to know he won't be bothering Dana at her home anymore."

"What?" Robert questioned and Jake realized that no one informed them about what happened in the early hours.

"Eric didn't tell you Henry attacked Dana at the house early this morning."

"What next." Robert said.

"How, horrible for Dana," she turned to Robert. "Why didn't you tell me?" She looked insulted, that he would keep it a secret from her.

"I just got home this morning and know as much as you do." Robert claimed.

"Robert, I can't take any more of this. I'm going to go home and rest for a bit." She reached up and kissed him.

"I sorry honey, you must be exhausted. Thank you for being here for mom." He took her hand. "Let me walk you to the elevator. Detectives, would you mind waiting here?" Robert asked.

"Take your time." Thom answered, than turned to Lindsay before they left. "I'm sorry miss but you look very familiar do I know you."

"I'm not from around here, so I don't see how you could, detective." She developed a fake southern drawl and left on Robert's arm without a second glance back. Jake couldn't understand how anyone could end up married to a woman who could turn an accent on and off in a moments notice.

He waited until they turned down the hallway to the elevator and checked to see that the nurse had gone back to her station before he turned to his father.

"What was that all about?"

"I can't place it now but, I've met her somewhere before."

"There are a million women like Lindsay around. Some people like to call it high class, if you seen one you seen them all." Jake looked around to make sure the nurse wasn't listening to their conversation.

"I guess so," Thom chuckled.

Robert came around the cornered and waved at them to follow him.

# Chapter 101

"It's right over here." Robert picked up the files from his desk and handed them to Jake.

"Did you look all the way through it?" Jake asked as he took a seat and opened the file.

"No, I found it too disturbing and needed to start my mother's treatment."

"How is she doing?" Thom asked.

"She had large traces of poison, I believe someone was trying to kill her, but she's going to be fine."

"Do you know who might want her dead?" Jake asked.

"It might sound bizarre, but after reading these files, I think Eric is."

"Why do you think that is?"

"I don't know. He's my partner, and I thought I knew him better, but reading his notes proved me wrong."

"This is strange. Why would he write this down?" If Jake didn't know any better he would have thought that a madman got hold of the file and scribble his insanity over it.

"Let me see it," Thom asked and Jake handed it over to him.

"We will have to check it for prints." Thom flipped the pages over using the top corner of the page. Half way through he stopped.

"Hold on what is this?" He laid the file flat on the desk and pointed to a piece of flower paper. The three stared down at it as though it were something contaminated with the worse kind of disease imaginable.

Jake finally read the words so everyone could hear.

'You must choose; to wed or die;

To wed in riches or die a pauper in castles surrounded in death, I will take your final breath with my kiss upon your lips.' There was no mistake, the limerick, was written for Dana.

"This is Dana he's referring to." Jake surmised.

Turning the page more notes revealed what happened to the others.

'Sally, (mistaken identity) her neck so smooth,'

'Tina, (tempting beauty lost in her own conceit)

'Henry (willing sacrifice).

'Dana, (your music will play forever in my heart.) Dead or Alive, hidden riches will belong to me."

"I found these in his desk also." Robert pulled out a black music box and set of keys with 'Sally' written on the tag.

"We have the wrong guy." Jakes insides felt like a giant fist grabbed hold of them and twisted. *'I pushed Dana to the killer.'*

"My partner is a killer." Robert rubbed his hands down his face.

"Robert, what are the hidden riches he's talking about?" Jake questioned.

"I have no idea."

"Once we know that we have our motive. Thom stated.

"How could I have been so stupid?"

"I'm going to get an officer to stay in the room with Dana and your mother?" Jake said.

"Dana's not with my mother. She's with Eric." Robert almost yelled it out.

"Do you know where they are?" Jake panic when the realization of Dana being with Eric hit him.

"They could be at the house." Robert said.

"We need to get out there right now." Jake said.

# Chapter 102

Pulling in front of the house gave Jake some hope when he noticed the lights on and no car in the laneway.

He parked on the road up a ways from the house just in case Dana was alone and Eric had slipped out for coffee.

"That's strange the light is on in the attic." Robert said as they climbed the steps to the porch.

"We don't know what to expect, so let's go in quietly." Thom recommended.

Robert fumbled in the dark, with his keys unnecessarily, because when he went to unlock the door it pushed open.

"Let's hope Dana's home alone." He whispered before leading them into the entrance hall. Light were on in every room and it looked like the place was ransacked, drawers were opened and paper thrown all over.

"What the hell is going on here?" Robert questioned as he led the way into the kitchen. No matter where they looked things were pulled out of there place. Cupboards doors were ajar, and the shattered remains of a teacup mixed in a white power were shattered on the floor.

"Someone is looking for something." Jake said. 'Hidden riches,' he thought and watched as Robert reached up and brushed his index finger through a white powder.

"You may want to rinse your hands off." Jake cautioned Robert. "My guess would be it's rat poison. We need to leave it until the lab does a run through." Jake said and Robert put the bag back where he got it and gave his hands a quick rinse.

"Does Dana use the attic often?" Jake questioned in a low tone.

"None of us did."

"Can you get to the attic from this side of the house?" Jake asked.

"The entrance is right there when you reach the second floor." Robert confirmed.

"You two take the stairs here and I'll go around to the ones by the entrance." Thom said. "This way if anyone tries to sneak out the front door, I can surprise them." Thom patted his side where a gun sat snug in a holster.

"We'll meet you at the top." Jake nodded and watched as his father disappeared down the hall.

"Stay behind me." He cautioned Robert before they started up the stairway.

"If Eric did anything to harm Dana, I'm going to kill him." Robert confessed.

"You won't have to." Jake whispered. *'I may do it before you get a chance.'* Jake thought.

Thom made his way down the hall towards them.

"In my wildest imagination as a child I never would have come up with this scene." Robert said. "When this mess is all over, I'm taking Lindsay, and my mother, along with Dana on a long..." He stopped short when a low murmur of voices could be heard coming from the attic.

"We ready?" Jake whispered and motioned towards the stairs leading to the attic.

Robert followed between the two detectives, his stomach twisted in knots with the fear of what they would encounter when they reached the top.

# Chapter 103

The stairs curved around then opened up to the pinnacle part of the house.

Rounding the corner Robert's jaw dropped, "What the hell is going on here?"

Nothing in the world could have prepared him for this.

A light filled the room, displaying her sprawled on the floor, with half her body stuffed in the trunk.

Only Thom recognized the strange woman hovered over her barking orders. "There's over ten millions dollars, so don't miss any of it."

Too preoccupied to notice the men approach, the older woman continued to scream, Robert stared stunned by what he was seeing.

"What are you doing, Lindsay." His voice was low and demanding, she jumped up letting papers fall to her feet. She tried to push them aside with her foot unsuccessfully, while the older woman tried to blend into the shadows.

"I came to see if Dana was here." She spoke slowly as though trying to search for excuses.

"Who is this?" Robert pointed to the female, holding a handful of notes from the chest.

"That is Margaret Lewis, your wife's mother." Thom answered for her. "I couldn't place her face at the hospital but it's very clear now. You're older than the picture sitting on the desk at your mother's house, but the eyes never change."

"I don't know what you're talking about." She snapped at Thom.

"You don't need to know, I'll take a bet that Dr Rycker is the brother." Thom hazarded a guess.

"Is that true," Robert, questioned Lindsay, the anger dripping off each word, but she didn't answer. "What are you looking for in the trunk?" He demanded to know.

Jake walked over and picked up a handful of paper.

"It looks like a fortune in Bonds and T-Bills. Jake handed them to Robert. "Hidden treasure I'd call it."

"I would say a trunk full of treasure is motive enough." Thom added.

"Where did this come from?" Robert asked.

"Look honey, we're rich." Lindsay scooped up more bills and ran to Robert offering them up to him as a gift.

"You're good Ms. Lewis, you had me believing you were the poor grieving mate." Thom directed at Margaret.

"I'm only taking what's rightfully mind. I knew Ralph Reed was a stupid man the first day he came into the bank and started to buy these things years ago." She kicked at the floor. "He won money and invested but the old miser refused to spend a dime."

"So you knew his worth all along?" Jake stated.

"I'm a smart woman so yes I did, but even after we dated and I agreed to marry the repulsive man, he insisted, his brother's kid would have it all." She looked over at Lindsay. "So when he bragged that his nephew was going to attend the U of T, I had Eric do the same."

"So our meeting was all a setup." Robert looked disgusted at Lindsay.

"That was Eric's plan." Lindsay said.

Margaret shot her a hate stare.

"It would have worked if you had more brains and found the chest before now." She hissed at Lindsay.

"No if Eric wouldn't have gone on another one of is killing sprees, it would have worked." Lindsay screamed back at her mother. "And if you would have been a better lover to Ralph he wouldn't have dumped you." Lindsay said. The three men watched as the two women turned on each other.

"The old miser deserved to die. First, he flaunts his millions in front of me then a week later he tells me the wedding is off."

"My mother and Eric planned it all. She even had Eric kill Ralph Reed." Lindsay ran over to Robert and clung to his arm.

"Shut up you stupid child." Margaret yelled at her.

"She knew he would do it because he strangled all those women in Toronto." She turned to Thom, "I'll tell you everything." She spited out at him then turned to Robert. "Darling lets go home, I'm tired." She sounded desperate.

"Get away from me you fraud." Robert pushed her from him. "You made me believe your mother died."

"She's dead in my eyes." Lindsay clung to Robert's arm again and he peeled her fingers away. "I'm innocent, they tried to make me kill you but I refused."

"Right, sweetheart, and who fed the old lady this tea laced with poison?"

Margaret tossed the box of tea at Robert and laughed. "She has been lying to you from the very beginning." Margaret snorted.

"My mother sat out front behind huge sunglasses spying on the place to make sure I was doing what she wanted."

"Dana saw through your lies." Jake intervened.

"Robert, I'm your wife, are you going to let him talk to me like that." When he shoved her away from him, she turned on the three. "This is harassment. I'm not saying another word."

"You don't have too." Thom said looking around the room. "We caught you two in the act."

"Motive enough for murder." Jake said.

Robert openly cried. "How could I be so stupid? You set me up and played me, all for stupid money."

"Where are Eric and Dana?" Jake demanded. The air was stale and silent, except for the whimpering sobs that began to escape from Lindsay.

"Lindsay, where has Eric taken Dana?" Robert growled at her to answer Jake.

"I don't know." She snivelled.

"The note said if they didn't wed she would die in castles surrounded in death." Thom recalled the limerick Eric wrote in the file.

"That can only mean one place." Jake looked at Robert. "Mullins Funeral Home looks like a castle." He turned to his father. "Can you call the station and have these women escorted to the jail house." He turned to Robert. "We don't know what these two are capable of, can you stay and help until the police arrive.

"Definitely," He said and watched Jake join them together with handcuffs.

"Have them wait for about fifteen minutes before they send anyone to the Home. I don't want the sirens to tip Eric off, making him act more stupid than he already is."

"Be careful, son. This guy is deadly."

"One more thing dad," He stopped for a moment in the door.

"What's that?"

"Tell them to set Henry free."

# Chapter 104

Dana chuckled at Eric flirting with the waitress while she counted out his change.

"Can you believe this beautiful woman refused to marry me?"

"She must have her reasons." The young girl said, but looked at her as though she were crazy.

"Thank you." Dana smiled at her.

"Would you have turned me down?" Eric flashed a killer smile causing a slight blush to colour the girl's cheeks.

"I'm going to run to the washroom while you work your charm on this poor girl." Dana laughed and pushed her chair back from the table.

"Ahh, if the green eyed monster of jealously is biting at you maybe it's time to reconsider the offer." Eric grinned across to her. "It's still on the table." He winked at her.

"Think of all the women that would miss out on getting to know you if I take you out of the single ranks." Dana chuckled when he made a face at her.

"While you freshen up, I'm going to check my message, so take your time."

*'I must be mad, an absolutely, gorgeous, funny doctor wants to marry me and I turn him down.'* Dana thought, *'but, the fact I'm not bothered by his flirting, tells me a lot.'* She headed to the washroom thinking what a good friend he is and how much he helped her since her father died.

So many things that ate away at from her past now seemed trivial, thanks to Eric. He enabled her to let go of past resentments, but the romantic spark wasn't there for her.

There was no desire or connection, like the night Jake rushed to her apartment and stayed sleeping on the floor. *'We had fun at his house until the nut case came, stating, misguided, claims on him.'* She missed Jake and wondered when he would get back.

# Chapter 105

The waitress was over at another table, while Eric paced in front of the door talking on the phone.

He glanced up at her and snapped the phone shut. The strained expression on his face told her something was wrong.

"What's the matter," she questioned, her body began to
tremble.

"We have to leave." He placed a gentle hand on her back and escorted her outside before he spoke.

"Robert's been trying to get a hold of us all night."

"Why?" She asked.

Instead of answering, he shoved her into the passenger seat where the night air chilled her body. Shivering she could barely sit still long enough for him to get in behind the wheel.

His attitude frightened her, but sitting in silence was worse.

"Eric, what did Robert say to you?" She demanded. He took a deep breath and turned to her taking both her hands in his he looked her straight in the eyes.

"I don't know how to tell you." Tear welled in his eyes and Dana started to cry.

"Tell me, what."

"Your mother took very ill this morning. Robert arrived home from the conference early and found Lindsay trying to revive her. They rushed her to the hospital." Eric started to cry, her body went numb with shock.

"What's wrong with my mother?" She held her breath waiting for what he would say next.

"I'm sorry Dana. It isn't good." He pulled her to him and held her tightly against his chest. "She passed away about ten minutes ago."

"No, she was fine yesterday." Dana cried.

"They're going to take her body to the funeral home. Did you want try to catch them at the hospital or just head over to Mullins?" Eric asked still holding her.

"We're so far way, let just go to Mullins." Dana pulled away and sat straight up in her seat. '*This has to be a mistake, maybe, Eric misunderstood Robert's message.*' A deep sob escaped her, as the reality of Eric's words hit her. '*My mother is dead and I never said good-bye.*'

"Let's get out of here." Eric flicked on the lights and sped out of the parking lot. '*Tonight you are all mine,*' Eric laughed inside.

# Chapter 106

The drive that took them an hour earlier cut in half as Eric busted every speed limit out there. Pulling into a darkened lot, he drove up to the front door. No way could he describe the excitement building deep within his gut.

"It's so dark. Shouldn't they be here by now?"

"Let me try the message center to see if Robert called in." He opened his phone and hit the speed dial. Unaware, that Eric held his finger on the off button, Dana stared out at the old decrepit building hating the sight of it.

She wiped at the tears trickling down her cheeks, "I can't take anymore." She whispered.

"This Dr. Rycker again, has Dr. Reed called in yet." He spoke into the dead phone. "Are you kidding me, I left a message almost an hour ago for him to call me." He sucked in a deep breath. "What the hell, are you people doing down there?" Eric screamed into the phone. "Yes, I'll hold for a minute."

'*I'm so good I have myself believing my tale,*' Eric thought and almost laughed out-loud.

"Nurse Randal, called twenty minutes ago to say Dr. Reed left for the Funeral Home." Eric let out a long sigh. "Thank you, I'm sorry for yelling at you but this is very stressful for the family." He said, and snapped the cover closed on the phone.

"Apparently they left almost half an hour ago. They usually bring the bodies in through the back of the building." Eric paused and turned the key in the ignition. "Should we go and see?" Eric asked, but she remained quietly staring out the window.

"Dana, are you okay?" Dana slightly nodded, her energy slowly drained from her. "Dana I think you're going into shock."

"I'm okay, Eric, I just can't believe this is happening." She cried.

"I'll take care of you." He reached into the back seat and retrieved his bag.

"No more pills." She held up her hand.

"This is a mild sedative it will be like drinking two beers. I'm going to take a shot also, we can both use something to help get through the rest of this awful night. It's like our family is falling apart." Eric said.

"I just can't believe what's happening." Dana said.

"I feel empty." Eric rubbed his hands over his face and started to cry. "I'll go first." He said and slowly eased the liquid heroin into his veins. It felt so good and heightened his feelings. Resting his head against the seat, he let out a sigh.

"It's the only way I can get through this nightmare." He took her hand.

"You're right I could use something to ease the tension and pain from my gut." Dana said.

"It's the only way we will get past this horrible night." Eric said and took her arm and pushed her sleeve up. 'I should take up acting when this is all over. How many killers can get their victim hold out their arm willing to shoot them up with a drug?' Eric thought as he watched her winced at the pinch of the needle breaking through the flesh.

Within seconds, she felt light-headed, but still had a good control of her movement. Eric was right the pain disappeared immediately.

# Chapter 107

The headlights danced on the gravel as Eric slowly manoeuvred the road to the back entrance.

"Shouldn't I be seeing flashing lights and cars all around?" She questioned holding her head.

"I'm sure they are on the way." Eric stopped by a large wooden door.

"Wait here, I'm going to look around." He said, reaching behind the seat, he took out a bag.

"What is that for?" She asked thinking it strange that he would need anything.

"None of your business," he snapped at her and left.

"What!" Her voice echoed in her ears as though she was in a tunnel. *'This must be joke, my mother isn't dead.'* She chuckled. *'Eric is playing a joke on me.'*

The headlights showed him struggling to get something out of his bag. *'What a hurtful joke,'* she surmised thinking nothing made sense anymore. *'Why would he do that to me,'* she questioned and opened the door stumbled out and staggered towards him.

"Eric, what are you up to?" She called but her words sounded hollow and empty, *'and what the hell, did I let you give me.'* She wondered.

"The Mullins gave me a key," he frightened her the way he glared at her. "I send lots of customers their way." He smirked, with a slight push the door squeaked opened.

"I'm going to wait in the car." Eric grabbed her hand before she could move.

"And chance Sally's killer getting you also." He ran a finger along her neck then shoved her into the darken building.

"Eric you're scaring me." At least being in the dark, she avoided the distortion from the drugs.

"Where's the trust gone, Dana? I'm good enough to be you're protector and hero but not husband."

"Are you doing this because I won't marry you?"

"Would that make you change your mind?" An insane laugh echoed through the room.

"No, I don't love you like that." She cried.

Suddenly he was behind her whispering in her ear.

"Sally died for you." She jumped at the realization that he easily moved behind her without a sound.

"What are you saying?"

His breathe was hot against her flesh. She shivered as he slid something silky around her neck and let it dropped. Dana shook her head, everything was distorting. *'Those are the words the killer told me the night he called.'* Dana cringed.

He laughed again, and moved into the only hint of light that shone from his car. He snapped the nylon roped in front of him before kicking the door shut.

"Oh my God, you killed Sally." *'I have to get out of here.'* Her mind screamed. She started to panic but forced herself to stay calm, she was sure the medication he tricked her into taking was actually helping her.

"Mistaken identity," he howled like a wolf who trapped it's prey, "how was I to know you had a twin who drove the same stupid little red Volkswagen. You should have heard her begging for her pitiful life. The funny part was hearing her beg for her man, who slept through her final moments, to come to her rescue.

Then there was Tina, although she filled a need she became obnoxious and had to go."

"Why," Dana needed to know the reasons.

"Your family is so pathetic, especially Robert he is just like your dead Uncle. I bet none of you would have ever figured out that he sent you millions of dollars and you don't even know where it is." She could hear him clicking his tongue like a parent disciplining a child. "It really does, belong to my family, my mother paid for it every time she crawled into bed with the disgusting little man, and then he threw her to the side. Sickening!" He snickered, "Oh by the way, sweetheart," he chuckled and Dana turned to the sound of his voice and tried to see him. "You read Lindsay like a book. She's my sister, you know."

*'He's crazy, I have to keep moving,'* Dana thought.

"To let you know your mother might not be dead yet, but when Lindsay called me at the restaurant she thought Mom would call it quits before morning. I have to tell you, she sure is a tough old lady, hanging in there with all the poison Lindsay pumped into her." Dana wanted to lunge at him but the drugs were making her weak.

She wished he would stop laughing. He sounded more like someone playing the part of an insane person in a low rated movie.

"Oh yes, your boyfriend went to the hospital to let Robert know you all can rest easy because they apprehended Henry. Doesn't that make you feel warm and fuzzy all over, knowing he's out there protecting us."

Dana slid back into the darkness and slowly moved towards the door. Eric kept talking as if he were having a conversation on the couch with a friend. "Don't you hate it when someone steals your parking spot?" he let out a sigh, bringing up Sally again. "Well believe me that bitch won't be taking anyone else's spot again." He yelled.

Things went quiet for about thirty seconds and Dana froze to the spot not to make any noise to clue him into where she was. "Huh, but after tonight, you won't need to worry about that, will you?"

She heard the zipper close on the bag, *'oh no, he's going to try to shove more drugs into me. I have to get out of here.'* She thought. She slid her hand along the wall, if, she could get outside her chances of survival would increase. Her hand hit the roundness of the door handle. *'I can do this,'* she felt hope,

"One, two, three," she counted under her breath then yanked back on the door and bolted.

# Chapter 108

Running Dana fell behind the car. Hopefully, by the time he found his way out of the place he would think she was high tailing it to the wooded area.

He was faster than she imagined, he rushed out the door, barely giving her enough time to conceal herself. Standing in the headlights, she could see him, holding a thin nylon rope folded in half, snapping it together. It resembled the one she seen around Tina's neck the day they found her dead.

"You are my first." He raised his voice while holding the rope over his head. How could he claim that she would be his first when he just finished bragging about Tina and Sally? Shaking Dana tried to control her breathing. Eric was crazy and clearly intended to take her life tonight.

"The first woman I was willing to marry."

'Lucky me,' she thought.

She had never been more frightened, especially since no one was aware of her plight. More than likely, he lied and everyone one was at home carrying on as though life was great; and it was, she told herself. No matter how miserable she felt wallowing in a past that wasn't near as bad as she imagined, she loved living and had no intentions of giving her life up without a fight.

Feeling along the ground, she wrapped her hand around a small rock, it wasn't the biggest but with it she might be able to inflict enough pain to slow him down so she can get away.

The fear mixed with a chilled night air sobered her up a little from the effects of the drugs.

Concealing her weapon tightly in her palm, she stood up to face him and slipped her hand into her pocket.

"I knew you didn't go far." He smiled at her as if they were playing an innocent game of hide-and seek.

"Eric, why are you doing this?" She pleaded.

"All you had to do was marry me and none of this would have happened." He yelled at her.

"Eric, There are so many women out there who would marry you tomorrow if you asked. I'm not stable enough to be a wife to you. It wouldn't be fair to you." She tried to reason with him. Who would have thought the Eric she knew would have flipped because she rejected his proposal.

"What you don't understand, is I have to marry you." He laughed and slapped his hands on his legs. "If I want to share in the money your uncle stashed away in his trunk."

"What money?" Dana was even more confused then before.

"It doesn't matter." He snapped. Dana had to do something to get him to change his mind.

"Eric, I made a mistake when I didn't take your ring."

"You've got that right." He smirked at her.

"I said no because I'm not good enough for you." She tried smiling at him. "You're this handsome, smart doctor, and I'm a no body, I'd end up ruining your life." His eyes stared out into the darkness. "It takes a special woman like Lindsay to be a doctor's wife."

"Huh, is that how you really feel." His voice softened.

"Yes, I just didn't know how to tell you. But maybe if we have all that money you're talking about I can learn." She hoped he would fall for her bluff.

"That's how you really feel?" He questioned again.

"You know how insecure I am," she stepped out from the shadows and stood only a few feet from him. "Let's go home and forget all this happened." She forced a smile.

"What have I done?" He fell to his knees and held his arms out to her.

"I don't want you to ever think you're not good enough. You are better than Lindsay." He reached into his pocket and pulled out the ring he offered her earlier and motioned for her to come.

With a deep breath, she went to him and knelt down beside him. She had to make him believe her. She wrapped her arms around him. He pulled her close to him and kissed her.

"I'm so sorry, please be my wife?" He pleaded and she held out her hand for him to slip the ring on her finger.

"I can't believe you still want someone like me." She continued the lie.

"More than ever," he said holding her hand.

"Then yes, Doctor Eric I will." She smiled fighting the repulsion she felt by his kiss. He stood up and helped her to her feet.

"I only said that I killed Sally and Tina to scare you, I didn't kill anyone." Eric tried to convince her.

"Darling, I didn't believe you did. You're a Doctor. You save lives not take them." Dana took his hand and started towards the car. "Come on let's get out of here before the Mullins arrive and charge us with break and entry." She forced a laughed.

Laughing, Eric picked her up in his arms and twirled around with her. She hoped he didn't notice her tense up when he did.

"I want to make love to you, right here." He dropped to the ground with her.

"Please darling, I want our first time to be perfect, with candles and wine. Can we go back to your place?" His weight was heavy on her.

"I'm ready now. We can do all the other stuff once we get back to my place." His voice was heavy as he kissed her neck.

"But, for you darling, I can wait." He rolled off her and helped her up.

"I do love you." She smiled at him.

"You wait for me in the car. I have to grab my bag." He motioned towards the car. Nervous to turn her back to him she waited until he picked up the velvet case the ring came in.

"Don't want to leave this behind." He chuckled. Dana smiled at him and for a split second turned away.

In that time, he grabbed the rope he had earlier and ran at her knocking her to the ground.

"Eric," she screamed as she fell.

"How stupid do you think I am?" He pulled her to her feet by her hair. She struggled to get her hands into her pocket as he wrapped the rope around her neck. Twisting it around his hand he left enough space for some air to keep her from passing out.

Pressing his lips to her ear, he whispered. "Not only are you the first woman to get me to slipped a ring on her finger, but you're also the first to know I'm going to kill ahead of time." He pulled her head back and kissed her again. This time she spat in his face. She felt her knees buckle and her consciousness slipping. She imaged voices calling through the dark.

# Chapter 109

"Eric, let Dana go or I'll shoot you."
She gasped in air as the rope loosened.
Eric pulled a scalpel out and held it up to
her throat, not his preferred method but
just as efficient.

"Looks like you have a hero after
all." He spoke through clenched teeth. His
eyes were black beads staring out into the
dark. "I hope you can see how sharp this
thing is that I have kissing her lovely
neck, Detective. Cooperate or you're going
to taste her blood as it splatters all over
you." He pushed the edge deeper and Dana
winced when it broke her flesh.

He looked in the direction of Jake's
voice. "I recommend you come into the light
where I can see you and slide that gun over
while you're at it." Eric ordered.

"Look darling, your Superman just flew
in," Eric twisted her to face Jake once he
stepped out of the shadows, "now the gun."
When Jake hesitated, drops of blood dripped
down her neck, as he applied more pressure,
to prove, he would enjoy slicing her up.
"I'm beginning to think your boyfriend
prefers his gun over you, darling."

"Here," Jake bent down and slid the
weapon across the gravel.

"Now, isn't that a good Superman."
Eric planted a kiss on her temple before
shoving Dana towards Jake. She stumbled and
Jake grabbed her and pushed her behind him,
while Eric snatched up the gun.

"Stay there," was the last thing she
heard before a shot rang through the air
sending Jake to the ground.

"Jake," Dana fell beside him.

"I'm okay, he hit my leg." Jake sat up in pain.

"Isn't that cute," Eric stood over them. "Now get your boyfriend up or I'll take out his knee cap." He yelled at her.

Jake struggled to his feet and leaned on Dana while Eric forced them towards the building.

"I have to apologize, Detective, we weren't expecting company, isn't that right sweetheart." He laughed like a mad man. "So, the problem is, I only prepared one resting place tonight. But I'm sure you won't mind sharing with Dana."

"You don't have to do this, Eric." Jake tried to reason with him.

"Oh please," He said. "Dana's already tried the sweet talking speech and look where it got her. So don't waste your breath." Eric said and kicked Jake forward with his foot. "Get in there." He yelled.

He reached over and flicked a switch and light filled the room.

"See that door?" He pointed to the far corner. Dana nodded. "That is where they bring the dead bodies through. So, get your boyfriend over there." Jake slid his arm along a table to alleviate some of his weight off Dana.

"Jake, you're bleeding badly." She whispered.

"My leg is the least of our worries. We need to turn this around before we get into that room." Jake spoke softly hoping Eric wouldn't hear. He searched the area for any thing that would work as a weapon.

"Are you two doing some love bird cooing?" Eric grabbed Dana's hair and she screamed when he pulled her back to him. "A little security in case you're planning to take me down, Detective." He aimed the gun and fired a shot into Jake's calf. A groan escaped from Jake, but he continued to hold onto the table.

"Eric, stop it." Dana screamed.

"I'm sorry sweetheart is this upsetting for you." He pushed her forward. "Now run and open the door before I feel the need to take another shot."

Without another word, Dana moved past Jake and pushed the door. A clinical stainless steel chamber opened up to them with a large slab table in the middle of the room. Off to the side a coffin lay on the floor.

Eric shut the door behind him and took a moment to inhale a deep breath.

"Death is all around, smell, the invigorating scent." He was too far gone to reason with, his eyes held a distant crazed appearance as though he were reflecting on past killings.

"You see darling, I know the place like the back of my hand. Every time I lose a patient, I pay a visit to the Mullins. They're very accommodating for us Doctors. So when I asked them for a tour they were more than please to take me around."

He pointed the gun in the direction of the coffin. "Now show me how much you love your new bed and crawl in." Jake hopped on his one good leg.

"Eric, the police are on their way, so you won't get away with this." Jake tried to reason with him.

"No one is good enough to catch me. I even sat in the police station back in Toronto ten years ago and went on the

search for the last missing girl I killed."
He laughed hard and tears fell down his
face. "Hell I even pointed the cop in the
right direction to find her. Then he went
around acting like a big hero for
discovering the dead body."

"There is something wrong with you,
Eric." Jake said holding on to Dana.

"There is nothing wrong with me." He
screamed and ran at Jake.

The butt of the gun hit hard against
Jake's head and he fell back into the
coffin and didn't move. Eric lifted his
legs and tossed them over the edge so he
lay straight.

"Eric, please, don't do this." Dana
looked into the box and could see blood
from the bullet holes in Jake his leg
seeping into the white velvet material.

"Cry on some one else's shoulder,"
Eric said and pushed her on top of Jake. He
groaned as her weight fell on him.

Eric pulled over a contraction that
resembled an IV used at hospitals to feed
saline into people. He ran a hose with a
needle attached to the end of it, into the
box.

"What is that?" Dana questioned.

"I'm glad you asked. It's a mixture of
formaldehyde, I set up with a slow drip so
it will take a while before the smell gets
too unbearable." He tucked the tube near
their feet. "That should give you some time
to make your move, Detective. Just remember
I kissed her first." Eric laughed as he
pulled the lid shut.

"It's okay Dana, breath into your
sweater." Jake voice was a low whisper and

he struggled to move his arm around her. It sounded so good to hear his voice.

"Jake you're not dead." Dana cried and ran her hand along his jaw.

"Not yet."

"What are we going to do, he has that stuff dripping into the coffin, if, we don't get out of here soon the smell will kill us." Dana cried.

"The police will get here before that happens." Dana took comfort from his words but feared they wouldn't get there in time as a strange stench began to replace the air in the coffin.

The drugs Eric gave her earlier were making her sluggish, as her mind drifted deeper into sleep she imagined voices. A loud shot fired, and then something that sounded like wood cracking, outside her deathbed.

Jake was losing a lot of blood, and the smell was overpowering and she was helpless as she began to slip into a sleep.

# Chapter 110

"Stay still, I hear the sirens," a wisp of fresh air rushed in as the lid lifted. Dana's eyes flickered to see an image hovered at their feet.

Coughing she tried to sit up, how long before the stench would leave her nose.

She focused in on Henry unravelling the plastic tube from the coffin. His shirt was turning red by his left shoulder.

"Henry, what are you doing here?" Dana asked in a raspy voice. "Where is Eric?"

"You won't have to worry about him." He motioned over to where Eric slumped in a pile on the floor with a large hole in his head. A blood stained board lay next to him.

"I'm so sorry, Henry." Dana cried, holding onto the edge she tried to pull herself up.

"Stay there." Henry said wrapping a tourniquet around Jake's leg with the nylon rope Eric tried to kill her with earlier.

"Is he going to be okay?" Dana shook Jake to wake him.

"He lost a lot of blood." He tugged on the ends of the rope. "This should stop the bleeding.

Jake moaned again, and his eyes flicked open for a moment.

"Are you alright," he whispered to Dana.

"Yes," Dana said and he went unconscious again.

"Henry, you're bleeding." She reached for his hand and he balanced her as she stepped over Jake.

"Yeah, the Bastard tried to kill me."
He nodded in Eric's direction. "I doubt
he'll ever take another life again." Henry
said and held his shoulder.

"How did you know we were here?" Dana
asked grateful.

"I was arrested and in jail when the
call came in to release me, when I was
leaving they were putting a pose together
to come here."

"Will you ever forgive me?" She
covered her face with her hands.

"You were only trying to help Sally."

"I can understand if you never speak
to me again." Dana cried.

Before Henry could answer, a door
busted open and the police rushed in with
the Mullins trailing behind them.

# Chapter 111

Television crews swarmed the building with cameras waiting like vultures. After a month of trials, the deliberations ended in two short days, the jurors were ready to pass sentence. The whole town rushed to the Courthouse for the final verdict.

Two large officers rushed Dana, Robert and their mother through a gauntlet line of Newspaper and Television crews screaming questions at them, and shooting their pictures.

Inside things didn't get any better. The room was teeming with people who pointed in their direction as they walked to their seats.

Her mother appeared frail, but she was recovering nicely and getting stronger every day.

Robert was a stronghold for the family, the glue that kept them from falling apart.

The room was huge with dark brown wainscoting, covering the walls, the mundane thought of how difficult it must be for cleaners to keep if so shiny, briefly occupied Dana's mind.

Dana, Robert and their mother slid into a bench beside Henry and Linda, his girlfriend. He stood and wrapped Dana in a tight bear hug and whispered in her ear.

"Redemption, this is it, girl." Henry said.

She was glad to see him, over the month they spend many hours together talking and sorting things out. It amazed her how forgiving and kind hearted Henry was.

Phil sat across from them with Sally's family. He lost weight and his eyes held a distant look. She wondered if he would every get over his loss.

A tall, pretty woman with long blonde hair approached them and Robert left his seat to meet her. Dana recognized his divorce lawyer and guessed his marriage to Lindsay would be over with soon.

The Prosecutor showed up and stopped to shake hands with them. Shortly after that a side door opened, and the loud murmuring of voices ended instantly, the moment everyone waited for arrived. Two guards escorted Lindsay and her mother into the room.

They looked like twins dressed in colourful orange prison overalls. The Media dubbed them the 'Black Donnelly's of Chiapas Falls'. The law obviously agree, the two women arrived with hands cuffed and feet shackled.

The shuffle of their feet sliding across the floor echoed through the Courtroom.

Lindsay suddenly stopped and looked directly at Robert and mouthed the words 'I love you'.

When he lowered his, eyes she glared at the blonde sitting beside him before the Bailiff moved her along to her seat.

Dana took Robert's hand, *'is the woman that stupid,'* she wondered. Does she not realize life, as she knew it is over? Both her and her mother we going to jail.

Each member had their own legal representative, Lindsay and Margaret joined their solicitors. An empty chair by the third lawyer represented Eric, who wouldn't be making an appearance.

He now lay imprisoned in his own mind. The hit Henry applied to his head left him a paraplegic, the left side of his body paralysed. Eric would live out the rest of his life locked to a wheelchair, where he could reflect on the twelve women and the lives he robbed from them.

Dana's inside were turning, the Jury entered the room, she glanced back at the entrance, '*he's going to miss it.*' She thought.

"All rise." The Bailiff called out and everyone stood for the Judge to make his entrance.

"Sorry, I'm late." Jake slid in beside her and planted a quick kiss on her cheek.

"You may be seated."

Dana looked down at her family, it was a long journey about to end and they survived. Each of them joined hands, even Robert's lawyer held onto his and Dana wondered if a relationship was forming between them.

A member of the Jury stood.

"In the case of Margaret June Lewis, how do we find the defendant for first degree murder of Ralph Reed?

"Guilty, your Honour," a murmur washed over the crowd.

"In the case of Lindsay Gale Reed, how do we find the defendant for the murder of Ralph Anthony Reed and attempted murder of Nancy Ellen Reed?"

"Guilty, your Honour," at the announcement a loud wail escaped Lindsay and the crowd went wild applauding.

"This is a courtroom. I will not have it turned into a circus. Keep it down or I'll have everyone removed." The Judge ordered and waited until the noise subsided before turning to the Juror again.

"In the case of Eric William Rycker, how do we find the defendant for the murder of Sally Lynn Lauren?"

"Guilty, your Honour," Sally's family and Phil hugged at the sentence.

"In the case of Eric William Rycker, how do we find the defendant for the murder of Tina Michelle Wakefield?"

"Guilty, your Honour."

"In the case of Eric William Rycker, how do we find the defendant for the attempted murder of Jake Thom Turner and Dana Susan Reed?"

"Guilty, your Honour."

The Judge inhaled a deep breath, and turned to the group of twelve.

"Thank you, for your assistance, you are now relieved of your duties to the Court." He looked over the crowd and some of the newspaper crew rushed out not waiting for sentencing.

"Will the defendants please rise?" The Bailiff requested.

The Judge glared down at the group standing in front of him.

"I will not spend more time then necessary, I am appalled at what had driven you two women to murder." He glared down at them. "Greed," the Judge shook his head. "A lesson needs to be made here." He looked at Lindsay.

"Lindsay Gale Reed, you are sentenced to twenty years without parole for the murder of Ralph Anthony Reed and the attempted murder of Nancy Ann Reed." A scream from Lindsay echoed through the Court.

"Margaret June Lewis, you like wise are sentenced to twenty years without parole for the murder of Ralph Anthony Reed."

"As for Eric William Rycker, I believe he already is serving a sentence for his crimes but will not do it outside the walls of a prison. For the murders of Tina Michelle Wakefield and of Sally Lynn Lauren, I sentence him to two life sentences."

The Judge took a moment to address Eric's lawyer, "I believe there will be a trial in Toronto following this court, concerning the similar murders of ten women in that city."

"That is correct, your Honour."

"He looked at Jake and Dana in the front row.

"As for the attempted murder of Jake Thom Turner and Miss Dana Susan Reed, I sentence Eric William Rycker to twenty years without parole." He stared out over the crowd as reports rushed from the room, "This Court is dismissed," he finished off then left for his chambers shaking his head.

"Greed."

THE END